The
Negative

The Negative

Michael Covino

VIKING

VIKING
Published by the Penguin Group
Penguin Books USA Inc., 375 Hudson Street, New York, New York 10014, U.S.A.
Penguin Books Ltd, 27 Wrights Lane, London W8 5TZ, England
Penguin Books Australia Ltd, Ringwood, Victoria, Australia
Penguin Books Canada Ltd, 10 Alcorn Avenue, Toronto, Ontario, Canada M4V 3B2
Penguin Books (N.Z.) Ltd, 182–190 Wairau Road, Auckland 10, New Zealand

Penguin Books Ltd, Registered Offices: Harmondsworth, Middlesex, England

First published in 1993 by Viking Penguin, a division of Penguin Books USA Inc.

1 3 5 7 9 10 8 6 4 2

PUBLISHER'S NOTE
This is a work of fiction. Names, characters, places, and incidents either are the product of the author's imagination
or are used fictitiously, and any resemblance to actual persons, living or dead, events, or locales is entirely
coincidental.

Grateful acknowledgment is made for permission to reprint an excerpt from "Desert Places" from *The Poetry of
Robert Frost* edited by Edward Connery Lathem. Copyright 1936 by Robert Frost. Copyright © 1964 by Lesley
Frost Ballantine. Copyright © 1969 by Holt, Rinehart and Winston. Reprinted by permission of Henry Holt and
Company, Inc.

LIBRARY OF CONGRESS CATALOGING-IN-PUBLICATION DATA
Covino, Michael.
The negative / by Michael Covino.
p. cm.
ISBN 0-670-85078-0
I. Title.
PS3553.O884N4   1993
813'.54—dc20   92-56914

Printed in the United States of America
Set in Electra
Designed by Brian Mulligan

For Connie Hatch

I have stretched . . . golden chains from
star to star, and I dance.

—*Arthur Rimbaud*

They cannot scare me with their empty spaces
Between stars—on stars where no human race is.
I have it in me so much nearer home
To scare myself with my own desert places.

—*Robert Frost*

Acknowledgments

I wish to thank Lisa Beerntsen, Bart Bull, Dorothy Covino, David Littlejohn, Mike McGrath, Karin Myhre, Todd Nolan, John Raeside, and William Zander for giving me critical compass readings at various low points, high points, points of zero visibility, switchbacks, fallen logs, and tollbooths along the longsome and sinuous road that was the writing of this novel.

I am especially grateful to Nina Sonenberg, Gary Young, and Ramsay Bell-Breslin for munificence with their time and their intelligence above and beyond—far, far beyond—the call of friendship. Whenever I got lost in the forest, one of these knights-errant would lead me back to the road. Or, if it was called for, slingshot me back into the forest.

I also want to thank the following for sharing their film expertise with me at different times over the years: Brad Fuller, Robert Hillman, Errol Morris, Constance Penley, Chris Rush, Charlie Silver, Craig Valanza, and the late Melissa Gold.

And thanks of a whole other order to Ann Beattie, who knows the variable nature of sunsets, from exhilarating to exhausting, and to Lynn Nesbit and Dawn Seferian.

Part One

The Gangster

C h a p t e r 1

$\mathbf{W}$hile I waited for the professor, who was already fifteen minutes
late, who had suggested this meeting in the first place, who in fact I
had never met, I sipped my second Scotch and in an effort to assuage
my irritation watched the sun spread reddish light over the San Francisco skyline.

The waters of the Bay shimmered radiantly. The downtown office
towers glittered darkly. The last rays spilled through the Golden Gate
like a torrent of sunshine. Christ, it is a lovely view, a view that you
cannot appraise, that you cannot quote a figure for, that is beyond
price—though, to be frank, I know a little something about what an
upscale sunset view, presented to prospective buyers in the proper light,
will do to enhance the value of a house on the high end of the real
estate market.

My attorney had arranged the meeting. He had called me from his
San Francisco office. "Who is this guy? What's his story?" I had asked.
The good man put a phone shrug in his voice and said, "I don't know.

He seemed on the level. I don't believe he's a fed trying to set you up." A reflective pause followed. "Said he teaches at Hayward State, which checked out. Claims he read about you in that magazine article several years back and thought he might have something of interest." Something of interest! A professor with an angle. Well, why not?

I finished my Scotch, then turned from the twilight view to observe the traffic in the Claremont's Terrace Bar. The place hummed with the mellifluous voices of young professional types. The Friday-evening press of lawyers, execs, stockbrokers, systems analysts, real estate salesmen in tasseled Bally loafers.

I was once among them. No one looking at me would have guessed that three years earlier, *California* magazine had profiled my own meteoric career as a real estate salesman—or, rather, real estate swindler. My ex-wife, that traitorous bitch, that double-dealing swine, that heartbreakingly beautiful blonde, had been selling real estate on Long Island when we first met, at a party in Oyster Bay. We looked into each other's eyes and recognized each other's soul, and before the night was out we had hatched a scheme wherein we would rent great big houses on pricey patches of turf like Grosse Point, Michigan . . . Shaker Heights, Ohio . . . Key Biscayne, Florida . . . and Hillsborough, just south of San Francisco—rent mansions, then sell them for a mint.

The beautiful thing about homes in the two-to-four-million-dollar neighborhood is that buyers lay out at least one-fourth the loot instead of the usual ten or twenty percent for the middle-class suburban tract home. So if we sold a house for two million we were able to walk away with a cool $500,000 (minus first and last, operating expenses, etcetera, etcetera) before the sheriff gave the bum's rush to the bewildered buyer. My wife posed as an escrow officer, I as a real estate broker. Or vice versa—depending on the sex of the prospective buyer. Flirtation sometimes figured in our pitch.

Make no mistake. Plenty of fancy paperwork was involved. But we were hard workers, and we enjoyed our work. We enjoyed leading a prospective buyer through a rambling eighteenth-century Connecticut farmhouse and fingering the handsome stone fireplaces, insisting that the client climb up on a chair, the better to admire the grain in the exposed ceiling beams. We delighted in wandering through a renovated

North Carolina colonial and nodding at the antique marble fireplace in the master bedroom, remarking how pleasing it would be to read to the children on a rainy day in the upstairs glass-cathedral-turret sitting room. We relished equally the stately Tudor charms of yesteryear found in a mansion nestled behind stone walls and pine woods in Westchester, and the contemporary lines of a Norman Jaffe house in Westhampton Beach, whose pitched skylights admitted the heavens. We loved our work, and we never sold a house that was ugly or in poor taste. In nine months of unloading homes in some of the better neighborhoods of this fine nation, we cleared $1.9 million before selling a mansion in Hillsborough to a wealthy couple, portrayed with unsettling gentleness, with an effective lack of showiness, by two FBI agents who had truly given themselves over to their roles (they even gave us a little sales resistance, insisted we first modernize the kitchen).

It should have been a simple case of white-collar fraud. But my wife, a breathtaking lady, offered to cooperate with the authorities in return for a lighter sentence, and so laid at their feet as sacrificial offering certain facts about my background. I had no record, but she told them to push harder, and sure enough, my name—or, rather, my father's name, Frank Furio, Sr.—popped up on the wonderful Quantico computer (terrific speed, tremendous memory), and so it was established that I was the son of an old-line capo in the New York Capriccio family. The feds, boys fresh out of Boalt, became delirious. They thought they had netted a big one. They stamped "OC" all over my file, and it became an *organized crime* case. It wasn't. But it did me no good to protest that I had no part of the family fiefdom crap, the medieval shenanigans, that I was interested in money, not fealty. In truth, I am not a violent man (although growing up I have gleaned a few tricks from people around me regarding insurance fraud, forging new identities, making paper companies appear like magic out of janitor's closets, etcetera, etcetera).

I was sunk. *The Village Voice* ran a piece identifying me as one of "the new breed of white-collar Mafioso." *New York* magazine said I belonged to "the yuppie wing of the Capriccio family." *Vogue* called me "a New Wave gangster-entrepreneur" and discussed my suits, shoes, and well-groomed looks. So when a writer from *California* made a pro forma request to my lawyer to interview me, he was pleasantly surprised that I agreed. Quite frankly, I felt the need, if not to set the record straight, then to tend to my image before my case came up before the Northern California federal judge handling the trial. Unlike my father's people, who have a tropism for the dark, away from the glare of the spotlight, I thought the media were there to be played, to the advantage of the best player. That's what a college education will do for you.

And it worked. The writer took the high road and rhapsodized about how I had attended Cornell (School of Labor Relations—I didn't tell him about my scheming father's plan to found a local Teamsters dynasty). But the Ivy League had no need to get its guard up. I comported myself with dignity, mostly. I read Proust. I ate up Emile Durkheim and Thorstein Veblen. I analyzed frame by frame *The Birth of a Nation* and *Citizen Kane*. I studied everything except labor relations. That pensioneered public menace, my father, ranted at me for wasting his hard-earned money on *art history* and *literature* and *sociology*. He couldn't understand my desire to broaden myself; the pure development of the intellect meant nothing to him.

The article went on to give my father's curriculum vitae. The usual: bank robbery, extortion, bookmaking, loansharking, suspected murder, and so on into his black night. I, the article said, was not into any of these things. The piece also said (ho ho ho) that I had no plans to return to real estate.

But I didn't think it was real estate that caught the eye of the professor, who—I glanced at my watch—was now twenty minutes late. For the article also alluded to a vague interest on my part in movie production; and the professor, one Wilbur Blackfield, was, to be exact, an assistant professor of Cinema and Popular Culture. He had told my lawyer he might have something that would interest me. That meant I had something that interested him.

Whatever the article's effect, the judge felt inspired to pity me and rejected the prosecutor's contention that I was OC (and therefore deserving of a stiff sentence). I pleaded to conspiracy, tax evasion, and defrauding homebuyers in several states, was ordered to make restitution, and was sentenced to six years in Allenwood Federal Prison, a so-called country-club can, where I did an easy two. And then, because

I had liked the Bay Area better than anywhere else in this splendid nation where I had pushed my unreal real estate, because I wanted to avoid New York, where attempts would be made to bring me under the wing of the Capriccio family, and because I still retained some financial interests out here, I resettled in San Francisco.

Across the bar I now spotted the professor—at least I thought it was the professor—threading his way through the tables toward me. Wilbur Blackfield was large and broad, and radiated a kind of sly professorial shabbiness. He shuffled, he shambled, he lumbered, he padded along like a cunning Saint Bernard. The man lacked structural harmony. Under his wrinkled blue oxford shirt breastlets were starting to bud. And his eyes, in marked contrast to the slowness of his body, his deep-set eyes darted left and right, alert and shifty. He looked, say, five or so years older than me, about forty—not a good forty, a *bad* forty, the last decade filled, I suspected, with academic frustration and backstabbing. He didn't wear his clothes so much as look as though he were bivouacking in them.

The reason I thought it was the professor was simply that I had seen him once before, though it was only now that I was able to attach a name to that flabby shrewd face. It had been a month earlier. I had driven across the Bay Bridge to the Pacific Film Archive in Berkeley to see an obscure 1951 gangster movie starring Robert Mitchum called *The Racket*. My father had recommended it, and this strange man now shambling toward me had spoken before the picture was shown. Christ, had he spoken! That night he had gotten carried away by enthusiasms. Beneath that shifty look passions boiled and roiled. His screed took in World War I, German Expressionism, the 1930s migration to Holly-wood of top German film talent as the Nazis rose to power, Hitler, the Holocaust, the dark night of the world-soul, and then he was off and running on twentieth-century madness, which, he passionately explained, is different from the madness of any other century, that in this poor century madness has crossed a threshold, has had to reinvent its terms *yackety-yackety-yack*, and how strange and terrible and beautiful the planet has become in the late twentieth century. Yes, on and on he raved before the audience—a *paying* audience—an obsessed, completely self-absorbed fellow, interesting up to a point I suppose.

But that point passed, and the audience started to get restless. Loud coughing up front. Muttering way in back. An ostentatious clearing and clacking of throats somewhere off to the side. The professor, no nitwit, picked up on the hostile currents, wrapped up and bowed out.

Now I glanced at my watch, then up at the professor as he reached my table and smiled brightly.

"Frank Furio?" he said, offering his meaty, sweaty hand. "I'm Wilbur Blackfield." I nodded, ignoring that meaty, sweaty hand. With a stentorian sigh he lowered himself into the chair opposite mine and gazed out the window.

"What a stunning sunset!" he exclaimed.

"It was more stunning twenty minutes ago."

He fluttered his hands and said, "I read all about your impressive career a few years back."

"So my lawyer tells me. But you shouldn't believe everything you read, Professor."

"Please. Call me Wilbur." He added, "Of course, I'm as skeptical as the next guy. But it did make for interesting reading. Then, just a month ago, I saw a small item in the *Chronicle* saying you'd been released. A model prisoner."

I looked more closely at Professor Wilbur Blackfield, who, smiling pleasantly, sat studying me, Frank Furio, model prisoner. If you didn't kill someone you were a model prisoner.

The waitress came for his order. "A pousse-café," he said, and then spelled it out in mind-numbing detail: "From bottom to top: grenadine, crème de cacao, maraschino cordial, curaçao, Crème Yvette, and brandy." Rapidly scribbling, she made a face, but this didn't seem to register on him. "And please make sure the bartender gets the sequence right—specific gravity and all that. I don't want one layer sinking into the next." As she walked away, hips swinging, he sighed with sexual melancholy.

"I saw you speak once," I said. "At the PFA."

"No kidding. During the *noir* series?"

"Some Robert Mitchum movie—"

"*The Racket*. What'd you think?"

I shrugged. "Justifiably obscure. Certainly no neglected classic."

"No, no—of my talk."

I smiled. "It was interesting. You know your stuff." I let it go at that, and then just sat there studying Wilbur's creased fleshy face in the fading twilight.

"I believed a lot of that article," he said. "That you weren't, you know, Maf like your old man. You were independent. No middlemen; violence is for schmucks. In a technocracy gangsters have to use their brains."

Had I said all that? I hadn't read the article in years. I'd have to go back and look at it so I didn't have strangers quoting or misquoting me to my face.

"You know, our fathers had something in common."

"Yeah?"

"Your old man robbed banks, mine worked in them. Wells Fargo."

"They'll have to get together some time."

He smiled pleasantly and got down to business. "I think I have something that could help you. In fact, I'm sure of it. The newspaper suggested that between fines and legal fees, you're now in the poorhouse."

That wasn't strictly true. I had about ninety thousand a year coming in from a few far-flung investments set up through childhood friends and college buddies before I had trooped off to Allenwood. A rental property in Mill Valley. A lingerie store in a Pleasanton shopping mall ("Pleasant Lingerie for Pleasant People"). Stocks traded under a false name. But I wasn't as liquid as I like to be and I was lying low, living comfortably but not luxuriously in a condo on Telegraph Hill. The prison business and the resultant IRS attentions crimped my life style, no question about it. I had to take my profile down a few pegs.

So I shrugged modestly, sipped my third Scotch, and waited to hear the professor out.

"You *would* like to make some money?" he asked.

"A rhetorical question."

Professor Blackfield nodded, glanced toward the bar to see how his drink was coming along, then smiled disarmingly and asked, "You know who Doug Lowell is?"

"Of course," I said, a touch annoyed. Who didn't? Doug Lowell was big, a world-class moviemaker, maybe even an artist. Fabulously rich, he was one of the most powerful people in the movie industry, yet a maverick in the bargain. He lived not in Los Angeles but on an estate in the Santa Cruz Mountains. Six or so years ago he had made a small bundle on a violent but clever low-budget thriller called *The Black Pig*, whose ground-level high-velocity tracking shots, along with a shrewd, supremely conscious manipulation of the *noir* genre, had blown away many critics. The movie had been a hit out of left field, the money had rolled in from the action houses, and Doug Lowell was on his way. That picture gave him the clout to make his next one, the medium-budget *The High Plateau of Stars*, which blended Homeric epic with science fiction and turned out to be a blockbuster. It put Doug Lowell over the top in a big, big way. You couldn't talk about the state of American movies—that is, American mass culture—without taking sides on him, on whether *High Plateau* had transcended the *Star Wars* genre by infusing it with a new kind of visual poetry, or whether he was just further dumbing and doping the already skewed sensibilities of American youth. People couldn't make up their minds on what he stood for; the jury was still out. I recalled reading in the gossip columns recently that he was having difficulties with the sequel, *The High Plateau of Stars, Part II*, that it was more than a year behind schedule and fantastically over budget; and since he had taken a gamble and practically financed the movie out of his own pocket, with minimal studio backing, there was even talk he might go belly-up. I didn't believe that for one instant. People like Doug Lowell never go belly-up.

The professor said, "I'm sorry. I didn't mean to offend you. Of course you know who Doug Lowell is."

"That's all right."

"What did you think of *High Plateau*?"

"It wasn't bad."

"C'mon," the professor said slyly, coaxing. "You could do better than that."

He was pushing it. Okay then. "The movie was Spielberg but with an existential pang and a neo-Marxian feel for the modern machinery of simulacra. He understands we live in an age in which artifice has triumphed over the real. The picture was fun, yet a touch baleful. As if we were seeing an outer space that had become haunted, burdened with history."

He nodded. "There are some who say that Lowell could have been a major painter if he had wanted. An avant-garde character who would've caused a stir in the art world. Or at least every time he strutted into a SoHo bar. He lived in lower Manhattan for a while, you know, painting and diddling in experimental films. Sometimes even hand-painting his films frame by frame. You know the type. They spend two years making a five-minute movie that's then seen by twenty people in New York and fifteen people on the Coast. But then he saw the light. He looked around and decided the pond was too small, the stakes too slight. Standard-issue avant-gardists struggling to free themselves from the prison of tradition, when mainstream American movies are freer than anything else in sight. Lowell wanted the world to be his field."

"Still, there are others who say he's nothing but a con artist grafting highbrow stuff onto lowbrow entertainments, for the cachet."

"What do you think?"

I shrugged. "I haven't studied the matter."

He accepted this and nodded. "I also read in the article that you'd like to get into movie production."

"Just something I tossed off."

The professor gazed thoughtfully at me. Was Wilbur Blackfield aware of my own career, however modest, in moviemaking? Because, to tell the truth, I hadn't just tossed it off. I had once gotten into movie production in a half-witted swindlelous sort of way and had rather enjoyed it. While I was at Cornell a childhood friend, Tony Fino, had called to ask if I knew anyone who made films. In fact, another childhood friend, Arnie Goldblatt, after studying with Martin Scorsese at NYU, after getting thrown out for plagiarizing a paper on Pudovkin, was churning out porno films from a Bronx warehouse near the Throgs Neck Bridge. I brought Tony and Arnie together. Tony had picked up the American distribution rights to a low-budget Eurotrash slasher called *Crazy About You*—I never understood how that had come about except it had something to do with several kilos of heroin processed at a farmhouse outside of Palermo that had then been lost in transit to

JFK. At any rate, Tony had the intermediate English-dubbed copy and no idea what to do with it. So the three of us sat in the warehouse on a gray rainy day and watched it on Arnie's editing table. The movie had a classical plot: Boy meets girl, boy chops girl up. This sequence was repeated ten times with modest variations and using ten different models, all of whom were attractive in a low-budget sort of way.

Make no mistake. It was a stupid bloody monotonous film, horribly dubbed, too. But there is a market, however marginal, for stupid bloody monotonous films. Our problem was to come up with some gimmick that would convince an American distributor to pick it up. We needed a positive differential. That afternoon we sat around drinking beer, smoking pot, scheming.

Then I had an idea. I suggested we find some semiretired semicelebrity—someone washed-up and down at the heels but with lingering if steadily eroding name recognition. Someone we could coax before the camera for, say, forty thousand dollars for a day or two's work.

Then Arnie thought of Bruno Zopp. Praised by Lotte Eisner in her classic work *The Haunted Screen*, he had migrated in the late 1930s from Nazi Germany to Hollywood, where Fritz Lang helped launch him on a second career starring as a mad German scientist in B horror movies. Arnie made a few phone calls, and the next day I jetted out to California and found the poor bastard holed up in a rented one-bedroom condo in a West Hollywood high-rise, where the refugee from Nazi Germany was killing his last days drinking Bombay gin and watching American soap operas. Isn't the USA a big grand surreal operation! Bruno was down-and-out. Not much remained of the old German exile gang to keep him going or even to provide company (actually, the day I saw Professor Blackfield speak at the Pacific Film Archive he mentioned Bruno in passing).

So it was on a bleak cold November day that Bruno Zopp—once directed by Max Reinhardt, once a supporting actor to Greta Garbo—so it was on a bleak cold November day that a painfully grateful Bruno Zopp, talked down to twenty-five thou, found himself in a Bronx warehouse in the shadow of the Throgs Neck Bridge surrounded by the sons of Bronx wiseguys. He was magnificent. He stormed back and forth across the cold concrete floor, pouring his passion into a moronic monologue hastily penned by Frank Furio, Jr. He accepted like a gentleman, without complaint, pointers on locution and tips on the Stanislavsky method from Arnie Goldblatt, whose previous screen credits included *Rubber Dreams*, *Latex Lovers*, and *Hogtied*. There he stood, a grand noble relict of German Expressionism, flanked by whips and chains and handcuffs and dildos, which Arnie had decided to leave lying around to add, as he put it, to the "demented atmosphere." It was demented all right.

Arnie took this material and cut it into the original movie, interspersing it between the murders. It provided the film with a sort of goofball narrative framework: events recalled in tranquillity from the bughouse. It was sick, silly, ridiculous. All told, Bruno Zopp wound up with eleven minutes of screen time that were scattered like golden raisins throughout the deadly dough. But it was good enough to sell the movie in this country.

But we also had a stroke of luck. On his flight back to the West Coast, Bruno Zopp's sad German Expressionist heart-in-exile caved in on him. Farewell Bruno! So not only was Tony able to find an American distributor on the basis of Zopp's name, but the movie, which we retitled *Love You to Pieces*, was promoted as the last movie of the one, the only, the legendary horror-screen great Bruno Zopp.

Love You to Pieces played in grind houses across the nation for several weeks. It turned a modest profit and attracted a few kind words. A *Daily News* critic called it "mesmerizing in its awfulness but not without some glints of humor." *The New York Times* said that "though the film is invested with the stink of the slaughter yards, Zopp acquits himself with elegiac twilight dignity." Later in video it even developed a modest cult following (every rotten thing these days develops a modest cult following). Tony paid me thirty-five thou and I received my first and only screen credit: *Frank Furio—Creative Consultant*. And I felt a certain sorrow, genuine if not especially deep, that Bruno was not with us to share in this final triumph.

Ah, Bruno Zopp! You deserved better than Arnie Goldblatt, Frank Furio, Jr., and the sad old postexpressionist, poststructuralist, post-everything Bronx.

But that was years ago. This evening, this strange professor nodded oddly and said mildly, "Just something you tossed off. Well, perhaps we can get into movie production together some time." Abruptly he changed the subject. "Four hundred thousand dollars. Not a bad payoff for three months' work on that Key Biscayne house. Of course, there was a lot of paperwork. Drawing up the phony mortgages. Setting up the phony escrow. Why, it's as much fun as doing your own income taxes."

"You tenured?" I asked suddenly.

He shook his head no.

"How much do *you* make for three months' work? Three *years'* work?"

Wilbur sighed. "Not enough, Frank. Not enough to live comfortably in the Bay Area these days. Why, the cost-of-living index is even higher than in New York. Just consider your basic material necessities: A six-bedroom redwood shingle in Pacific Heights with a hot tub on the sun deck and an unfiltered view of the Bay. A BMW in the garage and a Volvo station wagon for the groceries and the fucking kids. A summer cabin up the coast and a ski condo in Tahoe." He sighed again. "Way out of the reach of a professor without a parish."

The guy was diverting. He glanced again toward the bar to see how the bartender was coming along with his freakish concoction.

"You have any idea what *High Plateau II* cost?" he asked.

"He's gone way over budget," I said. "I read the papers same as anyone."

"Sixty-seven million," Wilbur said thoughtfully. "It was supposed to cost thirty or forty. And you know what? He put up most of the cash himself. Can you believe it? That's something even people like Lucas and Spielberg shy away from, and that Coppola tried, nearly bankrupting himself in the process. And Coppola did that while the economy was still going like gangbusters."

I let my gaze drift around the bar. Soft mellow jazz wafted through the air. A waitress with a punk went around lighting the candles on the tables, now that the sun had disappeared completely behind the dark Marin hills. The flatlands of Berkeley and Oakland, spread out below, glittered in the late dusky April glow. And on the lit courts immediately below us, two sports in tennis whites swatted a ball back and forth.

"Professor," I said, rising, "it's been a pleasure, but kidnapping is not my game."

"No, no, no," he said, laughing good-naturedly. "Please, sit. We're both educated men. I would never insult you with such a proposition. I wouldn't dream of that. The violence. The media attention. The FBI."

"What's on your mind?"

Wilbur scanned for the waitress, then sat up straighter, assumed a more properly professorial attitude. "Okay. A movie is shot, the action recorded on the roll of negative in the camera. Usually there's three to six times as much negative footage as eventually makes up the actual film. In the case of *High Plateau II*, there's a lot more. The positives are developed at a lab and the negatives stored for safekeeping—"

"At the lab or at the filmmaker's place?"

"Doesn't matter for our purposes. The director and his editors get the developed film back. They look at it, pick out what they like, set aside what they don't like, and edit it down till they have something resembling the movie they had in mind. This is called the final cut. It is what the movie will look like. It *is* the movie." Wilbur closed his eyes against the last light, as though recharging.

I checked my watch. I had a dinner date at Donatello's in San Francisco with a noted stock market swindler. I had a nightclub date afterward at DV8 with a young woman, a Bechtel engineer who might be able to give me some inside info on subcontracting bids I could pass on to friends in construction. "Get to the point, Professor."

His eyes blinked open. "This print is shipped off along with all the stored negative footage to an independent contractor called the negative cutter. In this case the negative cutter is in San Francisco. She match-cuts. What this means is, she carefully slices out all the bits of negative that match the final positive. She then splices these bits together, and the final product is called the matched negative. This matched negative is then sent to the lab, where dupes are made, to preserve the original, and two thousand or so release prints are struck off for the theaters." Wilbur smiled inwardly, a pedagogue warming to his subject. "You understand? Everything boils down to the matched negative—a dozen or so reels you can hold stacked like plates in your arms."

"Please. Don't keep it simple for me."

"I'm not. By the way, I very much admired your work on *Love You to Pieces*." I stared at him. He smiled exquisitely and rolled right on: "Now, before any prints get struck, the matched negative is *the sole record* of three years of backbreaking work. Of millions of dollars worth of superstar fees. Of A-list technical talent. Of millions of dollars more worth of stunning set designs, of all that difficult location photography in Antarctica, the Sahara, the Himalayas, and the South Bronx. Of still millions more worth of complicated postproduction work at Lowell's facility in the Santa Cruz Mountains, where an army of technicians has spent the last year round the clock editing the mountain of footage down to a manageable two hours of fast-paced, crowd-pleasing stuff. At least, so they hope."

"How come you know all this? That the match-cutting was done up here instead of L.A.? That it's just about finished?"

"It can be gleaned from the gossip columns. From casual conversations picked up on the film-party circuit. Besides, Lowell prefers the Bay Area talent pool. It makes him feel less Hollywoodish. Plus union regs are looser." Wilbur paused to look out the window. "What I'm saying is—"

"I know what you're saying."

"—for a short period of time, just several days before it's shipped to the lab, the matched negative represents *everything* that has gone into the production. It is the sole record of all the work. The whole sixty-seven-million-dollar investment." All of a sudden he looked straight at me. "Two guys posing as Doug's people," Wilbur murmured. "No guns, no rough stuff. They're sent to pick it up. Do you understand? The movie is scheduled to open in two thousand theaters across the country in just five weeks. It's booked solid from Bangor to San Diego, from the inner cities to the suburban multiplexes. These two guys would have Lowell's back against the wall—let's say, a two-and-a-half-million-dollar wall. The theater owners will be screaming if they don't have the prints for the start of the summer season." Finished, Wilbur cracked his knuckles and smiled modestly.

"How do you know he even has that kind of money? The movie's supposed to have pretty much tapped him out."

Wilbur said, "A guy's two thousand in debt, he'd probably have trouble raising two million. But somebody who's seventy million in debt, he'll always find another two million."

I asked, "Just suppose, for the sake of hypothesis, he goes to the cops?"

Wilbur shook his head. "He won't. That's the beauty of it. It's not like a kidnapping, things go wrong, someone gets killed. He won't go to the cops or even to the insurance company that holds the completion bond on the film. For one, he won't want to draw attention to the theft. Show business sorts might be obsessed by profile, but not of this kind. No, he'd be the laughingstock of the industry. Besides, he's already gotten enough bad PR for his budget overruns. But more importantly, he has to figure whoever took it will have less qualms about whacking a negative than whacking a hostage. Then where'll he be?" Wilbur leaned closer. "Far better to just quietly absorb the ransom demand into the already inflated budget. Another business expense."

"You said something about insurance."

"Okay. Technically he probably wouldn't be out sixty-seven million. The film's bonded. But they're not going to reimburse him just like that. They might even insist he reconstruct another version from the outtakes. So he'd be out his original movie. The bottom line is, it'd be more cost-efficient to pay us. Otherwise the movie gets bumped back to Christmas, and you better believe interest accumulates pretty fast on sixty-seven million. Insurance won't cover that."

I wondered aloud why nobody had ever done this before if it was such a cinch. He had an answer, he had two. In the early seventies in a little-publicized case in Italy that was even less publicized in the United States, a gang of neo-Fascists had stolen the work print to Pier Paolo Pasolini's last film, *Salo*, then returned it for five hundred million lire and mutual assurances to avoid publicity, which would benefit neither party. But more to the point, Wilbur went on, it was not the sort of heist that would occur to your ordinary gangster, no, he wouldn't get it, he wouldn't appreciate the beauty of it, the poetry, he wouldn't be able to put it all together, it was too sublime, too avant-garde, it required thinking of a very high order.

Which is not to denigrate gangsters, Wilbur hurriedly went on. But they're usually into pedestrian stuff, like knocking off an armored car or a Teamsters local, or rigging a construction bid.

On the other hand, the people to whom it *might* occur—industry people, journalists, academic types—wouldn't have the requisite stamina. You needed imagination and cowboy courage to get in the game.

"So what I'm wondering is," Wilbur said finally, "might this interest you?" The professor had finished his presentation. He smiled at me, his student.

I crossed my legs. I leaned back. I delicately sipped my Scotch. "Tell me this is a joke, a colossal put-on."

Wilbur took a pipe from his tweed sports jacket, tapped it in the palm of his hand, packed the bowl with tobacco, placed it in the corner of his mouth—but then didn't light it. I almost shook my head in admiration. The guy was wonderful, an absolute treasury, a depository of professorial gestures.

"No joke, no put-on. You interested or not?"

I have spent a fair part of my life in the company of psychopaths. As a baby I was rocked on the knees of psychopaths. At Christmas psychopaths would give me pigskin footballs and shiny new bicycles. On my birthday psychopaths would take me to Coney Island and, holding on to their fedoras, ride the savage roller coaster with me. At Thanksgiving I'd watch psychopaths, whistling while they worked, carve up the turkey. Yes, I am thoroughly familiar with all sizes and shapes of psychopaths—but none that I'd ever met hailed from academia.

"Why me? Why not a friend, someone you trust?"

"I liked the sense of you I got from that article. Cool, smooth, and educated. I liked your background. A mix of Ivy League and the streets. You need the first to understand this, the second to pull it off. I suspect you'd be very good in working out the logistics. You understand these things. You even understand movies. As for friends, all mine are mild-mannered academic types who don't know intrigue from ivory."

"Who else have you shopped this to?"

"What did I just say? Where am I going to shop it? The faculty club? Tack a card up on the bulletin board?"

I could hear cocktail chatter at the tables around us. Brokerage and bond reports. Corporate capital gains and tax-free growth. Whether a Carrera Targa depreciated more quickly than a Carrera Cabriolet.

"How you going to contact him? We're talking about Doug Lowell. I don't suppose he's in the White Pages."

"I was at a party recently. A sound editor who once worked for him. I had to make a call. There was a Rolodex by the phone. I let my fingers do the walking." Wilbur paused, then said, "You're not hesitating because of moral objections?"

"Of course not," I said indignantly.

Wilbur smiled. He saw he could get to me. The lights in the place were dimmed. "A more romantic mood," he said. "All business discussions should be coming to an end." He nodded thoughtfully. "It's quite wonderful, actually. You look like a young stockbroker or something."

I glanced at my Rolex, then quietly said, "And you look like a professor. A greedy, stupid, rumpled professor. You having that much trouble getting tenure?"

"A million tax-free dollars," he said pleasantly.

"Running out of colleges in the Bay Area to teach at?" I asked, putting down a twenty and rising to go. "Afraid you'll wind up dead-ended at some two-year cow college in the sticks?"

"Think about it. But please don't take too long."

Just then the waitress arrived, balancing the professor's multilayered pousse-café concoction in a tall pony glass. A real treat. In layers, in floors, in tiers from the ground up: red, brown, white, orange, violet, and amber liquids, with an overstory of whipped cream sprinkled with chocolate curls, all crowned by a maraschino cherry. Gingerly, she set it down in front of him.

"May I?" I asked, reaching for the drink.

"Uh, sure."

I grabbed a spoon and vigorously stirred the contents, clattering metal against glass. Like a rainbow whipped through a blender, the colors raced together. I took a long draft. Then shook my head as I handed the drink back to a stricken Wilbur Blackfield.

"It's mundane," I said. "It needs something."

C h a p t e r   2

The Berkeley campus was just coming awake when I arrived at the library the next morning—the library where I would spend the next two days researching Doug Lowell. The musty air made me gag; the amazing vitality of young miniskirted coeds revived me. And on and on I worked, scribbling notes like a gentleman and a scholar.

There was no shortage of material on Doug Lowell. People loved to read about him, to monitor his fortunes, to ventilate on his extravaganzas. I pored over clippings from *The New York Times*, *The Los Angeles Times*, the *San Francisco Chronicle*, and *Variety*, I read interviews with Lowell in *Film Comment* and *American Film*, profiles and glossy write-ups in *Esquire* and *Vanity Fair*, career overviews in *The New York Times Magazine* and financial profiles in *Forbes* and *Fortune*.

Time described him as being in his late thirties, with a master's in architecture from Harvard's Graduate School of Design, and a distant cousin of the late American poet Robert Lowell. *Newsweek* described him as forty, a graduate of the Carpenter Center for the Visual Arts at Harvard, and a descendant of the poet Amy Lowell. An investigative update in *The New York Times* said he was in his mid-forties, had taken a summer course at Harvard, and had been expelled from the University of Southern California for stealing film equipment. His name, the *Times* reported, might have been Anglicized not on Ellis Island but in an obscure courthouse in New Jersey that had since burned down, taking boxes of records with it. And he had gall. In a *Film Comment* Q & A the interviewer had asked, "What do you owe your father, who started out as a carpenter and now does set designs for your pictures?" Lowell, usually generous, had snapped, "I owe him nothing. He owes me. I am not a chip off the old block. I'm a block off the old chip." No patrician airs about Doug Lowell, nothing humdrum about the guy. And he was recognizable, physically. Photographs in the magazines showed a bearish fellow with a dark beard starting to gray and shrewd broad peasant features animated by a carnal playfulness, as though the whole world made him randy. He was casual about his wear, inclined toward faded blue jeans, ragged crewneck sweaters, and always the same navy windbreaker.

Then there were his eyes. In every photograph his eyes registered as though they were on high beam—these incredibly clear light blue eyes. A sadistic lucidity shone in them. Yet they were kindly (but a shade more pigment and they'd turn you to ice). Doug Lowell looked radiantly concentrated: engaged, yet free of it all; calm, yet as if his mind were as busy as Times Square, as Macy's just before Christmas. And in the outer corners of those eyes twinkled a huckster's alertness to being found out. What he didn't look was self-absorbed or egotistical. He was too big to be egotistical; he knew exactly what size shoes he wore. In other words Doug Lowell looked like a real workout.

I learned that in addition to his estate in the Santa Cruz Mountains, he kept a cottage in Malibu, condos in San Francisco and on Central Park West, and a ski cabin in Vail. But it was the Santa Cruz estate that dazzled me. Although Lowell was usually willing to meet with reporters, he kept his combination estate–production facility strictly off-limits. So to oblige the curious, the tourists, the straphangers, the inheritors of Thomas Paine's *Rights of Man*, the *San Francisco Chronicle* one day rented a helicopter and sent it thwok-thwoking into the air space above Lowell's estate. The helicopter had hovered while the paper's photographer hung out the door, dangling from a rope ladder as he shot the place through powerful telescopic lenses. The next day the aerial photographs appeared on the paper's front page, along with a map pinpointing the location of the hidden entry gate on Bonny Doon Road, the security gate a little farther up the driveway, the lake, the main house, the guest house, the carriage house, the swimming pool, the old stone stable that housed his cars, the editing bunker and storage shed built into the side of a mountain . . . all laid out along a one-way road that looped through the pleasant, rolling wooded grounds. An arrow at the top of the map was labeled "North." A road that ran below the estate was labeled "To Highway 1." The thing was a blueprint, an engraved invitation *Come on in!* for burglars and kidnappers. Unbelievable! But that wasn't what I was up to.

The centerpiece of the estate was the white Victorian mansion. Built from the ground up in 1986, the forty-room house was a first cousin of its nineteenth-century predecessors in every last detail. The elaborate workmanship of that era, tens of millions of dollars' worth of painstaking little touches, the sixteen chimneys, the bow windows, the stained glass windows, the carved friezes, the veranda, the conservatory—Lowell had re-created a classic detail by detail. How I would have loved to have sold that house to some Silicon Valley "computer genius"! It is one thing to hear that someone is worth a hundred million; it is something else to see such money in action.

But now all this, or much of it, was threatened. Sailing along on the success of *The High Plateau of Stars*, blithely indifferent to finances, Lowell had spared no expense on the sequel, which had become as overextended as the economy. And because it was an independent production, no budgetary watchdogs from the studio had shown up at the far-flung location sites to see that principal photography was progressing smoothly. Nor had studio executives spent hours each day viewing the rushes, or dailies—footage shot the previous day. In short, no controls had been placed on Doug Lowell, and so the money had bled from him. By the end of principal photography, industry insiders were whispering, "*Cleopatra . . . Heaven's Gate . . . One from the Heart . . . Ishtar. . . .*" And the gossip columnists were hissing, "*Disaster . . . disaster . . . disaster. . . .*"

In fact, hints of the madness to come could be found in press notices before the sequel even got off the ground. A scouting trip for locations was described in *Esquire* as "Around the World in Eighty Ways." Lowell had spent a month traveling all over, making test shots to determine if the quality of light met his specifications for that "high plateau" look. He traveled by mule pack in the Chilean Andes, by kayak in the Arctic, by camel across the Sahara, by dog pack in the frozen interior of Antarctica, by raft through the tropical heart of Borneo, by pedicab in the Philippines, and by bulletproof Mercedes-Benz through the South Bronx.

The *Esquire* piece set the tone and it never got better. The press loved Lowell; he was colorful, rich yet bohemian, and had a license to act nutty. Just prior to two months of very tough shooting in Antarctica, he had a compound of Quonset huts constructed in the snowy wastes; one hut enclosed a Finnish sauna for his use and that of the stars. A scene required Eskimos, which Antarctica lacks, so a hundred and fifty of them were flown in from Alaska. Another scene required elephants with fur glued to their flanks to make them look something like mastodons, so he leased an LC-130 to fly in a couple of elephants from India. He had a snowfield spray-painted blue, because "White creates too much of a glare." "Isn't this getting expensive?" an AP reporter had asked. Lowell riposted, "A lousy picture at ten million is worthless, a great picture at sixty million, priceless."

His success had made him dizzy, turned him into a megalomaniac, according to some reports. Others held him to be a genius and insisted that in the end all would turn out well. But who could tell? Film exposed in the Antarctic was processed in a lab in New York, then assembled in Santa Cruz, which meant that Doug Lowell on location couldn't review the daily footage the next day, or even the next week, as is usual. And then at costs of $457,000 per day he had kept the crew and cast around an extra week in order to capture the beauty of the sun setting finally in the Antarctic at the start of the long winter darkness, a sunset that Lowell insisted would be more magical, more heartbreakingly dusky, more twilightish than any regular old polar dusk. He explained to *The New York Times Magazine* that "such a dusk would feel the pure weight of all those months of darkness it would be pulling down with it; it would be a sad melancholy poetic dusk, a dusk with self-knowledge of its own demise, aware that the curtain is dropping for a long, long time." It got pegged in the press as "The $3.2-Million Heartbreak Sunset."

From the Antarctic the production repaired to the Sahara, where Lowell had air-conditioned circus tents pitched. And when a volcano erupted spectacularly in Fiji, with fireworks and molten lava flows and

lunarscapes at noon, he had the second-unit camera crew rush there
to record it. All the wonders of the world, millions of years in the
making, became backdrop for Lowell's cinematic blowout.

And at the opposite extreme of Antarctic twilight poetry were
the "high plateau" sequences shot amidst the rubble, the squalor, the
tenement wasteland of the South Bronx, where it was rumored Doug
Lowell had paid a Mott Haven street gang to maintain security. It was
the sort of streetwise gesture for which Lowell liked to be known, to
balance his image as poet of the polar dusk. An outraged Bronx City
Council member, José Vásquez, complained to the press and to the
Bronx DA's office, urging an investigation. But when a picture of his
Rockland County rural manor appeared the following week in *The
Village Voice*—it was not his listed Simpson Street registered voter's
address—his voice shrank to a frail, hoarse whisper.

The start of production was supposed to be February 4, completion
of principal photography July 30, the first cut ready by September 15,
and the final cut by November 30, just in time for Christmas. It never
happened. According to *Film Comment*, Lowell was averaging one
minute of usable material for every ninety minutes of film shot. Too
many exterior scenes subject to the whims of the weather. Too few
interior scenes parceled out to the sound stages of Burbank. The shooting schedule and the budget had expanded exponentially, and when a
reporter asked, "What's taking so long?" Lowell shrugged, smiled wear-
ily, and said, "Well, you know. I want to get it right." And as costs
soared, Lowell mortgaged almost all his holdings, including the gem,
the Bonny Doon mountain estate.

The reports grew dreamier as I progressed chronologically through
the clippings. A *San Francisco Chronicle* columnist published a staff
memo from Lowell that said, "*From this day forward* all memos are
to be NEATLY handwritten on 3-by-5-inch WHITE, LINED index cards."
The original line producer quit and promised never to speak to Lowell
again except through a battery of lawyers. *Variety* reported that the
replacement line producer later left the set and had been checked into
a private sanitarium in upstate New York by his wife. According to
New York magazine, a disgruntled extra had been picked up by an
Argentinean naval patrol boat floating in a kayak off Tierra del Fuego

and raving with hallucinatory vigor that the picture was monstrously out of control and that Doug Lowell had set up a black altar at the South Magnetic Pole to communicate with Satan, who was the picture's secret backer. Said Lowell to inquiries: "Feasibility and cost are mere technical questions, of no concern to the committed artist."

But the American Humane Society became concerned when a hathi elephant was discovered wandering in a daze through the slums of the South Bronx, its flanks spray-painted with colorful gang graffiti (the Bronx Zoo issued a laconic statement saying the animal had not escaped from there). The Alaskan branch of the American Civil Liberties Union filed a suit on behalf of thirty-seven Eskimos who claimed that they had suffered such a shock when they had been flown without their understanding first to Antarctica, then to the Sahara, that upon returning to Alaska they could no longer distinguish between the forty-three different types of snow (Lowell brought in a philologist to testify that in fact such linguistic distinctions don't exist in either Inuit or Yupik).

Principal photography ended with the movie way over budget, far behind schedule, and—so went the rumors—not quite looking like it was supposed to. Then followed an additional eighteen months of quiet, guarded postproduction work at Lowell's editing facility in the Santa Cruz Mountains. Costs continued to mount, and the heaps of footage were slowly reduced to a movie. And from the Polo Lounge to the Russian Tea Room, Lowell's detractors wondered if the movie was even releasable.

Of course other industry insiders believed that Doug Lowell, maverick extraordinaire, would pull it out of his hat at the last moment and stun the world with a movie whose gross would surpass even his previous blockbuster. For in the original *High Plateau* he had done new things with the genre, created characters who could stand up to the special effects, and added a self-reflective element that didn't in any way slow the picture down or dampen its commerciality.

Finally, Lowell announced that his movie was completed and would be released May 23, Memorial Day weekend, in time for the traditional start of the summer season. A "Talk of the Town" writer from *The New Yorker* asked, "What will you do next?" Doug Lowell was described as having smiled softly and said, "I might want to make a small, serious picture."

◆ ◆ ◆

After a day in the library I had something of a feel for Doug Lowell, after two days I felt I knew him. Closing the last magazine and going out into the warm spring sunlight, I couldn't imagine a moviemaker in the whole history of cinema who would feel himself in a less negotiable position—he'd trade his kids and throw in his wife to get that negative back. Then too I agreed with Wilbur's assessment that Lowell would not go to the police or call in private investigators. He had too much to lose, too much creative and capital investment at stake. The theft would be a large humiliation, not to mention the fact that public knowledge might prompt destruction of the negative.

However, I would be untruthful if I did not admit to a large and sneaking admiration for Lowell. For as a result of my readings I also suspected that Lowell himself, however perversely, would, in an objective sort of way, be amused by what we were plotting; that at the core of the man's ambitious being—beyond his talent, beyond his money, beyond even his ability to hustle the world—that at the core of the man there resided a true sport, a devoted joker, a fellow with a feel for the low comedy of life. Yes, beyond his shock and astonishment he would appreciate, perhaps even admire, our heist on the aesthetic level.

A Palermo gangster once said of a Sicilian Mafia chief: "Inzerillo died at thirty-seven, it's true. But his thirty years amount to eighty years for an ordinary person. Inzerillo *lived well.* He got a great many things out of life. Other people will never get even a hundredth of those things. It's not a shame to die at that age if you have done, had, and seen everything Inzerillo did, saw, and managed to get. He didn't die weary of life or dissatisfied with it. He died *full up* with life. That's the difference."

Full up indeed! And I admired the movie mogul for that same breadth of scope and vision, that same crazy sense of risk, of steely willingness to live life on the high wire. Yes, I admired him for that very same readiness to gamble that fuels and fires the gangster. The provisional life style of one is not so different from the existential business shenanigans of the other. For sure, the movie mogul and the gangster share a fundamentally religious belief in the big score, the jackpot, whether it be the summer blockbuster that will put him over the top, the Academy Award sweep that will give him his pick of work for a decade, or the multimillion-dollar armored-car heist, the megaton shipment of uncut China white sitting on a freight ship from Palermo docked at a pier off West 47th.

So then, I silently tipped my hat to Doug Lowell, for I would enjoy stealing several million dollars from him, and he would enjoy—perhaps not as enormously—having it stolen by me.

However, I was not done. There remained Wilbur Blackfield, that strange itinerant crank professor, who himself needed to be checked out, albeit as inconspicuously as possible. So the next day I made a few phone calls and visits to campuses. I posed as a concerned parent whose child was considering Professor Blackfield's courses at Hayward State in the fall. I spoke earnestly to department chairmen, flirtatiously to secretaries. Where was he educated? Where else has he taught? Has he published? What has the man *done in life?* I learned of a B.A. from UCLA, a Ph.D. from USC, a one-year teaching stint at Sonoma State University, six months at S.F. State, a triquarter lectureship at the San Francisco Art Institute. Never offered tenure, always moving on. A good engaged lecturer—perhaps too engaged. Always bringing passion to his subject—perhaps too much passion. I ran a data-base search and learned of an article in *Film Quarterly* in which he analyzed the *film noir* genre as a reflection of unconscious American sexual anxiety about the atomic bomb—an article that, according to his contributor's note, he was expanding into a massive tome. The book never came. I learned from a chatty secretary at Sonoma State that while there he had left his wife for a pretty nineteen-year-old coed who had been swayed if not by his good looks then by the passion and power of his words. Two months later when the semester ended, she left him for a lifeguard at the campus swimming pool. Whereupon Wilbur, shaken and bereft, tried to return to his wife, who would have no part of him. He spent the next semester in the Napa State Mental Institution.

Professor Wilbur Blackfield seemed a touch off balance, but then I had grown up in the company of people who were as explosively unstable as nitroglycerin. What counted was that he had schemed madly, creatively, beautifully. Did I myself have any qualms, any doubts, about the viability of the project? No. My primary concern was: What are the risks and are they worth the rewards? My mind is sharp, my intellect well informed, my body fit and hale. I felt keenly alive to the possibilities before me. As the hanging judge said to the murderer before passing sentence: "You have shown no sense of guilt. You have expressed no feelings of remorse. You have demonstrated an utterly depraved indifference to human life." That is extreme. I am no murderer, and I love the blue-green coniferous mountains, the waterfall that thunders out of the clouds, the diminishing light at play on the pearly lake at dusk. But the conventional indignation of the judge gets the point across. I have no qualms. Yes, I had done my market research and I had considered the target. When I looked at Doug Lowell I saw an occasion, an opening—and if the professor was right it would only be an occasion, an opening, for a day, two at the most.

C h a p t e r   3

I woke at dawn in the guest house in a cold sweat, the sheets soaked. Once again, that damn nightmare had scaled the walls of my sleep. I was in a cave stumbling along lost, holding a candle to guide me as I followed a long, unspooled strip of 35mm motion-picture film that for some dream-reason I believed would lead me out of the cave—and into the blinding light of day. No such luck. Gleaming stalactites, dewy with sweat, descended from the ceilings. Great stalagmites, sharp as spears, thrust up from the cavern floor. And the strip of film wound on and on, snaking through the tunnels. It rounded bends. It ascended cold clammy vertical fissures. It descended into tight crevices. And wherever it went I followed.

I would walk upright. I would walk crouched over. I would crawl on my hands and knees, and then, when I could no longer crawl, I would wiggle—wiggle through dark, narrow passageways with sharp *things* sticking out of the walls. My clothes were wet, torn, and muddied, my knees black and blue, my hands cut and bruised. Sometimes it would take me hours to inch along through some hellishly narrow crawl space. *But the strip of film did not lead me out.* No light shined at the end of this tunnel, or the next, or the one after that. The film wound on and on, beckoning to me, teasing me, leading me deeper and deeper into the bowels of the earth. But never out.

Then I would notice that my candle had melted all the way down. The flame would begin to gutter. Abruptly a night worse than blindness would drop, as though a medieval executioner had yanked a hood over my head.

And once again I would sit bolt upright in bed and stare shivering out the window at my mansion, which loomed like a ghost house through the drifting mist.

Perhaps you wonder, *Why does he sleep in the guest house when his mansion, his beautiful mansion that cost nine million to build, is just fifty yards away?* But I have always felt myself to be a guest, an outsider, a visitor—a guest of the film industry; a guest of my talent, which I sometimes feel is merely on loan to me; a guest on this planet; and a guest of my wife, my adorable wife, who fled back to Cleveland, to the ancestral home of her father, the Shaker Heights textile king, who despised me the moment he laid eyes on me, when his daughter had fallen in love with me and my net worth was fifty cents and his was five million. Now I am worth fifty million, or maybe a hundred, and he is still worth five million, and he hates me more than ever.

So my wife had retreated to her ancestral home to take a sabbatical from me (I needed a sabbatical from myself) while I finished "tinkering" (her delightful word) with my film—finished editing it during those last weeks when I had become so locked in to my work that I must have appeared mad to her.

Let me tell you about *tinkering.*

During those last weeks in the editing bunker as I worked myself into a frenzy of aesthetic creation and destruction, my editors started to whisper that I was "crazy," "mad," "obsessive," "violent," that my *film* was "crazy," "mad," "obsessive," "violent"; yes, behind my back, but in *sotto-voce* stage whispers, they would talk to each other in this insidious way, they would speak as though I had become the movie, the movie had become me, me and the movie had become interchangeable, you could thread me on the wheel's sprockets and run me through the projector, you could seat my movie in the screening room and have it watch me; and so, after working and driving my editors as though they were slaves, after refusing to let them leave the bunker, after refusing to let them eat, sleep, shave, shower, attend their children's wretched birthday parties, visit parents weaving macramé nooses in old-age homes, after driving them, working them, whipping them into a frenzy for weeks on end, I suddenly *reversed* myself, yes, I drove them *from* the bunker, I expelled them—because suddenly I realized they wanted to destroy my film, my delicate film, which they could do just by looking at it, just by *breathing* on it; because suddenly I realized I needed to clear my head of all their inane imbecilic suggestions; because suddenly I realized I needed to secure my film against them, stand guard over my film like a sentry on night duty whose vigilance the lives of others depend upon; yes, I realized then and there that in order to preserve my film's purity I needed to keep the film to myself for as long as possible—*don't let go of it*—for my editors don't understand the creative process, the destructive process, that first I grope, I pick my way through the footage, poke around—but then, as I get the lay of the land, as I pick up the trail, why, then I press harder, I sift through the footage, I probe, I ransack, I arrange, rearrange, *derange*, I go *deep inside* the film; yes, I *slash* this scene but *amplify* that scene, I *scale down* this sequence but *soup up* that sequence—no matter what the cost in money or health or sanity—my sanity or that of those around me, whose sanity, like my own, is expendable, yes, constrained by neither law nor conscience, for the only law, the only conscience, is the law, the conscience of my movie—yes, I realized I couldn't let my editors near it any longer as I trimmed and pared and *cleared the decks* of excess, but also as I augmented and reinforced, as I perfected; and I realized I couldn't let the studio executives, those professional know-nothings, look at my film either, couldn't let them *set foot inside* my film, for they would say, in trying to prove their worth, how I should have *slashed* this scene but *amplified* that scene, *scaled down* this sequence but *souped up* that sequence; nor could I let my poor vulnerable film be press-screened for the critics, those professional parasites who live off not their own creations but mine, who would dine off my film for the three or four days between the press screening and the official release date, three or four days during which they and they alone (more or less) could boast, "I saw *High Plateau II*, and let me tell you—," who would say, without shame, but also without passion, what I should have done, how I should have *slashed* this scene but *amplified* that scene, *scaled down* this sequence but *souped up* that sequence; nor could I even rely upon the general public to understand what I was doing, for the general public is no longer so general, what with the proliferation of *classics sections* in video stores, and *film studies programs* in the universities, and *film critics* (rather than movie reviewers) on every small-town newspaper in the nation, there no longer are *un*professional viewers, the whole world's gone professional, from the teenager in Harlem to the corn farmer in Iowa, from the Westchester suburbanite to the Oregon logger; and so the *general public* would sit in movie theaters across the land suggesting to each other while picking popcorn kernels out of their teeth how I should have *slashed* this scene but *amplified* that scene, *scaled down* this sequence but *souped up* that sequence; and in saying all these things, all these people would've destroyed my film; better I hold on to it forever and ever, or at least until I had perfected it, made it so absolutely pitch-perfect that I would preempt all of them, for perfection is nothing less than a preemptive strike, yes, criticism everywhere must be brought to its knees, hounded and beaten into submission, thrashed, crushed, pulverized, *smashed*.

That is, I just want everyone everywhere to like my modest little entertainment.

At any rate, three days ago I at last finished it and had it packed off to the negative cutter so that the final negative could be assembled and rushed to the lab, where prints would be struck for the theaters— the theaters that were expecting it in less than four weeks, that *had been* expecting it for two and a half years now. The film was supposed to have been released the Christmas before last. Then it was supposed to have been released last summer. Then last Christmas. It had required a superhuman, a Herculean, a *Nietzschean* effort for me to finally say, "My film is finished."

In fact, I hadn't said that, not at all, I hadn't said any such thing.

I couldn't bring myself to say that. Rather, my lawyer, Paul Meltzer, my financial manager, Phil Rosselli, and my lieutenant, Jerry Fugle, had told me it was finished. One by one they visited me in the isolation of my mountainside bunker and gently told me, as though offering condolences in a funeral parlor, that it was finished. They told me that it *had to be* finished (no way around it). That due to contractual obligations, I no longer had a choice. First my attorney had sat me down and showed me a schedule of which lawsuits I could expect to be hit with on which days if the final negative did not arrive at the printing lab in a week and a half. "First Constellation," he said of the studio distributing the film. "Then the major theater chains—Cinerama, Cineplex Odeon, RKO, United Artists—which have booked the movie. Then the toy manufacturers licensed to sell the products that tie in with the movie—products that, incidentally, have been gathering dust in warehouses across the nation for a year and a half now. You will be hit with lawsuits from people—actors, executive producers— all of whom have point participation in the profits." Then my old friend, my old *lawyer*, smiled maliciously. "You will even be hit with lawsuits by whole nations, for you have apparently sold the sequel rights to more Western European countries than exist in all of crumbling Europe." Whereupon he shuffled his papers, crammed them back into his briefcase, buckled it, and with a slightly supercilious smile left my mountain.

Next my accountant tiptoed in. He opened *his* briefcase. He took out *his* papers. Then he, too, convincingly demonstrated why my film was finished whether I knew it or not. "It's really quite simple. You are hemorrhaging money. The movie, originally budgeted at thirty-two million, has cost you closer to seventy million. Now it is time for you to release it and get blood transfusions from movie theaters all across the nation."

Finally, Jerry, my lieutenant, my counsel, my aide-de-camp on matters of *aesthetic import*, trooped in. Jerry's tack was a thing of beauty to behold. Nothing about money, lawsuits, contracts, obligations. Rather, he told me the film was beautiful, that it couldn't possibly be made any better, that therefore, ipso facto, it was finished.

So it was finished. And so I had hoped that after sending off the final work print to the negative cutter, I would at least be delivered from those lost-in-the-cave nightmares that had been tormenting and torturing me for so long now.

It hadn't happened. The nightmares continued as forcefully as ever.

I got dressed and slipped outside. I wandered across the grounds. I roamed around in the early-morning mist, my hands sunk in my pockets. How had things gone so wrong? How in the world had I let things get so badly out of control?

Even now that the film was out of my hands, I felt the urge to hop in a car, drive up to San Francisco, get it back, and set furiously to work re-editing it. Yet I couldn't do that. *I couldn't do that.* So I was left to ponder whether an angel had sat on my shoulder during the shooting or the devil's own monkey. At times I thought *The High Plateau of Stars, Part II* was one of the loveliest movies ever made— deeper, more stirring, lusher, richer in characterization, more passionate than the original *High Plateau*. Other times I thought it was rank with death-stench.

I had made my first feature, *The Black Pig*, in a dark, diabolical, even sinister mood. My father had told me I was no good. The dean of USC had kicked me out. My girlfriend's father had told me I was a bum, not fit company for a decomposing corpse, let alone his marvelously composed daughter. And she herself was unhappy living with me in a cluttered loft in lower Manhattan while I went through my *avant-garde phase*, defiantly making films that no one in his or her right mind would pay a nickel to watch. I was down but not out. I was filled with a youthful rage, the fury of a young man determined to show the world.

So I compromised, we moved back West, and I made *The Black Pig*—a sleek distillate of my favorite crime movies—on a shoestring budget with money raised from figures operating on the fringes of Hollywood, the sort of people who start out in flea markets and carnivals, fringe money for a fringe movie. They thought they could control me. But I proved tougher than they were, I fought like hell to make it my way, and I succeeded. Wintry, bitter, ironic, but also permeated with a manic energy, *The Black Pig* was constructed out of the dark geometry of fatalism and determinism. It became a success.

It made me a small millionaire. And afterward the job offers poured in from the major studios, and the film scripts piled up in my mailbox. I had, as they say, arrived.

But after its success, after its commercial and critical triumph, that reservoir in me of rage, of anger, of cynicism just drained away with a *whoosh*, as though someone had pulled the plug. I emptied out, then filled right back up with a clear sweet high energy. I was accepted and now wanted only to please, to show the world my gratitude. I wanted to Christo-wrap the world with rainbows.

Constellation agreed to back me for a medium-budget movie. I recalled the Viking sagas of my childhood that I had loved so much —*The Vikings* with Kirk Douglas and Janet Leigh, *The Long Ships* with Richard Widmark and Sidney Poitier—and I hit upon the idea of crossbreeding them with the more recent crop of space adventures to come up with a movie about warrior-explorers who are holy fools traveling out on a thunder road through the cosmos. "You must be crazy," said one executive, reflecting on my screenplay. "You've won a shot at the mainstream. Everyone expects you to do a big crime movie, and this is what you come up with—a sword-and-sorcery space epic?" He threw his hands up in despair.

Yet I prevailed. I talked up a storm, I acted out scenes in the executives' offices, playing all the parts myself, and eventually my infectious enthusiasm overcame their doubts.

But after its monstrous success—a success that made my first success look puny, a success that startled me, that startled Constellation, that startled the industry—a different set of emotions took up residence in me. Instead of feeling elated, I became depressed, impotent, *scared*. I had originally planned that my next project would be a small delicate somewhat experimental feature about my childhood, something that would have a limited run in the so-called art houses. But suddenly it seemed *too* small, *too* delicate, *too* experimental. I worried that others would view it as a retreat.

So *I* retreated. I drank. I swam for hours in my pool in the chilly misty dawns. Studio executives would helicopter up from Burbank and Culver City, Universal City and Century City, hoping to ignite my enthusiasm for their projects. Now *they*, in their three-piece suits and ties, acted out wacky scenes in *my* office. And I would respond politely, with measured appraisals, saying that I needed to *think it over*. Then they'd readjust their glasses, pump my hand, and leave, and I would never call them back. Instead I'd grab my old ratty sleeping bag, which had begun to disgorge feathers, and hike ten miles across the Santa Cruz Mountains and sleep in the woods by myself.

The money had poured in from *High Plateau* as though God in heaven had opened a trap door. Constellation controlled the film, but I had a large point share. In addition, I had insisted on owning the merchandising rights (which they mistakenly had thought would be negligible). Moreover, I had insisted that I own the sequel rights and that Constellation serve only as distributor (again, the studio had mistakenly thought there'd be no sequel, that after getting this space nonsense out of my system I'd settle down and start churning out more *Black Pigs*).

So I became rich, I became a large grand *huge* millionaire, I went from marginal man to mogul man.

Rich and paralyzed. Finally, I convinced myself that I had *no choice* but to do a sequel, that once I had put an equally or even more successful sequel under my belt and my net worth had jumped from fifty million to a hundred and fifty million, *then* my position in the industry would be unassailable. *Then* I could make my *small delicate childhood movie*. Yes. From the fortress, the citadel, the castle of my hundred and fifty million dollars I could do whatever I wanted. Whereas from the slit trench, the ditch, the foxhole of my fifty million I would be vulnerable to assault.

But first I built my house on Bonny Doon Road in the Santa Cruz Mountains, on a parcel of land I had purchased earlier with *Black Pig* money. I wanted some distance between myself and Hollywood.

But not too much distance. I was, after all, dependent. And so I settled on the Santa Cruz Mountains. How I had longed for this mansion! In Los Angeles I had always rented, but now I decided it was time to *live on my own*. And my wife wanted it, too. I experienced a longing, a homesickness, a pure craving for the majesty, the nobility, the courtliness, the sublime grandeur such a mansion would confer upon me; and so, more or less on a whim, without counting the cost,

I had a Victorian mansion, perfect in every last detail, erected from scratch.

But when the house was finished I stepped back and looked at it and suddenly experienced a dread, an architectural apprehension, a *grandeur* phobia, an absolute terror at the thought of sleeping there. *The house wasn't me.* Even while my wife was tastefully furnishing the master bedroom, I was insisting we *sack out* in the guest cottage— where we have been *sacking out* ever since. And so the mansion has remained empty, more or less. My wife saw to it that the main living room, the dining room, and the kitchen, as well as a few bedrooms for guests, were properly furnished so we could entertain. But basically it became an instant ghost house. By building it I had satisfied my yearning for grandeur.

But by building it I had also realized that I didn't really *yearn* for grandeur. In fact, building the house had nothing to do with grandeur and everything to do with my trying to avoid directing, my trying to avoid *building* the *High Plateau* sequel. My fear of inhabiting the big-budget mansion was in fact my fear of inhabiting, of *directing*, the big-budget sequel, whose contracts had already been drawn up. Yes, and my inhabiting the small guest cottage symbolized my desire to inhabit, to *direct*, the small, personal childhood movie. It was so obvious! Why spend a hundred dollars an hour babbling to a shrink when you can spend nine million on a house that serves the same purpose?

An old Chinese folk tale tells of a warrior who dropped his sword overboard while riding in a boat. The warrior then notched the gunwale at the spot where the sword fell into the sea so he would know where to look for it later. *I became that man.* You do something right once in your life—in my case twice, *The Black Pig* and *The High Plateau of Stars*—then you spend the rest of your life racking, ransacking, *pillaging and raping* your brain in an effort to remember how you originally did it.

Nothing went right. And I still don't know whether I put a great film in the can or a pile of ashes. The newspapers and the magazines had a field day. Yet they didn't even begin to capture the madness that went into the making, the construction, the *miscreation* of the film. Yes yes yes, they recorded my little contretemps with the Eskimos, the

ACLU lawsuit on their behalf. But no one, not even the *National Enquirer*, picked up on the incident involving Tommy Mace, that craggy space explorer, and the sweet little Eskimo boy.

Often when we were about to shoot a scene in the Antarctic, working under the most horrific conditions, I would turn just before the camera was to start rolling and look for my *star*, my *leading man*, my *bankable asset*. He was nowhere to be found.

"Where the hell's Tommy?" I would yell. Standing there in my goose-down parka, stomping around in my boots to keep warm, holding the battery-powered megaphone in my gloved hand, I'd be all posed, *raring* to go.

And through the gusting snow, my assistant would yell back, "He's in the trailer again. With the Eskimo kid."

I would sigh. Tommy had shacked up with a thirteen-year-old Eskimo boy. This occasioned much debate, academic haggling, epic clashes around the set between gays and straights, men and women, those favoring the acting out of every sexual impulse and those condemning such behavior as a descent into the maelstrom of barbarism. Earlier, in the South Pacific, Tommy, not one to discriminate, had shacked up with a thirteen-year-old Polynesian girl. So now self-exculpating debates raged back and forth between the different camps as to what was more heinous, sodomizing a thirteen-year-old boy or statutory-raping a thirteen-year-old girl, arguments that were not exactly lucid and learned, in which one sexual sophisticate would say that it was antihomosexual prejudice that made most of us condemn Tommy's cohabitation with the boy more harshly than with the girl, and that all of us had just been brainwashed into sexual conformity. And then someone would argue back that in a basically heterosexual culture isn't it more criminal to seduce a same-sex child, since, as studies have shown, this would predispose the child toward homosexual and abusive sex as an adult, and that this had nothing to do with being antigay, it was just a practical matter of humanity given that gays have it rougher in our culture, blah blah blah. And in this way, filled with hubris, deluded about life, they would argue, so empty-headed, so bankrupt, and so intellectually oppressive.

Me, I thought the arguments beside the point. I couldn't care less what Tommy did, how he expressed his sexual proclivities, he could have worked out an arrangement with a penguin for all I cared. *But butt-fucking thirteen-year-old Eskimo boys was not good PR.* Never mind that the kid was underage. Never mind that Tommy, as an ambassador of Western culture, was imposing a vast and deranging cross-cultural psychosexual neocolonialist ad nauseam trauma on the Eskimo culture. Never mind that neither Margaret Mead nor Claude Lévi-Strauss would have approved. What troubled me was that the *National Enquirer* would not approve.

Finally the day arrived when we were to pull up stakes and head to the next location, the Sahara Desert, which would put Tommy in the mood, *in the market*, for Bedouin kids. So he bid farewell to his brokenhearted Eskimo boy, who begged Tommy to take him to the desert; and when the kid finally realized that he had been spurned, that he was as disposable as a tissue, that Tommy was through with him, that the pivotal experience of his life had just come and gone, then the youth went into Tommy's trailer and—he had picked up Western ways rather quickly—gobbled down fifty sleeping pills.

He survived. But it cost me and Tommy Mace $25,000 each to hush that little incident up, that little *near-death*. I had the kid on film in one negligible scene; and sometimes I would sit in the dark of the editing room, in the quiet of my mountain, running that haunted scene over and over, freezing the frame on the kid's dark smiling friendly open face. Looking at him, I could only think that *Nanook of the North* seemed so long, long ago. To Tommy's credit, he exhibited the appropriate forms of distraught behavior: he started drinking a fifth of vodka per day, he stopped cruising new locations, and he took to brooding round the clock. "That Eskimo kid was pure," Tommy would say to me. "He loved me for myself. He had never seen the original *High Plateau*. He had no idea how famous I was back on planet Earth. He'd never been exposed to the media or the influences of Western civilization." And I would nod sagely and pat Tommy Mace, that cultural ambassador, that emissary of good will, that *colonial agent*, on the shoulder.

The film progressed bumpily. When I worked on my earlier films I had felt so confident, so relaxed, so *on*, that I would only shoot two or three takes of a scene. My cameraman would complain that we needed more coverage. My editor would complain that the available footage wouldn't cut smoothly. My actors would complain that they could've gotten it right on the next take. To no avail. I felt so on top of things, so dead certain of my craft, so energetic, so high, so charged up, so *calm* that I knew when just one take would suffice. Later, after viewing the scene, the way it fitted into the movie, my cameraman would apologize and tell me that that's why he's only a cameraman and I'm the director. My editor would apologize and say that the frustrating thing about working with me was knowing that he would never have the opportunity to save my movie in the editing room, so perfectly did all the pieces fit together, like a magnificent jigsaw puzzle. Even the actors, those boorish prima donnas, those strutters of the boards, would say I had made them look good. And they were right. No one did it better.

But on *High Plateau II* I lost my magic touch, I started to *lack confidence*. I would shoot so many takes of a scene that my actors would whine of exhaustion, my cameraman would say we weren't going to capture anything that hadn't already been captured, my editor would complain that he would need a decade just to review the footage, let alone whip it into shape. And I would keep shooting, the film would keep piling up, and the money, *my* money, would tick away like a taxi stalled at a red light in hell. Alfred Hitchcock shot *Rear Window* so economically that it yielded only a hundred extra feet of footage. My poor *High Plateau II* yielded a million.

One scene in particular generated tens of thousands. Vincent Hail, huge and menacing, portrayed Stenkil, who heads a famous clan of space warriors that captures a rival spaceship. He takes as his prisoner Estrid, portrayed by the lovely Marilyn Brewerton. In the abduction scene that I had written, Stenkil, avenging an ancient slight, throws her across his bed, which is covered with the furs of some galactic beast, and rapes her. Now, I intended to shoot the scene so that it implicitly conveyed a denunciation of carnal colonialism, an impeachment of sexual imperialism, yes, an *indictment of libidinous brutality*. That was the game plan.

I looked through the viewfinder to check the composition before commanding the action to begin. I consulted with my cameraman, Mike Peterson, about the shot choice, angle, and lens; and Mike, the perfect craftsman, listened carefully. He had shot my two previous films, and with each one his own stature in the industry had grown. We had established a solid working relationship.

But this day he was unhappy with me. For he had already worked in 128-degree heat in the Sahara Desert, he had already lugged a hand-held camera along a narrow icy ledge in the Antarctic, he had already crawled through a snow tunnel pushing equipment ahead of him, he had already been sniped at in the South Bronx by an angel-dusted gangbanger. So he was not pleased by the time we got to the rape scene even though we were shooting on a sound stage in the safety and comfort of Burbank.

We didn't get it right on the first take. We didn't get it right on the second. We didn't get it right on the third, fourth, fifth, tenth, or twentieth take. I ordered Mike to dolly the camera in closer, and then I checked through the viewfinder. I had the camera dolly back and checked again. I moved in imitation of the camera to show Mike how I wanted him to pan the scene. I ordered him to try various angles, different heights, directly overhead, almost under the bed. I was looking for just the right blend of pearly white thigh and luxurious dark animal fur, just the right mix of fetish and fury, of passion and passivity, *of venery and venom.*

Then I called for a hand-operated Titan crane, with its twenty-foot-long mechanical arm. Mike Peterson, his camera operator, the first assistant, and I all squeezed onto the crane's platform. I ordered the scene shot from a high angle and back, to drag out the rape, to suggest frustration and impotence. I ordered the scene shot at close range and from a low angle, to capture the violence and intensity. I ordered the camera to crane right down into her face, to show its psychological landscape, to capture the cataclysmic tracks of her tears. I ordered the camera to start high up and far back, then to crane down and in for an extreme close-up—only not of her face but of her fist clenching so hard that her knuckles were turning white.

I got rid of the crane and had Mike Peterson switch to a hand-held 35mm Arriflex, whose ragged jumpy motions would exaggerate the violence of the rape. I had him strap on a PanGlide, to suggest a smooth sinuous evil. I ordered zip pans from face to face to suggest violence and rapidity. I ordered a hole cut in the bed and the camera situated *inside the mattress*, staring up, the lens poking right into Stenkil's enraged face, so that he appeared to be raping the camera, so that he appeared to be raping the audience, yes, I was looking to effect a transference, I wanted to wound, I wanted to violate, I wanted to traumatize, I wanted to smash the proscenium arch of the frame and *prey on the mind* of my audience.

The set had fallen deathly silent. The onlookers—technicians, extras, assistants—had grown from the usual bored crowd of fifteen or so to more than fifty, then multiplied and swelled to a hundred attracted repelled hypnotized spectators. I kept shooting. By now it was not Estrid but *Marilyn* who was weeping. By now it was not Stenkil but *Vincent* who was screaming. And still I ordered Mike to keep shooting away. Sixty takes. Sixty-five takes. *Seventy.*

After the seventy-fifth take I turned to Mike Peterson, who was tired, exhausted, *used up*, but that was his problem, not mine, and I said that the solution was to remove the studio's roof and use an F. & B./Ceco Aero-Vision mount on a helicopter. I explained the shot I had in mind. We would start with the helicopter hovering just a few feet above the bed, then pull farther and farther back, higher and higher into the sky, *up and away*, until Stenkil, Estrid, the bed, the spaceship were all just infinitesimal dots, the whole scene rendered with a melancholy distance.

Mike Peterson looked at me. Then slowly, taking his time to enunciate, he said that it wouldn't work because we didn't own the studio but were merely renting the sound stage, so they probably wouldn't appreciate us ripping off the roof. Moreover, he said, as the helicopter pulled away, the camera, no matter what kind of lens we used, would inevitably take in the environs of contemporary L.A., thereby shattering that lost-in-space quality so essential to the mood. And, he added, we were too close to the Burbank airport to get permission to stick a helicopter up in the air space, anyway.

I nodded and said, "Okay. Let's do another medium-angle head-on shot." Groans, sighs, and ugly silences greeted my request. But no matter. Everyone took up their positions. For *I signed the checks.*

And during that shot, *Marilyn* screamed out so painfully, so violently, so appallingly, that only then did I emerge as from a hallucinatory trance to realize that I, soaked with sweat, flushed and trembling, was the only person besides my film crew who was actually watching the scene, that in the shocked silence that had been building and deepening and intensifying on the set, the one hundred appalled spectators were watching *me*, that I, off-camera, had become *the center of my own movie.*

"Cut," I said quietly. "That's enough for today." And then I hurried off, embarrassed, humiliated, and humbled. And I knew then that the movie had gotten out of hand, become ungovernable, for *I* had gotten out of hand, become ungovernable. *And nobody had tried to stop me.* One hundred various human beings—big small smart dumb brave cowardly strong weak generous mean handsome ugly talented untalented—one hundred various human beings had stood around watching, and not one had possessed the courage to yell, "Enough already." That is when I realized that I—the film—(I *am* the film) was in trouble. They were terrified of me. I terrified myself.

Now here is the amusing part. Months later, when the arduous task of editing down the mountain, the *Himalayan range* of footage had begun, I spent one entire day reviewing all seventy-six takes of that scene in the dark quiet of my editing room in the bunker. I had ushered my editor and assistant editors out, for I wanted to review the rushes in peace and not relive the humiliation of that day; and as I reviewed them I realized with dawning astonishment, with growing amazement, with *absolutely cool-headed comprehension,* that the seventy-sixth take, the take where *Marilyn* had screamed out in genuine pain and agony and humiliation, where *Vincent* had shouted and heaved himself on her in a genuinely murderous rage, I realized that the seventy-sixth take was *the best take of all.* Holed up in my editing room I had the dismal realization that this ugly brutal unsettling scene, this scene that I would have to use all my powers to persuade the MPAA rating board to allow me to keep without forfeiting an R, I realized that this scene, the seventy-sixth take, *worked*; that I had been right and the one hundred appalled spectators wrong. *I had found the sword that had fallen overboard.* Sitting in the dark in my mountain that day, I experienced a small bleak misanthropic lift.

Now I wandered past the old stone stable, with its timbers and mossy rocks, which actually is not old, which in fact I had built from scratch to *look* old, to reek of antiquity, to stink of venerableness. I wandered past the stable filled not with the finest Arabian thoroughbreds but with the most high-tech cars on earth, including my Corvette ZR-1 which could outrun, outperform, *outclass* my Testarossa and my Countach, which itself had a "teeny-teeny" dent in its rear right headlight well, as my wife so delicately, so *delightfully*, put it, in defense of our boneheaded son. The boy is spoiled, he thinks it is nothing, perfectly ordinary, for a sixteen-year-old to say to his father, "Hey, Dad, I'm taking the Countach. I have a date tonight." Whereupon *Dad* will *toss him the keys*, yes, toss him the *eighty-thousand-dollar keys*, and then he can't even park without smashing into a wall in a Carmel parking lot. It's difficult to believe that just six years earlier he was overjoyed to receive on his birthday a movie makeup kit with fresh wounds so he could transform himself into a victim of the Black Pig's butchery. Now for his birthday he expects a Ferrari. Would it do any good to explain to him that I won Mom's heart with a blue, banged-up Volkswagen bug?

All quiet. No one was up yet besides me and my ghosts. The lights were not on in Werner's bedroom above the stable, the mechanic I had imported from Munich, who has such a poetic feel for the big epic engines of my Mercedes-Benzes and my Porsches as well as for the moodier, more complex engines of my Ferraris, Maseratis, and Lamborghinis. He loves rolling up his sleeves and sticking his arms elbow-deep into the entrails of my cars. It makes him pig-happy.

Nor were the lights on in the dormitory where the help lives—cooks maids gardeners janitors—the González clan from Guatemala, or El Salvador, or Nicaragua, or one of those places, some of whose members were refugees from the death squads that love to roam the palm-studded countrysides of those delightfully squalid tropical paradises. Or maybe I have it mixed up. Maybe they were ex-members of a death squad who had fled their homeland without properly securing a pension or a numbered Cayman Islands account, fled from the peasants who had risen up in righteous indignation. Yes yes yes, I know it is terrible to mix these things up, to make light of such tragedy, that one Central American culture is completely different from another, and that we need to respect one another's differences *blah blah blah*. After all, several slow-witted reviewers had gently criticized *The High Plateau of Stars* for its "ahistorical irreverence," when in fact they didn't have a clue as to what I was up to with my *historical dislocations*.

Nor were the lights on in the mansion where my lieutenant, Jerry, had spent the night sleeping, no doubt soundly, undisturbed by those nightmares that without warning launch midnight ground assaults on my sleep, yes, spent the night with his wife, or concubine, or succubus, or whatever that creature is to him (wife: I remember now). I had not *asked* Jerry to spend the night. But he had taken it upon himself, *of his own free will*, to spend the night, to stay close to me in my hour of need. How touching. I suspect that my lawyer and my accountant put him up to it, told him to *keep an eye on me*, to make sure I didn't snatch back the negative and set furiously to work on the movie all over again. Yes, they were *all* conspiring against me because they feared *I* would conspire against them, because my art is a conspiracy against them, because my art is a conspiracy against the industry, because my art is a conspiracy against *the world*.

Dead silence in the misty dawn. Vapors rose from the pool. A rubber raft drifted in the middle. One ridiculous newspaper account even claimed that I stock my pool with dolphins. The papers exaggerate everything, blow everything out of proportion, I have but one solitary dolphin.

And sometimes I wonder why I didn't simply quit, pull up stakes after the success of *High Plateau*, do a vanishing act that over the years would acquire the power of myth, of legend, of an industry folk tale. Why did I feel this sick perverse need to duplicate my success on a yet grander scale?

In the beginning I *knew* just how good I was, long before the world knew. I worked on the screenplay for *The Black Pig* in a primitive cabin in the Sierra Nevada that had neither telephone nor electricity nor running water, just a fireplace and a propane stove. I would sit scribbling at the kitchen table, the only human being for miles around. And when I went to bed at night, I would lie in the close darkness listening to the primordial quiet—no sound but a branch creaking in the wind, a night owl hooting, a raccoon foraging through the underbrush.

Lying there in the dark, I would project myself into the sky, where I would float, spreading like a stain, like a slow dreamy shadow across the nation, from dark restless sea to dark restless sea, infusing, *penetrating* the dream life of the continent. I was that supremely confident. Drifting off to sleep in that dark cabin, I *knew* I would make cinematic history, that my force would explode through the walls, that even while the international hotshots lunched and dined and partied in New York, in Los Angeles, in London and Paris and Rome, something was incubating in the isolation of that mountain cabin, something that would eventually overwhelm the world.

Four years later, the success of *High Plateau* overwhelmed *me*. Suddenly I really *was* everywhere. My face stared up from the covers of magazines as the commuters hurried home through Grand Central Station. My eyes blazed back from rack after rack in airport magazine shops across the nation. My image had moved like an occupying army into all the neighborhoods of Media City, and I became a prisoner of my own voguish inflation. A critical success combined with a commercial success makes people think the filmmaker is a genius, a magician whose art just incidentally throws off money. Networks and magazines stumbled over each other in their rush to get the scoop on me. I was the man everyone wanted to be, everyone envied, everyone coveted intellectually, sexually, artistically, financially. At night as I lay in bed in my guest house I would feel myself drifting, floating up into the sky—but this time *they* would stretch me out as though on a rack across the whole country. This time I was not a haunting presence. This time *I* belonged to *them*, I was a receptor, *they* dreamed *me*. Their dreams flew up and rearranged my very molecules.

I looked at the pool, at the silhouettes of stalwart redwoods looming through the mist. Loneliness and melancholy clung to their boughs. Even if my film bombed, even if it failed to recoup its costs, I could probably, after selling off all my other real estate holdings, pay my debts and still hold on to my estate.

Would I like that?

Yes. I would drop out of the film business, the film *racket*, altogether. I would turn the estate into a campground, the mansion into a bed-and-breakfast, and the guest house into my office-residence. And in the early-morning hours before the tourists awoke I would wander down to the pool with a butterfly net and scoop twigs, leaves, and pine boughs off the surface. That way, by the time the guests did wake, the surface would be clear.

And maybe one early riser would notice me, a middle-aged man scooping leaves out of the pool, and he would feel pity. He would never suspect that this fellow, who had shaved off his beard, was the acclaimed director of *The Black Pig* and *The High Plateau of Stars*. He would never suspect that this unassuming man skimming the pool with a net had dined with kings and presidents, slept with starlets and famous harlots, rubbed shoulders with the best of them, *for he had been the best of them.* No, the camper would simply see *the man with the butterfly net* and experience mild pity tinged perhaps with distaste for this poor fellow who had to get up at dawn to tend to the pool before the guests commenced splashing around. He wouldn't realize that in the cool misty mountain dawn, by the simple act of skimming leaves and twigs off the pool's surface, the poor fellow had at last found something resembling inner peace.

The mist was beginning to break up. To come apart in great cottony tatters. To divulge a patch of blue sky directly overhead. A stand of redwoods looming on my right. A granite overhang thrusting straight out of the hazy light.

A new day was beginning.

I didn't have a thing to do.

The Gangster

C h a p t e r   4

The professor hung up, then lumbered out of the phone booth outside
De Lauer's Newsstand in downtown Oakland.

"The negative's ready."

"She give you any trouble?"

"Nope. She said she thought we were picking it up tomorrow. I
explained there'd been a change, the lab had forgotten to take Labor
Day into account, blah blah blah."

"Blah blah blah? Labor Day's in September. You meant Memorial Day."

"Oh?" Wilbur shrugged. "She knew what I meant."

I pondered Wilbur Blackfield as he hauled himself up, limb by
limb, into the van's passenger seat. An academic phenomenon, a quick
study in absurdity. We had both dressed casually, but Wilbur, perhaps
out of some deep dramaturgical sense, had insisted on a disguise. So
he'd yanked a lumpy blond wig over his unruly brown hair, slipped

blue contact lenses over his good brown eyes, then wrapped Ray-Ban mirror glasses around those.

"You should've tied a balloon to your head."

"A balloon to my head?"

"Forget it."

We rumbled across the Bay Bridge to San Francisco beneath clear cerulean skies. It was unseasonably hot. The Transamerica pyramid building tapered to a needle point on the edge of the downtown financial district. Farther back loomed the tall dark Bank of America headquarters. How comforting it looked! How solid! How I would have loved to tunnel my way into its vaults with a water-cooled core drill and oxygen lance, and get at all those lovely negotiable instruments!

I glanced at Wilbur. His fingers drummed nervously on the dashboard. We had borrowed the van from an old college buddy of mine who lived out in Walnut Creek, where he installed windows. After picking up the negative we planned to transfer it to my car, then drive up into the Sierra Nevada, to Lake Tahoe. That had been my idea. Use the rugged terrain to our advantage in working out a drop point, a safe getaway route. The negotiations, I had calculated, would take three days, four at the most. Tahoe would allow us to squeeze in some fishing, hiking, fine dining, and gambling. Make it a working vacation.

"What happens," Wilbur asked, looking at a patrol car ahead of us, "if someone gets suspicious, writes down our license plate?"

"I switched plates."

"What do you mean you switched plates? On your knees, in the open . . . ?"

"I drove out to SFO yesterday and walked around the lot till I found a black 944 just like my own. Not terribly uncommon. Then I unscrewed the plates—"

"Won't the owner—?"

"Shut up and let me finish, okay? Next I unscrewed a set of plates from a nearby Toyota and attached them to the other 944. The Porsche's owner won't notice he has someone else's plates for weeks. As for the Toyota's owner, who the fuck cares?"

"So if CHP runs a computer on your plates—"

"—they'll come up with a black 944 but not one whose owner has a rap sheet stamped 'OC.' And I did the same with the van."

"I'm glad you're on my side, Frank."

My side? I felt there was some fundamental misunderstanding here but said nothing. Besides, misunderstandings are sometimes to be preferred to clarity of desire. I steered the van off the bridge ramp into the area south of Market. Drove past Slim's nightclub. Past Hamburger Mary's. Past Stormy Leather, a hardcore fetish boutique my ex had discovered shortly before the feds took us down—good for a few last wild-assed nights. Then found a parking spot at the yellow curbed loading zone on Folsom, right outside the industrial building where the negative cutter's studio was located. In another age the place had been a gay bathhouse. I killed the ignition, and then we just sat there, breathing quietly, Wilbur staring grimly out the windshield.

"Last chance to pull out," I said.

He seemed trembly, on the verge of hyperventilating. The professor took a deep breath and hissed, "Let's go." Then thrust open his door and hopped out, forcing life and swagger into the slump of his shoulders.

"Remember," I instructed, as the old battered freight elevator cranked us up to the fourth floor, "let me do the talking."

The gate creaked open. We stepped into a ramshackle vestibule. Framed movie posters appointed the peeling walls, among them *The Black Pig* and *The High Plateau of Stars.* I pressed a buzzer, and a woman said over the intercom, "Yes?"

"Hi. We're here to pick up *High Plateau II.*"

She came out, her hair thick and dark, wearing glasses over bright violet eyes, dressed in corduroy jeans and a black pullover, and picking bits of film cement out of the threads of her sweater. "Hi, I'm Gina. I'd shake hands but"—smiling, she displayed her palms—"they're kind of sticky. You guys work with Doug?"

I nodded. "I'm George, this is Steve," I said, introducing Wilbur. "I do some line producing for Doug."

She gave me a long look, grinning. "You don't do *your* job very well. I can't believe how much footage he shot," she said, laughing. "Unfucking real."

"Well, Doug's a bit bullheaded, you know," I said easily. "Fancies himself something of an *auteur.*"

She smiled nicely. Cutting and matching negatives probably brought on eyestrain, but the glasses gave her an attractive, bookish look. "I would imagine he'd be difficult to work with," she said sympathetically. "Anyway, the boy will start bringing it out in a minute. If you have any questions, I'll be in back." She turned and walked off.

"*Start?*" Wilbur murmured.

"Hey," I called out. "Can I get your phone number? Maybe next time I'm in San Francisco . . ."

She smiled over her shoulder. "You already have it, remember?" She disappeared through the door in back.

"Are you nuts?" Wilbur said. "We're robbing her, you're gonna ask her out?"

"Hey Wilbur, if everything goes according to schedule, she's not even gonna know we robbed her. And what was that about 'start'?"

He didn't seem to have heard me. We stood in the vestibule, Wilbur sweating profusely. "I've never done anything like this," he muttered, glancing worriedly around. "I'm a professor, for chrissake. What the hell am I doing here with some maniac who tries to hit on a woman during a heist?"

Just then the teenager appeared, wheeling in a handcart stacked with ten boxes. Under their weight the handcart squeaked and groaned. The kid wore earphones, tight black Levi's, and a black T-shirt emblazoned with "Smegma." A wire extended from his bulging right pants pocket, ran up into earphones, and from there into his brain, causing the kid's head to jerk up and down to an invisible erratic beat.

"Is that it?" I asked.

The kid grinned foolishly. I leaned forward and—with both hands—gingerly removed his headphones. "Is that it?" I repeated.

"Well," the teenager said, still grinning, "each box contains ten reels of negative footage. And there're a hundred and forty more."

"Reels?"

"*Boxes.*" The kid laughed nastily and shook his head. "You could tie a bow around the equator with this stuff and still have leftover for shoelaces."

I glanced at Wilbur. His color had gone south.

"Well, let's get on with it," I said.

While we waited for the elevator, Wilbur muttered, "This is un-believable. There must be two hundred and fifty hours of film—a hundred and twenty-five for every hour finally used. What a fucking nightmare it must've been to edit."

"And you think we're going to transfer this to the Porsche? We'll be lucky it fits in the van."

The professor scratched his sweaty forehead. Furrowed it in thought. "Well, we don't *need* the excess negatives. Logistically un-wieldy. The only thing that counts is the matched negative. But we don't want to preserve the stuff, either."

"I don't follow."

"Suppose we take off for the mountains with the matched negative and store the extra footage somewhere down here. Then Lowell hires detectives who somehow locate it. He'd be able to patch together a passable second matched negative from all the second, third, fourth, and twentieth takes. It'll cost him time and money, and it won't look as good as the original. But he'll be back in business and can tell us to fuck off."

"You already told me it'd be easier just to pay us."

"But why take chances? We don't need the extra footage, and God knows *he* doesn't need it."

I shrugged. The elevator gate creaked open.

It took six trips to load up the van. Finally, only a few boxes remained. The teenager stacked those up in the vestibule, disappeared in back, then reappeared, bopping behind the handcart. Stacked on it were four padlocked octagonal metal canisters. Two larger octagonal canisters joggled on top. "These four"—he pointed—"contain the twelve reels of the matched negative. These two, the six reels of the final work print."

I nodded and glanced at the four cans. "Pretty casual, huh?"

The teenager laughed. "Lowell's cutting it damn close." He handed me the clipboard. "Well, just sign here," he said, and I scribbled "Michael Ovitz."

"That's it?" I asked, handing it back.

"That's it," he said, and clamped the headphones back over his ears.

Then Wilbur and I waited in silence for the elevator. Eyes fixed on the overhead floor indicator. The elevator was on the ground floor. It decided to stay there a while. It seemed to have pitched tent on the ground floor. The sweat poured down Wilbur like spring runoff from the Sierra. The indicator light advanced to two . . . three. . . . Then, like a blip moving off a radar screen, the light blinked out. Vanished.

I glanced at Wilbur. You couldn't call him a portrait of grace under pressure. On the contrary, he looked like the lunatic in Edvard Munch's *The Scream*. Behind the Ray-Bans his eyes were panicky and delirious, his face flushed and sweaty, his mouth twisted in anguish.

Gina reappeared through the door. "Damn, is the elevator broken again? Third time this week. If you'd like to wait there's a—"

"Shit, lady!" Wilbur exploded. "This is supposed to be in the theaters in four fucking weeks." The big man leaned down and, grunting like a sumo wrestler, with a tremendous effort, picked up all the remaining cartons. He staggered toward the stairwell, full of purposeful action. Gina stood there, hands on hips, staring at Wilbur but with a new kind of expression, one that was thoughtful, even curious. Doing a new read on him.

"Thanks, Gina," I said, "but we'll take the stairs."

"Your buddy's an asshole."

"He's been under a lot of pressure lately," I said. Then bent over and picked up the six canisters, following Wilbur into the stairwell.

Out on Folsom I banged open the van's side door. My nerves were pulsing all over the place. As we rammed and crammed in the remaining cartons I kept glancing all around.

"Hurry up, goddamn it," I snarled.

"I'm hurrying."

"You didn't have to blow up like that."

"Fuck her."

"No. *Fuck you.* The idea is *not* to call attention to ourselves. *Not* to cause the lady to remember anything about us. *Not* to stand out in topographical relief in her memory. What the hell is the percentage in being confrontational?"

"*Don't* call attention to ourselves? You asked her out, for chrissake."

"That's different. Shit. Come on. Hurry up. We can't afford to hang around."

I eased the van into the flow of midday traffic. Massive and brooding, Wilbur sat hunched in the passenger seat, the film canisters heaped at his feet and piled in his lap. He looked tired, shaggy, pulverized. Driving through SoMa, I turned abruptly several times, monitoring the rearview mirrors. No one. Finally, I drove up Harrison onto the Bay Bridge, heading toward the East Bay at three in the afternoon.

The professor remained quiet. We boomed through the Treasure Island tunnel, across the bridge's lower deck. After a while Wilbur said, "You have any idea where to get rid of all this stuff?"

I considered. "Out in the Livermore Valley, near Pleasanton, there's a toxic-waste site. I think we can get in there, just dump the boxes."

Wilbur nodded. But it wasn't until we bounced off the bridge and were highballing it east on 580 that the color returned to his face. The green wooded Oakland hills rolled by. In another month the sun would have sucked the chlorophyll right out of them—they'd be dry as straw. *The golden hills of California.* High up in the hills, the huge white Mormon Tabernacle temple gleamed. Newcomers always look at it and exclaim, "My God, I didn't know there were so many Mormons in the Bay Area." There aren't. It's just that nobody erects *Triumph of the Will* monstrosities the way the Mormons do. Religion as show biz. Pure white as the color of cleanliness, purity, hysteria. We sped on. On my right, the small slummy pastel-colored tract houses of East Oakland. Farther back, along the shoreline, the huge gantry cranes that unload the container ships entering the port of Oakland. They look like the metalized skeletons of Trojan horses, and people say they were the inspiration for the giant mechanical monsters in *The Empire Strikes Back.* Nothing to it: "Hey, let's build fifty-foot-high mechanical monsters that clomp around in the snow." Moviemakers as magicians working in the realm of the big-budget surreal.

I glanced at the canisters piled in Wilbur's lap and heaped at his feet. Then at Wilbur. He was snoring softly, sonorously, brokenly. A scholar with a criminal kink. With whom I had cast my lot. If I'd had my wits about me, I'd've kicked open his door and pushed him out then and there.

C h a p t e r 5

So, so peaceful.

Yet as I wandered through the woods in the misty dawn, I realized that the *objective* peace of the woods did not find its *subjective* correlative in me, that I was not at peace, I was at war—at war with myself, at war with my movie. For the movie was still not completed. For the movie was *hardly* completed. For all that had taken place so far were mere skirmishes, *less* than skirmishes.

Yes, the more I thought about it, the more I realized that numerous scenes could be improved by recutting the footage in radically different ways, *shuffle the deck*; that I could deepen Stenkil's melancholy upon leaving home for a distant universe by substituting Sir Adrian Boult's sublime rendition of Vaughan Williams's Third Symphony, with its visionary contemplativeness, for Sir Neville Marriner's more mainstream interpretation of Vaughan Williams's *Fantasia on a Theme by Thomas Tallis*; yes, and that big intergalactic battle scene ought to be moved *en bloc* from the end of the picture to the very front, *before the credits*, to get the ball rolling pronto. All these things needed to be done, yet here I was roaming around in the misty dawn, hands sunk in my pockets, as though I didn't have a care in the world, as though I were walking through a *peaceful* forest, rather than picking my way across a murderous minefield.

Just consider the scene where my penguin-monsters appear suddenly on a ridge of rubble. I had sought the type of effect that John Ford achieved in *Fort Apache* when his Indians appear suddenly on horseback high along the ridges overlooking the valley through which the U.S. Cavalry so obliviously gallops. It is a famous shot. When the Indians come into view, the moviegoer's heart stops with fright. But now, thinking back, I realized that *I had not achieved the same effect*, that my penguin-monsters, despite their ferocious makeup, despite the fangs glued into their jaws, did not appear as intimidating, as frightening—let alone as noble—as John Ford's Indians. For one thing, despite weeks of instruction, *months*, by a top animal trainer, the penguins still *waddled*. We never had been able to make them—not a single damn one of them—give up their ridiculous waddles. And the waddle, that silly swaying from side to side with each tiny step, detracted from the atmosphere of serious menace that I had been trying to create. Yes, I had failed to achieve a *penguin effect* that was equal in power to the *Indian effect*. I had hoped to give the culture a new mythical monster, a creature on the order of a Cyclops, a dragon, a Gorgon, a Homeric addition to the pantheon of great miscreations. Instead, I wound up with a flock of whangdoodles and whiffle-birds waddling across the rubble of the South Bronx.

I decided to drive up to San Francisco and retrieve my final print. To hell with my creditors. To hell with my distributor. To hell with the domestic exhibitors. To hell with the foreign exhibitors. To hell with the toy manufacturers, the point participants, my employees, the great (and not-so-great) moviegoing public—to hell with all of them. My movie, my poor fragile art, came ahead of the whole long line of them.

But first, breakfast. I wandered across the misty lawn into the main house, into the *breakfast nook* on the glassed-in portion of the veranda. My lieutenant, Jerry, sat at the table, sipping coffee and reading the

San Francisco Chronicle. And that oddity to whom he's married, with
whom he's *reached an accommodation,* sat there too, pale Margot,
dressed in sepulchral black, as is her wont, leafing through a Japanese
graphic novel. Jerry looked up and asked, "You have a good night's
sleep?"

I nodded crankily.

"So. You decide to do promo for *High Plateau II?*"

Again I nodded.

"That's good," Jerry said, and meant *That's bad.* For it meant that
I had decided to demean myself by jetting all over the country, plugging
the movie on talk shows, granting interviews to pushy *print* journalists
in New York and Chicago and Los Angeles, in *Kansas City* and *Cleveland* and *Cincinnati.* It meant finally that I felt I *needed* to promote
the film, which, properly translated, meant that at heart I felt the movie
was incapable of promoting itself.

He asked, "Did Beth"—my personal secretary—"arrange the
schedule?"

"Yes. Tuesday and Wednesday I do the East Coast. I do Gene and
Roger on Thursday—"

"They both loved *High Plateau.*"

"—the rest of the Midwest on Friday. The following Monday I go
to San Francisco to do Morgan and Alfred—"

"They loved *High Plateau,* too."

"—then Wednesday I wind up in L.A. for a round of interviews
and, if I can stomach it, a press conference."

Jerry nodded. Jerry is always nodding. A clause in his contract says
Nod all the time.

"What are you doing today?" he asked casually.

I shrugged, trying to convey in that economical gesture a general
but not unpleasant vagueness, a jaunty carefreeness, the good-humored
information that I was at loose ends but of light heart, so it didn't really
matter at all.

For if I blurted out to Jerry my true intentions—or even if I just
calmly explained my true intentions—if I told him that I aimed to
drive up to San Francisco, retrieve the final print, and set furiously
to work on it all over again, why, Jerry would have called the men in

white, had them measure me head to foot for a straitjacket, then bolt me to my bed. It is a peculiar situation. *I* am Jerry's boss, *I* am the president and sole shareholder of the company. Yet at the moment, because of the shakiness of the company's financial condition, I have somehow become the prisoner of all these people with whom I have surrounded myself.

In fact, I don't exactly know how I wound up with Jerry, except that I recognized in him some quality—an ethereal social quality, a *crazed* ethereal social quality—lacking in myself. Please don't misunderstand me, I don't mean to suggest that I'm a wallflower, certainly I know how to pour on the charm when it comes to sweet-talking studio executives into forking over millions. But Jerry is in a class by himself. I could be walking down a street in Tangier, or Bombay, or Nairobi, and people will recognize me because they have seen my picture in newspapers and magazines. Jerry walks down a street in Tangier, or Bombay, or Nairobi, and people recognize him because somehow they actually know him. The man carries around in his head a Rolodex thicker than the Manhattan phone directory, and he works the telephone like a politician canvassing his district, which just happens to be the world. Indeed, at times I think Jerry isn't real but a superbly tooled response-machine, programmed to mimic the well-adjusted personality—provided the social interactions don't get too complex.

Yet he is oddly modest. He maintains a low profile, always stays in the background, does most of his work behind the scenes, sub rosa, and would never think of upstaging me.

I don't know when he sleeps. The man runs around the country, the *planet*, attending film festivals everywhere. He could well be a secret lobbyist, an influence peddler, a pilot fish for real estate interests: he helps start up a film festival in a remote wilderness area of the Northern Cascades, and several years later, like dark magic, ski resorts, condo compounds, and chichi restaurants are multiplying in the wilderness. He helps start up a film festival in a Florida swampland, and several years later, just like that, a vacation resort has mushroomed out of the marshes, complete with paved streets, palm trees, and houseboats gliding along the canals. Christ's miracle of fish and bread is nothing compared to Jerry's miracle of film festivals.

Then, too, he has brought small foreign and domestic independent films to my attention, which I have then, on his recommendation, picked up for distribution. I usually take a bath on these films to the tune of a quarter million, they play modestly in the art houses, but they do garner critical accolades, which accrue to my own status, to my own artistic savings account.

But there is a problem, and it is this: a subtle contempt emanates from the man. I can't put my finger on it, but it's as though he secretly despises me, despises my films, as though he considers himself a superior outsider, a covert agent of refined taste who has somehow infiltrated the industry, to use me as his instrument to reshape it, to make it more worthy of high culture; or at the least he's signed on to serve as the conscience of my *avant-garde days.*

His wife now said, "Dougie, be a darling and pass the sugar."

I glared at her. She smiled innocently at me. But then I thought *What is the use?* and passed her the sugar. My wife doesn't call me "Dougie." My *mother* doesn't call me "Dougie." And this is what amazed me more than anything else: I did not understand how my lieutenant, this bright vibrant articulate man, this *well-adjusted personality,* could have wound up with this woman, she was the stumbling block to my originally hiring him, I couldn't understand how such a man could make such a mistake. I remember the first time I met her—actually, met her voice. I arrived at a party, a gala affair attended by hundreds of *gala affair* people; and clear above, or rather, clear apart from all the chatter and tinkle of glasses this one otherworldly voice—not particularly louder than anyone else's but somehow shriller, keener—knifed cleanly through, like a falsetto through a thicket of bass, like a laser through genital flesh: "Oh, what beautiful plates. How can you even bear to eat off of them?" And: "Oh, you're a vegetarian. That's marvelous. But how do you do it? There is so much wonderfully fresh meat and fish available on today's market." It was only later that I was introduced to the body attached to that voice, a moderately attractive body with frenzied black hair, mad bright unfocused eyes, and a grand white smile that somehow always managed to stay out of sync with the conversation its mouth was engaged in, like a sound track misaligned with its image track.

That first time I met her she was dressed all in black, too. Sheathed in black, I should say. *Shrink-wrapped* in black, to be more accurate. She seemed stylized. Margot was, I later learned, in mourning. Yes, mourning in skintight black stretch velvet, skintight black leather, skintight black lace, for all the world looking in mourning as delectable as a shiny purple plum.

Margot has been in mourning for two years now, ever since her fool older brother trooped off to some miserable atoll in the South Pacific to do sound recording for a *socially relevant* documentary on nuclear testing in the 1950s—a documentary that would demonstrate to the world how the U.S. government had lied to the native peoples and stolen their islands for a pittance and treated the natives like guinea pigs in order to study the long-term effects of radiation poisoning. Yes, he had gone off to evoke sympathy for the natives, and then he had OD'd on heroin one night while carousing with the natives. Nearly pure white heroin from the Golden Triangle. Some of his poor deluded friends on the production team had even suspected it was the dirty work of the CIA, that it was a Machiavellian plot to discredit their documentary, which would strike a blow against American neocolonialism—their poor documentary, which will never get enough credit to be discredited, which the CIA could care less about. Of course, the answer to his death was probably much simpler and sadder. The poor fool didn't realize that heroin scored in Micronesia, because it is that much closer to its source, because it had been handled by fewer middlemen, might not have taken as many cuts of lactose as the diluted junk he was used to scoring on the Santa Cruz boardwalk.

I can forgive various addictions, sexual perversions, unadulterated greed—but I have no tolerance for stupidity. These people, these *filmmakers*, they troop off to places like the Mururoa atoll or the Fangatau atoll, to places like Yap and Hao and Alofi, they land on the shores with a ton of equipment, their own little D-day invasion; and the idea, *their* idea, is to show how the United States (Britain, France) has exploited the poor native peoples. It is incredible. More documentaries have been made about the exploitation of these islands than nuclear bombs detonated on them in the fifties and early sixties. These raggedy-haired film crews go down there with their subsidies from anti-imperialist fairy godmothers like the Rockefeller Foundation and the Guggenheim Foundation and the National Endowment for the Humanities, and they shoot their little documentaries, and then they wreak havoc among the native peoples (of course, I should talk, with the Eskimos coming after me). They rail against the West for shattering the natives' peace of mind with *nuclear bombs*, for breaking down the natives' rustic communal-living style by introducing *fences*, for teaching nut-gathering communities how to plant *barley* and *corn*, for giving *designer jeans* to people who were content to frolic and gambol beneath the swaying palm trees in loincloths cut from the hides of local lizards. Yes, the narrators of these films, who always speak with stern impeccable Anglo enunciations, tell of how the islanders' "traditional way of life is threatened by Western social forces," and then in the evenings these *Western social forces* get down and party with the locals. Let us be frank. With friends like these, who needs the CIA?

In fact, I wouldn't be surprised if one day Jerry were to inaugurate a film festival on Bikini atoll, *the Radioactive Film Festival*, he could alternate movies like *Guadalcanal Diary* and *PT 109* with documentaries on Yap and Mururoa, then condominiumize, *colonialize*, the surrounding atolls, and instead of smoke detectors the contractors could install Geiger counters.

But back to Margot. At first I couldn't understand why Jerry was with her, she is not a human being anyone can possibly get close to, I believed she was evidence of a fatal flaw in the man's character, a conception of self that spoke to some unfathomable abyss.

Then I got to know Jerry better and couldn't understand why she was with him.

For the man has girlfriends all over the country, all over the planet, which keeps his wife at a constant pitch of anxiety and terror. Yes, Jerry is a great one, a magnanimous, *large* human being. Just last year this *well-adjusted personality* arranged an AIDS benefit at the Palace of Fine Arts in San Francisco, enlisting for the festivities all his avant-garde filmmaker friends, each of whom contributed a single indecipherable film short to the program (Jerry even made me dust off one of mine for the show). And in this way, in the local media, Jerry was viewed *socially*, Jerry was hailed as a *responsible* human being, a human being concerned about his fellow men and women; but, in fact, I *know* that Jerry, who will fuck anything that has two breasts and a pulse, or at least is still warm, who never considers that he is AIDS-bait himself, who never considers the consequences of his own actions for himself, or, more importantly, for others, particularly Margot, is just the *opposite* of what he appears to be, is a deeply *anti*-social human being, someone who knows a hundred thousand people broadly but no one deeply, someone who in public life seems to be concerned about his fellow human beings but who in *private* uses and exploits his fellow human beings mercilessly, who cares nothing about them, who to this one dispenses herpes, to that one chlamydia, to the one over there condyloma.

Yet I think I keep Jerry around not because he enhances my artistic portfolio but because, what with all his girlfriends, some kind of interestingly bad melodrama is always unfolding between him and Margot, some kind of *tortured but sophisticated* love triangle that I, observing from the sidelines, find fascinating, entertaining, and oddly exhilarating.

Just then Margot, sitting across from me, cackled at something in her Japanese comic book. I glanced at her. I glanced at my bowl of corn flakes. I glanced out the window at the redwoods that, given half a chance, will outlive all of us. Abruptly I rose from the breakfast table—she and Jerry looked up, startled—but I had no time to socialize this morning, I had things to do, shot sequences to go over, *a whole movie to retrieve and revamp.* I headed through the mansion and up the stairs to my office.

My secretary, Beth, blond Beth, sat at her desk in the outer office, radiating high competence and bloom. I like Beth. A bright literate woman, she offers insightful comments on my screenplays, has called my attention to several novels for possible option, and whenever I am out of town she takes great care in watering my bonsai, which are way too delicate for the slashing shears and the gushing water hose of the González clan's gardener.

She looked up and smiled. "Morning, Doug."

"Messages?"

"Several journalists requesting interviews. A diplomat from Uganda wanting you to serve on the board of"—she arched her eyebrows—"a new film festival they're starting up in some jungle outpost this fall."

"Cannes–on–Lake Victoria. The hot new tourist attraction, to replace the diminishing elephant herds. Jerry have anything to do with that?"

She laughed. "I don't think so. Also, Reed called"—Reed Sternwood, president of distribution for Constellation—"to make sure you sent the print off to the negative cutter."

"You assured him I did?"

"I told him the truth. That the watchdog from Crown Completion—"

"Bulldog."

"—actually accompanied Jerry up to San Francisco to make sure it got delivered. And half a dozen calls"—she frowned—"from Nancy."

I nodded. Nancy was Tommy Mace's agent. She felt I owed Tommy a million or so dollars in point money. I felt differently. "Tell her I died," I said, and headed into my office.

I sat at my desk. I opened a drawer and got out a dog-eared copy of the shooting script to refresh me on my original intentions. That way I could run the film on the projector in my head while driving up to San Francisco to retrieve my final print—which, of course, was anything but final. *Tommy Mace suing me!* Unbelievable. I *found* him. I *made* him. I remember when he was just another young megalomaniac on the hustle. He had landed a string of supporting roles in three low-budget flops: a teen slasher, *The Sorority House on Dead End Street*; a crime caper, *The Big Elevator*; and a teen romance, *Tender Is the Dawning Heart*. Three rotten performances in three rotten movies in a row. He was dead in the water, finished before he started, passed out of the picture before he'd even starred in one. After that he got a few screen tests but showed up miserably. Nobody wanted him. At that point, if he had any future it was in films like *Naked Meatpackers 2* and *El Paso Wrecking Company 3*.

But in the teen slasher, in one fleeting instance, when the crazed killer went after his girlfriend, in one unguarded moment, the camera caught, by sheer accident, completely unintentionally, a look on his face of haunted pride, of uncanny majesty, of a spooky possessed rage. And in that one fleeting expression I *saw* who Tommy Mace could be. I saw my lead.

I wanted a fresh face too. The studio had tried to impose, to *inflict* on me, several big stars, but I rejected them. The budget would have shot up, and the stars would have brought along their own script doctors, their own script quacks, who would have "remedied" my script by prescribing dollops of glop and goo. I knew what I wanted, and it was Tommy Mace. I am good with actors, which is rare for movie directors, so many of whom lack a background in theater, so many of whom view actors merely as pieces of furniture and the director's job as set decoration, as deciding how to *arrange* the pieces of furniture. Naturally, the studio executives thought I was mad.

Tommy, that footstool, almost self-destructed. My agent contacted his agent saying I wanted him to do a screen test for a role in my upcoming film. My agent got back to me saying Tommy refused to test for anyone, let alone some B-list director he'd never heard of. The moron, I thought. The suicidal prick. So I called him up myself, I praised him, I cajoled him, I flattered him . . . and finally he agreed to the screen test.

The next day he stood in his torn leather jacket, ripped Levi's, and faded black T-shirt in front of the video camera on the bare sound stage; and I, feeling prankish, asked him to do a line reading from *Hamlet*.

He did it from memory. "To be or not to be," he began, "and sorry I could not travel both." And from there it went downhill. *Hamlet* turned into *Hambone*. The man was as eloquent as a flumdiddler. Jerry thought he was hopeless; he didn't understand what I was up to, what I saw in him. *No one understood what I was up to, what I saw in him.* In fact, I started to have my own doubts.

After lunch, I sat a sullen Tommy down in front of the video monitor and—it was not pure sadism on my part, though there was a touch of that—played back his performance. During the viewing he squirmed and fidgeted, he crossed and uncrossed his legs, he slumped, he sank, he slouched down in the chair in his torn leather jacket, his ripped Levi's, and his faded black T-shirt (now he wears thousand-dollar custom-made Italian silk sports jackets over that same $5.99 faded black Fruit of the Loom T-shirt).

"Not bad," I said.

"You don't want me, just say so," he said, rising to go. "I don't gotta sit through this shit. Especially by some guy whose only movie is some violent low-budget piece a shit."

I put my hands on his shoulders and pressed him back down into his seat. Then I looked with scorn into his eyes, I *penetrated* his eyes with my scorn. For I knew just how good *The Black Pig* was; the part of the world that counted knew just how good *The Black Pig* was; and Tommy saw the scorn in my eyes, the deep contemptuous scorn, and realized that he had goofed, that he had made a mistake even if he didn't understand the how of it.

"Look at this," I said, and ran on the video the scene from the slasher where for one unguarded moment he had shone. He watched it, then said, "Yeah, so?"

"You were good there," I said. "For five seconds you owned the fucking screen."

He squirmed some more. The stupid bastard didn't see it. When he was good he didn't see it, when he was bad he didn't see it.

"So what do you want?" he said finally, with sullen resignation.

"I want you to take this video, go home, and—"

"I don't have one."

"What? A home?"

"A VCR."

I calmly took out my wallet—I wasn't going to let this moron throw me off my rhythm—and handed him three hundred dollars. "I want you to go home. Look at this scene over and over. *Study* it. I want you to figure out how you can duplicate what you see there. If you can't recall what you were thinking, what you were feeling, what emotions were firing you up at that exact moment, then at least figure out what you have to do with your facial muscles to mimic that expression. Then come back and tell me we're in business."

I didn't hear from Tommy for three days. During that time I studied other faces, other *mugs*, in the agents' casting books. But not one of them had the magic, not one of them was *a magic mug.* Then Tommy came back. He had figured it out. How, I don't know. But he had changed. His *being* had changed. He had taken those five seconds and tried them on and grown into them and liked the way they fit. He had adopted them. He had *become* them. And he apologized for his earlier rudeness and paid me back the three hundred dollars.

On the set Tommy was an angel. He never complained, he never whined. If I needed extra takes he always did them willingly. If I suggested a different way for him to read his lines, he took my advice without argument. And during the long stretches of boredom between camera setups he sat in a chair quietly reading Sonia Moore's *Training an Actor,* Stanislavsky's *An Actor Prepares,* Michael Chekhov's *To the Actor.*

So how did he repay me for rescuing his career?

The second time around, Tommy Mace was not such an angel. The second time around he fought me over line changes. The second time around he argued about camera placements. The second time around, instead of reading self-help books for actors between camera setups, he hounded Eskimo boys and Bedouin girls.

Then, one day after we had completed principal photography, I sat looking at the rushes and realized that I needed one brief scene to bridge a gap in the narrative. I called him up and said, "Tommy, I need you in Burbank. Think you could make it down next Thursday?"

Silence. I listened carefully. The silence swelled and expanded, it inflated like a black balloon. Then—he stuck a pin in it. "Sure. For one and a half million." "Excuse me?" I said, certain there had been some mistake, that I was on a party line and some joker had jumped in. "I have fulfilled my contractual obligations regarding *The High Plateau of Stars, Part II,*" he said, speaking no longer like a Sunset Strip hustler but like a Philadelphia lawyer, "and anything additional constitutes overtime to be renegotiated for a new fee." I hung up. Furious, I called his agent. The mad bitch hewed to the same line. I threatened to sue, to ruin him. She said the sequel would guarantee he was too big to ruin. She was right, *I* was making him too big—and if I didn't acquiesce, she warned, a second sequel would never get made.

I remember discussing with Jerry how to get around using Tommy Mace. He jokingly suggested, "Why don't we get some geezer who can play Tommy's character in old age? You can have the guy tell the story from a retirement home on Saturn. He can supply the missing pieces."

"Great," I said dispiritedly, and this is what I mean about a subtle contempt.

"It'll be like that horrible movie six or so years back," Jerry went on, unaware he was depressing me—or maybe he was aware he was depressing me, maybe he *enjoyed* depressing me. "That Italian slasher—what was it?"

"Bruno Zopp's last one?"

"Yeah. *Love You to Pieces.*"

I ended up shooting a modification of the scene, using a body double who was viewed only in long-shot. It was crude but effective, and we got the scene done for $95,000—*my* $95,000, but at least I hadn't caved in to Tommy Mace's extortionist tax.

And now it occurred to me that after driving up to San Francisco and retrieving the film, I should recut it so that Tommy Mace's role diminished, so that it shrank—but why stop there?—indeed, I would make Tommy Mace disappear, vanish into thin air, cease to be, yes, I would *disappear* Tommy Mace from my film, leave his handsome face, that magic mug, littering my editing-room floor, to be swept up at the end of the day by one of the Gonzálezes, who, it is rumored, used to be in the business of disappearing people themselves in Central America. Yes, I would become the *director–as–death squad*, I would nullify Tommy's existence. And why not? He was *my* creation. Now I would *un*create him.

No good. I could get around a mediocre scene or a mediocre supporting actor in the editing, but Tommy was in almost every sequence, and I could not get around the entire picture.

Still, other vital work remained to be done.

"Beth," I said on my way out, "I'm just going for a drive in the countryside. I need some fresh air but should be back in half an hour." I said that poorly. She nodded but gave me a fishy look, as though she had located in my stilted *just* and in my ponderous *but* the fuzzy phraseology of deception. And, indeed, as I closed the door to the outer office behind me, I could hear her picking up the phone.

I strode briskly to the old stone stable. I entered and surveyed all my beautiful pieces of machinery, my beautiful pieces of automotive *sculpture*. My accountant thinks I buy these cars as investments, and it's true that in the rare-car submarket prices can shoot up fifty percent in a mere six months. But the deeper truth is that I buy these cars as objects of aesthetic contemplation—fast-moving objects of contemplation, to be sure. And anyway, what would I do otherwise? Buy more stocks? I can't tool around the mountains in my investment portfolio.

I decided to take the twin-turbo 911 Gemballa Mirage coupé, with its all-white leather interior. From the key rack near the entranceway I removed the Gemballa's key. I opened the door. I climbed in. I turned the ignition and revved the engine. What a beautiful primal roar! I turned on the six-hundred-watt stereo system by pressing the wireless remote-control button on the steering wheel. What will those incredible Huns think up next! The spaceships in my movies are not so luxuriously appointed. I started to drive out.

Suddenly a figure materialized in front of the stable's door, silhouetted in the hazy sunlight, waving its hands around like crazy. The silhouette had a configuration remarkably like that of my lieutenant. I braked and lowered my window. I adjusted the volume. I smiled and said, "What is it, Jerry?"

"Doug, where're you going?"

"I thought I'd take a spin on the Coast Highway."

"Please, Doug. You can't," the silhouette said. "It's finished. That's it."

I sighed. They were on to me. I asked the silhouette, "Do you like my film?"

"It's a great film, Doug. It's your best work yet."

I squinted into the sun, trying to get a purchase on my lieutenant's eyes, to see if he actually believed what he was saying. I could not tell. *I could not tell.* Even when you can see them, the smooth surfaces of my lieutenant's eyes yield nothing, they go deep, there are depths to those eyes, but they don't invite you in. It is the problem when you have surrounded yourself with yes-men over the years as I have done. You don't start out surrounding yourself with yes-men. You start out surrounding yourself with tough sharp characters like yourself, friends who will give you a fight, who feel comfortable giving you a fight, who aren't afraid of being critical with you, since the critical faculty is a crucial component of the creative faculty; and for a while I enjoyed the push and pull, the give-and-take of arguing movie points with my old friends.

But then something happens. You have a success, your old friends start to get petulant, they turn jealous, they feel that your success is more their success than you're willing to admit, you feel that your success is more yours than they're willing to admit. So what was once a fresh, open, spontaneous dialogue between old friends soon becomes freighted with doubts, burdened with ulterior motives, shadowed by subconscious hostilities. You begin to question their very intentions when they criticize what you are doing. Whereas once you trusted their opinions, now you are skeptical, deeply wary; and in the meantime, you have grown more sure of yourself (your success gives you that surety). And so you begin to weed them out. You begin to slough off your old friends, your old *traitors*, the ones with cheek, who give you back talk, who aren't awed by you, who have the audacity, the nerve, the colossal gall to contradict you. So you weed out your old friends, the *no-men*, and gradually replace them with *possibly-men*, and these, in time, with *probably-men*, and eventually these with *yes-men*, with sycophants and toadies and bootlickers, with parasites and barnacles and leeches who fasten themselves to you with the gooey mucilage of *yeses*. Finally, you have become so accustomed to fawning, groveling behavior that you believe it is the norm. The end result? The next time you hear the smallest echo of a doubt resounding from deep within yourself, no one is there to help bring that echo to the surface. It is lost, and you are lost.

I squinted more closely at my lieutenant's silhouette and repeated, "You really liked it?"

"I loved it," the silhouette's voice said. "It's the movie you've had buried in you all your life."

I nodded and smiled. Framed by the rustic doorway, my lieutenant's silhouette perceptibly relaxed. The sun had burned off the morning fog and now hovered directly over the mountains behind my lieutenant's backlit figure, limning his curly hair a soft glowing yellow. It was a lovely confluence of umbras and radiance, and I knew in my heart that if I ever directed another crime drama, I would find a place in it for just such a composition.

Abruptly I revved the engine. "Out of my way," I roared. "*Out of my way, you miserable fuck.*"

The Gangster

C h a p t e r 6

"You'll like the Double-O. It's your kind of place," Wilbur said as we sped north up the Livermore Valley toward the toxic-waste dump.

I nodded, though I doubted it. Earlier that day I had parked the Porsche farther up the valley, in the gravel lot of the Double-O—a windowless cinderblock bunker that houses the last topless bar in the East Bay. It was not out of our way. The professor had explained that he was researching the decline of the topless craze for a paper he was slated to deliver at a Popular Culture conference in Madison, Wisconsin, that fall. This might well be his last opportunity to pursue his research. "Besides," he'd said, "it's important we keep up appearances."

I didn't argue. "Sure. Why not? We'll grab a drink, then continue on."

I had seen enough of the professor by now to know he wasn't kidding about this stuff, either. He brooded over American culture and what had been born and what had died in the suburbs. According to Wilbur, the rise in the 1970s of strip joints in suburbia, which was then assimilating in a half-assed way the liberating currents of the sixties, figured in the clinical crisis of Western culture. Spouse swapping. Orgies. The disintegration of the family. The pornography explosion. The birth of new diseases and of a provincial cosmopolitanism. But then the decline of strip joints in the 1980s somehow figured still further in the deepening malaise, as suburbia, realizing it had taken a wrong drift, went about rezoning and barricading itself but without properly defining the perimeters of a new erotic *anima mundi*. Wilbur took it as his job, his mission, to explicate the meaning, to clarify the bright but elusive flame of existence for the people who dwelled there, indifferently yet uneasily, in a state of vague gnawing itchiness of both the soul and the libido.

First, though, the toxic-waste site. As we drove up the valley, the newer suburbs—the ones that had sprung up within the past decade, the condo colonies, the middle-level-executive homes—flashed by. They made me, in spite of myself, think of my father. A middle-level Capriccio executive in this fading suburban century. I wondered what he would think if he ever got wind that I'd gone partners on a scheme with a college prof. For years he'd been worrying when would I shape up, show my stuff. He saw me, at thirty-four, diddling in stock frauds and no-budget horror pictures, securing loans with counterfeit notes. And worse. Reading Schopenhauer, taking solace in Picasso and Segovia, going to bed not with nice Italian girls from the old neighborhood but with Irish, Jewish, and Anglo trash. Something new in the evolution of his species. Not a serious man. I was as baffling to him as a visitor from Mars.

I said to Wilbur, "You talk much with your father?"

He shrugged. "I call him on his birthday, Father's Day. Why?"

"Just wondering." Whenever I looked for a Father's Day card, I always got one as neutral as possible. None of this "To the Best Dad in the World" crap. Neither of us was particularly sentimental. I watched the scenery whiz by.

◆ ◆ ◆

We arrived at the disposal site. It had been a while since I'd last passed this way, and some construction had sprung up in the meantime. A brand-new suburban tract development came right down to the edge of the toxic-waste dump, separated by a nice high white fence. Next to that, a brand-new elementary school. Next to that, a brand-new golf course, whose grass looked too green, slightly eerie. And next to that, a brand-new shopping mall, anchored at one end by Macy's, at the other by a ten-screen cineplex with a marquee out front that boomed: "COMING MAY 23RD!!! HIGH PLATEAU OF STARS II."

I drove the van through the unattended gate into the disposal site —actually, a vast network of crisscrossing canals. Then parked parallel to a trench filled with stagnant, stinking, iridescent goo. A posted sign advised:

NO SWIMMING

NO FISHING

Just as well, I didn't have my bathing trunks. Wilbur slid the side door open and we worked quickly and quietly, grabbing boxes from the van and chucking them into the canal. In no time, a hundred and fifty boxes littered the surface of the chemical quicksand—boxes filled with hours upon hours of footage shot in the freezing white grandeur of the Antarctic, boxes brimming with the shifting sands of the Sahara, boxes redolent of the golden sunlight and warm tropical breezes of the South Pacific, still more boxes containing the astonishingly photogenic rubble of the South Bronx—all that splendor, all that work, all that multi-million-dollar magic and mayhem now slowly sinking.

"What about the work print?"

"Dump that, too," Wilbur said. "No, wait a sec. Maybe we'll want to look at it later." Wilbur smiled dreamily. "Should we get bored."

We stood for a moment at the edge of the canal, watching the boxes sink into the oozing toxic muck. A gurgling noise would be followed by another, then another, as the gunk ingested, then sucked down the boxes, the iridescent slime percolating and surging around them like a slow-motion sea. The gunk would then drain back into the impressions left by the boxes.

I glanced at the professor. He looked thoughtful, serenely meditative, at peace with himself. Wilbur removed the pipe from his pocket, packed the bowl with tobacco, placed the stem in his mouth, then struck a match, lit it, and—"No!" I yelled—tossed it into the canal.

Whoosh! The chemical river flashed to life, flared up in twenty-foot-high chartreuse sheets of fire that put fingers to the wind, then raced north and south, fanning out—*roaring*—through the network of ditches.

"Jesus," I shouted above the roar. Instantaneously I felt the whomp of the heat.

We scrambled into the van, then bounced along the access road between undulating walls of fire. I felt like I was trapped inside some maniacal Looney Tune. We rocketed through the gate and back onto 680, speeding north toward the Double-O. Already acrid black smoke was inundating the sky behind us.

"You stupid fuck!" I yelled, pounding the steering wheel with one fist. "The hell is your problem?"

"Oh, I'm such a wretched fuckup," Wilbur wailed, and he himself started to pound the dashboard with both fists. "What in the world is the matter with me?"

I stared incredulously at him. Was the son of a bitch poking fun at me?

Already I could hear the distant wail of sirens. I fought off the impulse to accelerate and instead drove steadily, my eyes going to the rearview mirrors, on the lookout for flashing lights. Nothing. Nor did the freeway motorists cruising beside us—commuter vans, elderly shoppers in shiny German sedans—take undue interest in our welfare.

"What next, Wilbur? Stop at a 7-Eleven, clean out the cash register—"

"I'm sorry."

"—burn down the shopping mall for an encore?"

He didn't answer.

"Christ."

As soon as we pulled into the Double-O's lot, I began transferring the film canisters to the hatchback of the Porsche. I felt shaky. A powerful throbbing rocked my skull, as though some ancient warlock were swinging a club back and forth between two enormous gongs, each located exactly behind my temples. It was too much. Finishing up, I tucked a blanket over and around the canisters, then slammed down the rear-deck lid. Wilbur watched me, puffing on his pipe.

We went inside. Six customers—traveling salesmen, construction workers—sat scattered around the dim club. Up on the stage, a plump platinum blonde in a sparkly G-string was finishing her stand-up routine. "They're sixty-eight triple-E and weigh forty pounds each," she squeaked. "As you notice, the left one's a little larger. That's cuz my boyfriend sleeps on it. He's roving 'round here somewhere. He's the one with stretch marks 'round his mouth."

Wilbur, holding a Scotch, shook his head. "This place. Striptease is dead in the suburbs. A year from now this will probably be a yogurt shop."

Just then an attractive stripper in her mid-twenties, with auburn hair that streamed over her shoulders, took charge of the stage. She scanned the audience with a critical eye, panning the suburban element slowly, then narrowing that critical squint to the bulk of Wilbur, nothing else. In the close darkness I saw a slight smile curl Wilbur's mouth. She smacked her lips, turned quickly away, then launched into her dance routine, to the Talking Heads' cover of "Take Me to the River."

The gloves went first, then her blouse, followed by her jeans and brassiere. The dancer's shoulders had a stylish sag, and I liked the swing and swivel of her hips. This was a woman I would have noticed in an upscale restaurant in San Francisco or New York, let alone a dingy suburban nightclub east of Oakland. She gyrated at the edge of the runway beneath the red lights, shifting and pivoting, bumping and grinding.

"What do you think?" Wilbur asked.

I shrugged. "She gives an honest performance."

In truth, I stared at her. She was there and not there, her face registering with the most subtle tilt of the chin, the slightest arch of the eyebrows, the whole gamut of the disdainful, the sensuous, the exquisite, and the undivulgeable—every modulation of emotion that a two-bit stripper in a two-bit nightclub did *not* need access to. She was a Vermeer in a mall gallery filled with velveteen. She was vexing.

"You got a paper and pen?" Wilbur asked.

"What for?"

"C'mon. Cut the first-degree."

Wilbur jotted something down, then folded the note and signaled our waitress, whom he instructed to give the note to the young woman as soon as she decamped the stage. To show that he was a man of the world, Wilbur also tucked a five-dollar bill into the elastic top of the waitress's fishnet stocking, which snapped back over the fiver. She rewarded him with a cool smile as she walked away on high heels.

Instantly my mind filled with visions of the professor on all fours crawling toward the stage, like Emil Jannings on his deranged journey toward sadic Marlene Dietrich. Trying to keep the alarm out of my voice, I remarked, "Wilbur, ordinarily I'd say go right ahead. She strikes me as a fine young woman. But not tonight. If you recall, we're about to embark on delicate ransom negotiations."

"Frank, it's not what you think."

"Yeah? What is it?"

Wilbur said nothing. When the song ended, the woman descended the steps at the side of the stage, wrapping a silky kimono around her slender figure, and was handed the note. She read it and smiled. Generous stockinged thigh flashed through the kimono's slits as she walked friskily toward our table, where, to my astonishment, she installed herself with total familiarity in Wilbur's lap.

"Hey, Wilbur. Terrific. So it went okay?" She put her arms around his neck and kissed him.

"What went okay?" I said, sitting straight up. Alarm bells began clanging in my skull.

"Frank, this is Jolene. She's a student of mine at Hayward State. She's working here undercover for me. Part of her term project. Like when Gloria Steinem went undercover at the Playboy Club disguised as a bunny."

"Undercover?" I muttered. *"What went okay?"*

"Frank, now don't get bent out of shape—"

"WHAT WENT OKAY?"

"Well, you know . . ."

"You fuck," I said in a low controlled voice. "You miserable fuckup. *Asshole.*" A rage, a towering funnel of anger, a black storm cloud, descended upon me. "Who the fuck are you? What sort of unpredictable basket-case piece of shit did I hook up with, anyway? Shit."

I sat there shaking, trying to think clearly, the blood pounding through my skull. Should I take the negative and run? It would be fair play. But where would I run to? Besides, this goofball—possibly both of them—knew who I was. I would have to kill them, and I did not want to kill anybody, not today, not tomorrow, it was bad style, an indication of poor form, crude workmanship, lousy work habits.

I took a long draft of my beer in an effort to soothe my frayed and frazzled nerves. Jolene, still installed in Wilbur's lap, stared at me. Faint alarm had registered on her fair freckled face.

"Jolene," I said in a tight voice. "You're very pretty, and I'm sure if I got to know you better I'd discover you're a marvelous human being. But just now I need to speak to Wilbur in private. You think you . . . ?"

"No problem," she said, springing up from his lap. "Wilbur, I'll be in the dressing room." She looked over her shoulder at me. "I'm okay, really," she said, then added fawningly, "Wilbur thinks very highly of you," and disappeared through a side door.

Bong! Bong! . . . Bong! Bong! . . . The warlock was beating double-time on the gongs inside my skull, which had become a vast empty echo chamber. I massaged my temples with the tips of my fingers. Then carefully said, "This is turning into a crowd scene, Wilbur. A mob scene. And I don't like mobs. They make me feel claustrophobic."

"I'm sorry," Wilbur said contritely.

"I don't think you understand, Wilbur. I just don't think you get it." I said this gently, softly, with a certain autumnal melancholy. Not a trace of threat. His eyes widened, he got it. "I'm only going to ask once. Are there any more cute surprises in store for me?"

"I swear, no."

"Because if there are, I want to know now. So I can decide what to do now."

"Frank, that's it, I promise. And I'm very, very sorry. I didn't mean to upset you so. Please. Let's go on with our relationship from here."

I shook my head. "Like I don't have enough worries, you blowing up the dump back there." I said, "You fucking her?"

Wilbur flinched, momentarily affronted. "We're romantically involved. We love each other. What we feel for each other cannot be contained within the traditional parameters of the professor-student relationship."

"She do Greek? French? Turn into a regular linguist in the sack?"

"Hey, hey, let's not get personal."

"What's your girlfriend, nice college girl, think about her prof shaking down a moviemaker for several mil?"

"She thinks it's great. She loves it."

"You trust her?"

"Of course I trust her. I said we're in love."

I gave Wilbur a long look.

"Hey, the girl takes off her clothes for the sake of research, she can get into this." Wilbur ventured a smile, allowed it to broaden. "Cinema 201. The Economics of Moviemaking. Field trips required."

"So you're in love." I sighed. "Like you were with that coed at Sonoma State? The one you left your wife for? Who then took off with the lifeguard?"

Wilbur started and drew back, he stared heavily at me, he regarded me through a frog-lidded squint. "Where'd you get that?"

"You think I was going to get into this without digging a little into your background?"

He studied me uneasily for a minute. Then his large ungainly body untensed, he unscrewed his eyes, relaxed. "What else?"

I shrugged. "An itinerant professor in search of tenure. And three months at Napa."

"You heard about my breakdown." Wilbur shifted uncomfortably, a log readjusting to the flames. "I thought we could use a girl Friday. Errands and stuff. Don't underestimate her, Frank. Good grades, sharp mind. She'll be transferring to Berkeley in the fall."

"You should've told me before we started."

"You're right, Frank, and I'm sorry. I apologize. But I didn't want to scare you off. The money will still be divided fifty-fifty, of course."

I sipped my beer. That wasn't even worth acknowledging. I said, "It's time to call Mr. Lowell."

Wilbur nodded. We had figured it was imperative we reach Lowell before the real couriers showed up the next morning; that way he could at least keep news of the theft from getting out—which would just complicate life for everyone. We had also agreed that I should be the one to telephone, since the professor's voice had something of a professorial timbre, more nasal twang than guttural gruff, it wasn't intimidating enough, it didn't sound as though he gargled with gravel in the morning. Not that mine did, but it was more in the neighborhood. At any rate, making the calls suited me just fine. It would give me more control—something I wanted, especially after the Jolene surprise. One large shock to my electrical system was enough.

He said, "I'll be in back with Jolene."

I nodded and watched Wilbur shamble off, shoulders stooped penitentially. How in the world had Wilbur—sheepish, wheedling, half-assed, half-sneaky Wilbur—achieved lustful success with that marvelous-looking woman? (No one is that hard up for grades.) For that matter, how in the world had I hooked up with him? What could possibly have been on *my* mind? If I didn't have the instinctive aversion of the ex-con to shrinks, this would've topped my list of questions.

I headed toward the pay phone at the side of the bar. Picked up the receiver and cradled it between my shoulder and ear as I fished out change. Then dropped in a quarter, dialed the estate, and heard a synthesized voice ask for $1.50. I deposited six quarters and waited. After four rings I expected to get an answering machine or voice mail, or hear a servant or secretary pick up. But the phone just kept on ringing. Eight, nine rings. Then—a man's voice:

"Yeah? Who is this? Do you know the time? Why, it's—no, wait. That can't be right. Is it really only seven? *Hello?*"

It was Doug Lowell. I recognized the voice, full of itself, from the television talk-show circuit. Gracious Doug, the bearded artist-martyr in jeans and windbreaker, explaining to the host how at one point on his first film he'd run out of money and finished financing it with *his own credit cards*, but he didn't mind because he *believed* in it. Plain Doug, the humble entertainer, telling another host that no, he wasn't ashamed that his second movie had grossed so much money, it was fun, and besides, he had no illusions about being an artist, he was just an entertainer, a mere entertainer, let the cultural historians of the future decide who the real artists of the day were—and so on until the commercial break.

"Doug, fuck the time and listen carefully." Up on the runway, under the dim red lights, a woman did a sluggish bump-and-grind, like she was on Percodan. Very erotic. She had the animation of a banana slug. I turned my back so I wouldn't get ill. "The matched negative to *High Plateau II*," I said. "It's vanished."

A perplexed silence followed. A soulful, charged, *complex* silence. Then:

"You got it?"

"Afraid so. But don't worry. I'm handling it with sterile gloves, the way a surgeon handles a rich man's heart." I signaled to the bartender to refill my glass.

"I'm pleased to hear that. That's very reassuring. But tell me about yourself. Do you work for me? Do I have your résumé on file? How'd you get my number?"

"We've never met. Getting your number was the least of it."

Another silence. Longer and, it seemed, more thoughtful. I switched the phone to my other ear, glanced at the runway. The manager was holding up the dancer as she descended the runway stairs under the red lights, smiling dreamily and attempting stage bows. Scattered laughter and applause. Christ.

Then: "Let me get this straight. You stole the negative to my movie?"

"That's right, and we want—"

"What about the rest of the negatives? There must be crates of the stuff."

"Dead weight. Excess luggage. Who needs that shit? Not you, not me. Gone. Kaput. Up in smoke. Literally."

"No kidding. Let me get back to you."

"Wait a—"

Click.

Doug Lowell had hung up.

C h a p t e r   7

I stalked off into the woods, angrily waving people away. Behind me I could hear Werner driving the Mirage, *my* Mirage, back to the stable. Did I say "my Mirage"? Let me elaborate, let me diversify. The man driving it is *my* Werner.

It had been futile on my part. I had arrived at the front gate only to find that it had been locked and the guard given strict orders that under no circumstances was I to be allowed to leave. So what could I do? Crash my car at ninety-five miles per hour through the wrought-iron gate? No, if I had done that the gate would have yielded slightly, then sprung back—and *I* would have been catapulted at ninety-five miles per hour through the gate. So I had stopped and the guard had emerged from the booth and kindly asked, with a doff of his cap and the most humble smile—I tip the old gent well at Christmas—if I would be so kind as to step from the car and leave the keys in the ignition. Which I did, feeling like a criminal. And then Jerry and other courtiers had come running out from the stable and the main house, walkie-talkies in hand, and I had stalked off into the woods.

Incredible! Impossible! I, the king, imprisoned in my own castle! What great distances I have traveled in the past decade, and yet what small wretched piddling distances—they can be measured with a piece of yarn. It reminds me of my early days when I was trying to get *The Black Pig* off the ground and some independent producer was footing my bill at the Chateau Marmont while arranging meetings for me with various industry people—footing my hotel bill and nothing else. I became *The Prisoner of the Chateau Marmont*. I was so broke I used to filch apples and oranges from the bowls of fruit arrayed for decorative purposes in the lobby. And I couldn't leave. *I couldn't leave.* For fear I might miss that one phone call that would transform my life, charge me with aim and purpose. I felt like a refugee, an undocumented alien, an undesirable quarantined in purgatory. I waited in my bungalow at the Chateau Marmont for days, *weeks on end*, waited for calls from studio executives who were certainly in no rush to see me, who weren't even *aware* they were in no rush to see me, who were benignly indifferent to my arrival in town—the moment was not captured by the paparazzi (though now if I smile unconsciously at a woman a picture the next day identifies us as Couple of the Week)—indifferent to the sad story that my rental car and restaurant tabs and airline bills had already skyrocketed past my credit-card limits. It was torture.

And the hypocrisy. During my sojourn at the Chateau Marmont I couldn't get my phone to ring if I called myself from next door. But after the success of *The Black Pig* my rate of returned phone calls increased tenfold; after *High Plateau*, a hundredfold. All I had to do was ring someone and leave my message, and the head of International Creative Management would get back to me in fifteen minutes, Steven Spielberg in eleven, and the President of the United States in six. I know, because one dull drizzly afternoon I clocked them.

But maybe it isn't hypocrisy. Maybe this is just the way of the world. After all, if my secretary tells me that Joe Schmo is on the phone and has a great idea for a movie, do I enthusiastically grab the receiver and say, "Okay, Joe. Let's hear it. Take your time, I want you to get it right"? No, of course not. I have my secretary jot down a message, and then I crumple that message up, dribble my imaginary message-ball downcourt across my office, feint a jump shot, then drive and slam-dunk that crumpled ball of paper through the hoop of my wastebasket.

And who can blame me? After the success of *High Plateau* I was besieged by all sorts of hustler-artists, dissembling screenwriters, cinematic carpetbaggers, and plain run-of-the-mill con men with a thousand schemes for making my money grow by leaps and bounds—my poor vulnerable money, which would have melted away like a Teamsters pension fund.

"Doug!"

I didn't turn. It was Jerry, the well-adjusted personality. I continued to plunge through the woods, *my* woods.

"*Doug!*"

I kept going. Behind me I could hear the well-adjusted personality crunching pine needles underfoot as he tried to catch up. "Doug, please. You know you can't work on the film anymore. It's finished."

He drew up alongside me. I slowed down. We walked through the woods in silence, our hands clasped behind our backs, two brown-robed Franciscans sunk in profound monastical thought. After a while I asked, "Are you angry I tried running you down?"

"Of course not." The well-adjusted personality laughed. "All in a day's work."

"That was a pretty good dive. Maybe I can give you stunt work in my next picture."

Jerry smiled. He had actually had a bit part in *High Plateau*—as a cybernetic yes-man who does nothing but nod and smile. A little in-joke that everyone, including his wife, got, except him.

We emerged from the woods onto the dirt parking lot that handles the overflow when I throw parties. In its center, plunked down on a pile of rocks as though it had crash-landed there, is the original spaceship from the first *High Plateau* movie—dented, battered, and artfully antiquated to give it the feel of a vehicle purchased off a used-spaceship lot in East L.A. After the movie's success, Constellation's executives had presented it to me as a gift, as a token of their appreciation. In truth, I didn't know what to do with it, I would have preferred an

Audemars Piguet watch, or a desert island, I was sick of the damn thing, I didn't want to look at it anymore.

So I had tried unloading it on the Smithsonian, figuring that if that noble institution had accepted into its halls the psychedelic bus, the psychedelic *heap*, of Ken Kesey and his Merry Pranksters, why, then —but they were not interested. I offered it to the President as a curiosity for the front lawn, but as much as he had enjoyed the movie, he regretfully didn't feel that 1600 Pennsylvania Avenue was the appropriate final resting place for it. Of course, I could have found an eccentric buyer for it somewhere—a Canadian billionaire, a Silicon Valley whiz kid—but I felt my spaceship deserved to be domiciled in as special a showcase as possible. All or nothing!

It was to be nothing. Finally, I rented a flatbed truck and had the Gonzálezes load the spaceship onto its platform one night, then drive the thing out to the Mojave Desert and just dump it. Two weeks later I got a call from the State Highway Patrol saying that they had investigated a UFO sighting and found my stolen spaceship instead—I had never reported it as stolen—and were returning it to me. The next day their tow truck lugged the battered, sun-blasted spaceship, now dappled with vulture droppings, onto my estate. The driver stuck his head out the cab window and yelled, "Where do you want this thing?" The only place I could think of was the dirt parking lot. I directed him there. And there it's been ever since, a two-ton conversation piece that arriving party guests *Ooh* and *Aah* at.

I now asked Jerry, "How much do you think I could auction that off for? Enough to buy a few more days to work on the sequel?"

"Doug, the movie doesn't need any more work. But more importantly, you don't want to auction that off. It means too much to you. It's invaluable. The memories."

I, a sentimental fool, a nostalgic mooncalf, nodded.

Six o'clock. I wandered into the mansion, into the main living room, where Jerry sat in front of the forty-two-inch SONY TV screen, eyes riveted on the KMUT evening news. Huge clouds of black smoke mushroomed into the sky. Traffic jams on I-680. Cops shouting through bullhorns. Suburbanites rubbing their reddened eyes. Panicky crowds stampeding through a shopping mall. Men dressed like astronauts hosing streams of chemicals into a roaring fire. Ambulance sirens . . . horns honking . . . mass evacuation . . . total chaos, a real mess. It looked like a medium-budget disaster movie helmed by a B-list director.

"What happened? Was there a meltdown at Lawrence-Livermore?"

Eyes transfixed by the spectacle, Jerry said, "Some toxic-waste dump caught fire."

The scene switched back to KMUT's studio, where the anchorwoman, Cindy Anderson, gave the latest on the blaze: "Investigators now say it may take weeks to discover the cause."

Cindy Anderson: a warm yet reserved smile, one blue and one green eye, and a pleasingly roupy voice. Thin and sharp-boned, she wasn't the prettiest anchorwoman on the air, yet she was made beautiful by a keen intelligence that quickened, that animated her lodestar eyes. Jerry had once told me he'd heard she'd originally co-anchored a news show in Washington, D.C., but had been packed off to an affiliate in San Francisco—something about sleeping with too many politicians who *were* the news. At least that was what Jerry had heard: Jerry was a veritable lending library of shoddy fictions, warmed-over gossip, and garbled fairy tales. On top of that, the owner of KMUT, a master bamboozler, wasn't above leaking such a canard on the media cocktail circuit if that's what it took to adrenalize his station's ratings.

"You ever sleep with her?" I asked Jerry.

"No." He laughed. "I invited her up to cover the Northern Cascades Film Festival once, but she didn't bite."

I nodded. Shortly after the success of *The High Plateau of Stars* she had requested an interview, and I'd readily agreed, inviting her to drive down for lunch before the rest of the TV crew arrived. I gave her a quick orbit of the estate, and we eventually wound up in the editing bunker in my mountain.

"Such a boy," she teased, watching as I fiddled with the controls on a new piece of equipment.

"It's not a toy," I said, slightly miffed. "This editing table is going to revolutionize filmmaking, allowing instant video playbacks of cuts before they're actually made."

"Will it make your movies any better?"

"No, but it will allow me to assemble them more quickly. More economically." I paused. "So actually, yes, it might make them better."

"Speaking of economics, I hear you're bankrolling the sequel yourself."

"Film is a collaborative art," I said, "and one's chief collaborator is always finance. If I finance it myself, then I can collaborate with myself and no one else."

"And so you don't collaborate?"

I said nothing. She nodded thoughtfully, then said, "You started out as an independent, saying you wanted your freedom from the studios and that besides, Hollywood was no longer what it once was. Yet in the wake of your success, old colleagues are accusing you of having become more Hollywood than Hollywood."

"Has the interview begun, Ms. Anderson?"

"Just trying to get a feel for the territory before the camera starts rolling."

I watched her walk over to an editing rack, from which strips of *High Plateau* outtakes dangled. She began examining one strip, holding the frames up to the light, trying to discern what discarded dreams and drama they might yield. I examined Cindy, trying to discern what upcoming dreams and drama she might yield. She looked lovely in a houndstooth-check blazer that flared over her hips and a tight-fitting black skirt. Idly, I wondered if KMUT provided her with a wardrobe allowance, if the station manager would fire her if she showed up just before airtime wearing old blue jeans and a ratty sweater. I stepped closer behind her, hesitated—then folded my arms around her, amazed at myself as I tried gathering her to me. Yes yes yes, my maneuver was completely clumsy, strictly amateurish, the move of a bungling Lothario, a total misadministration of my hands—

She stiffened. Without dropping the film strip, she said, "Doug, no."

"Cindy—"

"I mean it."

I removed my arms and stepped back. "C'mon Cindy. Be a sport. I'll give you a cameo in my next picture. Cindy Anderson, newscaster from Neptune."

She turned, laughing. "Hey, Doug, didn't anyone ever explain how it works? I ask *you* for a role. *You* say, only if I sleep with you."

I laughed, too. (What else could I do?) Then, trying to recover, I said, "So, who'd you sleep with to get your job?" And realized as soon as the words left my mouth that I'd just jammed my foot in deeper.

"Nobody. I went to the Columbia School of Journalism, then interned at a station in Washington. Who'd you sleep with to get yours?"

I was not extricating myself from this gracefully. In fact, I seemed to be doing an exquisite job of entangling myself even further.

But just then, to the rescue, Orson padded out from behind some stacked reels of old film, meowing.

Orson. The name had been my wife's idea. She thought it would be "cute" if we named *our* pet after *my* favorite movie director (my favorite of the week). So now I'm stuck with a longhaired, flea-infested tabby named Orson.

"Oh, he's adorable," said Cindy, scooping him up and stroking his soft fur. Instantly he began purring, the affection-monger. "What's his name?"

"Orson."

She gave me a long look. The look demanded explanation. So I told her the story, which I thought for some bizarre woman-reason might put me back in her good graces, as though the information that I disliked the cat's name as much as she did might establish a bond of intimacy between us from which my poor wife, felonious labeler of felines, would be excluded.

She didn't comment—and instantly I realized I'd just added insult to injury, affront to indignity, silent-comedy stumble to cartoon pratfall by disobliging my poor defenseless wife.

"Let me show you something," I said suddenly.

"What?"

"Just watch."

I took a videotape down from a shelf and stuck it in a VCR. Warily, bracing herself for the worst, Cindy settled into a chair to watch.

Moments later Tommy Mace, garbed in blue jeans, black T-shirt, and torn leather jacket, appeared on the monitor. Standing by himself, hunched over, ill at ease on a bare sound stage, Tommy Mace said, "This is just bullshit, you know. I mean, I've studied with—"

My voice, off-camera: "Just get on with it, Tommy, okay? Pretend you're at the dentist, something that's got to be done."

Tommy cleared his throat. "It's been a while."

My voice: "I understand. Are you sure you remember it?"

Tommy nodded, coughed, and cleared some more mucilaginous debris out of his air ducts; and then, with one hand to his chest, began to declaim:

> To be or not to be—and sorry I could not travel both.
> Whether it is bolder in the mind to suffer
> Like Saint Sebastian the arrows of outrageous infidels
> Or to ask arms for the poor. Or
> To die—to sleep the sleep of reason
> All through the furlough of our discontent.
> And by a sleep we mean to say
> The heartburn of bare bodkins, the grunts and sweat,
> And the thousand natural shocks
> That flesh adheres to. It is a consummation
> Passionately to be wished for—the rub—Soft you now!
> Now hard the mortal coil! For who would gladly borne
> The whips of fair Ophelia. Yea, me! For
> Surely some revolution is at hand
> From the undiscovered country, from whose bosom
> No traveler returns—That furry traveler
> Slouches toward Denmark to be born.

It was not merely the perfect recollection that made Tommy's recital so enchanting but the absolute certainty of his delivery as well: the whirlwind of his passion, never a pause, never a tripping over the tongue; the way he stormed back and forth across the bare stage; the manner in which he'd roll his eyes heavenward and saw the air with his hands, then touch one hand to his heaving chest, extend the other straight toward the North Star; the way he'd drop suddenly to both knees, place both hands over his heaving heart, then slowly spread his arms; the fine manner in which he'd modulate his voice, one moment a whisper, the next a roar like a rhinoceros. Yes, never the exaggerated emphasis, never the excessive deliberation, but always with an approach to the language of real life.

When this little video show was over, I turned to check Cindy's reaction. Knees clasped to her chest, Cindy Anderson rocked back and forth unable to stop laughing. "Bravo," Cindy cried, tears streaming down her cheeks. "Encore."

"He told me he used to perform in Ashland."

"As what? An usher? My God. This is priceless. Why, this is better than discovering some X-rated thing from his past." She shook her head and said, "Can I borrow it? I want to make a copy. Just for friends, I prom—"

"Forget it. You know I can't do that."

And she did. "He's good-looking, though."

"What're you, twenty-eight? You're over-the-hill. The guy likes tykes on trikes."

She laughed. And when her segment on me aired several nights later, it was good: artful, intelligent, and engaging. (And nothing cutesy about me and my meow-pal, Orson.) I called and thanked her, and that was that. We hadn't spoken since, though lately she'd been trying to set up an interview for the sequel. This occasion, though, I declined through my secretary, for though Cindy Anderson had been gracious the first time around, I felt sufficient uncertainty about the sequel to want to keep my distance from her. Ethical people are too unpredictable.

On the TV screen she now said, "That's the six-o'clock evening news. We'll be back at ten with the latest update on that fire still raging out of control at a toxic-waste site in the Livermore Valley. Good night."

I rose to leave. "See you later," I told Jerry, who, riveted to the set, nodded. I walked out of the mansion and crossed the lawn to the guest house. I was not done yet, not by a long shot. I would go to sleep early, set the alarm for four, wake up and slip on my old jeans, a sweater, and sneakers. Whereupon I'd steal through the woods and scale the wall at the edge of my property. Then I—Doug Lowell of the celebrated sports-car collection—would hike up to the Coast Highway and stand like a vagrant at the edge of the blacktop, my bare thumb stuck out in the chilly early hours, trying to hitch a ride north to San Francisco. With luck I'd get there before anyone noticed I was gone, and before my people arrived at the cutter's studio to pick up the matched negative.

As I hurried across the lawn, a twilight breeze struck up and cut clean through my bones (I thought I could hear it whistle). I started to feel depressed, anxious. Shivering, I rubbed my hands together and hurried home to the guest house.

I wandered lost in a cave, holding a candle to guide me as I followed a long, unspooled strip of 35-millimeter motion-picture film that I believed would lead me to the light of day. Gleaming stalactites, dewy with sweat, descended from the ceilings. Great stalagmites, sharp as spears, rose from the cavern floor. And the strip of film snaked on. It rounded bends. It ascended cold clammy vertical fissures. It descended into tight crevices. And wherever it went I followed. *But the strip of film did not lead me out.* No light shone at the end of the tunnel, or at the end of the next tunnel, or—what's that? Something was ringing, far, far away, in the opposite direction, like the ringing of—of—*a telephone.* I struggled to turn in the tight dark narrow crawl space that I suddenly realized I had wedged myself into—impossible!—I squared my shoulders, I exhaled to narrow my chest—*umph!*—no good—I wiggled with all my might—the ringing continued, *louder*—dear God, I was going to die here wedged into a cold clammy crawl space with a strip of orange celluloid running beneath me like a stream of plastic piss—the ringing continued—an overpowering sensation of suffocating, like someone was mashing a pillow over my face—total claustrophobia!—and like I was drowning, too—*the ringing*—I struggled, I twisted, I brought all my concentration to bear *ummmmmmm-ppppppphhhhhh*—

I looked groggily around. The telephone on the nightstand was ringing—the old-fashioned white rotary-dial telephone with its loud, grating, old-fashioned ringer. I sat up. I listened to it ring. I watched it ring. I put my hand on the receiver and *felt* it ring. Finally, I picked it up and said, "Who is this? Do you know the time? Why, it's"—I looked at my watch—"no, wait. That can't be right. Is it really only seven?" I felt as though I had been sleeping for days. *"Hello?"*

"Doug, fuck the time and listen carefully," a voice said. "The matched negative to *High Plateau II.* It's vanished."

What was the gentleman saying? Must wake up completely. "You got it?"

"Afraid so. But don't worry. I'm handling it with sterile gloves, the way a surgeon handles a rich man's heart."

Was this a joke? Certainly the man on the phone—*a rich man's heart*—displayed a modicum of wit. But his voice? I couldn't place it.

"I'm pleased to hear that. That's very reassuring. But tell me about yourself. Do you work for me? Do I have your résumé on file? How'd you get my number?"

"We've never met. Getting your number was the least of it."

I still felt woozy, groggy, cloudy, but the ground fog that enveloped me was beginning to break up. The caller, who had a slight Eastern accent—actually, New York—did not *sound* like a practical joker. Still, this had to be taken slowly. One day at a time. "Let me get this straight. You stole the negative to my movie?"

"That's right, and we want—"

"What about the rest of the negatives? There must be crates of the stuff."

"Dead weight. Excess luggage. Who needs that shit? Not you, not me. Gone. Kaput. Up in smoke. Literally."

"No kidding." The full import of what he was saying finally dawned on me, finally *struck* me. Amazing! I felt like the drowning man who sees the narrative of his life flash before his eyes.

Except this was different, in two respects.

First, it was not my whole life that flashed before my eyes but rather just the past three years: I saw all the debilitating fights with Tommy Mace—shouting matches in the Antarctic, petulant high-noon silences in the Sahara. I saw my fanged but feeble penguin-monsters waddling so stupidly across the rubble of a collapsed 161st Street tenement. I saw myself in Burbank calmly, madly, asking for the seventy-sixth take of Stenkil's rape scene while the cast and crew looked on appalled. I saw myself signing, with a Hancockian flourish, papers for a third mortgage on my estate, for a third mortgage on this, for a third mortgage on that, while my financial manager looked on appalled (and there is a direct causal link, it turns out, between seventy-six takes and a third mortgage). I saw my imported Eskimos melting like candles in the desert beneath the blazing *Lawrence of Arabia* sun. I saw a hathi elephant, plucked from the jungles of India, wander off into the jungles of the South Bronx never to be seen again. I saw the onset of the long melancholy polar winter night, the red orb pulling down with it like a black shade all those months of darkness that would follow . . . along with $3.2 million of my own money. I saw myself in my editing room, haggard and drained, unshaven, unbathed, my eyes bloodshot, my beard matted, attempting to project a businesslike air as I methodically, systematically, *desperately* tried patching together the endless mess of celluloid in which everything I owned was invested. And finally, I saw in my office a walnut filing cabinet that contained a manila folder that held my insurance contract with the Crown Completion Bond Company of Beverly Hills—my contract that guaranteed that should any unforeseen eventualities cause my film not to get finished, why, then Crown would have to pony up eighty percent—or was it eighty-five percent?—of the bill.

Yes, like a drowning man I saw all these things flash before my eyes.

However, *I did not feel like a drowning man.* Just the opposite. What I felt was that I had been drowning, suffocating, choking for breath for the past three years, but suddenly I had swum up, up, *up* and broken through the surface to gulp in huge lungfuls of fresh exhilarating life-giving air. *Eighty-five percent!* And the air was the gift of this man, this kind stranger at the other end of the line, this savior, this unwitting deliverer, this—this—this *liberator.*

"Let me get back to you," I said, and hung up.

Part Two

C h a p t e r   8

I sat in a rocking chair on the lit porch of the guest cottage, in the deepening dusk, gently rocking back and forth. In my lap, the Crown Completion Bond Company insurance policy. In one hand, a Canon pocket calculator. In the other, a refreshing glass of bourbon.

The movie had personally cost me . . . factoring in the still-accumulating interest on the assorted mortgages . . . roughly $75 million. In its capacity of distributor, Constellation was contractually committed to picking up the costs of eighteen hundred prints, saturation promotion, and lots of very expensive TV advertising . . . roughly thirty million. That is, a bit under half of my $67-million negative cost. A film returns about forty-five percent of its box-office revenues to the studio—which is to say, to me and to Constellation. Of which amount Constellation would be entitled to, based on their investment, approximately thirty-three percent.

Did I think *The High Plateau of Stars, Part II* would do well? No. In my heart of hearts I did not. I am at times a grandiose man, I am

Michael Covino

at times a paranoid man, I am at times a manic man and at other times a deeply depressive man, and at any of those times I can even be a deluded man. But at the moment, ever since that bracing phone call, I felt myself an exceptionally *lucid* man. The fog had lifted, the sun was shining, birdies were tweeting on their branches! *High Plateau II* was a *terrible* movie, a miasma of blackdamp and plague spores, and it would be an unmitigated box-office disaster. As the sequel to a smash hit, it would clean up at the box office in its first week of release, fall precipitately the second, and plummet by the fourth. If it did seventy-five million in receipts I would be astonished—rotten sequels to *Jaws* and *Star Trek* had not been so successful—and this, *my* movie, was much worse. I know. I *made* it.

But let me be generous, let me give myself the benefit of the doubt, let me presuppose it would do, say, a hundred million in tickets—an amount that would put most movies in the black. Subtract the forty-five percent from that, and you have $45 million (no calculator needed for that one). To Constellation would go thirty-three percent, or roughly fifteen million. Out of the remaining thirty million, *my* thirty million, I was contractually obligated to pay Tommy Mace's five percent of the *gross* points—five million. Another dozen people—top producers, top technical people, and two other lead actors—would divvy up between them an additional five percent of the gross: another five million. Put simply, if *High Plateau II* did $100 million at the box office, which was breathtakingly unlikely, I could expect to see personal returns of . . . twenty million. The film would leave me in the red. I would lose $55 million.

Of course, there would be ancillary markets—foreign distributors, videocassettes, cable, satellite—but I, in my infinite wisdom, in my slyly selfish calculations, in my *supreme arrogance*—had refused to let any of them put up anything other than the most meager guarantees, insisting instead on increments of percentages tied to the movie's profitability on the American market. The returns from these dribbling in over the years would barely outstrip the interest payments on my mortgages. As for toys and other spinoffs, the business they did would be directly tied to the business the movie did. In other words, *I* had structured everything, all the deals, all the arrangements, all the stipulations, so that I would retain total control of the film and receive maximum profits—the obverse of which was that I was also responsible if the film went over budget, and stood to suffer maximum losses. I had structured the whole shebang so that the very infrastructure of my empire now lay exposed, ready to shake, totter, and splinter thunderously asunder.

Twenty million dollars! As good as broke. (And if *High Plateau II* did do under $75 million, I would in fact be broke.) I, who in a single bound, with a single picture, had made my position in the industry so firm, so complete, so totally unassailable—well, with a single other bound I would be *infirm* and *incomplete* and *totally assailable.* Indeed, I would be moving *down in the world.* The whole industry would see that I was on the run. The whole industry would *laugh* and *throw things* at me. Yes, they would take advantage—God, how they would take advantage. *I* would be the one who would have to helicopter down to Burbank—*drive* down to Burbank—and act out scenes from prospective projects in the offices of vaguely interested executives. No longer would they helicopter up to Bonny Doon to act out scenes from *their* prospective projects in *my* office. I would be at *their* mercy.

I sipped my bourbon. I listened to the crickets. I felt the cool twilight breeze touch my cheeks and forehead. Was I upset? Did I feel frightened? No. I sat on the porch in a serenely meditative state, calmly, *happily,* punching out numbers on my little Canon calculator.

I had told Crown that I was budgeting my film at $32 million, but their accountants had read my script—read it with their own calculators in hand—and said, "Forget about it." Too many far-flung locations. Too many opportunities for bad weather. Too many weird intergalactic effects (but I drew such godly power from saying, "Dead aliens, resume your positions"). They estimated costs of fifty to seventy million. I protested. I hadn't yet been classified as "difficult," or as a "perfectionist." I had come in fast and just a touch over budget on my first two films, so I was able to get the bond. But because I was taking the unusual risk of backing the film as well as producing it, Crown said they would insure the production for only up to what I was personally worth, which they figured to be $70 million. I was my own collateral. Crown would sell me the policy at the usual six percent of the film's budget—the budget I had sworn by—but because Crown considered the enterprise so risky, they would adjust the rate upward as the budget soared, culminating in fifteen percent should I reach the $70-million ceiling. Above that, Crown would take my film away from me.

So. If the negative were to be destroyed, Crown would have to reimburse me eighty-five percent of the cost of the final negative, or $57 million—which would be a loss, but still, I'd be better off than with just $20 million. I would not only be able to hold on to my estate—and, to be truthful, I like my estate, it comforts me, it gives me a sense of coziness and solace—but I would also be able to prevent foreclosure actions on most of my other properties while I worked my way back to profitability on my own terms. As for the taxes, writeoffs, and deductions involved in all this—well, my accountant could dope out the details later.

In other words, it made sound financial sense for me to ensure, to encourage, to promote, to gently shepherd, to nurture along *the total destruction of my negative.* For only that act would leave both my empire *and* my reputation relatively intact.

Who was behind the theft of the negative? Who was my poor unwitting benefactor, my ministering angel? It did not matter. I'd worry about that later—or, more accurately, I'd leisurely contemplate that later. Now I had work to do, lists to draw up. First thing in the morning I needed to tell Jerry not to bother picking up the negative, that Greg, one of my producers, who lived in San Francisco, would. Jerry might feel a tad suspicious, but my own continuing presence in Bonny Doon would reassure him that nothing was amiss.

Next, I would have to prepare myself for the grand role of victim, a complex and quite demanding role, for when this extortionist called back to negotiate the return of the negative I would have to shuttle between nonchalance and solicitude, between disdainful lack of interest and anxious concern, yes, I would have to blow hot and cold, swing crazily from one emotion to another, wobble and seesaw to keep him off balance, to *disorient* him. For this was the delicate part, this was the tricky part, this was the *artful* part. I would have to bring the guy to as high a pitch of frustration as possible—but that is something I am used to doing to get the performances I want out of uncompliant, *uninspired* actors. Of course, this time I would only be allowed a few chances to motivate the guy to give the desired performance, which was to *totally destroy the negative* in a grand fit of picturesque rage and pique. My chief concern was that, in frustration, he would turn right around and try to deal with the insurance company.

But that was no worry, no worry at all. For it might not occur to him, or it might but he'd be too scared to deal with those boys, or he would deal with them and it would work out. In which case? In which case I'd be back where I'd started, *back in the nightmare following an unending strip of celluloid through dark, dank caverns.* I had nothing to lose. I would just be stuck with a bad movie, a $67-million white elephant. No gain, but no loss either. Actually, if I could stick Crown for the ransom bill, whatever that might turn out to be, I would at least be that much ahead.

Dusk was deepening into night. The trees were becoming less distinct, shading into piney silhouettes. I could hear the distant muted roar of the Pacific drifting up the coastal canyons. So soothing, so comforting. I planned to be listening to that roar for a long time to come.

I looked again at the insurance policy to ascertain exactly where my obligations ended and Crown's began (but the law is never exact, ambiguity is the trough lawyers feast at). I read through the pages of unendurable small print. I examined obscure clauses to determine what exactly Crown might try to evoke. I considered contractual asides for how Crown might try to interpret them in ways disadvantageous to me. There was the usual. Coverage would be rescinded if it was learned that during the period of principal photography the director or any of the lead actors had engaged in free-fall parachute dives, ascents of El Capitan, or deep-sea diving off the Great Barrier Reef. Coverage would be rescinded if proof was established of serious heroin or cocaine abuse on the set. Coverage would be rescinded if the principals took unescorted walks at three in the morning through East Oakland, Harlem, or Chicago's West Side. (The language wasn't quite that colorful.) Any of these things, and production would be shut down, left without a shred of coverage.

In the light of the porch my eyes continued to scan the pages of small print. One section—one sentence—caught my eye. *And should the negative be lost, or destroyed, or irrevocably damaged, then every effort must be exhausted, in all conscience, and within reason, to replace it with a plausible facsimile of the original material.* I slowly read that sentence again . . . *in all conscience . . . within reason . . . plausible facsimile.* Out of such equivocalities do suits and countersuits spring eternal. Well, no need to mince words in court for several years while my fifty-seven million stagnated in Crown's passbook account. I knew what that meant. It meant that I would be expected to salvage another final negative out of the excess negative footage. Of course, I would argue in court for all I was worth that such a negative would not be the same as the lost one, would not be as great as the original. And, of course, their lawyers would argue, for all they were worth, that given how many takes I had shot of each scene I could indeed *reasonably* assemble a *plausible facsimile* of the original negative—indeed, could reasonably assemble *twenty* plausible facsimiles. My lawyers would put honorable directors up on the stand to testify as experts in my behalf, their lawyers would put directors—petty envious mean directors—on the stand to testify in their behalf. And so "artistic integrity" and "fiscal responsibility" would get kicked around quite a bit in the old courtroom.

But if the joker on the other end of the line had been telling the truth, he had already destroyed all the excess negative footage. Gone. Poof! Up in smoke. No possibility of assembling a second cut, a *plausible facsimile*. Which was a relief.

However—*however*—one poor dim dismal possibility still existed that Crown's no doubt highly unscrupulous lawyers might try to seize on: that I salvage a negative from the *positives*. My editing room, the bunker I'd had carved into the side of a mountain, still contained miles of leftover positive footage. A negative could conceivably be made from the positive. Of course, my legal argument against salvaging a movie from the positives would be even stronger. First, the newly assembled movie, as in the case of assembling from the leftover negative footage, would not be the same as the movie that had been stolen. It would only be a facsimile (plausible or not was another question—legal to them, aesthetic to me). But secondly, the negative then made from the positive would never yield as good a quality theatrical print, since it was now removed *two* generations from the original. A print could be struck, but it would be of mediocre, *inferior* quality. Slightly fuzzy, like it had been blown up from 16mm. And that's not what people expect from Doug Lowell.

I had no doubt that I would eventually win such a case in court. However, their lawyers would still flog *in all conscience* and *plausible facsimile* to death. They would try to force a settlement out of court. It would cost time and money.

Yet I could dispense with this little matter very easily, in a single lightning-swift stroke.

A fire. Tonight. An accidental fire in my editing room. Completely inconsequential. And a week from now, after the extortionists had in frustration savagely destroyed the negative, I would break the news of the theft to the insurance company and place the time of the extortionist's first phone call at . . . let's see . . . some time early tomorrow morning . . . just before I informed Jerry not to bother going up to San Francisco . . . but after the fire! Bad luck. Terrible coincidence. Lousy bit of timing. But nothing to be done about it. *Now can I please have my $57 million?*

As to the fire itself.

I rose from the rocking chair and headed across the lawn to the mansion. I stole into the kitchen. I opened a cabinet door. Nobody around. From the top shelf I removed a container of Pounce—"The Fun Food That Cats Love to Eat"—and slipped several moist meaty pellets into my shirt pocket. Then I returned the container to the cabinet and left, heading across the dusky lawn toward the deep dark woods.

"Here, kitty kitty kitty. Here, Orson. Come to papa, Orson," I sang, walking slowly through the forest.

My wife had called a week earlier from her father's Shaker Heights mansion—called collect, since that starchy skinflint refuses to pay for her phone calls to his son-in-law. And the first thing she had asked was not "How're you doing?" or "How is your film coming?" but "*How is Orson?*"

Orson had been, technically speaking, a wedding gift from her father to me. The witless fool, who likes to think he's as cagey as a fox when in truth he's stupid as a cow, had told her, "Watch how he treats the cat. It will be an indication of how he'll treat your children [unspoken: *if you ever get that far*]." Which, though she wasn't supposed to, she proceeded to share with me, as though she were letting me in on some private joke just between the two of us, though *her* unspoken message was *So please, honey, don't fuck up*. And I had replied, without a glimmer of humor, with a distant chilliness, "Cats are not children."

In any event, last week when she had called and asked, "How is Orson?" I'd deadpanned, "Orson's fine. Editing this film has put him in a frenzy, made him impossible to be around—you try to pet him, he claws and bites you. Totally unbearable. But the end is in sight. Orson, that *auteur*, has seen the light at the end of the tunnel and is padding happily toward it."

She laughed and said, "I'm happy to hear that."

"You miss me?"

"Yes, I miss you." She paused. "But then I've often felt more for you at a distance. I fell in love with you at a distance, but . . ."

"But up close I always seemed a little . . . *raw*."

"I started out at college admiring you at a distance. You were the guy who told the professors they were wrong while everyone else was sucking up and slaving to get A's. Then I fell in love with you at a distance. But up close, especially when you're working hard, you can sometimes be . . . scary."

"It's sad."

"Is the film really almost done?"

"Yes."

"Good. Let me know, and I'll be on the first flight out of Cleveland." There was a pause. "I love you."

"I love you."

"And kiss Orson for me. Good night."

"Good night."

That was a week ago. Tonight, like a hunter in the forest, like the Big Bad Wolf, I was stalking Orson. In truth, furry playthings make me peevish, they are an inconvenience, I neglect them. She had named the cat "Orson" thinking to please me. But I have never cherished a particular affection for pets, not for the faithful dog, nor for the sagacious cat, unlike my dear sweet wife, who never appears so blissful, so happy, so *gratified* as when she is opening a can of Friskies Salmon Dinner, or caressing that affection-monger till he purrs disgustingly, or cleaning out Orson's stinking, piss-soaked litter box.

So basically it became her cat.

"Here, Orson. Here, Orson Orson Orson," I said, strolling through the dark woods, trying to radiate an air, an aura, of great harmlessness, of sentient innocence, to send out great soothing emanations, as if I wanted nothing better than to do Orson a world of cat-good.

"Here, kitty kitty kitty. Come out wherever you are, you miserable little—"

Orson stepped out of some bushes off the path just ahead, sniffing cautiously. I smiled and proffered my palm, luring Orson with five pellets of Pounce, which I then let tumble to the earth. Orson padded forward, pawed and sniffed the pellets, then began eating them, one by one. As he finished, I gently lifted Orson, stroking his soft fur. I carried the cat back through the woods, toward my editing bunker.

I was going to frame Orson for the crime of burning down my editing facility.

We emerged from the woods. Straight ahead in the moonlight, carved into the mountainside, was the editing bunker. Fifty yards away, also carved into the mountainside, was a larger structure that served as an equipment storage shed, as well as housed my own modest sound stage and film library. We, Orson and I, entered the bunker. I switched on the light. Tall shelves lined two walls—shelves filled with slender boxes of positives from *High Plateau II*. All around, editing disarray: reels, cores, Dust Off, film cement, splicers, tape rolls, and more. Celluloid strips of positives dangled from the portable racks. Pieces of positives filled the canvas trim bins, cluttered the editing tables, littered the floor. All the dead soldiers from my movie.

Orson was beginning to get antsy, trying to clamber out of my arms. His whiskers twitched. Gently I stroked his soft fur. In one corner of the room, an old refrigerator wheezed. Alongside it, a table with a coffeemaker. Alongside that, a half-used bag of charcoal briquettes and a plastic container of lighter fluid. Often when my editors have reached the end of their rope, when they're haggard and drained and totally exhausted, when their nerves are on edge and they're beginning to snap at one another inside the cramped editing room, I, also haggard and drained and totally exhausted, will suddenly rub my hands together and shout, "Hey, I'm hungry. Let's have a barbecue"—not because I am hungry but because I am the guy who's supposed to be the leader, who's supposed to know how to charge up everyone else, who's supposed to be the source of boundless energy. And so I will take command of the whole bogus enterprise, piling up the briquettes in the barbecue pit, dousing them, lighting them, flipping the steaks, even putting on one of those ridiculous white chef's hats as a joke (but who puts them on seriously?), revitalizing everyone with my (hopefully) infectious energy, and, failing that, with my juicy New York steaks.

Now, I scattered a bunch of newspapers all over the floor. I flipped open the lid on the lighter fluid and began squirting the shelves lined with the boxes of positives, squirting the racks from which strips of positives dangled, squirting the floor, squirting the walls, squirting the editing tables, squirting everywhere.

Orson started to meow, tried to disengage himself from my one-armed iron grip. Then—Orson leaped. I seized him—pinned the poor beast on his back—grabbed from atop the refrigerator a box of wooden matches—got one out with my teeth—lit it—and then, with a perfectly rational mind—I had never felt more lucid—I singed Orson's two front paws, first the brown-and-tan paw, then the—*damn it*, the match blew out, I struck another—then the solid brown paw, with which he likes to experimentally poke his food. Yes, I singed his two front paws while the poor beast howled and wriggled and twisted and, with his teeth and claws, tried, quite understandably, to inflict wounds upon my hands and wrists.

Do not think that I'm proud of this, do not imagine that I derived a Sadean thrill, but the truth is, tears did not stream from my eyes, nor did remorse fill the chambers of my heart. No, this was strictly business. But then I saw in my mind's eye my wife's father—this was *not* business—and I thought, "How I treat the cat is an indication of *how I treat the cat.*"

But then, almost simultaneously, I had another thought—no repressions, no sublimations here—what I thought, quite consciously, was *I am setting my father-in-law on fire.* And I enjoyed that feeling, I luxuriated in it; but, more importantly, even as I enjoyed that feeling, even as I luxuriated in it, I was big enough, objective enough, to realize that the feeling was lagniappe, that the important thing was that this act had become *absolutely necessary.* I had nothing personal against the cat, it had given me no cause for offense; the cat just happened to be a convenient fall guy, my burnt offering at the altar of the silver screen. Besides, artists are born killers. Dante killed a man in the Florentine cavalry charge at Campaldino. Villon killed a priest in a Paris street fight outside Saint-Benoît. William Carlos Williams no doubt let one or two slip away on the operating table, to see what it felt like. After all, what better way for the artist to fathom the mystery of life than by extinguishing it. Anyway, I was hardly killing Orson.

Next I squirted lighter fluid on his long tabby coat of fur and then flung the howling beast toward the door, so it could drag itself outside, away from the scheduled conflagration. After all, if Orson burnt to an unrecognizable crisp, his ashes in a Ziploc bag might not be admissible as evidence. I lit another match and tossed it into a pile of soaked newspapers. The room flared up. I fled.

I fled through the dark woods. I decelerated to a trot. I slowed to a pleasant early-evening jaunt across the lawn. Then I headed, unobserved, back to my guest cottage, to my home. I entered, and the first thing I did was pour myself a good stiff shot of Jack Daniel's. *Gulp.* Like a liquid meteor it blazed a fiery trail down my gullet and lit a warm furnace, a happy camper's bonfire, in my gut. Good. It might be a long cold night. I scrubbed my hands clean of lighter-fluid smell. And, still dressed, I stretched out on the bed in the quiet darkness, rested the back of my head on the pillow—it was limp, lacking in springiness, like a sack of mashed potatoes, I needed to go to Macy's and buy a new pillow—and then I composed my thoughts and waited.

I listened to the crickets.

I thought about my life.

And as I let myself drift happily, teasingly, at the threshold of dream's wondrous door, I considered how, once I laid my hands on the insurance money, I would reshoot *The High Plateau of Stars, Part II.*

◆ ◆ ◆

Five minutes later, on cue, someone pounded on the door of my cottage. "Doug, wake up!" Jerry screamed. "Doug, the bunker's on fire!" I rushed out, I made a show of rushing out, Jerry and I rushed through the woods, two frantic comrades in arms. Through the dark swaying pine boughs, I could see flames leaping from the bunker. We emerged from the woods. Smoke poured out of the editing facility. Just as I'd expected, just as I'd *pictured* it, several of the Gonzálezes hopped around the bunker at a cautious remove. Señor González squeezed the lever and aimed the nozzle of a fire extinguisher, whose thin stream of ammonium phosphate didn't even reach the bunker—he might as well have been watering hell with his dick. The rest of the Gonzálezes had formed a bucket brigade, passing pails of water forward and pitching them into the roaring conflagration.

I checked my watch. Any minute now I should be hearing— *wait!*—I cocked my ear—then—I heard it, the wail of sirens closing in on their objective. A minute later a red hook-and-ladder truck, straight from central casting, screeched through the front gate, tires squealing, firemen hanging off its sides. I made a mental note that in my next movie I'd toss in a bright blue fire truck, gratis, without comment, just to throw people for a loop, a kind of Jacques Tati visual joke, or actually, perhaps it would be viewed more sophisticatedly, as a kind of Brechtian alienation device, yes, good old Brecht, living in East Germany with his West German passport and his Swiss bank account. Brecht was a bit of an alienation device himself.

The firemen jumped off the truck. They began busily unwinding their hoses, adjusting pressure gauges, extending ladders into the night.

"Want me to deal with this?" Jerry asked.

"Please," the movie mogul said vacantly, eerily calm, beyond weeping, beyond despair, deep into some sort of shock.

Jerry left my side and began acting as liaison, the role he was born to. The poor fire chief didn't know it yet, but he would probably wind up as Jerry's guest of honor at the next Northern Cascades Film Festival, where he would somehow be pressed into service to give an edifying little lecture on how David Selznick burned Atlanta to the ground in *Gone with the Wind* while fifty firemen from the L.A. Fire Department stood around, axes at the ready, insuring the safety of the production.

It was too late, though, to insure the safety of tonight's production. Firefighters, having fanned out, knelt and stood directing powerful jets of water into the blazing bunker. I, the stunned victim, stayed in the background and just watched. About twenty yards off to the side of the bunker I saw a fireman lean over and reach into the grass, then come up stroking a cat. But all the shouting and clanging of equipment made it impossible to tell, at this distance, if the poor animal was crying.

Jerry returned to my side. Part of the bunker collapsed in flaming wreckage, creating a sudden uprush of sparks. But the firefighters were starting to bring the blaze under control. Charcoal gray smoke was winding and curling upward, thinning as it rose into the hard luminous night.

"Well," Jerry said, "it was time to upgrade to laser-video editing equipment, anyway."

"What caused it?" the dazed movie mogul asked.

"I don't know. But thank God you finished the film."

Jerry was right. That was indeed something for me to be thankful for, and it softened my despair over the loss of my editing facility. I nodded and, surrendering finally to a flood of emotions, sobbed, "Thank God."

The Gangster

C h a p t e r   9

I stood next to the bar, in the dim red glow of the strip club, staring at the dead receiver in my hand as though it were some unsavory object, say, a used tampon. Up on the stage, a sullen suburban striptease act. Slumped in their seats, exhausted traveling salesmen brooding Willie Loman thoughts over flat five-dollar beers. What the hell was going on? Did Lowell think this was some prank played by one of his court jesters?

All right. No need to come unhinged. I would give him a few minutes—no, hours—to check out my story before I called back, swung open the bomb bay, and dropped the $2.5-million demand-bomb on him.

In the meantime . . . Jolene's dressing-room door was ajar. Through the crack I could see my new partner, now more modestly attired in tight-fitting Levi's and a pink V-neck sweater. She sat on a couch facing Wilbur, consoling him. "It'll work out, don't worry."

"But he was so angry."

"He had every reason to be. If he hadn't been, *then* I'd worry. I'd be wondering if he was a flake. We thought it would be good to have someone like him helping us. Now live with it."

"I should've told him beforehand."

"Yes, you should've. That's what I suggested. But he's not about to be dealt out, not with that kind of money at stake."

I knocked discreetly. They looked up. I stepped into the room.

Wilbur asked, "You call him?"

I nodded. "I'd like to tell you the guy's sweating, and he just needs a little time to put two million together. But he hung up before I got to the ransom part of the conversation."

Wilbur looked thoughtful, then shrugged. "He probably wants to check it out, that's all. I wouldn't worry."

"Do I look like I'm worrying? *Should* I be worrying?"

"No, of course not. That's not what I meant. I'm sorry."

I considered the professor; he was too apologetic, too conciliatory for his own good. We went back out into the club, where a young woman stood at the edge of the runway, disrobing to a Muzak version of "Yesterday" while crooning the lyrics. Dazed and passionate, she was missing the tune by a mile; her voice would shoot up like a roller coaster, crack horribly, then disintegrate into warbles and moans. The terrible thing was, she meant every word.

"You know," Jolene said, watching the stage, "she never even had formal training."

I stared at Jolene. She turned and met my stare with an askew smile, her intense green eyes on twinkly high beam. "A joke, Frank. That was a joke."

Jolene is a sport, I said to myself. Well, well, well. Life might become interesting with her on board.

◆　◆　◆

Wilbur drove the van, Jolene and I drove the Porsche, as we caravaned up 680 to Walnut Creek, to return the truck to my friend before continuing on to Tahoe. I had asked her to ride with me: there was the little matter of getting to know my new partner better.

"This is nice," she said, bouncing in her bucket seat. "Leather." She leaned forward and looked at the speedometer, whose numbers climbed to 170.

"I've never gotten it over one-thirty-one," I said. Then, before she found out for herself, "The back seats are vinyl."

She nodded without saying anything.

"I used to drive a Ferrari," I added, and felt lame the instant it was out.

"Career setbacks, huh?"

I didn't answer. The buttery aromatic leather reminded me of my ex-wife, of a tight-fitting leather skirt she frequently wore that drove me mad with desire for her. But it was the back seats, the vinyl seats, with their sour repellent odor, their malodorous scent of thermoplastics and polymers, that reminded me of her soul, of her laminated molding-compound soul. My dear ex-wife, who knew everything about real estate and nothing about the human heart—except insofar as she considered it another piece of real estate to be bought and sold and sub-divided and time-shared out and eventually torched as a slumlord might.

Jolene said, "Speaking of career setbacks, did you ever try tracking down your ex?"

Spooked, I stared at her. She looked mildly curious—no more. "No. Aside from the fact that it would've been impossible, it wasn't even like I would've known what to do if I'd found her."

"Strangle her?"

I shrugged. "I wanted explanation. Clarification. I wanted her back. I mean, I wanted to know *why* she did it. She knew I wasn't hooked up with my father's people. We were always honest with each other. I would just like to sit down and *talk* with her. Ask, Why did you betray me when you loved me? It made no sense."

"Would that have helped?"

"I don't know. But after we were arrested I never had the chance. The feds, the lawyers, they all got between us. There was a lot of unfinished business, and it'll probably remain unfinished forever."

In the dark of the car Jolene said, "I don't mean to be indelicate, but why did you expect so much honesty from her? After all, the two of you were engaged in a con—selling the mansions and all."

"There's a difference between a social lie and a private lie. This is a woman who was constantly telling me how much she loved me, how we were going to start a family in a year. We felt the same about things. Then, at the first sign of trouble—*boom!* She turns to ice, doesn't know me."

"It must've hurt."

"Allenwood was nothing. I could have done a dime in Leavenworth standing on my head. It was trying to figure what was going on in her mind, what she was feeling, that made me crazy."

Jolene shrugged. "I don't know. This distinction between a social lie and a private lie—maybe you and she just had different philosophies."

"Thanks." There hadn't been enough detachment in my words. I realized I was getting into a state—always happened when I talked about her.

Jolene was quiet a moment, looking soberly in the dark at me. Then she said, "I'm sorry. That didn't come out the way I meant it. I just meant maybe you didn't know her as well as you thought."

I nodded grudgingly. But the conversation was suddenly over.

We pulled into the BART parking lot, several blocks from my friend's house. Wilbur drew the van up alongside the Porsche and climbed down. I raised Jolene's window, then lowered the driver's just a crack. "Jolene, stay put a moment, okay?" She nodded and I got out, held open the door, and said, "Wilbur, do me a favor. Get in." Though my request puzzled him, he obliged, sliding into the driver's seat and squeezing his ungainly carriage behind the wheel. I locked the door behind him. Both he and Jolene peered up at me through the smoked glass, as though from deep within an aquarium, somewhat perplexed. I took the remote from my pocket and set the alarm.

"Look," I said, bending down to the crack, "I have to return the van to my friend. It'd be better if I went alone." They nodded, still

puzzled. "However, the car alarm is touchy. If you try to get out and
stretch, the thing's liable to start shrieking like an air-raid siren. You'll
have cops crawling over you in a second."

Behind the glass, Jolene looked thoughtful. "It's great the trust you
have in us."

"Excuse me. I believe we just met an hour ago, Miss Jolene, and
now we're partners in crime. Besides, maybe we have different philosophies."

She shot me a look. "Just hurry up."

"You bet."

◆ ◆ ◆

I drove the van to Wally's place, an attached redwood condo with a
garage, and parked in the driveway. We hadn't had much chance to
talk that morning. In fact, we hadn't talked much since I'd gotten out
of Allenwood. Wally, a big, good-natured California blond, had line-
backed for the Cornell Bears.

"So," Wally said, greeting me, drink in hand, "you use my van to
pull off a bank job, or what?"

I laughed good-naturedly, the fuck. "Hey, you're mixing me up
with my old man. After Allenwood I follow the straight and narrow."
I nodded soberly, a serious man. "Thanks for sending me those books
when I was in there." Czeslaw Milosz's *The Captive Mind* (bedtime
reading after lockdown). Vaclav Havel's *Disturbing the Peace* (a suspicious warden tried confiscating it). But I didn't want hard work; all
I wanted was Stephen King and Elmore Leonard, for the diversionary
value. But Wally had me pegged at Cornell as a man of action who
liked words and ideas. Jesse James with Nietzsche in his hip pocket.
Al Capone with a jones for the Ramones.

"No trouble. It must get boring, even in a Club Fed." Wally smiled.
"We had some times, didn't we? Moving grass in Collegetown. Remember that crazy Rastafarian, used to bring up weight from Jamaica?"

"Sure do. Along with reggae imports you couldn't find in Ithaca,
or even New York."

Wally stood there grinning, remembering. Then, "Shit, what kind of host am I? Let me get you a drink. What're you having?"

"Scotch over." I walked around his living room. "Window installation looks like it's been treating you well. Do you ever miss the action?"

"Action, hell. There's plenty of action installing windows. One day it's a new wine boutique in a mall, some pretentious little asshole wants half-moon windows. Next day we go out to Blackhawk, take a look at a nine-hundred-thou Disneyland Tudor. Guy wants us to knock out the shower wall, install a big plate-glass window so he can watch 'em tee off on the ninth fairway while he scrubs his balls."

"Different people's ideas of heaven."

Over in a corner of the living room, on a tiered cart with rollers, the walnut-veneer TV set was on. Wally glanced at the screen and said, "Check this out. News in my little corner of the world."

The anchorwoman, Cindy Anderson, was reporting that a big fire at a toxic-waste disposal site in the Livermore Valley late that afternoon had filled the sky with thick clouds of noxious-looking smoke and sent thousands of local residents fleeing, creating a massive traffic nightmare on 680. "At this moment," she continued, "authorities are pouring twenty-six tons of neutralizing chemicals into the site's canals. No one knows how it began. A few dozen people are being treated at local hospitals for respiratory ailments, but so far no one has been seriously injured." A shot followed of a perspiring state official who cleared his throat, then said that the dump site, the Livermore Valley Sanitary Landfill, had been cited seventeen times in the past year for violation of the Toxic Ponds Cleanup Act, and that it might take investigators weeks to penetrate the twelve-to-fifteen-foot-thick toxic goo in the canals to determine the cause of the blaze. *Weeks.* That was good. A comment followed from a Sierra Club spokesman, who compared the disaster to the meltdown at Chernobyl—which caused the anchorwoman to arch her eyebrows, slightly askance.

Wally said, "Any fine the EPA levels against the bastards will probably only be ten percent of what they figured they could make breaking the law."

"Calculated costs of doing business in these times."

"Hey, Frank. Why don't you stay for dinner?"

"You know, all this is giving me an appetite."

◆ ◆ ◆

It was several ticktocks past eleven when I arrived back at the BART lot. Wilbur and Jolene sat scrunched in the Porsche, looking distressed. Swaying pleasantly, I took out the remote, beeped off the alarm.

"You have a nice dinner?" Jolene said levelly. Wilbur looked miserable but remained quiet, perhaps recognizing when penance for a pernicious existence has been served.

"I couldn't get away. It'd been a while since—"

"Drink a few good bottles of Cab, toss a nice Chateaubriand onto the Weber?"

"Guy did us a favor, I had to—"

"Shoot the bull with your college buddy, recall old times?"

"Hey, this business of ours is no lark. You could stand to learn a little discipline, some patience. It's work like anything else."

"I suppose we're even now."

"It's a start."

C h a p t e r   1 0

So we left the Bay Area late Monday evening and drove east to the mountains, to Lake Tahoe. I still felt irritated, Jolene was unnecessary, a complication. But no matter. We were on our way and Wilbur was in fine spirits, in a very high manic place, indeed. He regaled us nonstop with esoterica, on and on he jabbered about forties *film noir* and the decline of the American thriller; how American TV commercials have insidiously affected the editing of movies, causing a kind of factory speedup; how there was no longer any inner life in American pictures; about Fitzgerald, Faulkner, Chandler, and West in Hollywood, and how Hollywood, in fact, had treated them royally, better than any American university had—and in the telling I got the feeling that Wilbur considered himself an ill-used beneficiary of the dubious graces of the American university system.

As we crossed the Sacramento Valley and passed through Sacramento, the level delta land started to roll, then grow hilly. The Sierra Nevada scaled the skies in front of us, the distant snowy peaks glowing under the fluorescent moon. Wilbur poured it on. "The Sierra Nevada are simply steeped in culture," he proclaimed, reminding us of the notorious jumping frog of Calaveras County and Twain's discovery of American vernacular, of Bret Harte and "The Luck of Roaring Camp" and how Harte dealt with the carnality that had eluded Twain. "Have you ever seen," Wilbur asked, "the photographs taken in 1876 in Yosemite Valley by a photographer riding on a stagecoach that got held up? Why, they're amazing photos. The highwayman is pleased as punch that the guy wants his image. He preens, he poses, he has no idea what photographs mean, they're so new—no clue that one day they'll be used against the likes of him. And speaking of photos, Ansel Adams had the right idea, he understood instinctively that Yosemite would photograph better in black and white, that in truth the beauty of the place lies in its contrasts, not in its colors. It's actually pretty monochromatic. And no American moviemaker has ever had the guts, the balls, to push the light values in the lab the way Adams did. If even one had dared, the whole course of American moviemaking might be different. But instead of great moviemaking, we got great coffee-table books.

"As for Tahoe, after Twain's two-month respite on the lake shore in 1858, which he wrote about in *Roughing It*—the restful vision of that grand lake would fuel him with the equanimity needed to ground his fury for the next decade—after Twain, the place had to wait a whole century before culture rediscovered it, and then it was claimed not by the movies but by TV, by 'Bonanza,' whose exteriors were shot in the Tahoe basin. That's right," Wilbur declared, "that's a Tahoe alpine meadow we used to see Ben Cartwright, Adam, Hoss, and Little

Joe ride across as the credits rolled at the start of each week's show. But it took Francis Coppola to capture the haunted beauty, the spooky grandeur, of the place in *The Godfather II.* Just picture that scene where Michael Corleone stares out the big glass window of his shoreline estate as his henchman takes his brother Fredo out fishing—then shoots him and lowers Fredo's body into the water.

"It's a long shot," Wilbur said. "Plus the setting sun's reflecting on the windowpane. You're liable to miss it. But when the gunshot rings out, Michael *lowers* his head. He didn't *want* to kill his brother, he *had* to because his brother had betrayed him. That's what everyone misses—the grim melancholy determinism of it—because most movie-goers aren't attentive to details. But Coppola knew what he was doing. The man's a fucking genius, or at least he was for three years in the early seventies when he made that pair of American beauties. The man *connected* with his material. He was *on.*"

We drove up, up into the mountains. Wilbur went on, on about the movies. To the west behind us lay the Sacramento Valley, the Coast Range, San Francisco Bay, then dark endless expanses of the Pacific Ocean. To the east in front of us the Sierra Nevada mounted higher and higher toward the stars, the dusty foothills covered with chaparral, the loftier mountains dark and piney, their peaks shimmering in the moonlight. I was starting to relax. Wilbur spoke of how no great American movies had been made during the Reagan years except for Martin Scorsese's *Raging Bull,* how the spectacle of the country as a bad B movie—"Not a *good* B movie, Frank"—had precluded any great movies getting made, and how, not coincidentally, it had been Scorsese's earlier movie *Taxi Driver*—"a *film noir* of sorts"—that had inspired Hinckley to try to assassinate the B-movie president, Ronald Reagan. "Scorsese felt under siege afterwards so he hit the TV talk shows and argued that there was no connection between his movie and the assassination attempt, that Hinckley was just plain nuts. But of course there was a link, and Scorsese should've been proud of it. He should've proclaimed, 'Yeah, my movie inspired Hinckley to shoot Reagan. So what? What of it?' And then he should've cold-cocked the world by announcing plans to make *Taxi Driver II.* He would've gotten the financing, too. Enough old-timers in Hollywood hated Reagan that much."

Wilbur was unstoppable. The fresh mountain air rushed in the open windows, and Wilbur gulped it down by the lungful. "Lenin was right, you know, when he proclaimed movies 'the most important art.' It took a wide-awake Marxist early in the century to recognize that the terrain had changed overnight, to name the new game in town correctly while university intellectuals just brayed and bleated and refused to acknowledge that the novel had been shunted aside, poetry relegated to the farthest margins of the culture."

Yet, Wilbur went on, what did the Soviet Union do with this dazzling insight of their founding father? "Why, nothing! An absolute zilch! Mosfilm was worse than Hollywood, a gigantic propaganda mill, and not even good propaganda. Is it any surprise that in 1926 that hack director Eisenstein's *Potemkin* was knocked out of the Second Goskino movie house in Moscow after a mere two-week run by Buster Keaton's *Our Hospitality*? No, of course not, the Russian people knew what they wanted. Lenin had the insight, but it was American artist-hustlers who took the ball and ran with it.

"But American politicians," Wilbur moaned. "What a bunch! In the White House screening room Kennedy used to watch Marilyn Monroe movies all the time. It pissed Jackie off, you know. Nixon watched Westerns. And *Patton*. He watched *Patton* over and over, thought it was the greatest movie ever made. Didn't realize it was a joke. Some joke. Influenced his decision to incinerate North Vietnam. And Reagan! Endless reruns of 'Charlie's Angels,' for chrissake. A straight T-and-A man who loved the happy ending. Impossible."

Jolene swept auburn hair out of her eyes and laughed. "You never delivered this one in the classroom. But what about LBJ?"

Wilbur shrugged. "I don't know. Lone Star kitsch. *Giant. Written on the Wind.* Dorothy Malone massaging the miniature oil derrick on her desk like it's earth's own hard-on. Maybe *Hud.* A consideration of Paul Newman as presidential timber. Most likely though, he watched that eight-millimeter film of Kennedy's motorcade through Dallas. Filmed by Zapruder, a mere spectator, an absolute nobody—and the guy comes up with the most famous snuff film in history! A gun-shot . . . another shot . . . a body slumps . . . the black limousine halts . . . a woman screams . . . the crowd roars . . . Jackie embraces her fallen knight, Johnny. *Yeah.* Johnson probably watched that over and over, in quiet awe, in reverential gratitude, freezing it repeatedly on Z-313—"

"On what?"

"You know, the frame where Kennedy's head explodes. Anyway, now any time the President pokes his nose out of his foxhole on Penn-sylvania Avenue, forty TV cameras zoom in. The networks never want to get scooped by an amateur again. So humiliating."

Wilbur slumped in his seat, exhausted. He was drained. He had poured himself out, he had illuminated the night—and the dark granite mountains had listened and still stood dark and granite for it.

I drove. The Porsche pounded up the mountains. I drove and directed my thoughts away from metaphysical ponderings on the de-cline of American culture and to Doug Lowell, who, in a certain sense I supposed, some intellectuals considered one of the architects of that decline. And perhaps he was. But that was neither here nor there.

By now Lowell's associates had no doubt confirmed that the negative to his new movie was indeed missing. And consequently Lowell's at-titude had—I hoped, I prayed—grown properly respectful of the people he would have to deal with. At any rate, it was time to find out.

The 7-Eleven stood on a deserted, wooded stretch of Highway 50 just beyond Placerville, set back from the road, all lit up in the night. Outside it, a phone booth glowed, as though beckoning the wayward traveler. I pulled into the lot.

"What's up?" Jolene said groggily.

"Time to check in on Doug," I said. Wilbur stirred and clambered out, padding after me to the booth. I dropped in the coins, dialed. Wilbur pressed both hands against the glass, staring in. On the fourth ring Lowell answered.

"Doug, it's me again. The guy with your dreams in twelve cans."

"Oh, yeah. I remember you. Now that I've looked into it, I have to admit that was a very inspired piece of work. But what is it I can do for you?"

This was not what I wanted to hear. I pressed on. "Two and a half million dollars. That's what."

"Sure. No problem." He laughed. "I'll have to run by my ATM first—"

I hung up. Wilbur was staring in at me, his eyes wide with dismay. Pushing open the door I said, "You sure we took the right picture?"

"Yes," Wilbur whined. "For chrissake, what happened?"

"A joker. Very cavalier. Certainly in no rush to negotiate."

Wilbur shook his head, mystified. "I don't get it. He ought to be hysterical. I swear there's no way he could have another copy. And the movie's scheduled to open in four weeks."

"Maybe it hasn't sunk in yet," I said, though, to be realistic, I thought it had. "Or he's bluffing, hoping to whittle down the price. He didn't get to the top by falling apart when the pressure's amped up." I nodded but didn't like the crack and strain I heard in my own voice as I stretched for the optimistic note. "I would also imagine, Doug Lowell being Doug Lowell, the guy has his pride."

"It makes no sense. Shit," Wilbur muttered, and we walked into the 7-Eleven.

"Get some beer," I said. He shuffled toward the cooler in back while I headed toward the newspaper rack, wondering vaguely if this whole thing had been a pipe dream, a chimera cooked up by a loopy professor.

A black-and-white photograph of Wilbur Blackfield appeared on the front page of the *Sacramento Bee*. Terrific. Lowell had gone to the cops after all, and they'd somehow made him.

But on closer inspection I could see that this was something different. Wilbur waved a revolver as he made people lie down on the floor inside a convenience store . . . *in Montana*. The picture had been taken by the store's surveillance camera, and its graininess made it look like a still from one of Wilbur's beloved *films noirs*.

However, on even closer inspection I could see that it wasn't Wilbur. As striking as the resemblance was, the man in the photograph lacked Wilbur's grand contemplative professorial presence. He looked stupid. Dubbed the "Convenience Store Killer," he possessed the same large hulking frame, the same half-cunning piggy eyes, the same sloping

Cro-Magnon posture, even the same disheveled way of dressing as Wilbur. According to the UPI story, the guy had been blazing his way across the United States, sticking up stores in Glens Falls, New York; Athens, Ohio; Iowa City, Iowa; Aspen, Colorado; and Missoula, Montana. His general itinerary, tracked on a map like the sweep of a hurricane, indicated a westward movement, and he was expected in California any day now. All surviving witnesses described him as monstrous, without a shred of humanity, evil incarnate.

Muttering, Wilbur strode toward the cash register with a six-pack of Bud. Behind the counter, his back turned, a teenager slouched on a stool, munching a donut and watching the news on a small TV that occupied a shelf at eye level. The station was replaying footage from the Montana 7-Eleven as the killer made two employees lie down. Mounted on the wall right above the TV, a surveillance monitor showed Wilbur striding down the aisle. The professor's muttering snagged the kid's attention, and he giraffed his head back to gaze at the monitor —did a double take—jerked his head down to the TV—and wheeled around, horrified, just as Wilbur plunked down the six-pack. "Gimme a couple of beef jerkies, too. And how about—"

"Anything you want," the kid cried, snapping off the TV, then grabbing the whole plastic canister with about fifty beef jerkies and shoving it across the counter toward Wilbur. "Anything," the kid howled, "just take it!"

"This is very peculiar service," Wilbur remarked as I joined him. He started to reach for his wallet.

"NO!" the kid screamed, flinging up his hands. "I mean, please, no. That won't be necessary."

"It won't?"

"No. Please."

The kid banged open the cash register and worked his way across the tray, grabbing all the twenties, tens, fives, and ones. He then lifted the tray and pulled out four one-hundred-dollar bills and some American Express Travelers Cheques. "Here," he said, thrusting the wad at Wilbur. "Take it. It's yours."

Wilbur turned and whispered, "Frank, what the fuck is going on? I don't like this."

"Do as he says and take it. I'll explain later."

Wilbur glanced nervously over his shoulder, then turned back to the kid. "Won't you get in trouble?"

"The owner'll understand, believe me. Anything else?"

Wilbur scratched his head. "Do you have the May *Playboy*? There's supposed to be an interview with Doug—"

"We don't stock those anymore," the kid cried, terrified, "but it's not my fault. These Fundamentalist types were putting up a howl." The youth mopped his brow. "But there's this store back in Placerville that stocks *everything*. Much finer stuff, if you know what I mean." He nodded frantically. "Just ask for Nasty Ned."

Wilbur scanned the store, bewildered. It *looked* like an ordinary 7-Eleven. Against one wall stood the newspaper stand. Facing it, the magazine rack. In back, the refrigerated glass case filled with sodas, beers, and wine coolers. To the side, the freezer filled with ice creams, TV dinners, and frozen pizzas. Even the kid—freckles, blond cowlick, Placerville High T-shirt—exuded a kind of post–Norman Rockwellian hyperrealism. Wilbur, having taken stock, turned and looked long and hard at me . . . but I just shrugged.

"Now, don't be alarmed by what I'm going to do," the kid said gently. "Here, watch." He picked up the telephone and gave the line a tremendous yank, ripping the cord right out of the terminal block. Then he proceeded to smash the receiver on the counter until the plastic splintered and shattered horribly. He swept the debris off the counter into the wastebasket. Wilbur watched, amazed.

I pointed at the camera. The kid looked up at it, petrified. "Right. That." He grabbed the stool by its legs and swung it at the camera. Like a wild man, he kept swinging and smashing away until the casing cracked open, exposing its workings. Then he righted the stool, climbed up, and removed the roll of film. He tossed it to me, and I pocketed it.

"*I don't fucking like this, Frank*," Wilbur hissed.

"Now, I'm going to lie down on the floor behind the counter," the kid said slowly, "and I'm going to stay that way for an hour. All right?"

He looked at Wilbur. Dumbfounded, even annoyed, Wilbur muttered, "Do whatever the fuck you want, sonny."

The boy looked at me. I kept my expression rock hard.

"*Two* hours," the kid said.

My face was stone.

"*Three* hours," he pleaded.

"Sure, kid," I said finally. "Anything you say."

◆ ◆ ◆

We exited the 7-Eleven into the cool Sierra Nevada night. Jolene leaned forward from the back seat and poked her head out the window. "What took so long?"

"Jesus, you wouldn't believe what happened in there," Wilbur said as we climbed in, and he began to relate the whole bizarre encounter to Jolene. I put the car in drive and cruised out of the lot, tooling along the winding mountain road. When Wilbur had finished, Jolene caught my eye in the rearview mirror and said, "All right. He doesn't know what went on. What about you?" I shrugged and told them about the story in the *Bee*. When I was through, Wilbur said, "Christ, you could've gotten me killed."

"Shut up a moment, Wilbur," Jolene said sharply. "Let me get this straight, Frank. The poor kid behind the counter mistook Wilbur for some crazy mass murderer. And so for the small sophomoric thrill of inadvertently knocking over a 7-Eleven for—what?—five hundred bucks and a six-pack, you would willingly jeopardize two and a half million dollars? Am I missing anything, Frank?" She shook her head incredulously. "And you think me and Wilbur are flakes? Let me tell you something. You belong in a fucking flake asylum for pulling a stunt like that."

I kept driving. Did I spot any patrol-car lights flashing in my rearview mirrors? *No.* Did I hear the distant wails of police sirens responding to a 211 that some dangerous career criminals had just knocked over a 7-Eleven? *No.* Just the wind soughing through the pines. I had no doubt that the poor kid would indeed hug the floor for the next three hours, then crawl to the phone booth just outside, flattening himself on the ground if a car motored up the road.

"I don't hear you, Frank. Nothing to say?" She shook her head.

The woman was unrelenting. "What do you say we look for another 7-Eleven? Turn this into a Charlie Starkweather *Badlands* kind of thing. A romantic crime run across the nation. You'd like that, wouldn't you, Frank?"

"Who said anything about romance?"

"That's not what I meant," she said, and turned away. In the close darkness of the car I noticed Wilbur shoot her a look.

"Jolene, relax," I said. "Where's your sporting blood? Life is interesting. Let things happen naturally. Be joyously amazed by the occasional serendipity of events."

"Yeah, I'll be fucking amazed all right." She shook her head again. "Shit."

C h a p t e r   1 1

We arrived at dawn, and from the crisp touch of the wind and the resinous scent of the air I would've known even with my eyes closed that it was spring in the Sierra. In the spreading light of the alpine morning we passed Echo Summit, more than seven thousand feet above sea level. Then turned a corner and, a good ways below, Lake Tahoe swung into view—two hundred square miles of shimmering blue mirror rimmed by pine-forested mountains.

◆ ◆ ◆

I parked in a far corner of the Ponderosa Lodge Motel's lot, away from the registration office. Inside, behind the counter, a young blond fellow minded the store; he flaunted a winter ski tan, wore a Chico State sweatshirt, sat reading the sports section of the *Chronicle*, and seemed politely indifferent to my arrival.

"I'd like a two-bedroom housekeeping cabin with a lake view."

He glanced up, looked through a chart, then swung around in his seat and took two keys off a hook on the key board. "No problem," he said. I registered us in a phony name and paid cash in advance.

"There's coffee in the morning, free copies of the Tahoe *Daily News*, and direct-dial."

"What about ice?" I said. "And of course we'll need an ice pick."

"The ice chest's across the auto court next to the soda machine," he said, already hunched back over the sports page. "As for the ice pick—man, don't bust my balls."

◆ ◆ ◆

Cabin 7 was at the back of the motel. You entered it through the small living room. Both bedrooms, furnished with TVs and queen-sized beds, faced the lake through curtained sliding doors that opened onto a connecting sun deck.

I walked to the glass door and pulled the cord that drew open the thick white curtains. Radiant gold light flooded the room. Then I slid the door open and stepped out. From the sun deck I could examine the sky over the Sierra Nevada on this dazzling day. The lake, cobalt and silvered, lapped right up against the sun deck's posts and extended seven miles across to the opposite beach; just a little farther back, the mountains started abruptly—rising from spring-green shorelines to, thousands of feet higher, wintry blue peaks.

Why was it that I wanted to listen to the lake, to be engaged by the mountains, and not by Jolene and Wilbur, who were, at that very instant, bickering about something in their room? I craved, at the moment, low stimuli. I just wanted to sit on the deck, eyes shaded, drifting. . . .

Jolene tramped into my room, snapped on the TV, flashed past CNN, MTV, HBO, then had her eye caught by some cable-network real estate station that advertised mansions in different parts of this great big scrambled country. She saw me staring in and called out, "This make you nostalgic, Frank?"

More than she knew. I remembered watching this program with my ex-wife as we geared up for our swindlelous project. You'd get a long shot of the mansion, followed by well-lit interior shots of all the rooms, with special emphasis on the marbled bathrooms and the huge kitchens with their walk-in refrigerators. The camera would stalk from room to room, like the camera in *Halloween* or *Friday the 13th*. I don't know if it was intentional, but a subtle hint of horror always tainted the air. A price would flash on the screen—"Only $3.4 million!"—followed by an 800 number to call. And sometimes, for study purposes, we would videotape the show, then call the number and record the sales pitch that followed. The show gave me a deep feeling for the various markets around the country: depressed in the Midwest, booming on the coasts, a minisurge around Atlanta, a deep slump around Dallas. I got a marvelous feel for the republic through my American Real Estate Studies. This land is *my* land.

"It used to be my favorite program," I said truthfully, stepping back in. "Ahead of '60 Minutes' and 'Monday Night Football.' "

Jolene said, "Just think. After you get your money you can buy one. Right here on Tahoe."

I shook my head. "Shoreline estates are on the pricey side. Two, three mil." I turned off the TV. "We have work to do."

◆ ◆ ◆

From the hatchback of the Porsche I removed the canisters that contained the final work print and lugged them to our cabin. Then jiggled the ice pick around till the lock on the first canister sprang.

"You learn that at Cornell?" Jolene asked.

I had a curiosity about the movie—I don't mean just the natural curiosity one would have for something with a $67-million price tag, but a sort of proprietary interest, the deep-rooted inquisitiveness of one who possesses something but doesn't know whether it's a dogstone or a diamond. I opened the can and removed the reel. Unwound about ten feet of celluloid past the leader and held the film up to the light that streamed in through the sun deck's doors.

"Do we at least have the right movie?" she asked.

"Oh yeah." I threaded a few more frames through my hands.

"Thumbs-up or down?"

"From this little bit it looks silly. But who knows?"

Jolene remarked, "Just remember what Barnum said and multiply it by today's demographics."

"Maybe."

◆　◆　◆

After lunch I decided to call Doug Lowell. A full day had passed, time enough for him to feel the rock of his resolution starting to crack. I left the cabin and strolled three blocks east to a shopping mall on Highway 50. Outside the Pay Less Drug Store, I found a phone booth, stepped in, and dialed the Bonny Doon estate.

"How you doing, Doug?"

"Oh, you. Want to hear something wild? Tommy Mace is suing me for point money owed from my last picture. I made the ingrate a superstar, a multimillionaire—"

"Fuck Mace. I want to talk cash up front, not points. Ready to—"

"I'm tired of it all. I don't want to be restricted by real life anymore."

"*What?*"

"Never mind. What's up?"

Christ. "Are you ready to discuss the negative?"

"I don't have much choice, do I?"

"You're finally getting the pict—"

"No pun intended. Did you know Mace is a pederast?"

"You sound homophobic, Doug."

"A broad-minded thief."

"First, we want the money—2.5 million—in unmarked twenties and hundreds."

"Nonsequential too, right?"

"Uhh . . . ?"

"Nonsequential. You know, where the bills all have different serial numbers so the banks can't list them on their hot sheet."

"Of course nonsequential. That goes without saying," I snapped, hearing my voice flush with indignation, almost crack. This wouldn't do, not at all. The son of a bitch was poking fun at me, playing me for a fool. I decided to assume the proper air of magisterial menace, of the professional persecutor, the accomplished animal. "Listen, you fuck. Who the fuck do you think you're dealing with anyway?"

"Calm down. I was just trying to be helpful." There was a pause. "What do you say we make it . . . one and a quarter million?"

I calmed right down. "No problem. You'll get back half your movie."

"Touché." Then: "For curiosity's sake, what if I don't pay?"

"Huh?"

"If I don't pay. Then what?"

"Jesus. What do you mean, then what? We destroy the fucking negative, that's 'then what.' "

"Okay. Continue."

The guy was taxing. I drew a deep Zennish breath and went on: "I want you to drive to Tahoe on 50. Stop at the phone booth outside the general store in Little Norway. You'll get further instructions there. Drive alone, and don't waste our time having the booth tapped. We're just going to send you to another booth—"

"Why don't I give you my cellular number? We can skip all this rigamarole about booths."

"Noon tomorrow, Doug."

"Tomorrow? Listen, I really don't mean to be troublesome, but I have an interview with some woman from *The Village Voice*. How about the day after?"

I didn't answer right away. Was Lowell kidding? The guy seemed to have his own calendar. "If you don't mind my saying, you have a pretty fucking laissez-faire attitude for someone who has sixty-seven million riding on a film due in the theaters in several weeks."

"Money isn't everything, you know," he said thoughtfully. "Artistic validation really means a lot to me."

"Hey, your show. Day after tomorrow, noon." I hung up and stepped out of the booth, feeling strangely enervated—peripheral, somehow, to what was going on. How had I gotten involved with these people? Who were they? The day was uncannily brilliant, the sky azure, the snowy peaks burned with a high white fire. I should have been *happy*.

◆ ◆ ◆

My companions had repaired to the sun deck. Wearing bright-red bathing trunks and Ray-Ban mirror glasses, Wilbur sat in a beach chair smoking his pipe, grading test papers, pouring strawberry margaritas from a pitcher, and watching a rerun of "Charlie's Angels" on the TV, which he had managed to crowbar loose from the dresser top and hook up to an extension cord out on the deck. Jolene looked up and said, "So, rain or shine?"

"To be honest—"

"Ssh." Wilbur put his finger to his lips; he focused on the screen with rapt concentration. "A woman has hired Farrah, Jaclyn, and Kate to find out who set fire to her film-producer son's office, not realizing he's been dealing in pornography and blackmail."

Ssh? I looked at the test papers stacked in his lap and littering the sun deck. Ketchup, mayonnaise, and gelatinous substances of indeterminable origins had dried, forming thin crusts over them. No wonder the guy never got tenure. He didn't grade his papers so much as attack them like some demented 1950s abstract expressionist, the kind who eschews the usual tools of his trade in favor of sticks, knives, trowels, fat tubes of dripping red fluid paint—or perhaps a heavy red impasto with sand, broken glass, bones, fecal matter, and other foreign substances mixed in. "Wilbur, I just spoke to Lowell."

But a commercial came on—for *The High Plateau of Stars, Part II.* I turned toward the set, curious.

It's hard to get a feel for a picture by looking at a trailer. As far as I could tell, though, *High Plateau II* looked like some bastard hybridization of the Sahara Desert and the South Bronx, with camels and angry-looking Puerto Ricans wandering around. A TV voice screamed: "COMING TO THIS PLANET MAY TWENTY-THIRD. CHECK PAPERS FOR THE THEATER NEAREST YOU!"

I looked at Wilbur, puzzled. "What was that about?"

Wilbur shrugged. "The trailers are put together months earlier. Lowell has nothing to do with them. Don't sweat it."

"Don't sweat it? I just said I spoke to Lowell. The meet's on."

"Terrific." In the burning overhead sun, Wilbur's flanks, thighs, stomach, and nose were starting to take on the neon hue of his strawberry margarita. He didn't seem particularly attuned to what I had just said. Wanted to get back to Farrah Fawcett.

"But he couldn't make it tomorrow," I went on. "He insisted on the day after."

Jolene jerked right up in her recliner, swung the hair out of her face. Even Wilbur turned from the TV. Jolene said, "What the hell could be more important than getting his movie back?"

"An interview with the *Voice*."

"Bullshit. It's a trap," Jolene said.

I shrugged. "I'm not worried about a trap. It's our game. We control the board. It's his contempt—or maybe just lack of concern—that bothers me."

Jolene stared at me, her green eyes bright and hard. "Okay, Lex Luthor, it's not a trap. But even if it is, you know how to outsmart them. So maybe it's time you unveil your plan."

Jolene and Wilbur sat on the couch in the living room, looking at the U.S. Geological Survey map and a sheet of drawing paper on the coffee table that showed the layout of a motel and the location of a nearby phone booth—complete with lines and arrows indicating Highway 50, as well as secondary roads. "I rent a ground-floor room in this place, just up the road from Little Norway," I said, tapping the paper. "It has a back window I can slip in and out of easily. Wilbur, listen up. You take up a position on Talking Mountain. You'll have a police scanner, binoculars, and a walkie-talkie. From there you'll command a clear view of the road and be able to monitor Lowell's approach from the west."

"How do I get up there?"

I stared a moment at Wilbur. "Call a taxi."

He looked puzzled. "Won't that—"

"There's a fire trail. I'll drive you." I breathed in slowly. "Now pay attention. Next, Lowell stops at this phone booth. Wilbur, you'll radio me he's arrived. From the motel room I call Lowell and tell him to proceed to a second booth in Phillips, *west* of here but still in your sightline. Even if the first booth is tapped, there won't be time to tap the second. And by sending Lowell *back*, you'll be able to spot any unmarked car that U-turns behind him."

"In which case I contact you on the walkie-talkie?"

"No. I'm going to give you a Remington bolt-action. You stop the fuck's clock."

"You're joking, right?" Wilbur said, wiping his brow.

"Yeah, I'm joking." All this serious talk was making the professor simple. "Okay. Once Lowell arrives in Phillips, you radio me again. I call Lowell with instructions, tell him to proceed to the motel. He parks, gets a key from the manager, enters the room. He leaves $208,300 on the bed—"

Jolene said, "Why that amoun—"

"—which is one-twelfth the total take. He locks the door behind him, returns to his car, and waits fifteen minutes. All the while, Wilbur, you're monitoring him. Then he re-enters the room and finds the first of the twelve reels on the bed. After satisfying himself that it's his movie, he leaves another $208,300."

Jolene nodded. "Got it. Back and forth, back and forth. Twelve times at fifteen-minute intervals over the course of the afternoon." She said, "It'll put us in danger for three hours, though."

"It'll keep us safe for three hours. This way neither party can effectively double-cross the other. At the slightest sign of trouble, or even something just a little out of the ordinary—say, Lowell forgets to lock the motel door behind him, or a Jehovah's Witness turns up selling subs to *The Watchtower*—at the slightest sign of something just a little out of the ordinary, Wilbur radios me, I scramble out the back and jump in the car. Which will have you at the wheel."

Jolene said, "They'll spot us getting on the road."

"I've gone over the map, checked out the terrain. Just ten yards from the motel a fire trail starts. It connects up with other fire trails that cut through the forest to Highway 89. Tomorrow we're going to practice those trails till we can run them blindfolded."

"Then what?" Wilbur asked.

"I take the money to Wells Fargo, ask for the manager, and explain that I would like to open accounts in all our names."

"Won't that—" Wilbur stopped, frowned, saw Jolene was laughing.

"Wilbur," I said, pointing out toward the deck. Test papers were blizzarding everywhere, the wind kiting them over the lake. "Jesus!" Wilbur cried, jumping up and racing outdoors, clawing at air as the papers sailed out of reach. *"Don't just sit there."*

◆ ◆ ◆

That night I couldn't sleep. I lay in bed, not just tossing and turning, but feeling my very ions careening randomly, madly about, throwing out crazy fields of energy that pulsed and raged around my body like an electromagnetic tempest.

Sitting up, I surveyed the room in the dark. My bed, I noticed, stretched east to west. I debated getting up and rearranging the bed so that it ran instead north to south. In Allenwood a convict doing time for possession of stolen bonds—he had no idea how they came into his possession—had taken me aside one day and asked if I had by any chance noticed which way all the cots faced. No, I hadn't. He smiled, leaned closer, glanced over his shoulder, and then told me that they faced, every single one of them, east to west; and that this was deliberate, that they were aligned perpendicular to the Earth's true magnetic field so that *our* magnetic fields would not be aligned in our sleep with the Earth's; so that, in fact, they would clash; and that this was a subtle form of institutional coercion pioneered by the CIA in the 1960s, to create magnetoelectrical chaos and static in our bodies that would keep us from functioning at optimal capacity. I remembered nodding and smiling, and thinking, "So this is what prison does to a guy."

But maybe he was right. Maybe he was on to something and that was why now, as I lay wide awake at three in the morning stretched out east to west, I felt so disoriented. And maybe that's why, now that I thought about it, my ex-wife and I had started fighting more frequently when we moved into that Hillsborough mansion, that *haunted* mansion, why things had started to disintegrate, to feel so wrong even before we sold the place to that charming FBI couple. Because now that I thought about it, our big brass bed ran *east to west,* counter to the polar flow of our sexually charged ions.

I got up. I paced back and forth. This sort of magic thinking, of sophomoric late-night solipsism, wouldn't do at all. I was losing my mind. I tiptoed over to the wall my bedroom shared with Wilbur and Jolene's bedroom, and pressed my ear to the plaster. Nothing. It was dead in there.

I continued pacing back and forth. Lowell had agreed to the meet but had then postponed it a day. Why? Perhaps Jolene was right and it was a trap.

All right then. I would analyze this. The moment of the exchange is always the most dangerous:

—That is the moment the hidden sharpshooter picks off the terrorist.

—That is the moment the roadblocks go up barring all escape routes.

—That is the moment the helicopter with megaphone and spotlight swoops in out of nowhere.

I combed my plan for flaws. From his mountain redoubt, Wilbur would be able to monitor all activity. In addition, the steep terrain and the narrow gorges ruled out the use of a helicopter. Furthermore, the exchange would take place *indoors,* in the motel room, in such piecemeal fashion that Lowell and I would never come face to face. He wouldn't even be able to identify me for the sharpshooters.

But most importantly, Lowell simply couldn't risk not getting the whole film back. If anything went wrong, he'd be the big loser. And in this scenario the only time something could go wrong was not during the exchange but immediately afterward, when he already had the entire negative back in his possession.

I pondered this. The wording, I thought, contained a clue. *Entire.*

I walked to the sliding glass door and opened the curtains. Moonlight furrowed the lake. I slid open the door, stepped onto the deck. The brisk mountain air braced me.

My freedom for the next ten years, I decided, was worth more than the last installment of $208,300. There would be no final exchange. After collecting the eleventh payment I would simply clear out of Little

Norway. True, Doug would be horrified when he entered the motel ten minutes later and discovered that the eleventh reel (not to mention the twelfth and last reel) wasn't on the bed. It would be a shock.

But I had no wish to cheat him. I have my professional ethics. I would call the next morning and tell him which San Francisco Greyhound bus terminal locker contained the last two reels—hey, they're on the house.

Such a strategy had the added benefit of insuring me against a double-cross from Wilbur and Jolene, who wouldn't learn of this final twist until the whole transaction was just about completed. Not that I didn't trus—

A glass door slid quietly open—the door to Wilbur and Jolene's room. I turned. The white curtains billowed out, Jolene stepped barefoot onto the deck. In the moonlight her eyes shone above those high sculpted cheekbones of hers, that slightly askew smile.

"I thought I heard a prowler," she said.

Fine way to greet a prowler, I thought. You greet a prowler with a baseball bat, or by loudly racking a twelve-gauge shotgun. You do *not* greet a prowler wearing white nylon bikini panties and a snug lambswool V-neck sweater whose V plummets and rappels down the amazing cleavage of your perky breasts.

She brushed past me and hopped onto the deck railing; her pert firm buttocks rested on the cool metal, her hips swelled up to the sides . . . and there she sat facing me, legs parted, those exquisite thighs reflecting moon sheen, the white nylon—so exceptionally translucent!—puckering around her flossy vulva.

I remained standing, idling, *loitering*. I tried to keep my eyes off her luminous thighs, off the shiny white nylon stretched across her belly, off her accentuated hips, her lambswool breasts, her smooth creamy throat—dear God!—sooner stick a pyromaniac in a watchtower in tinderbox season and expect hourly reports!

"A prowler," I mumbled.

"Frank?"

She was sitting on the balustrade, in those white panties, in that snug sweater, her head tilted to one side, smiling boldly. Now that she had my attention she gripped the railing with both hands and began swinging her legs open and shut, open and shut, in a friendly, easy sort of rhythm, like a ranch hand sitting on a corral fence.

"I was going over the exchange. Making sure we'd—"

"Frank, come here."

I stood stock-still in the moonlight, like a marble statue, completely immobile . . . except for the Gila monster waking up and stretching in my Jockey shorts. Jolene reached out and gently but firmly gripped my shoulder. Drew me toward her. Her legs locked like pincers around my waist.

"Uh, what about—"

"Shh." She touched a warm finger to my cool marble lips. "He's a marvelously sound sleeper."

And so, tilting windward into the balustrade, at a diagonal, at a *north-south* diagonal (I noticed), we had a ruttish romp on the deck overlooking moonlit Lake Tahoe.

The Movie Mogul

C h a p t e r   1 2

Everything was set. We were meeting tomorrow in Lake Tahoe. I would give him $2.5 million. He would give me my movie.

I sat at my desk and buzzed Beth: "Get me Tommy. And don't go through his agent."

"Yes, Doug."

I got up, walked to the window. Across the lawn, under a tree, Jerry sat in an antique blue Adirondack lawn chair, reading a book. He seemed so at peace with the world, so relaxed, so well-adjusted. Jerry *always* seems so at peace with the world, so relaxed, so well-adjusted, the man feels nothing, has no idea what it means *not* to be at peace with the world, to feel oneself in a constant state of turmoil, conflict, *war*. Good calm peaceful world-tranquil Jerry. Good loyal treacherous world–yes-man Jerry.

Treacherous? In recent years Jerry has shown his loyalty more unswervingly than anyone else, yet I deduce in that loyalty a fair measure of treachery, of fervent big-hearted duplicity—not conscious treachery,

——— 137

mind you, but treachery nonetheless. I suspect he is slyly observing me in my decline, in what he *mistakes* for my decline; he wasn't around for the heady ride up, at least he'll catch the intoxicating plunge down, the dizzy smash at the bottom of the shaft, and maybe even encourage that smash with his litigious loyalty (he's always wanting to sue this person or that on my behalf, I'm always having to say, "Down boy"), his sticky mucilaginous glue of *yeses*, his syrupy encouragement that I am doing good work when, in fact, I am doing atrocious work—and perhaps he himself even believes it.

Whereas my cameraman, Mike Peterson, has been loyal over the years, yet has never turned into a suffocating yes-man. He has always felt comfortable enough, relaxed enough, *free enough*, to offer me advice and criticism; and if in the past two years his criticisms seemed to have increased a hundredfold while the percentage of times I accepted his criticisms decreased a hundredfold, why, then it is only natural that a certain estrangement, a special kind of refrigeratory rancor, has set in between us.

My secretary's voice came over the intercom: "Line two, the president."

Christ. Reed at Constellation wanting to know why the negative hadn't arrived yet at the printing lab. I snatched up the receiver and, taking immediate command—you can't let executives browbeat you —barked, "Now listen here, Reed—"

"Hello, Doug. How are you doing?"

Wrong president. I switched the receiver to my other ear, then lowered my volume and readjusted my timbre so that my voice boomed—moderately—with cheer and good will. "Hello Mr. President. How can I be of service to my country on this bright sunny American day?"

And do not think that I was speaking facetiously, do not imagine that I was being flip. Because I understand the need of a man like the President to sometimes just pick up the telephone and ring up an artist, yes, I understand this need of his to occasionally have artists around, I understand this need to reassure himself that despite the pinnacles of power he has attained he hasn't grown remote, he has remained in touch with the real questions, the important issues, that at the highest levels we human beings still need to sort out life—and for that endeavor only art, humble art, will (at least so far) do the trick.

But then I have my own needs, my own requisites, my own agenda. Does the President have the power to destroy everyone on this planet? Fine. I have the power to entertain everyone on this planet. Of course, once you have destroyed everyone, you have also destroyed all the markets, and without the proper markets cinema cannot thrive. No more markets, no more sequels. Consequently, I try to stay on the man's good side.

"I want to invite you and your lovely wife to an arts reception on Thursday, May twenty-second, at my place," he said. "No need to bring wine or ice cream." The President laughed heartily—do Presidents ever laugh feebly?—and went on: "It'll be followed by dinner at the Kennedy Center. Boris will be there, as well as Andrés, and Piño."

A dinner party. What should I wear? "Mr. President, it is with great regret that I must decline and beg for a rain check. Unfortunately, *The High Plateau of Stars, Part II* opens the very next day. I will have my hands—"

"Oh, goodness, how could I have forgotten? Of course, Doug, of course. I understand."

"But I'll tell you what, Mr. President. As soon as I get off I'll arrange to have Constellation ship you a print so you can treat your dinner guests to a special private preview in the White House screening room that very night—the day before it opens."

"Why, that is most generous of you, Doug. How very thoughtful. It will certainly beat standing on a long line flanked by Secret Service men with MAC-11s bulging under their trenchcoats. And, by the way, I am sure the lines will be *very* long."

Suddenly it occurred to me that the whole purpose of this call was to wangle a print so he could screen my movie for his guests the night before *High Plateau II* opened; that he *knew* it opened the next day and that I wouldn't be able to attend his dinner and so had counted on my offering a print in my stead.

Moreover, the President did not *want* me at his dinner party. He had deliberately invited me on the one night of the year when he knew I could not attend (you do not get to be President for wanting in the

Machiavellian instincts). Of course, I would yet have the last laugh—
the President would not receive a print with which to entertain, with
which to *impress* his distinguished guests, because there would be no
negative to strike prints from.

"Well, I hope you enjoy it, Mr. President," I said cheerfully. "And
I hope to catch up with you sometime soon."

We chatted a little more, and finally, with a slight snicker, he said,
"And do say hello for me to the charming Mrs. Fugle. Good day,
Doug."

"Of course. Good day, Mr. President."

I hung up and went back to the window, where I stared down at
Jerry reading so peacefully beneath the tree in the antique blue Adirondack lawn chair. I would not bother to convey the President's greeting to his wife because, in truth, the President did not wish me to
convey his greeting. But I knew *why* he had said that, I knew *what* he
was referring to. In fact he did not want me at his dinner party precisely
because of the bad taste, the ill diplomacy, I had once demonstrated
in drawing up a list for my own dinner party.

It had been a political fundraiser, here at my mountain home in
Bonny Doon. At the time, the President was just plain James W.
Thomas, a Democratic senator from Iowa, or Indiana, or one of those
indistinguishable Corn Belt places where, when you're motoring
through, the scenery accumulates like wet cement in the stomach, yes,
a youngish middle-aged hustler, a traveling salesman trying to cadge
money out of the Hollywood crowd. Industry heavyweights from Los
Angeles and Northern California had been invited along with West
Coast politicos. I was riding high on the success of the first *High
Plateau*, and the fundraiser had been the idea of Jerry, who himself
had been a recent acquisition of mine, filched on a friend's recommendation from the American Film Institute. Jerry thought it would
be an excellent way for me to "expand my power base." My power
base! Why in the world did I even think I needed to expand my power
base? A hundred million Americans *paid* in the coin of the realm to
see my movie—which is as many as voted gratis, *free of charge*, for
both candidates combined.

At any rate, it had been considered quite a coup. Everyone in

Hollywood, young and old alike, had been after him; everyone invited that night thrilled at the prospect of meeting him; and everyone envied me, believing that I would later be the recipient of numerous White House dinner invitations, as well as get appointed to some prestigious governmental arts post.

The evening started off well. Big black Buick sedans, black Cadillacs, and white stretch limos, along with the usual run of sporty Ferraris, Porsches, and Maseratis haphazardly filled up the dirt parking lot in the woods around my battered spaceship. The senator stepped from a Fleetwood and sniffed the air. The senator sneezed. Too much of California had gotten into his nostrils. He appraised the lot's centerpiece and made an instant calculation: propping one foot up on the side of my dented spaceship, he struck an appropriately photogenic pose for his photographer and smiled. *Pop.* (The picture would later be distributed as a publicity photo.)

My wife, the perfect hostess, that four-star general of taste, of managing the rigamarole of silverware and foods, bustled about, a look of slightly worried yet rapt absorption in her eyes as she oversaw the staff and attended to the million details that make up the perfect gargantuan dinner party—the preparations in the kitchen, the arrangements of flowers and crystal decanters, the selection of grand old chinaware and porcelain (while I, who would have been content putting out crackers and onion dip, who feel so stupid in the social graces at which she is so adept, saw only to the selection of the wines). I positioned myself at the doorway to greet my guests: the beautiful and distinguished-looking movie people and their spouses, who returned my greetings with the offhanded naturalness, the spontaneous ease of old friends; and the less beautiful but distinguished-looking politicians and their spouses, who also greeted me with the offhanded naturalness, the spontaneous ease of old friends, though, in fact, unlike the movie people, they were *not* old friends, I had never met most of them, it was the offhanded naturalness, the spontaneous ease of *old politicians.*

Dinner—filet of beef Lucien Tendret—was served by the Gonzálezes in the large dining room. All those celebrities and political powerhouses assembled in my house! Never had I seen so much social wattage at one dinner party. It was difficult to say who produced more electricity, the political crowd or the Hollywood crowd. You could have lit up Candlestick Park that night with all those brilliant toothy smiles, all those oral cavities propped open by white picket fences . . . and yet the only thing I could think about was that I used to enjoy the old days so much more, just a small dinner party with a few trusted friends where the wine would flow freely and the conversation would be passionate, funny, and smart.

Some sixty guests were seated up and down a long spectacular banquet table that had been created out of a single slab of old-growth Coast Redwood that when felled had measured nearly three hundred feet in length and twelve feet in diameter. It had been chiseled and carved out by a carpenter—no, excuse me, it had not been chiseled and carved out by a carpenter, nor even by an artisan, or a wood-craftsman, but rather by an *artist*, a *sculptor*, a Giacometti, a Brancusi of *indigenous Californian materials*, yes, the table fairly glowed, you could ice-skate on it, a burnished pond of Redwood glaze; and the damn thing, for which I had to have a wall knocked down so it could be hauled in, had cost me a fortune.

But never mind. Let me establish the mood, the setting, the ambience. Paintings appointed the walls around the dining table. A gory Francis Bacon portrait, red splotches and hints of internal organs amidst the grizzly darkness. A big Julian Schnabel canvas bisected by some sort of voodoo doll and with pieces of broken dishware—plates and cups and bowls and saucers—glued onto its abstract background and then painted over, the brilliant slashes of paint fusing the brilliant broken dishware to the canvas. A fluorescent-blue David Hockney swimming pool, a lissome youth quivering on the tip of the diving board. And a somber black-and-red Andy Warhol portraiture of a dangerously erotic John Gotti, CEO for the Gambino group. (A critic once compared Warhol to Goya, saying that someday Warhol's commissioned portraits will look as deformed as Goya's portraits of the Spanish court, though it escaped Goya's contemporaries that they were deformed. And I sometimes regret that I never commissioned Warhol to do my portrait.) I had briefly considered removing the Warhol for the evening, in deference to the senator's war on organized crime. But then I'd thought, what the hell, a touch of the old *épater le bourgeois.*

On the other hand, I asked myself, why do I keep *any* of these things on the wall, I don't even really like them, they give me indigestion every time I sit down alone, as I so often do, to drink a beer and eat a ham sandwich at this huge, lonely-making table, at this *hundred-foot-long shellacked redwood sculpture-slab.*

Actually, I get a kick out of the Schnabel. Every time a dinner guest breaks a plate, or a cup, or a saucer, or a tureen, my maid María González, per my instructions, saves the pieces; and then afterwards, when no one is around, when no one is looking, I surreptitiously glue several fragments onto the canvas as a memento, then paint right over them; and in this way my Schnabel, a truly postmodernist work, grows in complexity and depth, becomes weighted with the associations it lacked when I had it wrapped and hauled home from the Pace Gallery.

The evening wore on. I watched the Corn Belt senator say, "We have to learn to trust the Russians, but at the same time we must not learn to trust them too well." And I watched everyone all up and down the table nod at this pontification, eyes fastened hungrily on the man, as though this astute political wisdom were issuing forth from a John Stuart Mill or a Thomas Jefferson—and I said to myself, I had an old-growth redwood tree, a tree that is a thousand years old, a tree that was alive when the Crusaders ranged across the Holy Land, a tree that was prospering when the Black Death was ravaging Europe, a tree that was growing larger when Columbus first sighted the New World from the crow's-nest of the *Santa María*, a tree that was continuing to expand and branch out while Kit Carson was blazing a trail westward through the wintry passes of the Sierra Nevada, yes, I had a noble, a majestic, a magnificent thousand-year-old tree chopped down and carved up by some *carpenter* possessed of the idea, the decidedly wrong idea, that he is a *sculptor*, I had this tree chopped down and massacred and pickled and kippered and mummified and then laid out in state so it could serve as a *food tray*, a *slop trough* for this collection of creeps and phonies and egotists and exhibitionists.

And I looked at Jerry, who was so thoroughly enjoying this evening, who was truly at ease, so well-adjusted, in his element, at home (*in my house*). While I, who felt misplaced, out of my element, *not* at home, listened as movie people recounted Hollywood stories to the politicos, who in turn recounted Washington stories to the movie people—a bit of confidential gossip about which actor was hooked on heroin while Steven Spielberg was shooting *Hook*, some inside info on a quietly brewing Washington sex-change scandal, an amusing anecdote about how the president of France had mistaken a Napa Valley Chardonnay for the finest Puligny-Montrachet. In this way each side entertained the other, fed the other's vanity, let the other side in on its little trade secrets, its trade *gossip*. But why not? After all, it was this free exchange of gossip (which, *everywhere*, has replaced the free exchange of ideas), along with bathing in the glow of the next president, that everyone was shelling out cash for.

Why not? A good question. Look at these people, I thought to myself, sipping my wine across the table, the redwood slab, the serving board, from the senator. There sits gnarled and handsome Sean Knoble, who goes at his food like he's in a Renaissance drinking song, who had started out as an acclaimed Shakespearean player, then descended to act, so to speak, beneath himself, in *cop* movies and *buddy* pictures, while the reviewers, ever mindful of his distinguished early career (the publicity packages would remind them), always remembered to write, "Sean Knoble brings a little extra something to the otherwise tritely scripted role of the homicide detective." Whereas in truth he never brings anything extra to the picture, all he brings is himself, just himself, because there is nothing else to bring, he left *everything* behind when he decided to cash in his chips at the silver screen's window.

And there sits Penn Arnold, delicately slicing his meat, whose gallant father had been blacklisted during the McCarthy years for his political beliefs, who himself should be blacklisted for his startling lack of talent (his father should have been, too, but that is another story), and isn't it wonderful that a man whose father suffered for his political beliefs—he lost his big mansion, he lost his big pool, he moved into a smaller mansion, he did laps in a smaller pool—should now be sitting at the same table as a future President . . . which, in fact, is the only reason he had been invited, so people could remark on this touching irony.

And there sits Radovan Slovikian, laughing and drinking, reaching for this and that, a one-time avant-garde Yugoslavian director widely credited with driving a breach into the fortress of conservative Eastern European cinema during the sixties and seventies, who then migrated to California, where he has lived ever since directing dreck soaked in PG-13 sexuality, and once again those imbeciles, the critics, mindful of *his* distinguished early career, always talk about how exalted the sex scenes are in his movies, when in fact his sex scenes are completely indistinguishable from the dreck of any successful hack director born and raised in Orange County—and that in fact is the compliment that would probably make him happiest (he loves this country, he laughs at his good fortune).

And there, talking comfortably to the man seated next to her, sits the lovely Melinda McCormack, who started out as the girlfriend of a powerful—and married—studio chief. No one would have thought twice about her after he dropped her and she disappeared from sight, but then she reappeared with a series of brilliant screenplays that she managed to get produced by a rival studio, the third of which she parlayed into her directorial debut, and she went on to become that rara avis, a female director of medium-budget, high-quality adult dramas; and there is something pleasing, when all is said and done and the bedsheets have been changed, about genuine talent.

And there sits Page Crispin, chewing his food meticulously, a tall man with decency etched into his fair watery features, who wrote award-winning poetry at Yale, then serious fiction that was published in the leading quarterlies, then a popular novel, then an Oscar-winning adaptation of that novel for the screen, and then for the last decade screenplay after screenplay, for which he is paid fabulous sums even though in that same decade not one of those screenplays has been made into a movie—but then, every so often, just to keep his hand in, he'll write some precious *literary* story about a sensitive fiction writer abused and misused by the clods and megalomaniacs in Hollywood, when in fact the clods and megalomaniacs are far more sensitive, self-aware, and generous than he is, the little prick.

And look at *those* people, I said to myself, scanning the politicos. There sits Frederick Waters of Stockton, warily rejecting a helping of artichokes, cagily shunting his string beans onto a siding of his plate, eyeing with suspicion an arrangement of broccoli florets. He had started out as a state assemblyman of such high ethical standards that no one thought he had a future. He then became a congressman of lesser standards, and finally found his calling as a senator-cum-bagman for Central Valley agricultural interests, for the manufacturers of *pesticides* and *insecticides* and *vermicides* and *rodenticides*, for those who have transformed the Central Valley into a vast *field of blood*, and I'm impressed that he can even bear to look at anything that's green.

And there sits the elderly Senator Stanley Allen, working on a tender red slice of beef, one of the most articulate liberals in the U.S. Senate, who got his start by blackmailing a senior colleague into stepping down by showing the poor fellow a photograph of himself, the big family man, caught flagrante delicto with a fuckably delectable fourteen-year-old girl (giggling, Jerry had told me that story, so maybe it's not true) —and that is why Senator Allen has never gotten further than the Senate, for as powerful as he is, too many people in his own party have it in for him.

And there sits Gloria Vandenberg, spearing a small sautéed rosemary potato, powerful congresswoman from San Francisco, whose position profits her gay, feminist, and multiethnic constituency, but profits even more, through her tangle of political connections, her husband, Donald Vandenberg, one of the biggest mall developers in Northern California, who sits next to her—spearing a *large* sautéed rosemary potato—a man who loves nature, who goes white-water kayaking every chance he gets, and who would think nothing of installing an air-conditioned, hermetically sealed, five-hundred-store shopping mall in Yosemite Valley if he could get the zoning permit.

And there sits Paul Smith, sipping mineral water, eyes darting left and right, *working*, perhaps the smartest of the batch, the handsomely rewarded Sacramento political media consultant, also known as The Invisible Man, who has handled the campaigns for many of these people, who himself always maintains a lower-than-low profile, an invisible profile, who will not *allow* himself to be profiled, who pays an L.A. public-relations firm to keep his name *out* of the news; a man who, by age nineteen, when he was organizing anti–Vietnam War demonstrations at Stanford, knew the deadlines of all the major networks in New York; who by twenty-five knew the unlisted home phone number of every major political journalist in the state, as well as that journalist's drink or drug of choice; who for several years worked for fifty dollars a week with César Chávez in the fields of blood absorbing United Farm Workers organizing techniques while fighting to protect the migrant farm laborers from the poisonous side effects of *pesticides* and *insecticides* and *vermicides* and *rodenticides*; and who now earns $250,000 a year applying those same organizing techniques to big-time political campaigns, including Senator Waters'.

And there, with the striking white crew cut, sits the elderly Thomas Ludwig, the distinguished Hillsborough banker, polished, imperturbable, urbane, and quietly arrogant—the food on his plate seems to vanish without his even touching it—a man born to great wealth and schooled in the art of the power broker, sometimes liberal, sometimes conservative, a major party fundraiser who could make or break a political career with a wag of his crooked finger. That he occasionally backs politicians who speak up, now and then, for the rights of poor black people while his banks redline the blasted inner-city neighborhoods in which these same poor people live is, of course, the kind of contradiction considered irrelevant, too simple-minded and trivial for words, by the cynical old buzzard, as well as by the rest of these sophisticates.

And should I, with all the resources at my disposal, be the one to point out such a truth in my humble art, in my multimillion-dollar entertainments? No. Better truths about outer space than life itself in all its enraging and maddening horrors. For if I ever stopped pretending to be one of these privileged people and instead made the movie I really wanted to make, the movie I swore I would one day make (before the success of *The Black Pig* dulcified my feelings), then I would have to retire to outer space myself, a place that, when all is said and done, frightens me with its desolate stretches.

And slowly, over the years, we change. Where once we were motivated by generosity and kindness and playfulness, now we are motivated by greed and selfishness, by a mad-making lust for power. We lower ourselves. We forfeit our good opinions of one another and of ourselves. Yet because we earn $20 million, or enough votes to get elected, we also earn a good name rather than a bad name; and in this way we elevate ourselves when, in truth, we are lowering ourselves; in this way we are able to move onto a *bigger* estate at a *higher* altitude in the hills (any set of hills will do) when, in truth, we have *fallen* from our high estate.

But never mind. Two actors present that evening, Sean Knoble and dear Tommy Mace, started arguing about what their Shakespearean dream role was—the Prince of Wales or Hotspur—while the senator, leaning forward, listened carefully. At the same time, though, he was casting an appraising eye over my paintings, pausing the longest to look at the Schnabel—to look, I thought, with a curious smile, a little glint of recognition, as though he understood that *I* had appropriated the Schnabel, turning it into my own personal pet art project, my own record of past dinner parties and of the grand old plates, cups, saucers, tureens, and bowls that had been martyred to those occasions. I recalled reading somewhere that the senator was as knowledgeable about cubism as clubbism. The two thespians kept arguing. Sean shouted, "To achieve true greatness in a role like that of Prince Hal it is necessary to keep one's distance from the theatrical and movie worlds, because so many people in these worlds are pretentious, self-satisfied, and smug, and those are the enemies of art." And Tommy, that Shakespearean scholar, responded, "But one must ignore the critics even more and continually take risks, and aim for a type of purity that has been lost in this century." And all I could think was, This dining table, this slab of redwood, this once-tree that had survived forest fires, droughts, earthquakes, insect infestations, survived all manner of natural calamities, could not possibly, were it still alive, survive the hot air of tonight's stovehouse.

But then, still listening to the increasingly heated yet curiously disconnected argument between the two thespians, the senator suddenly interjected, "My candidate for dream role is *President of the United States.*" And here he pounded his fist so hard that all the plates, up and down the one-hundred-foot length of the redwood table, jumped or jiggled. Immediately everyone chimed in, "But of course!" "What greater role could one aspire to!" "How clever!"

The senator was indeed a clever man. But something was eating away at me. Something petty. Something minor. Something, to me, of *huge consequence.* Here I was, riding high on the success of one of the biggest moneymaking machines of all time, hosting a political fundraiser, and everybody was paying attention to, hanging on the every word of, this man who might—only *might*—be the next President of the United States, and *nobody was paying attention to me.*

The guest of honor, to be sure a perceptive man as well as a clever one, seemed to read my mind. Affecting a tone of admiration, he modulated his voice into a softer key as he leaned across the table and said, "By the way, Doug, I have enjoyed all your works"—*works*—"but most especially the really underrated *Scintillate, Blue.* Yes," he said, signaling subtly to one of the Gonzálezes to replenish his wineglass, "it was, if I may say so, a small classic in its own right." He was referring to an abominable ten-minute experimental film I had made while living on Broome Street in lower Manhattan, a film that is still screened once in a rare while at USC or UCLA, and whose muddleheaded sophomoric opaqueness some so-called highbrow critics have mistaken for complexity and profundity. Yet I had to smile, I had to appreciate the wisdom of the politician who knows not just how to flatter, but to flatter so perfectly, so sublimely, so *politically.* Chances are he had not even *seen* the film, but it spoke well of his instincts in picking Paul Smith as his advisor, it spoke well of Paul that he should have gone out of his way to cook up this bit of truly subtle if preposterous flattery on which to coach the candidate, yes, I admired the future President and Paul at the same time that I knew them both for the pathological liars that they were.

At this point in the evening Margot, who had put away six or so glasses of expensive Stag's Leap Cask 23 Cabernet Sauvignon, staggered to her feet, apparently intent on imparting a bit of wisdom to the assembled. She was a sight. Margot wore a jet-black metallic dress with shoulder pads so mountainous they resembled *Saturn 3* booster rockets. So now Margot, shoving back into place a shoulder pad that had slid down on top of her breast, cleared her throat and said, in that charmingly eccentric register of hers: "Mr. President, in the movie industry we sometimes talk about the size of different men's endowments. For example, it is well known that both Chaplin and Bogart were rather well endowed."

Bong! Dead silence up and down the length of the redwood slab, whose high-sheen surface reflected back sixty faces that had been caught—food wine or words in mouths—in various attitudes of shock alarm anger outrage horror and giddy embarrassment. The only exception was Margot's husband, good old Jerry, who was grinning rather sillily, as though to say, *Isn't my wife something!*—as if she were some adorable pet who hadn't quite been housebroken. Oblivious to her stunned listeners, she pushed on: "Do you people ever carry on in a similar vein about former Presidents?"

I sank in my seat. I slumped down until my chin rested on the polished redwood edge of the table. I felt like a director whose production, so carefully planned and budgeted, has suddenly bolted from him.

But then, to my surprise, the next President smiled broadly, rose from his chair, reached for his wineglass—changed his mind and instead picked up his coffee cup—looked out over his guests with thoughtful speculation, and said, "My advisors had warned me that movie people could be—well, more *blunt* than the ordinary run of mortals. So let me answer just as bluntly. *Yes.* We discuss our predecessors' endowments in strategy sessions. We discuss them during meetings with pollsters. Indeed, we refer to them rather jocularly as"—he paused for effect, saluting Margot with his cup—"the National Endowment." Much laughter. Much *relieved* laughter up and down the redwood slab. "Benjamin Franklin discoursed frequently on this subject. In *The Farmer's Almanack* he perceptively wrote, 'No man should rule a nation whose own ruler is under eight inches.' Machiavelli said, 'Spare the rod and spoil the colonial nation.' He was speaking of sexual subjugation as well as military. Our friend here"—the senator turned to the Warhol on the wall—"Mr. Gotti once said—we picked this up from a wiretap—'Political power, at least in New York, grows out of the barrel of a gun.' Mr. Gotti also said, 'But personal power, the animal magnetism of the true leader, grows out of that other barrel.' " More laughter. "But I am here tonight—*we* are here tonight—to prove that political power grows out of a Hollywood checkbook." Everyone laughed, he got a hearty round of applause. The senator, however, despite a warning look from Paul Smith, did not avail himself of this opportunity to sit down. On the contrary, he was just warming up. The man was positively enjoying himself, delighting in the mild shock and titillation he was causing to some of the more delicate sensibilities present.

Then—he dropped his cup. It shattered on the floor. Everyone *oohed*. Except me. I wanted an instant replay, in slow motion, for I thought I had detected deliberateness in his bungle. My wife, pushing herself away from the table, said sharply to the maid, who stood ten feet away, "*María*," as though it were María's fault; and all the guests, up and down the length of the redwood slab, swung their heads toward poor María, to rain accusatory looks down upon her head. But the senator quickly, graciously, said, "Please. It was my fault entirely." His eyes narrowed to merry sharp flints, he bowed slightly and said to me, after a quick glance at the canvas Schnabel dish rack, "Perhaps I should have been an artist rather than a politician." He said this with a low twinkle in his eyes, yes, I was right, it had been deliberate, this was the senator's little joke, the senator's own knowing contribution to my Julian Schnabel, which with my additions I had appropriated and transformed into a *Doug Lowell*. And even as María began sweeping up the pieces of broken art-cup, pieces that, per my longstanding instructions, she would save, the senator, smooth as silk, resumed his bawdy discourse:

"Indeed, my friends, endowments are more than a subject of gossip and speculation. They are fit subjects for political analysis, for predicating foreign policy upon, for bearing in mind when discussing arms reduction, for drawing up psychological profiles of friends and foes alike. After all, endowments offer us"—here he wagged a finger—"clues to character. The great Texan, Lyndon Baines Johnson, for instance, was possessed of a large, paunchy, scarred affair—a long thick splotched purple shaft with a leathery head, lots of frontier foreskin, and an old battle wound that had healed to a raised ridge of scar tissue running along one side of its stem. He called it 'Jumbo.' (Texas Republicans called it 'Dumbo.') I have heard that the cowgirls used to find it more exciting than a ribbed and nubby condom.

"Nixon's, on the other hand, is said to be as gnarled and pimply as a witch's staff—it was that way when he was a lad—and atop its shaft, atop its head, a beady slit peers out from the oily tip."

Everyone laughed. He got a tremendous round of applause—and in that moment I knew that this brash man, this politician who knew when to heed his media consultant's advice and when to blithely ignore the stern look of warning, would win the election, that anyone who could bounce back like that from Margot's table-stunning idiocy would prove unstoppable.

Soon afterward the party broke up. All the big black Buick sedans, Cadillacs, and stretch limos, all the Ferraris, Porsches, and Maseratis emptied out of the dirt lot, stranding in the middle of it, all alone, my dull battered spaceship. I stood in the lot, waving to the fading red taillights of the last limousine, holding in my other hand a tumbler of bourbon. Suddenly it grew very still in the dirt lot. Black conifers grew out of the darkness around its edges. Constellations glimmered and whirled overhead. Crickets plied the night. I turned and stared at my dilapidated spaceship, the one that looked like it had been purchased off a used-spaceship lot in East L.A. I stared at its hulking silhouette in the darkness.

And then I climbed up its ladder, into its cockpit, and made myself at home in the pilot's seat. There I sat, feet propped on the dashboard, sipping my bourbon, thinking how strange and strange-making life is, listening to the crickets, looking at the stars overhead—the galaxies through which my spaceship was supposed to be able to plunge at twice the speed of light, the universes splintering and falling away from it— there I sat, smelling the pine-scented air infused with the salty sea breezes that drifted up the canyons, and I thought, *I feel sad.* I sipped some more bourbon. And then some more bourbon. And then finally, to the sound of crickets, I fell fast asleep, in the cockpit of my battered spaceship, parked in the middle of a dirt lot, in a pine forest in the Santa Cruz Mountains, beneath the vast empty starry spaces.

C h a p t e r   1 3

The President was right, I thought, gazing out the window now at Jerry reading beneath the tree in the antique blue Adirondack lawn chair. Several days after the fundraiser I had received a handwritten thank-you note from the aspiring candidate—"Next time let's do dinner at my place—the White House. But what do you say we leave the charming Mrs. Fugle at home?" Margot was not the sort of woman you wanted to take to the White House for dinner. But, of course, after her faux pas, her charming indiscretion, her blundering bone-headed solecism, the President, that Democrat, had no intention of inviting *me* to the White House, either. By letting her attend that dinner (but what could I do? the dinner had been her husband's idea), I had proven my own unreliability, my temperamental, artistic insta-bility. It is one thing for the senator to carry the day in front of political and industry insiders; it would be a whole other story to have to negotiate such a remark in front of Queen Elizabeth, or the President of France, or top officials from China or Russia. Expanding my power base! What a laugh. Good old Jerry. Well-adjusted Jerry. And I had *wanted* to visit the White House, I had *wanted* to install myself in the President's leather chair in the Oval Office, swing my feet up on the desk and make a study of the place, soak up all that historical furniture infused with power and get a feel for it—the megalomaniacal feel of the pol-itician, which is so different from the megalomaniacal mission of the artist. Good old Margot.

On the other hand, now that I thought more about it, I realized I had just the right role in a movie for her—a starring role opposite my own favorite actor, Tommy Mace. A kind of documentary, cinéma vérité style, concerning a stolen movie negative.

I said into the intercom, "Any luck reaching Tommy?"

"Doug, I've left messages in half-a-dozen places. I'm sure we'll be hearing from him any moment."

I returned to the window. Jerry still sat beneath the tree in the antique blue Adirondack lawn chair, but now he was leaning over to stroke Orson, my dear furry tabby, whose two front paws were bandaged up. Orson also wore a black patch over one eye, which made him look like Captain Hook's unsavory pet. Apparently in his panic to flee the burning bunker the poor cat had run smack into something sharp and poked out an eye. Orson, as might be expected, no longer evinced a tendency to follow me around. On the contrary, he now fled in terror whenever I approached, or, more accurately, he now limped off in terror to the safety of a distant shrub, out of which he'd glare at me with his one fiery red eye. Orson's recovery was moving right along.

My cinéma vérité documentary, my *premeditated* cinéma vérité documentary, would not, however, be a movie that I could entrust my old friend Mike Peterson to shoot. Because I respected him so much. Because I liked him so much. Because I valued him so much. I'd have to shoot this one myself.

In Antarctica I had put Mike through hell. That is all right. Hell can be good for the artistic constitution. But it eventually became too much even for prodigious Mike. When most of the Antarctic principal photography was finished and we still had a week to kill before we got to shoot the sun setting finally at the start of the long winter darkness—my so-called "$3.2-Million Heartbreak Sunset"—while we still had a week to kill I suggested to Mike that we—Mike, myself, and a stuntman—head off, *get away*, from the comfort of the coastal compound and push on into the wild frozen interior. In this way, I said, we might capture some extraordinary footage.

Mike was of two minds. A superb athlete and mountain climber, he *liked* adventure and had in fact first made his name in documentary photography. He'd shot films dangling from a helicopter ladder, hanging from ropes strung across roaring gorges, on parachute jumps, spelunking, deep-sea diving, and more. A low-key man, he inspired confidence and warmth in those around him, and I always felt he was in complete harmony with my desires. I experienced Mike not simply as a skilled laborer but as a kind of adjunct artist, exquisitely sensitive to my image-rhythms. He could use his camera like an electric eraser, a paintbrush, an airbrush, a palette knife, a spray gun, a bezel, yes, the man could capture the drama in a single snowflake and the poetry in a thundering avalanche.

"Why are we doing this? What do you think we're going to get that we haven't already gotten? Frostbite?"

I smiled pleasantly. But Mike wasn't in the mood, in the proper frame of mind, he didn't have the right *mental attitude*.

Before we left, Mike went into the equipment hut and got a PanGlide 35, for its smooth hand-held portability, then made the camera still lighter by drilling, hacking, and filing away its surplus metal. "Can I help?" I asked, watching him work. He looked up, his eyes met mine, he said, "No thanks." But in his eyes I read the information: See what I am doing. It is the opposite of what you are doing. I am stripping and streamlining my camera. You should be stripping and streamlining your movie, hacking and filing away all the surplus footage. But instead you are doing just the opposite, you are continuing to add new material, to build it up, to fatten it, to make it *potbellied* and *paunchy* and *abdominous*.

And I said back to him, through the force of my eyes: But that is how I work, that is how my art proceeds, I add, I subtract, it's a give-and-take thing, no artist simply subtracts, no artist simply adds, it is a dialectical process, a categorical procedure, it is finally a contentious and disputatious operation. I contend with and dispute myself, I contend with and dispute you, you are merely a technician, so you don't understand how my art thrives, how my art connives, how my art arrives finally at its diabolical destination.

Our eyes disengaged. Next I watched him wrap the camera in a few inches of foam rubber and tape for insulation, then thread the battery pack with several warm Thermos flasks worn on his belt. "Let's go," he said.

When Mike, the stuntman Max—for convenience' sake we'll call him Max—and I finally struck out from the compound it felt like old times, like when I used to go cross-country skiing in the Sierra up near Carson Pass and revel in the splendid solitude of the snowy woods. I wanted to capture something of those days—and at the same time get on film a rawness, a wildness that I felt could not be captured back at the compound, where we had some measure of comfort and always a hundred people on hand.

The temperature plunged to minus thirty-three degrees Fahrenheit. The winds soared to sixty miles per hour, sometimes gusting to a hundred. Mike skied and shot footage at the same time, balancing the camera on his shoulder while swishing across snowfields at twenty-five miles per hour.

"I want you to freeze to death, then come back to life," I told Max.

"Ha," he said nervously.

But other times Mike couldn't shoot. Icy mists would shrink visibility to nil. Or the glare would cause his exposure meters to go crazy. Sometimes the camera just stopped functioning; ice on the film jammed the mechanisms. And sometimes, despite all of Mike's precautions, the lens would grow opaque from moisture that had seeped inside. Mike would struggle with the camera for hours, holding the lens up to the sun's ragged rays, running the camera till it de-iced.

On the third night we pitched our tent, crawled into our sleeping bags, and then were amazed at the speed with which a storm descended, socking us in. Snow blasted into our tent. In the clangorous gloom small avalanches thundered in the near distance. Finally, the winds collapsed our poor shelter. We finished out the night tangled in the twisted wreckage, wet, cold, and depressed. My beard had turned into a filigree of ice that crackled every time I stroked it while ruminating on how I had gotten myself into such a mess.

Yet I knew how. *I knew how.* Mike said, "We are not making a movie. We are providing *material* for a movie. Like that rugby team whose plane crashed in the Andes. Starvation, death, the descent into cannibalism and madness."

I understood. I understood what Mike was saying, why he was complaining; it was like when we were shooting in the Sahara and Mike asked if the Mojave, at Los Angeles's back door, wouldn't have done just as nicely—and at one-tenth the cost. *But it wouldn't have.*

For the truth is, a shot of a bare stretch of Mojave sand that in every respect resembles a shot of a bare stretch of Sahara sand, a Mojave shot that is completely indistinguishable from a Sahara shot, a Mojave shot where the lighting, the angle, and the composition are exactly the same as in a Sahara shot—such a shot would nevertheless be *distinctly different*. For by pushing my crew and cast so hard, by putting them through such hell, by traveling so far from the comforts of L.A., by spending such an inordinate amount of money to get the shot, by risking exposure to foreign microbes as well as to some distant raging inscrutable guerrilla war, by dint of all these things the shot would *have to be different*, better, fresher, more confident, more alive. Yes, the shot might have looked *exactly the same*, but it would have been *a brand-new game*. And that's the long and the short of it.

The next day, after the sun had risen, the snow had stopped falling, and the icy fog had cleared, we saw that we had pitched our tent at the base of an evil-looking mountain that loomed some nine thousand feet above our camp. The mountain looked dreamy, the mountain looked dreadful, it looked outrageous, vile, abominable, it was all immense monstrous promontory peaks and execrable ridges of jagged sawtooth edges, rough sharp hellish spikes, yes, it was a cursed mountain, a mountain of malignancies piled upon malignancies, it was all dark whites and evil-hued grays, bristling with rank pinnacles and crags, it was a sinister mountain that resembled a Dark Ages fortress printed in negative, a mountain that whispered *Come play on my slopes* and then, in an even lower whisper, *I promise you a return of evil for evil*.

The mountain had *movie* written all over it.

"Christ," Mike said, gazing up and shading his eyes, which were already hidden behind polarized sunglasses. "Where'd that foul thing come from?"

"We're going up it," I said.

The stuntman turned and looked at me. Mike looked at me, then scanned the mountain. He pretended to take me at face value, he *humored* me. "Too dangerous. Icefields at the approach. Lots of verglas. Heavily iced grade-six pitches practically surround the summit. Forget it."

"We're going up it," mad Ahab repeated.

That day, two thousand feet up the mountain, halfway up an ice wall, the stuntman slipped. I had been watching him, forty feet above me, as he negotiated an ice bulge that dripped with spear-shaped icicles. He was laybacking up the tongue of ice, the front of a crampon barely finding purchase in the sleek, slippery surface. I watched from below, mesmerized as Max clawed his way up. Upon reaching the top, he hooked his ax over to catch the smooth ice of the dome and started to haul himself up, ever so slowly and painfully. The ax glinted with light, it shimmered and wavered. Then—it *eased* its way out . . .

He pitched backward—desperately smashed in his short ax, bought a purchase—got a refund. He flailed out with his ax to brake his fall, failed to find a grip, and dropped . . . plummeting right past me . . . for a split instant our gazes met, perfectly level, his eyes melancholy, mine full of benign curiosity . . . then *boom* he hit a ledge a hundred feet below, and I was sure he would bounce over the edge and hurtle to his death six hundred feet below that. I watched, totally mesmerized by something one hardly ever sees—a man falling to his death.

But he clung to the ledge with amazing tenacity. It was only then that I turned to Mike Peterson, roped into the ice wall ten yards to my left, and saw that Mike, aware he could do nothing, had made the split-second decision—a decision by reflex, as it were—the *professional* decision, to thrust aside his annoying humanity, whip the camera off his rucksack, and film the whole breathtaking descent, twisting his zoom lens to record the double's doomed plunge down the slope—

After Max recovered from his fall—the only reason he wasn't dead was because as a stuntman, as a professional himself, he knew how to land—he pulled himself painfully to his feet. Leaning against a rock for support, he brushed off snow and ice. Then, incredibly, *professionally*, he yelled up, "Did you get that?"

Mike yelled, "You bet." He turned to me and said, "This will print great. It's exactly the sort of thing that's impossible to fake. Like those chariots running over the guy in *Ben Hur*. Audiences will love it."

I nodded. I was indeed somewhat pleased. *Somewhat*. Because all the time I kept thinking that if only the double hadn't landed quite so much to the left of the ledge, where he had dropped from view behind a rock, if only he had thrashed around a bit more theatrically, if only he had *hurtled over the edge and plummeted another six hundred feet.*

I said thoughtfully, "How do you think he'd feel about another take?"

Mike looked at me and smiled. He continued to smile, but his eyes stopped smiling when, after a while, he realized I wasn't joking. Then he gave me a look—such a look!—that I hastily said, "Just joking." And I suppose I was glad that the stuntman hadn't died, though, to be honest, to be realistic, to be *unsentimental*, a falling stuntman is more easily replaced than, say, a falling PanGlide camera filled with indispensable footage.

The stuntman, it turned out, had broken a leg and several ribs, though he was able to limp, crawl, and drag himself back down the slopes to our camp at the foot of the mountain.

"We ought to head back, too," Mike said.

"We're going on."

"I have soloed grade-six routes in the Andes. I have climbed El Capitan five times—serious big-wall climbing. But I have never done anything this insane."

"Give me the camera. I'll do it alone."

"Do *what* alone?"

"It. Whatever."

We went on. Clouds gathered. Snow started to fall. Thunder cracked and boomed in the distance. Conditions deteriorated. And I felt lightheaded, free of gravity, giddy, like I was in a dream. The dream, to be sure, continued to deteriorate. We went on. Trying to put Mike's mind at ease, I said, "I feel like the hero of a Jack London story. Or maybe Samuel Beckett would be more apt. You know, 'I can't go on, I'll go on.' "

Mike looked at me icily and said, "We're going to have to make camp for the night. We're never going to get down while it's still light." He pointed to a ledge twenty yards above us, and then slowly, with painstaking delicacy, began hauling himself toward it. Working gently, he cut first one step, then another, and another in the rock-hard ice, until, one grueling, excruciating hour later, he had crawled atop the dome. Then he belayed me up the tight rope. We found ourselves on a small ledge that barely afforded room for one.

"Have you kept the camera dry?"

"Yeah."

We had hardly any food left, and what we had I hated: dehydrated beef, dehydrated vegetables, dehydrated this, dehydrated that, and a block of frozen bourbon. The climb had exhausted us, and the exhaustion transformed itself, *free of charge*, into depression, into gloom, into thoughts of isolation and ice-hell and ice-death. We felt tense, anxious, irritable as the long night set in. Huddled on the narrow icy ledge, I dreamed of my spacious mansion in the Santa Cruz Mountains. Dying of thirst on the icy ledge, I dreamed of my wine cellar filled with all those tannic monsters slowly, patiently maturing—wines that I now feared I would never get to sniff and drink. What in the world was I doing here? What had possessed me to risk my life for some trick shots whose place and purpose in the film I couldn't even envision? A dark thought was starting to take form inside me, to crystalize in the icy night. One is a multimillionaire, an acclaimed artist, a complete success, celebrated on both coasts, and so everything mitigates against such a thought . . . and yet there it was, assuming shape in the cold Antarctic night, yes, I was starting to think, *Maybe I am self-destructive.* I had already sunk just about all my fortune into this movie, this money pit, this yawning abyss, this Bassalia, this Cayman Island Trench of cinema that was swallowing me up financially, aesthetically, and spiritually. And now, on top of all that, I had gone out of my way to torture myself, to unnecessarily expose myself to danger, starvation, cold, dehydration, death—and for what? Toward what end?

The next morning—actually, the next late afternoon—as the sun started to rise, I felt better. I said to Mike, "Make sure you get this."

He looked toward the spreading pink polar light, then at his camera. "I can't get an exposure reading. The light's too fucked up."

"Fucked up and beautiful," I said. "Get it."

The previous roll of film had run out. Mike took another roll from his rucksack. And then, numbed by the freezing cold, balancing on his knees on the ledge's incline, battered by winds so fierce they would have blown us right off had we not been roped in, he began to remove the last reel from the camera—when his frozen fingers fumbled it— he lunged—*the ledge!*—the rope snapped him back—but the camera shot from his grip . . . along with the reel containing the irreplaceable footage of the plummeting stuntman. . . .

In the cold icy air at the bottom of the world the acoustics are really quite marvelous, clear as a bell. But there was nothing to hear. The camera plunged soundlessly through space, falling farther and farther away . . . down . . . down. . . . We never heard it land.

Neither of us said a word.

We spent the remaining daylight picking our way back down the mountain. Then, while doing roped pitches across an ice-blue crevasse—

"Jesus, look."

"What?"

"*Jesus.*"

Mike belayed me across to where he stood on a shelf, then pointed. Perfectly preserved in clear bluish ice: skin, hair, bones, a carabiner.

We spent the next hour searching the vicinity for clues to the end of an existence. We found a single Italian Alpine boot with a man's name stitched into it. Pieces of the rope he'd been rappeling with. An ice ax. And a leather-bound journal, its entries dated thirty years earlier. The man, it seemed, had been a Scripps Institute climatologist.

"Listen to this," I said, leafing through the journal. " 'Shot spectacular footage today as the storm descended. Now if I can only get out alive.' Christ." I turned to Mike. "The guy was *shooting* this place. Can you believe it? That means there's a camera around somewhere."

"See what the last entry says."

I thumbed through a week's worth of entries—day by day, the handwriting as well as the clarity of thought deteriorated—till I came to the last: " 'what kind of country is this, a victim is essential, I want to be punished, I'm not the first, I won't be the last, show me the door, despair my endowment, it can't be my turn yet, someone else's, can hardly stir, can't be me they're talking about, not me, find the ax, open the door, he's out there somewhere, made of silence, better than the lies, all lies, relief from the lies, still, I must say words as long as I still have some, until they find me, no, perhaps it's a dream, no, never dream again, everything's failing, it's too late, please, just show me the door' "

Shivering, I closed the book. It gave me the creeps, like some dreadful portent flapping out of the black night. Mike whistled softly. Then said, "The camera must be"—he scratched his head—"shit, it could be miles from here. It could be buried under twenty tons of snow and ice. A river of blue ice could've carried it off."

"Let's look for it."

Mike said thoughtfully, "It would be nice if we could find it. If the film was preserved, then at least he wouldn't have died quite so much in vain."

"Fuck that. Dead is dead. What I mean is, I can use his film in *my* film. Who'll know? Especially with you screwing up."

Mike looked at me. He said slowly, "Thirty years ago, figure he was probably using eight-millimeter. You're already blowing thirty-five up to seventy for a fourth of the theatrical prints. What're you going to do, blow eight up to seventy? It'll look ridiculous. The image density will be grainier than a news photo, like bad pointillism."

"It can be done. We can scan it into a computer, manipulate it digitally, whatever."

Mike said, "The guy's dead and you're going to exploit him?"

For one precious daylight hour we searched: no sign of the dead climatologist's camera. So the issue never came to a head. Nonetheless, a permanent chilly estrangement set in, like the long polar winter night, between Mike and myself. Later, back at base camp, at the foot of the evil-reeking white mountain, we fixed Max up on a makeshift sledge. I studied the map but could not locate the mountain on it—not that the nether regions of the earth have been all that accurately mapped even at this late date.

And as we left the mountain behind, as more icy fog stole in, I began to doubt the mountain's very existence. I felt it was a ghost mountain, a white phantom looming dimly through the grayness. And weeks later, when we were shooting in the sweltering Sahara, there'd be days when I would suddenly feel the presence of something immense and chilling behind me—I would whip around, expecting to see that foul mountain rising up from the shimmering desert floor. But I could never turn fast enough, it always melted away. And weeks after that, when we were shooting in the South Bronx, I would again suddenly feel the presence of something chilling, something immense and evil, looming behind me, rising up behind a row of gutted tenements—and I'd whip around. But again I wasn't fast enough, it would melt away. I doubted the mountain's existence. The mountain doubted my existence.

◆　◆　◆

For two days we trudged across the icescape, pulling the stuntman on the sledge. But we made it back to the compound in time for the last sunset.

And for that last sunset I had everyone assembled, cast as well as crew members. For even though the actors weren't required for this shot, I had insisted they stick around, I wanted that sunset to be internalized by them, I wanted that sunset to inform and speak to their performances for the remainder of the shoot, yes, I wanted that sunset to transfigure them, I wanted that sunset to *disfigure* their very souls, teach them loss and heartache and horror.

They complained. They grumbled at the inconvenience. They groused at my metaphysics of acting. They wondered aloud if the movie wouldn't be more profitably served by their moving on to the next location, where they could begin rehearsing.

But none of that mattered. *None of them mattered.* For finally it was time for the last sunset, the last polar dusk, the commencement, the onslaught of the long winter darkness.

"Shouldn't we have several cameras rolling?" Mike asked. "For insurance?"

"No, I trust you."

"Well then, how do you want me to shoot this?"

And that's when I said, "Oh, just give me your usual $3.2-million sunset shot."

And moments later, when it began, it was everything that I had hoped for and more; for the day was icily clear, the gigantic red orb of the sun hovered on the frozen horizon an instant—then started to dip; and as it dipped, as it descended, I felt myself drawn toward it, toward that cold fire, the red rays dancing and racing across the crystalline terrain, across that landscape of crimson glass, back toward their source, the starry heavens full of strange constellations expanding in the spreading darkness; and it was such a shifting alliance of light and dark, of pinks and blues—everything vibrating, everything shimmering, the whole universe a hallucinatory quiver—that I thought my haunted heart would burst; that I felt I was being transported to a place that no one had ever gone to before; and as the blue-black starry firmament closed in on the shrinking angry red spot on the horizon, as the pure weight of all those months of darkness to come began to exert its gravitational pull upon my soul, as the poetry that filled me magicked into melancholy, the thought rushed in—into the vacuum that was me—that such haunted bottom-of-the-world beauty is simply *not allowed* on film, *verboten*, it is prohibited, unsanctioned, *hands off*, the shutter slams down.

But just as quickly another thought, by sheer force of my artist's will, overpowered that first thought, and it was this: *Everything is allowed.* I am the boss-artist, I can capture whatever I want, the symphonies of the heavens, the radiance of swirling nebulosities, I can bring light out of the dark, blot out radiance and ring down the sable blackness—

Something went wrong. For that final shot Mike had used a Panaflex 35 with a 15-millimeter-wide lens, to take in the panorama. But moisture somehow stole inside, creating multiple ice fractures. A week later, when we viewed the footage on an editing table in an air-conditioned trailer in the Sahara, it looked as though someone had smashed a kaleidoscope into an ice-cube tray. A complete disaster. And to this day I still don't know whether the usually cautious Mike Peterson was just so exhausted by the previous week's adventure that he wasn't in command of his craft, or whether he deliberately screwed up as a way to extract vengeance for the hell I had put him through, as well as for my wishing to steal the dead climatologist's film, or whether he was angry at me for accusing him of professional incompetence in losing his camera, or—why not?—some furious calculus of all three. Anyway, something went wrong.

And in retrospect, from the tranquillity of my home in the Santa Cruz Mountains, I realized it was my fault. I had abused Mike Peterson.

I had expected too much of him. He was not an artist himself but rather the vehicle, the instrument of my artistry. *He wasn't as strong as me.*

I owed Mike. In his poor misguided estrangement lay his loyalty. I would make it up to him. Yes, after I received the insurance money I would storyboard the whole movie again, but with a lower, more practical-minded budget in mind.

And this time, when we returned to the Antarctic, we would get the sunset right. . . .

Beth's voice crackled over the intercom: "Doug, Tommy on line two."

I gazed out the window at Jerry, who still sat beneath the tree in the antique blue Adirondack lawn chair, stroking the one-eyed Orson. Jerry looked so calm, so at peace with the world, so well-adjusted. That's what happens when you don't have a thought in your head. Well, I would fix that. I picked up the telephone. "Tommy, how are you? Listen, I want us to put aside our past bad feelings." I laughed heartily. "*Why?* Why, because I have the role of a lifetime for you, old friend. A *dream role.*"

Yes, this time we would get it right.

C h a p t e r 1 4

"You see, you play an actor—"

"An actor?"

"That's right. The most challenging role an actor can assume is that of another actor." I said this into the phone casually, not wanting to appear too eager. "It'll be a dark brooding fatalistic look at the film world, like *Sunset Boulevard.*"

"God, when Gloria Swanson comes down those stairs . . ." He snapped to. "So, it'll be a kind of self-reflective thing?"

"Yes. I hadn't thought of it that way but . . . yes. Oh, sure, it'll outrage some industry starched shirts. But mos—"

"When do we begin?"

"Whoa! Not so fast." I cleared my throat. "I want you to take a screen test."

"You got to be kidding. No way I'm gonn—"

"Tommy," I interrupted, without raising my voice. "Personally, I think you'll be perfect for the role. But, Tommy, I don't want to mislead you. I have got to make sure. I have got to make absolutely one-hundred-percent certain. And this screen test—"

"I don't know, I don't know."

"—this screen test, I assure you, will be held in the strictest confidence—just you and me. That's why I don't want anyone else in on this yet. No agents, no publicists, no lawyers. I'm not out to humiliate you. But I also don't want any leaks to the press. One squib in a gossip column and the deal's dead. I don't want you telling your agent, business manager, or anyone else just yet."

"What about the money you still owe me for *High Plateau*? My agent's not going to appreciate my doing this, *if* I do this, before we've settled that little matter," he said. I increased by a good half-foot the distance between the receiver and my ear. "I mean there's this outstanding—"

"Just a second, Tommy." I put the phone down. I went over to the small office refrigerator in the corner, poured out a glass of mineral water, cracked an ice-cube tray and dropped in a few cubes, then returned to my desk. "Tommy?"

"Okay. Forget the money for the moment. Tell me a little more about my role," he said, more calmly.

"This movie, if we do it right, will gain both of us a tremendous amount of respect in the industry." This movie, I thought, if I do it right, will *clear the decks* of all the fools, charlatans, and con artists who have accumulated around me in recent years.

"Yeah?"

"It's Oscar material, Tommy," I said, my eyes on the door to the entrance to my office, or, more exactly, on the doorstop, a golden statuette, the figure's arms folded across its chest. I had received it for my screenplay for *The Black Pig*. Actually, I was even, much to my surprise, nominated several years later in the directors category for *The High Plateau of Stars*, though I knew I stood no chance of winning, no, not with that half-witted bilgebag Larry Stevenson up for *Fire-Run and Run-Rain*, the moderately moving story of a hearing-impaired woman who wins a bronze medal in the Winter Olympics. It didn't gross as well as *High Plateau*, but it did respectably enough. I had an aisle seat in the Dorothy Chandler Pavilion the night of the Academy Awards presentations, and when handsome Larry, beaming in his tuxedo, strode down the aisle to collect his Oscar, I whispered, "XYZ."

He stopped. "XYZ?"

"Examine your zipper."

He blushed, checked the mechanism—it was fine—and strode indignantly away.

"Oscar material," I repeated to Tommy, staring now at the doorstop. "I know how much having that gold statuette would mean to you, Tommy. Mean to *any* of us."

"You really think this will—"

"I know it will."

"I don't know, I don't know. Maybe you can just send me the screenplay."

"Can't do, Tommy. It's too secret. Too hot. It has to be done my way or not at all. If that's not acceptable, I'll understand, and there'll be no hard feelings. Though I would hate to have to fall back on . . . I don't know . . . Sean Knoble."

"Are you kidding?" Tommy cried, suddenly indignant. "He couldn't act his way out of a dumpling wrapper."

"He used to be a highly acclaimed Shakespearean actor."

"Yeah, a millennium ago—and his publicist never lets anyone forget it."

"Well, Tommy. I really want you," I said, noncommittally.

"Oscar material, huh?"

"A serious role. Just a second, Tommy." I went over to the stacked stereo system next to the refrigerator and slipped in a CD of Stravinsky's

Firebird, programming it for the "Danse infernale." I adjusted the volume and the treble, listened, readjusted the treble, listened some more, then returned to the phone. "Tommy?"

"I don't know. I'm tempted."

"And if you do this for me, Tommy, I promise I'll make a third *High Plateau*."

"For real?"

"For real," I said into the phone. I said this in a placid voice, in a level voice, in a voice dewy with sincerity. It is so easy to out-act an actor, to bowl over a performer with a second-rate performance. So anxious to please, so eager to be pleased. *Dream role.* I will give you a dream role. I will give you a surrealistic nightmare role. Besides, despite the success and the high visibility *High Plateau* had conferred upon Tommy, the offers had not poured in, the industry perception generally being that it had been perfect typecasting on my part.

Tommy said, "I know I made a fool of myself when I did that Hamlet soliloquy. I know that I came across as an arrogant young asshole." Ah, a bonus. He was connecting his Hamlet performance to my mention of Sean Knoble—a connection I had missed, but then that is one of the benefits, one of the prerogatives, of genius, these gifts that just fall into one's lap. "But that's in the past. You, me—we're both rich enough now that we don't *need* to do another *High Plateau*. We got rich, we got famous, now it's time we got good."

"Very nicely put, Tommy."

I sipped my glass of mineral water while Tommy said, "I've changed. I'm different now. I'm more serious about my work, more committed. And I will never stop being serious. I promise you that if I get this role, I will give you the best work of my life."

"Why, Tommy, I'm touched. That's extremely generous of you," I said, and even meant it for a second. Tommy's not so bad after all, I thought. He is showing a remarkable maturity, a generosity of spirit, a level of self-awareness which I would not have thought him capable of.

"When do you want to do this?"

"Why don't you drive up here—oh, the day after tomorrow, Thursday? Alone. Shoot for, say, three o'clock."

"Okay."

"One more thing. Wear a disguise—wig, beard, whatever—and give your name at the gate as . . . Larry Stevenson. That—don't interrupt—will preclude even your visit from making the gossip columns. Eyes and ears everywhere, you know."

"I'm glad things are finally working out between us, Doug. You know, I've always admired your work."

"I'm glad, too," I said, pleasantly recalling Tommy's description of my first feature as *some violent low-budget piece a shit*.

"A dream role, huh," he murmured.

"A dream role, Tommy. See you Thursday," I said, and gently put the receiver to sleep in its cradle.

I left my office, nodded distractedly at Beth—*deliberately* distractedly, so she could recall later at the inquest that her boss had seemed rather preoccupied, *disturbed*, that day—and then I headed across the lawn, scouting for Margot. Jerry looked up from the lawn chair and said, "How's it going?" Orson looked up, too, but he fixed me with his one good eye, glared, bared his fangs, hissed, then stumbled out of Jerry's lap, limping off as best he could toward a distant patch of shrubbery. "Orson hasn't been the same since that fire," Jerry said charitably.

"Orson's a fine feline, possessed of remarkable recuperative powers. Give him time."

Now, the easy thing would have been to ask Jerry where his wife was. But I did not want to do that. This was to be a surprise. So I limped off across the lawn, hissing as I went. Behind me, I could hear Jerry laugh uncertainly.

I found her, as I'd expected, lounging poolside in a chaise longue. Rather than saying anything I simply stood still for a minute dispassionately observing her. She was lying supine, eyes closed, inert, in the skimpiest of bikinis, the material glossy black; her body glistened with suntan lotion as she availed herself of the afternoon rays. Her arms stretched out along the armrests, her bony fingers, bejeweled with heavily lacquered raspberry-red nails, dangled languidly off the ends. The table next to her supported an ashtray congested with half-crushed cigarettes, a half-empty martini glass, and a half-read romance novel folded at the spine, facedown. Back issues of *People, Mademoiselle,* and *Elle* lay scattered about.

Then, as I drew closer, the piney scent of the woods dissipated, knocked out by the tangy punch of her tawdry perfume.

I stepped in between the sun and Margot, so that a shadow fell abruptly across her face. She did not open her eyes—a cloud, she must've thought, traveling overhead in its celestial orbit.

"A beautiful day," I said, gazing wondrously all about me. "Don't the pines smell terrific?"

She popped open her eyes. "Doug, what a glorious surprise," she said in that unnatural timbre of hers, registering a touch too much surprise in her face, as though she were an exile from her own processes of articulation. Across from us, at a distance of perhaps a hundred feet, a redwood forest began. Margot now sat slightly up, craned her neck a few inches, as though that would bring her closer to the piney air (and away from her overpowering perfume), sniffed inquisitively, her nostrils flaring and quivering. "God, you are right. Nature is putting on quite a show for all our senses."

A silence. I admired my surroundings. An exquisite day in the coastal mountains. A swimming pool warmed by the sun. A somewhat attractive woman. Should not the master of the plantation have been a happy man? Two yellow butterflies flitted past, tumbling over each other in the air. A few pine cones, far from trees, lay scattered about the lawn, placed here and there at my request by the González clan's gardener, for scenic effect.

I stepped suddenly sideways. The sun hit her full force on the bridge of her nose; she squinted and shielded her eyes. Excellent. Now that I had her attention I drew a deep mental breath and said, "Margot, how would you like to be in my next movie?"

Still shielding her eyes, she squinted up and said, "*Me?* In your big movie?" She studied me nervously. "I think you're teasing me," Margot said, smiling a little uncertainly.

"Not at all. I am planning a new movie, a sort of *film noir.* I think you would be perfect for the role of the femme fatale. The malefic moon of our *fin de siècle* moral ambiguity."

I stepped back in between the sun and Margot, so that my shadow crashed *timber* across her face. She stopped shading her eyes, which I now saw were filled with naked apprehension. "You're not perchance teasing me?"

"Why should I be? You're a very beautiful talented woman," I said, with a surfeit of feeling.

"I've never worked as a thespian before."

"No matter. You have great natural ability."

She took her arms off the armrests and hugged herself, as if she were suddenly chilly, despite the full radiance of the day. She allowed herself a small smile. "In actuality, I've always wanted to tread the stage."

"Exactly what I had surmised."

"Really?"

"It's in the way you talk, the studied naturalness of your gait."

"Is it that manifest?"

"Prima facie so."

Jumbled as her wits were, she was starting to understand, to organically grasp, that I, Doug Lowell, wanted her, Margot Fugle, in my next movie. She raised herself some more and swung her legs around off the chaise longue, planting her bare feet squarely on the grass. The lawn, I noticed, needed mowing. Then, in an unexpected gush of repellent sentimentality—which nonetheless I found quite touching—she poured out, "You know, part of me always wondered why you never offered me gainful employment on *High Plateau*—in costumes or set design or something. But a deeper part of me always felt a secret connection to you, Doug. That we were kindred spirits. I always felt that you saw through the surface me to the deeper, more spiritual me, and that you were always saving me for something special."

"Righto."

She glanced around nervously. "Has Jerry bestowed thought on this?"

"Jerry doesn't know yet. To be honest, I'd rather he didn't. At least, not just yet. It will be our sort of surprise to him—"

"A surprise." She nodded and even allowed herself a small conspiratorial smile, tinged with—Christ!—carnal complicity.

I quickly stepped aside so that the sun blinded her again, and said, "Yes, a surprise. And it will make Jerry especially happy, what with that little set-to on the last movie, where—"

"Well, you know what eventuated there—"

"That's okay," I said soothingly, reassuringly. "I know how these things go."

She nodded. "Who else will be performing in this venture?"

"Tommy. Only he—"

"Tommy!"

"Only he doesn't know yet that you'll be in it. Personally, I think you'll play beautifully opposite him. But to convince him of that I'm going to do a screen test first with just the two of you—only I'll tell him you're filling in for Julia Roberts because you're the only one available at the moment."

"Me and Tommy together," she murmured, with strange life in her eyes. She brushed some hair back off her forehead.

"And then when I play the videotape back for him he'll be amazed at the on-screen heat the two of you generate. Highly combustible."

"When will we do this, Doug?"

"The day after tomorrow." When Jerry would be safely out of town. Jerry was scheduled to jet off to Prague, ostensibly to check out some new Eastern European films for his Northern Cascades Film Festival, in truth to resume a transatlantic affair with some bantamweight Czech actress who lived in the sort of grubby but arty walkup garret where Jerry could imagine himself playing the part, however mistakenly, of the erotic hero of a Milan Kundera story.

"Doug, I feel such—gratitude."

"No problem."

But, suddenly, I did have a problem. Looking at her innocent, eager-to-please face, I suffered an instant of self-doubt, a poignant pang of guilt.

I turned from Margot to look at the pool . . . and flashed *the man with the butterfly net*. Simply call up the insurance company, tell them what happened, then let the chips fall where they may. If worst comes to worst and my film is recovered and goes on to bomb, why, then I could probably, after selling off all my other properties, still pay my debts and hold on to my estate.

Yes, I would drop out of the film business, the film *racket*, altogether. I would turn the estate into a campground, and in the early-morning hours, before the tourists awoke, I would wander down to the pool with a butterfly net and— *Stop!* Have you gone bonkers? What is this crap? Let's not hear any more of this butterfly-net nonsense. Inner peace is strictly for the birds.

Quickly I reminded myself, *Her husband encouraged me in my madness when I was making my movie* and *She cost me an invitation to the White House.* Thus fortified, I looked again at the pool's shimmering surface . . . and this time imagined Jerry and Margot drifting there, facedown.

"Doug?"

"Sorry. Just drifting."

Margot lifted one heavily penciled eyebrow—her way of indicating slyness—and said, "Will I be paid?"

"Handsomely."

She looked thoughtful, then, suddenly, worried again. Very, very anxious. It was finally sinking in. This was it, her big break, what she had been waiting for all her life, maybe. "The day after tomorrow?" she asked tentatively.

"Day after tomorrow," I said. "At three."

The Gangster

$$C \quad h \quad a \quad p \quad t \quad e \quad r \quad \quad 1 \quad 5$$

We went swimming. We lay on the beach. We sipped tall Tanqueray and tonics. Jolene wore a shiny white bikini. Wilbur watched her cavort Lycra-assed in the lake. It was love.

"Wilbur, I know it's not my business," I said, putting down the *Chronicle*, "but what do you plan to do with your share of the money?"

Lying flat on the sand, chin propped up on his fists, he regarded me for a moment, undecided whether to declassify such delicate information. Then:

"I know I came on strong with all that bourgeois nonsense about buying a redwood home and a BMW. But the truth is"—he drew a breath—"I want to make my own film. Not some existentially empty-headed Hollywood picture, unsuitable for the serious mind, but an artful documentary, an exposé in which I interview people who claim to have seen flying saucers. Of course, they haven't, they'll all be full of crap whether they know it or not. But what I'll be doing is laying bare their underlying loneliness. Typical *National Enquirer–Weekly World News* stuff on the surface. But, of course, that's not what I'm interested in. My real subject is estrangement, American division. The human spirit staring into the abyss, and out of desperation populating it with friendly little creatures from outer space. It'll be the antithesis of the kind of kitsch Spielberg, Lucas, and Lowell stupefy the American public with. Instead of the phony reassuring optimism of 'We are not alone,' my movie will shout out from the rooftops, 'We are all terribly, most decidedly alone.' Instead of serving up a stew of ancient myths seasoned and spiked with celestial mechanics, I'll—"

"You liked *High Plateau*. You thought Lowell went beyond the others."

But Wilbur wouldn't be stopped. "The scenes can whirl by without continuity. My film will be a protest against all forms of cinematic logic, and its intellectual audacity will startle the world."

I was quiet for a moment. I sipped my gin and tonic. Then I said, "What're you going to call it?"

"*Desperation.*"

I looked out at the lake, the distant blue mountains, the sky beyond those. "You know, there are foundations that give documentary film-makers money."

Wilbur nodded. "I've applied for grants from the NEH, Guggenheim, AFI, PBS. But they all turn me down. None of them *get it*. They understand films that examine racism, the plight of migrant farm workers, women in wartime factories, Japanese-Americans interned in camps during World War II. That they get. Yes, the hand-held camera descending into the mine shaft. But something like this is beyond them."

I didn't say anything.

"You think I'm a crank, don't you? Well, I'll tell you something. We *are* alone. Each and every one of us is—"

"Wilbur, listen to me. I speak as a friend. Invest your million in bonds, real estate, blue-chip stocks."

He sulked, pouted, frowned. He rolled over onto his side, away from me. Grains of sand clung to his bright-red flanks.

"You know, you should really put on some sunscreen."

"Fuck you."

I shrugged and returned my gaze to the wintry blue peaks several miles across the lake, which filled me with a deep inner calm, a kind of transcendental serenity. Then I dropped my gaze to Jolene twenty yards offshore, peppy Jolene splashing around in her bikini—she glistened with beads of Tahoe water—and my inner calm cracked.

Wilbur rolled back over. "You know, *The Black Pig* was haunting," he said. "Yeah, it had shootouts and car chases and all that stuff. But it was shot and edited beautifully. And a real melancholy underlay it."

"How can she swim out there? The lake's freezing."

"It didn't do badly at the box office, either, though it wasn't in the same league as *High Plateau*. I bet you didn't know that *The Black Pig* got written up in all the film journals. *Film Quarterly* devoted a whole article to an analysis of that rack-focus shot toward the end where—"

"Wilbur, let me tell you a secret. Lowell might've been the darling of the film scholars at one point, but I assure you, he's much happier now. He'd much rather have the world gasping in disbelief at the money he's making than a bunch of *cinéastes* chatting up his artistry in obscure film journals. He'd—"

Wilbur rolled back onto his side, away from me. I stared at his hulking dorsum. Perhaps I was being unnecessarily harsh. In a reconciliatory tone I said, "Maybe we should rent a VCR tonight, watch *The Black Pig*."

Wilbur rolled right back. "I don't think that's a good idea. We'd have to give them a credit card. After the exchange goes down and Lowell runs to the FBI, they might check video stores in the area to see who'd rented Doug Lowell films in the past week. It's an outside shot, but if they're hard up for leads . . ."

I looked thoughtfully at Wilbur. "Not bad."

Wilbur smiled, appreciated. "Besides, the motel gets cable. *Invasion of the Giant Spiders* tonight. Colorized." Then his smile faded and he gazed with great sad hungry eyes at Jolene as she splashed around in the drink. Did he have a melancholy intimation of last night? I let my own gaze drop from Jolene to the *Chronicle* . . . where an article leapt up at me:

UPI, Santa Cruz, April 26—A small fire broke out late Monday night at a technical facility on filmmaker Doug Lowell's estate in the Santa Cruz Mountains. Firefighters quickly brought the two-alarm blaze under control, and a spokesman from Lowell Productions said damage was minimal, under $40,000. Fire Inspector Donald Ingle said the fire probably started when a cat playing with wooden matches tipped over a container of lighter fluid. The cat suffered first-degree burns and other minor injuries. Otherwise no one was hurt.

Lowell's new movie, *The High Plateau of Stars, Part II*, opens nationwide in four weeks. It is the sequel to his blockbuster *The High Plateau of Stars*.

"Look at this," I said, shoving the paper in front of Wilbur.

He looked. He read. Then, "Yeah?"

"That's the night we first called him."

"So?"

"Doesn't that strike you as odd?"

"Coincidences happen. Lowell just had a run of bad luck that day."

"Maybe."

C h a p t e r 1 6

We needed walkie-talkies. It shouldn't have been a problem. Thursday morning before the exchange the three of us drove to the Radio Shack in Tahoe City, across the lake.

But before I could anticipate the professor, before I could intercept him, Wilbur shambled to the counter and got busy trying to impress upon the salesman, an attentive young fellow with glasses, who couldn't have been more delighted to hear him out, exactly what it was we were looking for. "Let's say, for instance, one is involved in—oh, say, a bank robbery," Wilbur explained in his professorial manner. "And your partner, whom you need to stay in contact with, is stationed several blocks away—"

The salesman, running his hand through his hair, watched Wilbur with a kind of clinical fascination. "Okay. Let me get this straight—"

"Sweetheart, stop teasing the man," Jolene said, laughing lightly, looping her arm through Wilbur's. She turned to the salesman. "Our son's on an orienteering relay team." From twenty feet away, by the phone accessories rack, I looked on, incredulous. Was this the same guy who, just the day before, had talked me out of renting *The Black Pig* because the FBI might later check rental lists in the Tahoe basin? Unbelievable.

I wheeled around and walked out. I didn't *know* these people. Keep going, I told myself. Get in the Porsche and drive straight to Reno. Play blackjack for a few days. Pick up a pretty cocktail waitress, one who's goodhearted and simple, without deviltry or kinks. Forget these characters—they're not even in the same street as you.

Instead I just sat in the Porsche, sinking deeper and deeper into the car's upholstery, recalling the moonlit night on the balcony with Jolene—her *unsimple* hands, her *complex* mouth—and thinking about all the moonlit nights a million dollars would buy.

"You okay?" It was Jolene. She stood alongside the car, jiggling a Radio Shack bag in her arms.

"He's out of control, you know."

She shrugged. "It's a good cover. He looks like what he is—a distracted professor lost in his own strange thoughts. The salesman didn't take him seriously." Abruptly she stooped down alongside the car window, bringing her calm green eyes, so intelligent and cagey, level with mine. "So don't you."

She stood up and shook the bag. "Hey, check these out. Walkie-talkies with a range-boost antenna system for extended signal reach in the mountains, and ceramic filters for increased selectivity. *And* a portable scanner for monitoring local police channels."

I nodded dully. "So tell me. Did he pay with his credit card?"

◆　◆　◆

Jolene and I sat in the Porsche in the shady lane behind the Shady Lane Motel. It took eighteen seconds to drive from the back of the motel to the road. It took twenty-three seconds from the road to the fire trail. We had driven it a dozen times. Nothing could go wrong.

"What time is it?" I asked.

"Relax. It's ten to noon. Wilbur will tell us when Lowell's arrived."

Nonetheless, I was feeling more and more unsure of myself, more and more wary of my companions. I was experiencing a crisis that struck at the very core of my identity, that *clobbered* my identity. The Radio Shack incident had shaken me, not just because Wilbur had almost blown it, but because *as a professor* explaining to the salesman what he was up to, he had somehow seemed—as Jolene had put it—too good, almost typecast. And so now as a gangster—as the son of a gangster—I experienced a peculiar wave of dread, a feeling that perhaps *I* was only impersonating a gangster. And as I thought back over the last few days, as I recalled Wilbur spinning out his far-flung monologues on American cinema, it occurred to me that Wilbur was only giving a mad impersonation of a professor; and that Jolene, at times listening attentively, at other times distractedly, was only giving an impersonation of the undergraduate enamored of, within limits, her professor.

We can go further. When she stripped on stage in the club, when she really *was* impersonating a stripper, she was, in fact (or in half-fact, or in hallucinatory fact), impersonating a stripper impersonating a student to please a man impersonating a professor.

And now that the three of us were in this together, I felt we had already crossed some boundary, passed into some fraudulent other dimension. So it was that when I got on the phone and shouted at Doug Lowell, I felt deep down that I was a fraud, that I was only summoning up a Mafia motormouth out of my childhood memory banks. Yes, I wasn't quite myself but a summer-stock company of all the assorted thugs and hoodlums I had ever met, they were using me as a stage to strut across and shout their bombastic nonsense, I was merely on loan to them, a playhouse for them to try out their stupid stunts and gangster gags, to do their mad characterizations, their—

"Frank, you okay?" Jolene was looking at me oddly.

"Huh? Sorry. I—"

"You seem distracted."

"Too much coffee." I dredged up a smile. "Don't worry."

I glanced out the car window. Need to get a grip on myself. Calm down. Set an example. After all, I'm the professional. Outside, hopping around on a low branch, was a bird with a crest, a dark bluish-gray back, and black cross-barring on its tail. What did the little beggar want? Breadcrumbs? I could never remember the damn bird's name. Just when I had learned the names of most of the common birds back east, I'd upped and moved west.

I reached for the Styrofoam cup of coffee on the dashboard. Three sugar packets lay next to it, each illustrated with an Audubon-style color portrait of a bird. One of them, I now noticed, had a crest . . . a dark bluish-gray back . . . and black cross-barring on its tail! I swiveled my head.

"Steller's jay," I said.

"What? Why are you drinking more coffee? Didn't you just say you'd had too much?"

I stared coldly at Jolene . . . but then realized she was absolutely right. Pull yourself together, Frank. Calm the nerves. Squelch them with great empty meditative thoughts.

I also realized, of course, that since our romp on the deck two nights ago, a great unresolved sexual tension now charged the air between us; that we hadn't yet discussed what had happened and what would happen; and that this area of romantic irresolution, this *arena* of romantic irresolution, of sexual infirmity of purpose, together with the business about to go down, was making us cranky and snappish.

So I turned and listened to the quiet hum of a warm spring afternoon in the Tahoe basin. I gazed at the forested mountain where Wilbur, invisible to the naked eye, had taken up residence.

Life was about to change. In a few hours we'd either have several million dollars and be popping open bottles of Dom Pérignon in the Forest Restaurant atop Harrah's . . . or we'd be sitting in more spartan accommodations, contemplating Steller's jays through the bars of the El Dorado County slam.

"Run a check on the walkie-talkie," I said.

"It's working."

"Just humor me, Jolene. Okay?"

She switched it on. Pulled out the antenna. "Come in, Wilbur. Come in, Wilbur. Jolene to Wilbur. This is a test. Do you read me?"

"Hey, how's it going?" His voice crackled over the walkie-talkie. "Can you see me?"

I raised the binoculars to my eyes. The mountainside jumped closer: sugar pines, incense cedars, tall columnar Douglas firs—and stout Wilbur Blackfield in a bright-red shirt. What was the use? What in the world was the use? "You were wearing a dark-green sweater when I dropped you off."

"It's gotten warmer."

"Put it back on." I switched off the walkie-talkie. Shoved down the antenna. "You're supposed to divide one and a quarter million with Wilbur. Your share will be 625,000. I say we take the money and split—that'll be an extra 312,000 for each of us."

She didn't answer right away. Then, "After this is all over, Frank, I want to be with you." She touched my hand. My penis engorged. "But I can't do that to Wilbur."

"Why? Where's it say you can't? What's he gonna do, nice prof? Go to the cops?"

"This was his idea. It'll be hard enough on him when I break the news about us. At least let him keep his money. It'll be a kind of consolation." She looked up at the mountain, then down at her watch. "It's noon. Suppose Doug doesn't show?"

"He'll show. Do me a favor. Think about it. Okay?"

C h a p t e r 1 7

Two hours later, back in our lakeside motel cabin, I poured myself a tumbler full of Bushmills.

"You're absolutely positive it was today?"

"You want to call him, Wilbur? Say, 'Hi Doug. I'm one of the guys snatched your film. But things aren't working out the way we figured. Why, Doug? Why didn't you show?' "

Wilbur glared. Then buried his face in his hands. "My God," Wilbur cried, rocking back and forth on the edge of the couch. "The FBI probably had the whole area staked out."

"Maybe he got hung up in morning traffic in Sacramento," Jolene ventured.

"Bullshit!" Wilbur cried. He was working himself into a state. "The bastard double-crossed us." Edgy, sweaty, his eyes deepening with panic, the professor rose and hurried over to the window, moving with nervous energy. From behind the curtain he grimly peered out. "I bet the feds have us surrounded," Wilbur said, nodding like a maniac. "Sharpshooters posed on the nearby rooftops. More sharpshooters on the lake disguised as yachtsmen. Sheriff's deputies armed with tear-gas canisters and flash-bang grenades. The other motel guests moved out." Wilbur collapsed in an easy chair and wrung his hands. "Christ! How'd I get involved in this crap? My life, though not perfect, was comfortable. Now I'm going to spend the rest of it locked up in some prison where the chow is dished out by the Black Guerrilla Family."

I said nothing, merely looked at Wilbur, wondering what, if anything, could be done about him. A man deeply familiar with the more shallow kinds of unhappiness, he had spent too much time in North Beach and Berkeley coffeehouses meditating on the meaning of genre movies that in their heyday had been churned out with unnerving speed. He had been at his best standing before a Pacific Film Archive audience and making fast, indispensable connections between disparate movies and the times that had spawned them, speaking with a mad delicacy of Cagney and Kierkegaard, *Nosferatu* and Nuremberg, Byron and Bogie. Yet it wasn't enough for this refugee from the dark night of suburban junior colleges. Looking for the exit sign. Trying to break out. A small-time intellectual who had somehow gotten it into his noodle to mastermind the heist of a big-time movie negative. But now things weren't working out, and he lacked the reservoir of experience that could be called upon to help him negotiate the passage. Two years at San Francisco State didn't prepare you for two years at Allenwood. Wilbur Blackfield's behavior filled me, it should go without saying, with a kind of aesthetic loathing. But worse, it endangered us.

As though she were eavesdropping on my thoughts, Jolene rose and went to the ice bucket. Dropped a few cubes into a glass. Splashed in some gin, a touch of vermouth. Then handed the glass to Wilbur. "Drink," she commanded.

Letting myself be momentarily distracted, I watched Jolene place her hands on her hips, admiring the straightforward way she handled Wilbur. She was wearing plain, tight-fitting blue jeans, beneath which she had apparently pulled on some sort of textured and embellished black nylon knee-hi's, for the material, seamed and sparkly, flashed out between jean cuffs and white Brooks running shoes, adding a fetishistic dash to her otherwise simple outfit. And looking at her now, listening to her, all I could think was, despite the accumulating frustrations, how glad I felt that Wilbur had brought her along—indeed, how much happier I would have been if just she and not Wilbur had accompanied me. Once again I wondered uneasily what she had originally seen in him, though the old goats and overweight wrecks that beautiful women will take by the hand and lead to the conjugal bed continually amazes me.

Certainly Jolene was caring, carnal, and criminal; and if my ex had left me with any lesson to ponder into the wee small cinderblock hours of the Allenwood mornings, it was that such a mix of ingredients doesn't always make for wife stuff, for the sturdy durable all-purpose material of marriages. Yet Jolene, I thought, seemed different.

Wilbur drank. He drank again. Then he drank some more. "Maybe Jolene's right," Wilbur said thoughtfully. "Maybe Lowell got hung up in Sacramento." Wilbur got a sly wheedling look, his eyes narrowing in on his nose bridge till the bushy eyebrows arching overhead actually met in a steep V at the start of the declension of his nose-slope. I made a mental note to invite him over the next time I got a high-stakes poker game going. Full of craftiness, he said, "Frank, why don't you go up to the mall and call him?"

I pondered the professor. What did the large ungainly man, so bright-eyed about movies, on dimmer about life, think he was up to? Did I care? "Sure," I said. "Somebody has to find out what happened." Getting away for a while struck me as a terrific idea.

I reached for the doorknob. Wilbur dove behind a chair, as though I'd pulled the pin on a hand grenade. Jolene stared at him. *I* stared at him.

Then I understood. The professor, schooled and steeped in *films noirs* and Westerns—Philip Marlowe shoving Eddie Mars out the door to his death in *The Big Sleep*, Butch Cassidy and the Sundance Kid stepping out into the South American sunshine to unwittingly meet their maker—the professor, scholarly gentleman that he was, with all sorts of dents in his doughy impressionable movie-mad cortex, really and truly thought that FBI agents were massed outside our door waiting to gun us down.

I sighed and stepped out. Golden Californian mountain light bathed me in its warmth and radiance. I strolled over to the mall. I bought a *San Jose Mercury News*. I stopped in at a bakery and had a Danish and coffee while I read the paper. I looked in a toy-store window filled with foot-high green plastic Five-Headed Vomit Monsters from the High Plateau. Each of the five heads, bobbing idiotically in a different direction and at a different altitude, could regurgitate a different color stream of vomit. I stopped in at a realty office to see what cabins went for in this neck of the woods.

Then, having composed myself with the calm pacing of these distractions, I stepped into a booth and telephoned Doug Lowell.

"Where were you?"

"Where was I?" His voice sounded genuinely puzzled. "What're you talking about?"

"The exchange, you fuck. Do you want your goddamn film or what?"

"Can I put you on hold? I've got the governor on another line."

"Wait a—" The connection broke, the line hummed. The man was impossible. I was about to hang up when Lowell, resuming the conversation as easily as if I were an old chum, confided, "It's incredible. The guy thinks—"

"*Fuck* what the guy thinks. Where were you?" I was fairly shouting into the mouthpiece. "Don't you want your goddamn film?"

"Damn. That was today we were supposed to meet, wasn't it? You know, I—"

"Mr. Lowell, opening date for *High Plateau II* has just been pushed back one week. May twenty-third is now May thirtieth."

I hung up. Stepped outside the booth and inhaled slowly. This was not comforting. My exchange plan, so lovingly crafted, had turned out to be a mere exercise. Lowell didn't seem to have grasped yet, except perhaps in the abstract, that we controlled the negative.

In Pay Less I purchased a meat cleaver. Fine tool for chopping up steaks, carrots, 35mm film. I returned to the motel cabin, where Jolene and Wilbur still sat in the living room; Wilbur, as though in a trance, sat watching the TV, which he had brought in from the sun deck. Some afternoon-talk-show host was interviewing teenagers who had murdered their parents. Wilbur did not look up as I entered. Jolene did and stared uneasily as I drew the dully gleaming blade from the bag and laid it flat on the table.

"So, did you reach him?" Jolene asked the meat cleaver. Her face was taut, her green eyes alert and watchful. She must have felt the need to distract me while she found out what I was up to, for she then engaged in a kind of carnal diversionary action. She hitched up the bottom of her right trouser leg, crooked that leg, so beautifully packed in blue-jeans casing, raised her right foot onto a chair, and leaned forward, elbow propped on the knee, chin propped in the palm of her hand, to see what funny business I was about—while distracting me with that funny business of her own.

"Yes, I did reach him," I said, momentarily diverted, as was intended, my eye following the line of her gam—flexed thigh, knee, long shank—down to her glossy sparkly black-nyloned ankle transmitting its lovely message of fetishistic longing. How indeed I desired her.

"And?"

Yet she was not, today, to hold my attention. In prison you could go crazy if you didn't get your mind right, if you let it wander off on some abject sexual tangent. So you learned a kind of jailhouse Buddhism—to blank out your mind in an instant, to empty it of all worldly distractions. That's what I did now. I willed her ankle into mere background music.

Then went to the closet. Selected at random an octagonal can. Picked the lock. Lifted out the top cylindrical canister.

"Jesus," Wilbur cried, at last awakened from his TV trance by the drama unfolding more immediately around him. "That's the negative."

"Frank," Jolene said, casually lowering her foot, a failure, from the chair. "So what did he say?"

I removed the canister's top. Lifted out the reel. Unwound the first fifty feet of film, which collected in a spiraled heap of coils on the tan acrylic motel carpet. Then used the cleaver to *thwock* sever it from the rest of the reel.

"Frank. Hold on," Wilbur cried, advancing across the carpet toward me. I turned, raised high the meat cleaver. He fell back, hands held up. "That's irreplaceable," he explained gently, retreating hastily.

I returned to the task at hand. Which scene was it? It didn't matter. I carefully laid out the strip on the table. Got a good firm grip on the handle of the beautifully weighted meat cleaver—strictly speaking not a precision instrument, but nonetheless the preferred tool of apprentice film editors everywhere. And then, trembling ever so slightly, in a joyous frenzy, in a liberating rage, in a transport of delirium and delight, I hacked, whacked, and chopped that strip to shreds.

Wilbur blanched. His mouth dropped open.

Grimly, Jolene said, "Saved in the editing room, huh Frank?"

Yet there was really nothing to get ruffled about. I didn't look upon myself as a culture vandal, an ape of wrath, like the dilettante who pranced into the Museum of Modern Art and spray-painted Picasso's *Guernica*, or Frank Sinatra the night he flew into a rage and slashed his friend's Norman Rockwell to ribbons. No, this was different, I was just making a few little surgical incisions, carrying out a bit of film-ectomy.

"Frank, I realize he's playing games with us, but—but—you're destroying a part of the film. Of film *history,*" Wilbur pleaded. "Once gone, it's gone forever."

I stood over the scrap pile of celluloid garbage, flushed, tremulous, still gripping the meat cleaver. I felt giddy, drunk, elated. Jolene stared, her green eyes wide, her nostrils dilating, as though she were having second thoughts about me, wondering if my train had jumped its track.

It hadn't, though. I tucked in my shirt. With both hands I smoothed back my hair. Calmly, coolly, I turned and looked at Wilbur; then I assumed a slightly injured air. In my most levelly chilly voice I said, "You're a man of taste, a professor in the humanities, an enlightened member of the cognoscenti. Me, I'm a thug, philistine trash from the Bronx—"

"No, no, Frank, that's not what I meant," Wilbur hurriedly said.

I softened. I tuned down the timbre of my voice. I said, more in sorrow than in anger, "Look. Do you think I enjoyed doing this? Do you think I'm insensitive? Well, I loved *The Black Pig,* too. I have a video library filled with the classics. Lubitsch. Von Stroheim. Wilder. Sturges."

Wilbur nodded dumbly. Jolene said nothing, still eyeing me warily, but a smile starting way back in her pupils.

"But you see, we have reached an impasse. Doug Lowell doesn't seem to *want* his movie back. Maybe he's off in his own world and hasn't quite grasped that we have it. So a radical measure is required. Do you have an envelope?"

Wilbur nodded again. He reached into his unbuckled briefcase crammed with student papers and handed me a plain manilla envelope. I swept the scraps in.

"Either of you want to take a walk?"

They both shook their heads no.

I strolled to Harrah's. In tree-shaded motel parking lots, here and there, the renegade piles of snow and slush squatted, diminishing day by day. Heaps of healthier white stuff still mantled the surrounding peaks. The sun was shining, the sky was blue. I whistled as I walked.

Then, at a counter inside Harrah's, I paid cash and posted the envelope Federal Express to D. Lowell, Bonny Doon Road, the Santa Cruz Mountains. If this didn't do the trick, nothing would. It'd be like receiving the hacked-off, surrealistic ear of a loved one in the mail.

God, I wished I could be there to see his face.

C h a p t e r   1 8

I sat on the veranda, in the shafts of redwood-filtered sunlight, watching the scraps of celluloid flutter like dying moths, like brittle brown bits of autumn leaves, to the wooden deck, my eyes welling up with tears, with dewdrops, with droplets that went *plop-plop*, with great pear-shaped tears of laughter that dripped and dribbled and dropped down the run of my cheeks. How I roared and roared. Oh, this was priceless!

But it could have been better. The extortionist, *my* extortionist, could have destroyed the entire film, instead of just—judging from the scraps—a mere fifty feet. Fifty down, nine thousand, nine hundred and fifty to go. Nonetheless, this was a start, this gave me a lift. The elderly gentleman posted at the front gatehouse in the stand of redwoods had signed for the Federal Express envelope, which he then passed on to one of the Gonzálezes, who trotted it up to me just as I was finishing reading an item in some syndicated Hollywood-gossip column in yesterday's *Chronicle*. The item related that the President and his dinner guests would be treated to a preview screening of *High Plateau II* a day

189

before the rest of the nation, courtesy of the President's dear friend Doug Lowell. Since it had been in yesterday's paper, which had been put to bed the night before, that meant the President's press secretary, that media manipulator, that communications conniver, had planted the item *before* the President had even spoken to me, so perfectly had he anticipated my offer. That gave me pause. Had I become that predictable? And what did it say about my art?

But then I remembered that the President would *not* be watching my movie, because there would be no movie to watch; and I immediately cheered up. And it was at that moment that Pedro, or maybe Félix, had come running up to the veranda with the package containing the first hacked-up scraps of *High Plateau II*, and I felt even better. *Even better!* No doubt the amusing fellow who had stolen my negative, after crouching on a mountainside for hours with binoculars (swatting mosquitoes, wiping sweat off his forehead, picking out ticks as they insinuated themselves in his hairy legs), had gone back to whatever dreary motel he was staying at after I had failed to show up, furious at having worked out some enormously elaborate, ridiculously baroque, foolproof plan for the "safe" exchange. That is the trouble with procedurals, they never proceed according to plan.

Lucia, the maid, stuck her head out the front door and said, "Collect call from Cleveland."

I picked up the flashing remote phone from the inlaid-marble stand beside my white wicker chair and, still chuckling, accepted the call. A distant voice said, "Doug, how are you?"

Distant voice! It was my wife. "Victoria, hi." I had forgotten all about her. I had forgotten I *had* a wife. One immerses oneself in one's work and goes for weeks and weeks without seeing one's wife (so married is one to one's work), and then when the wife calls one thinks, with altogether ambivalent feelings on the matter, *I am part of the human community. I have a wife.*

"I booked a flight back to San Jose for next Saturday. Figured I'd avoid the rush-hour traffic."

"Great. I'll pick you up. We'll have dinner on the way back at that little place you like in Saratoga, the—er—"

"Le Mouton Noir. Terrific. How is everything? Film ready to fly?"

"Or crash to the ground and burn. Will you still love me if it bombs?"

"Doug, if your next ten films bomb I'll still love you." She paused. "But that'll never happen. How's Orson?"

"Orson?"

She must have heard the catch in my voice, for she instantly said, "What's wrong?"

"There was a fire . . ."

"A fire! When? Where? Is he okay? Why didn't you call?"

"Well, it was no big deal. The editing bunker . . ."

"The editing bunker! What happened to Orson?"

"He's okay, relatively. Apparently, the fire inspector thinks Orson started it. He burned his front paws—"

"Orson started a fire?" she said. Her voice sounded incredulous. "That's the weirdest thing I ever heard. How in the world does a cat start a fire?"

"I agree. But there you go. Something about a box of wooden matches and starter fluid. He also lost an eye—"

"Oh, no!"

"—but otherwise he's just fine. Really coming along. How's your father?"

"An eye! Poor baby. How horrible. Doug, you should've called me right away. What's the vet say?"

"Well, Orson'll never see out of that eye again. After all, he lost it. But otherwise, the vet says he's just great. A terrific cat."

"Poor baby."

I finally eased her off the line after a bit of gassy conversation about some novel she was reading that she thought would make a terrific movie. Then I bent down and gathered up all the celluloid scraps, which I stuck back in the envelope. Next I rose from my chair, stretched, admired the redwoods climbing the mountains, and headed off through the woods.

To my left, carved into the side of the mountain, the burnt shell of my editing bunker. To my right, carved into the side of the mountain, the larger, warehouse-sized structure that contains my camera equipment, my film library, and my small sound stage. I headed toward that.

I pulled open the heavy door. Stepped in and switched on the light. Inside was another heavy door. I walked across the floor, stepping over cables and folded chairs. Arc lights to the side. Wooden scaffolding. A crane. Sets. Backdrops. Trompe l'oeils. It is so peaceful on a sound stage when there isn't a sound—when one can imagine all the scenes, all the sequences, all the movies that are *not* being shot, when the sound stage is blessed with silence, with sacred silence, with multiple silences, with all the silences of all the movies that never were and never will be. Archives and archives of silence. And sometimes when I'm feeling down, when my head roars with noise from too many hours spent in the editing room cutting and recutting and rerecutting too much bad footage, when my head aches from listening too intensely, too closely, to some hapless actor repeat the same sentence fifty times—each time indistinguishable from the last—listening until all the sentences run together like tributaries emptying into the same lower Hudson of phonetic garbage; yes, when I'm feeling down, when the roar is exhausting me, I will sometimes simply get up, leave the editing bunker, and wander over to the empty sound stage—and I will stand in the middle and let all the noise in my head just empty out, I will stand here on the sound stage gazing at the darkened arc lights and listening to the silence, where not an actor orates, nor a technician bustles about, nor an assistant shouts directions—I will stand here listening to absolute silence, to that strangely *resonant* silence, more peaceful than a primordial forest. And I will think, Here I am—alone with silence. And gradually, as the noise in my head fades, as everything that is unimportant falls away, I will feel comforted and sheltered by that silence.

But not today. Today I felt energetic, zippy, full of pep. Today I felt ready to *make things hum*. I opened a side door and went down a short hallway, then opened another door, into my film library—a mausoleum of footage that had been jettisoned from earlier movies, an emporium, a mall mart filled with leftover moods, shadings of characters, surplus scenes, unused locales, underlit interiors, overlit exteriors, California to spare, outer space to boot. Yes, all those reels of footage that had been kept in cans for years, wide-open vistas collapsed into canisters, light stored in darkness.

I walked around. I scanned the boxes and cans lining the shelves, and pulled out the one I was looking for—a reel of leftover 35mm footage from *The Black Pig*. I went back out onto the sound stage, pressed a button, and the special reflex screen of tiny glass beads descended from the rafters. I set up the highest-quality video camera I had in front of the screen, and then I set up a projector in front and to the side at a ninety-degree angle to the camera. Next I placed a semitransparent and semireflecting mirror at a forty-five-degree angle to both the projector and the camera; this would reflect the projected motion-picture images onto the screen. Then I calibrated the projector to run at thirty frames per second, so that I could interlock its motor with the video camera's.

Matching the perforations along the edges of the film to the machinery's sprockets, I mounted the reel on the projector. I turned the machine on. It whirred to life, shooting out light that hit the mirror as the leader ran through; and light seared the screen—the most perfect light of all—blank projection light waiting to be written on.

Then, the screen roared to life. Crashing waves. Tossing cypresses. Sea gulls wheeling overhead. The Mendocino coastline. In *The Black Pig* the doomed, illicit lovers meet in a motel along the coast. This, though, was just leftover mood footage—no lovers, no pursuers, no one, in fact. Just the surplus cypresses, waves, and sea gulls. Dislocated scenery in search of some characters.

I would stick a few branches in front of the camera, so it appeared to be camouflaged in bushes. Then to the side of the screen I would place a wind machine, its propeller spun by a deafening Rolls-Royce engine: it would sound like the wind combining with the roar of the ocean as it buffeted my two stars with wind and ocean wash.

But it couldn't be too deafening. After all, the shotgun mike would have to be able to pick up snatches of their conversation above the ocean's roar. And I would set up a rumble pot in front of the propeller, to create the impression of mist blowing in off the ocean. My little movie, however, would not require music.

I'd had so much trouble making *High Plateau II*, feeling less and less sure of my powers as I went along, less and less certain of my ability to just reach out and make the magical connections.

But I already felt better about this one. Much better. Yes, the heisters—Tommy, Margot (acting as liaison, of course, for Jerry, that born bagman)—they would all just be playing parts in a production, a movie, though they would not know it.

And what is cinema if not an imitation of life—better than life!—life's artistic perfection? After all, in cinema one gets more than one chance to make it right. And I'm never happier than when I'm working, than when I'm directing, for nothing matters to me more than my work. *I* decide I want my movie stolen. *I* decide I want my leading man to extort me. *I* decide I want my right-hand man and his wife to betray me for some imagined slight. It's my own little Shakespearean play-within-a-play, my little triumphant trompe l'oeil.

Yes, I would win yet, just as I have always won. I would show them all, I would make a movie outside of a movie, a movie in real life (but what is real when perception is everything?), with performances that pass, that *surpass* the test of real-lifeness; I would give them a movie like they had never seen before, a *slice of life*, as they say, a movie for the six-o'clock news, a movie that would have FBI agents lining up around the block, coming back to see it again and again, indeed, the blockbuster of law-enforcement agents everywhere, from sea to shining sea, all over this—

The screen went blank. Just light reflecting off the mirror onto the screen. The film had run out. I shivered, a foreshadowing of death, the bright blank shadowless screen of eternity. Bad crazy thought, I thrust it aside. I had only four hundred fifty feet—five minutes' worth—of that Mendocino mood film. So the script I wrote would have to be short: short, efficient, and incriminating. A small gem of compression.

My specialty.

The Gangster

C h a p t e r   1 9

At five the next afternoon I headed straight over to the mall to telephone Doug Lowell.

"Yes?"

"Director no longer has final cut," I yelled. "The fellow in black with the scythe has—"

"I was worried I wouldn't hear from you again," Lowell said pleasantly. "Like I'd pissed you off. Well, I'm pleased to say I agree. That scene with my space explorers chugging down the beer—that was the scene, wasn't it?"

"Excuse me?"

"You mean you didn't even look? Well, no matter. I always felt vaguely uneasy about the scene. There they are, my heroic space explorers drinking beer while steering their spaceships across the dusky sky of a foreign planet. I was going for one of those great bloody brooding world-historical twilights, the kind Paul Fussell writes so eloquently about. But something was off. I would—"

I gently replaced the receiver in its cradle. As I stepped from the booth I realized I wasn't the inspired sociopath, the accomplished animal, I prided myself on being—I was merely a moron.

I inhaled the crystalline mountain air. The day, I felt, exuded a certain dream-lit quality. I gazed at the snowcapped peaks of the Sierra, rising precipitously from the woods right behind the shopping mall. I felt a trifle vertiginous, queasy, though I suspect my condition went unremarked by the shoppers coming and going in their wood-sided station wagons and shiny four-wheel-drive vehicles. I couldn't quite digest—*metabolize*—the conversation I'd just had, if you could call it that, let alone think through all its possible ramifications. No, the only thing I could do was notice that the mountains looked extraordinarily solid, well made, *durable*. They seemed, in their modest way, to mock me, to stand as monuments to my own petty desires.

Then I stepped back into the booth. Dropped in more coins. Called information. Got an L.A. number. Dialed it. A receptionist chirped, "Golden Calf Productions."

"Is Arnie there?"

"Do you by chance mean Mr. Arnold Goldblatt?" Very snooty.

"Yeah, yeah. By chance I mean—"

"Whom may I say is calling?"

"Oh, for God's—*Frankie*. Frankie Junior from the Bronx."

"Thank you, Frankie Junior." I was put on hold. *Frankie Junior from the Bronx.* Christ, I was starting to sound like my old man.

Then: "Frankie, sweetie, is that really you?"

"Yeah, Arnie. How you doing?"

"Beautifully, man. Unbelievable. The VCR explosion—what a boon! Video transfers for *Latex Lovers, Hogtied, Rubber Dreams.* All of 'em. A whole second life for the Arnie Goldblatt oeuvre. *Auteur* classics otherwise lost to the cinephiles. Isn't this country wonderful? You sell something once, a decade later new technology makes it possible to repackage and sell it again. You have to be a moron you can't figure out an angle to get rich in this land. Hey, I see you had a little trouble with the law, something about selling houses that didn't belong to you."

"A bit of landlord-tenant confusion, Arnie. Property is theft and all that."

"Yeah, well . . . How's your old man? *Whoa*, did you hear about Sal Porcelli? Put Tony Fino away in Attica for *babania*, then disappeared into the Witness Protection Program?"

"Maybe he'll run into my ex there."

"Two days before he goes in, he's running around all five boroughs hitting on every loanshark he knows, ten thou here, twenty-five thou there, promising to pay it back within a week at a hundred percent vig. Took a quarter mil off the streets before he disappeared into the Program."

"Probably the biggest score he ever made."

"Yeah. Left a lot of angry loansharks behind, from Belmont to Bensonhurst. Boy, am I glad I got out of the old neighborhood. So, Frankie. What can I do for you? What have you been up to these days? These years, I should say."

"Arnie, I have a technical question. If you were making a movie and somehow lost the negative, could the film be salvaged from the positive?"

"A negative can be made from a positive," he said, instantly professional. "Hopefully, the positive is in pretty good shape, not too scratched up and all. But it can be done. It'll never look wonderful, but it can be done."

"How not wonderful?"

"The number of generations—the picture's quality will deteriorate with each successive dupe. You've made a print from a negative made from a positive of the original negative. So you've removed yourself . . . how many times already? And a print is made to certain specifications. So if you try to reverse it again, it may not come out, or just so-so. But it can be done. It has been done with reasonable results. But, hey—with porn, who gives a fuck!"

"And suppose the positives got lost as well?"

"Hey, Frankie. If the positives *and* the negatives got lost, it's like the wicked witch waved her wand. You know what I mean? *Poof!* The picture never existed, never got made."

"Thanks, Arnie."

"That answer your questions? Care to get more specific?"

"Can't just now, Arnie. Maybe someday, but not now."

"You in trouble?"

"Not yet."

"Good luck. And if you're in L.A. . . ."

"I will. Thanks."

I replaced the receiver. Dropped in some more coins. Called information. This time asked for a Santa Cruz number. Dialed that. A lazy voice answered: "Santa Cruz Fire Department."

"Hello. I'm Tom Finn of the *San Francisco Chronicle.* I'm doing a feature story on the moviemaker Doug Lowell, and I just wanted to clarify a few minor details. About that fire—"

"One second, please. You want Mr. Ingle."

I waited. Mr. Ingle came on the line. I asked, "That recent fire at a technical facility on Doug Lowell's estate. Which technical facility exactly was that?"

"His editing facility, I believe. The place where he assembles the film. You're from the *Chronicle?*"

"That's correct. You mean where leftover footage would be stored? Like all the positive work prints?"

"I don't know. Negative, positive. I guess so. I was assured nothing of any value was harmed. His new film had already been assembled and shipped out. That's *Ingle.* I-n-g—"

I hung up.

"Doug Lowell *liked* that you chopped a scene out of his film?" Wilbur cried. Then resumed pacing back and forth in the living room. The TV blared in the background; Morgan Meany and Alfred Egert, two middle-aged guys dressed like preppies, sat in wing chairs chatting about movies. "Well, that's just dandy. Maybe he should've hired you to be fucking editor for the film."

"Wilbur," Jolene said crisply. She sat in a chair across the room, studying him. "Lowell was being sarcastic, Wilbur. Sarcastic."

"Our plan was foolproof," Wilbur moaned, sitting abruptly on the sofa and wringing his hands. "We did all our homework. Where'd we go wrong?"

"Yes, Wilbur," Jolene said. "Our plan was foolproof. Except for one small detail we failed to consider—Doug Lowell might not *want* his movie back."

I said nothing. I walked to the sliding glass door and looked out. Low dark clouds were gathering around the peaks across the lake; the whole sky had darkened dramatically, and a spring thunderstorm seemed in the offing. That was good. I was in the mood for rain, for a drenching downpour that would cleanse the air. The lake looked dark and deceptively smooth, a peaceful ominous surface waiting to be shattered, to be punched full of holes, to be honeycombed by curtains of rain sweeping across the lake.

Looking out, I thought maybe I should just write the whole thing off to experience. Sell the blueprint for the heist to some people in L.A. Pick up a fifty-thousand-dollar finder's fee and let someone else try it out on the next big-budget picture to come along. But I *hated* giving up, not seeing this through, letting Doug Lowell put one over on me.

I turned from the window and said, "Lowell doesn't want the movie back. And I can think of only two reasons why. One, because he has or can get another copy. Or two, because he wants the insurance money." I looked straight at Wilbur. "Can he get another copy, Wilbur?"

Wilbur reddened. His brown eyes, sheepish, evasive, seemed actually to start, not crying, but sweating. Then he said, "You know, now that I think about this, there is a remote possibility that he could assemble another print from the leftover positives, then strike a second-generation negative from that."

"Is that so?" I said with cool detachment.

"But Frank, he'd have to be nuts to do that. It would look like shit. I swear. For the amount of time it would cost him and the loss in quality, he'd come out ahead buying the original back from us. That's why I never even mentioned it."

Jolene was watching us. Now she said, "That's what the fire at his estate was about, wasn't it?"

I nodded. "I called the Santa Cruz Fire Department and checked. It was his editing facility that burned down. Probably taking all the positives with it."

Wilbur stared at me, then said, "Why did you just—"

"Be quiet, Wilbur." Jolene turned to me. "Which means Lowell wants the insurance money."

"But that's insane," Wilbur cried. "All that time and expense. I mean that's his baby, his labor of love. Why in the world would he not want it back?"

I said, "Maybe Doug Lowell, having looked at his own film, knows something we don't know."

Rubbing his chin, Wilbur pondered. Then said, "So we find out who the carrier is. Deal with the bond company instead."

I shook my head no. "Doug Lowell is one thing. But the completion-bond companies—their policies are underwritten by insurance giants like Transamerica, Lloyd's of London, Fireman's Fund. And insurance companies are like crime families, capable of fielding their own private armies of investigators, bounty hunters, and all-purpose goons, none of whom will necessarily play by the rules."

"But they don't want to pay that scumbag sixty or seventy million!" Wilbur cried.

"That's true. But they don't want to pay us two and a half million either, not if they can help it. Bad industry precedent and all that. They'll pretend they want to deal with us, arrange a meet and so on. Then when we arrive—*boom!* They'll pounce on us like a pack of pumas—only it'll be bloodier."

"Shit. So we'll be extra careful—"

"Hey. You're not listening. They're not like police departments. They'll outspend the law, they'll put better investigators on the case, and they'll work it night and day until they've solved it. And you know why? Because it's not just a job to them like it is to the cops. It's their lifeblood."

Jolene said, "You really don't think we can outwit them?"

"Listen to me. In New York, several hundred people are associated in one way or another with the Capriccio family. Any one of them is capable of somehow winding up with, say, a stolen coin worth a million dollars. Or stolen jewelry worth two million. Or a stolen museum piece worth three. Yet not one of them would think of trying to sell it back to the carrier. You know why? Because they know better. They would all go through this one elderly gentleman, because that is what he does, that is what he has evolved into over the years. Whenever you got something that can't be cut, melted down, recast, or reset, he's the one knows all the tricks, all the laws, all the loopholes, just like a specialist lawyer. The guy's an institution, and the cops and the insurance people leave him alone. Sure, they watch him, but they work around him. They want something back, that's what he's there for. After they get it, they can go after the thieves themselves. But him they don't touch."

Jolene said, "I hate to be obvious, but why don't we go to him? Couldn't your father—"

"If the family got involved, our cut would go down dramatically. By at least half. This guy would take a large cut. My father, blood not withstanding, would take a cut. Capriccio would. And what's more, the police would know there was family involvement. And maybe they'd look and see who's out on the Coast, who's had past involvement with movies. And then whose name do you think they'd come up with? Wilbur Blackfield? Miss Jolene? So for all those reasons, no." What I left out: I also didn't want to admit defeat to my father.

Jolene said, "Maybe as a last resort."

"Maybe after the last resort."

"Okay. What're our alternatives?"

"I think maybe it's time we looked at the film itself. If Doug wants the insurance money, it's because he's decided it's worth more than the movie."

"Great. So we look at the film and agree."

"No. We convince him otherwise."

"How?"

I said nothing. Both Jolene and Wilbur stared quizzically at me. Then followed my gaze as I swung my head toward the TV set, where Morgan and Alfred, the two popular Bay Area film critics, sat arguing the merits of a new release.

"Six or so years ago," Morgan growled, his glittery pupils burning with a missionary fervor, "half the movies coming out of Hollywood looked like they were made by people ripped on coke. Now, half the movies seem to be about coke, while the other half still look like they're made by people ripped on coke."

Part Three

The Gangster

C h a p t e r   2 0

The Porsche pounded down the mountain road. White-knuckled, I clenched the steering wheel. Blood pounded around in my skull.

"Are you angry?" Wilbur asked.

I said nothing.

"You *are* angry, aren't you?"

Earlier that afternoon, back in our lakeside cabin after Lowell had failed to materialize, I had sketched out my extemporaneous plan—which, I thought, was touched by a cool dash of bravura. An altogether beautiful concoction. But when I was done, Jolene just looked at me and slowly said, "Your axle's bent, you know that?"

"Oh, c'mon."

She shook her head. "The world of men."

"What?"

"You think everything's a game—snatch the negative, that don't work, snatch a film critic."

But it wasn't a game, and it wasn't loony. I had started watching

Alfred Egert and Morgan Meany's popular local TV show, "Popcorn," shortly after I moved to San Francisco. Earlier in his career, Egert, no slouch, had published a handful of essays in *The Nation, Artforum, The Village Voice,* and *Film Comment* in which he quietly pounded away, again and again, at cognoscenti whose voices could only drip with sarcasm when they spoke about cinema as an art form. He would quote Georg Lukacs on the "trivial life" versus the "authentic life," then turn around and declare that Homer, who understood the art of the spectacle, would have gone straight from epic poems to screen-writing if some clear-eyed Aegean prince, weary of long-winded recitals, not in the mood for importing gladiatorial combat from Rome, had offered him an option on *The Odyssey.* Egert would expound on sex and violence as the ultimate commodity fetishes, but then say that this wasn't so bad as Adorno thought—that, on the contrary, a certain exhilarating breakthrough occurs when one consciously chooses to make one's bed in alienation and mystification—and then he'd remind people that Shakespeare had always been more than happy to pander to the groundlings at the Globe, and that it would've taken Billy no time at all had he found his way west to become the celebrated Bard of Burbank. And so forth. Somehow, Egert had managed to convert all this into a spot on prime-time TV (though for TV he left out the Hegelian hogwash). Meany—noisier, a failed performance artist or something (a dancer I'd dated had told me he'd had his coterie of groupies and hangers-on during a residency at New Langton Arts Gallery)—was sharp in his way: biting, nasty, rambunctious, gesticulative.

They had distinct TV personalities. Short, fair, and bouncy, Meany was effervescent, popping and crackling with nervous energy, a real live wire, he fairly shouted when he talked. Egert, by contrast—probably by calculation on the part of some wily TV producer—was mild, but there was forcefulness to this mildness. Heavy-lidded, mournful, and tall, Egert was full of intense reserve; he seldom raised his voice; rather, he commanded attention. He was the calm eye in the center of Meany's storm. One man was intractable, the other irrefutable.

Most important for my purposes, however, they were astute on how the industry worked, on predicting which movies would be box-office hits even though they were wretched, which ones would flop even though they were destined to become classics, even which "sure-fire" sequels would, in fact, bomb. For this among other reasons I thought I could divert the critical expertise of at least one of them.

My plan was simple and flexible. We would steal a KEM editing table, abduct one of them, and then with the critic in attendance view the movie on the editing table. My presumption was that the movie was bad. I didn't need a critic-hustler to tell me that. The question was, how bad? Was Doug Lowell, rumored to be manic-depressive, overreacting? If so, could he be turned, flipped, somehow convinced the movie would sell tickets? And if *High Plateau II* really was terrible, could the film critic—this was the tricky, *exciting* part of my plan— somehow be convinced, by one means or another, the carrot or the stick, cold cash in hand or cold steel on the throat, to go on TV and lie like a perjurer, to bear false witness and tell all the world—tell *Doug Lowell*—that Mr. Lowell had indeed delivered another masterpiece?

"We play it by ear. We ad-lib," I had said to Jolene back in the cabin.

"We play it by ear? Christ. You have any idea what you're suggesting?"

"We see what evolves. Maybe we have to cut him in, he goes on TV and praises it. Say, a quarter million. Makes Lowell believe he wants it back. Lowell has got to be persuaded he's made a great film, a moneymaker. That's our best shot." Then I added, "Also, someone on TV talking about a movie they've just seen, that Lowell says is lost, will stop the insurance paperwork cold. He'll *have* to deal with us."

In the shadows of the room, Wilbur, sunk in himself, said nothing, just puffed gloomily on his pipe. Jolene shook her head, said, "Too many ifs. This is getting complicated."

"In case you've been out playing golf, it's already complicated."

"How're you going to get them to come look at the film? Walk in their office, hand them engraved invites?"

"That's my problem."

Jolene's green eyes flared up, a dust storm on the planet Venus. "You get arrested for kidnapping, all of a sudden it's *my* problem."

"It won't be kidnapping—not technically."

"The judge will be amused by your explanation."

So it went, back and forth, on and on, until Jolene, worn down, unable to suggest a better plan herself, reluctantly acceded, or at least threw up her hands. At dusk, Wilbur and I quietly departed. Slumped in a chair in front of the TV, Jolene didn't look up, didn't say goodbye, good luck, good riddance, anything.

We drove off. I rerouted my thoughts to the tasks at hand. Stealing the viewing table from a Bay Area postproduction facility was just a detail—a felonious detail, but a detail nonetheless. However, due to the table's bulk, the operation would require Wilbur's meaty assistance. Stealing a movie critic would be trickier. That, though, would be my job alone, after Wilbur had trucked the table back up to Tahoe.

Now, as the Porsche descended the Sierra foothills, out of the blue Wilbur said, "Jolene's been acting cool toward me the last two days."

I looked at him.

"A bit distant. Critical of little things I do that she used to like."

"How so?"

"She used to love the way I tied my shoelaces, making two folds, then looping one through the other. Suddenly she's telling me I tie my laces like a kid." In the dark of the car Wilbur frowned. "I don't know what's going on. If it's because this stuff with Lowell isn't working out, or what."

Into a shrug I injected as much fake sympathy as I could muster. "Well, whatever, don't get bent out of shape over it. And don't push her. If she's acting like she needs a little space—okay, give it to her. Women are different, moodier. More at the mercy of their emotions, menstruation cycles, the stars. Stuff like that." Then I remembered something. "I used to know this woman. She told me how once she was standing on a beach facing the Atlantic under a full moon. Get this. She was having her period and she swore she could feel the lunar pull inside her womb, high tide rippling the blood around."

"You're kidding."

"That's what I thought. But, Christ, was she serious. I mean, how do you deal with something like that?" Actually, it was Jolene, her wide eyes shining strangely, who had told me that story the night on the cabin deck after we lay perspiring and exhausted in each other's

208

arms. She swore she'd never told it to anyone before—I chanced now she hadn't told Wilbur—and that I was the only man she'd ever made love to who she felt wouldn't laugh at her.

"Anyway, Wilbur, try and relax. Then one day, just like that, Jolene will be herself again."

"You think so?"

"Mark my words."

Wilbur, soothed and reassured, slipped off into the sheltering cavern of his Jolene fantasies. I drove. I drove and pondered Doug Lowell. That psychopath had not played by the rules. But soon Lowell was going to learn that there were newer, more terrible rules—the rules of the street, the rules of total warfare, the rules of blanket unpredictability. Yes, the rules of one who is committed to his goal no matter what the means, what the cost, what amount of chaos and destruction is left in his smoldering wake. I had never dealt with anyone like Lowell. But, then, Lowell had never dealt with anyone like me.

The Porsche was bearing down on a steep mountain curve. A granite wall suddenly jack-in-the-boxed up on my right. A precipitous drop yawned to the left. I shifted into fifth, accelerated, and thrilled to the thrust as we tobogganed into the curve at ninety.

"Jesus," Wilbur cried, yanking his unemployed seat belt across his stomach as the granite wall leered and bobbed and made faces outside his window.

I was starting to feel good about myself all over again.

Chapter 21

We arrived at Wally's Walnut Creek condo sometime after midnight. A company van sat in the driveway. A light shone in the living room.

"At least he's up," Wilbur said.

"Maybe."

It was not the best hour for borrowing a van, not even from an old friend. Wilbur stayed in the car while I walked up and rang the doorbell. I waited, then rang it again. After a while, the door swung open.

"Wally, how's it going?"

He stood in the doorway, listing to starboard, holding aloft a nearly empty tumbler. On the coffee table behind him, a nearly empty bottle of Stolichnaya.

" 'How's it going?' " he repeated dully, studying his glass. "*Salud.* Windows. I move windows. Windows on the world. My bid has just been accepted for the subcontract on that new development going up on the unstable hillsides of eastern Contra Costa, near Martinez. So I am celebrating." He took a sip. "Every night I celebrate. But that is unimportant. What is important is that my windows fill the frames of thousands, *tens of thousands*, of suburban households throughout Contra Costa; that my finely cut, properly fit windowpanes don't rattle in the wind; that they are installed in upscale shopping malls and pleasantly landscaped industrial parks throughout the length and breadth of the East Bay; that the corporate executive peers at the traffic jam below through *my* tinted plate-glass window in *his* office; that the busybody neighbor peers through *my* sturdy picture window in *her* living room to watch the mailman slip into the house next door while the husband's at work chipping away at the mortgage, though he's probably boffing his secretary on the side, too, sex harassment and all that crap notwithstanding. Windows on the world, I tell you." He held the glass up to the light and squinted into it. "No, none of it's very important. None of it, I'm afraid, means a thing or cuts very deeply. And if at dusk the setting sun reflects off all the windows with western exposures, creating a symphony, a crescendo and then decrescendo of light— well, what of it? All those windows. All those people staring out of them. Or into them. Always wondering if life is more exciting on the other side of someone else's window. It fills me with a loneliness like dusk, old friend. It chills me to the bone."

"Wally, old buddy. I don't mean to break your train of thought, but I'd like to borrow your van again. For a day or two, if that's okay."

Wally struggled to marshal his facial sinews into some semblance of cunning while blinking at me. The effort caused him to waver a bit. Slyly he asked, "Gonna hit a stable? Make off with a thoroughbred or two? Or maybe move some paintings out of the de Young? Or—I got it—drill into the vault of Wells Fargo?"

"Gotta move some more furniture, Wally. Pure anaphrodisiac."

"Will you do me a favor, Frank?"

"Anything you want, buddy. Say the word."

"Wanna do me something?" he said, laughing in a way that made me uneasy. "This life, man oh man. The adventures of window installation. And that's more exciting than sitting in front of a computer terminal all day watching amber numbers and letters wiggle across the screen." He shook his head. "People sometimes resist the truth without realizing it. Do me a favor, will you, Frank? The truth is, I wish you *would* go out and rob a bank. Will you do that for me, Frank? Will you?"

C h a p t e r   2 2

At two a.m. we pulled into the loading dock of a darkened Emeryville warehouse used by documentary filmmakers. I picked the lock; we quickly located a viewing table and dollied it to the van. Wilbur took off for Tahoe, and early the next morning I drove to a suburban shopping mall in Pinole.

There, at a counter in K Mart's toy department I purchased three Tommy Mace *High Plateau* Gunborga masks. At a counter in the hardware department I purchased a Black & Decker hacksaw. At a third counter I plunked down $185 cash, filled out a form saying I was not a felon, dope dealer or suffering from mental problems, and bought a 12-gauge Winchester Ranger pump-action shotgun and a box of standard shells.

In the shady corner of the lot where I had parked, overlooking the hurtling freeway, I put down my purchases and I took the shotgun out of its box. Then got out the hacksaw, braced my foot against the car's bumper, and sawed the shotgun's barrel down until sixteen inches broke off and clattered to the ground. Now I was ready. I didn't plan to use the sawed-off shotgun; it was just a prop to impress a man whose stock in trade was evaluating props, evaluating movies filled with props. Nonetheless, should a recalcitrant film critic or some busybody by-stander turn my grand scheme into a fiasco and it came down to ten years in the slam or using the shotgun, then—make no mistake—use it I would.

I did like the heft of it in my hands. It made me feel alive, bold, mean, stupid. Perhaps I should just load up the shotgun, yank down my mask, and storm back into K Mart for some more one-stop shopping. An old-fashioned stickup, where the rules of engagement are clear.

◆ ◆ ◆

It was Alfred Egert, proper as a mortician, mournful as a dachshund, who emerged from the KMUT studio building at close to nine, late dusk. I had parked the car, with its false plates, around the corner on a leafy side street. From the shadows of a doorway I watched him come out with co-workers, nod good night, and break off from the pack.

I stepped out. I followed him around the corner, strolled up behind him. Then poked the shotgun in his back.

"Don't turn. Don't say a fucking word or you get a twelve-gauge spinal tap. Walk to the corner, turn left."

"Is this some kind of—"

"The fuck I say? *Shut up.*"

We reached my car. Opening the passenger side while juggling the gun with my free hand—of course, I didn't want to accidentally shoot him, that would be disastrous—I leaned down and slid the seat back. "Get in. Squat on the floor." Then I handcuffed his hands behind his back and blindfolded those eyes with which he took the weekly measure of movie culture. In a way, all of this was unfortunate; I respected the man. When Egert talked on TV, despite the limitations of the format, he worked in literary and pop-culture references, brought up censorship and the arts, and spoke of the paradox that you could get away with anything in the movies—everything is permitted!—but that ideas, *real* ideas, were killed off or watered down by the built-in commercial strictures of the medium. There was no cunning conspiracy, it was just the way things were. Big investments demand big returns, and the bigger the investment the punier the ideas. Now the man sat scrunched up on the floor of my car, trembling, sweating, wondering what the score was. "Make yourself comfortable," I said, more kindly. "It'll be a bit of a ride." Off we drove.

After a while he said, "If you want money, you've grabbed the wrong guy. First, I am not paid anywhere near what the rumors have it. And secondly, I doubt KMUT will pay a ransom for me, though they'll milk my kidnapping for all it's worth on their newscasts."

I steered the car up the ramp onto the Bay Bridge. Across the water the hills of Berkeley and Oakland glittered with the lights of residences.

"Alfred, listen up. This isn't, technically speaking, a kidnapping."

"No?" A confused pause clouded the air. "Then it's worse. You're some movie nut who wants to chat."

"No. I—"

"I *knew* it. This has something to do with my crazy ex-wife."

"Alfred, I'm about to give you the scoop of your career."

"I bet."

"The High Plateau of Stars, Part II."

He was silent. After a few moments he said, "You're not going to hurt me?"

"Stop shaking. You're not in any danger."

"Then I don't get it."

"Which part don't you get?"

"About *High Plateau.* A number of articles have appeared over the last year making extraordinary claims about the production of the movie. Even wilder rumors have circulated." He shrugged. "But that's Hollywood. What do I have to do with this?"

"I'm taking you to see *High Plateau II.* A private preview just for you. You will be the first critic in the world to watch one of the most talked-about movies in years."

He nodded thoughtfully but without demonstrating, I felt, the requisite enthusiasm. Blindfolded, Alfred asked, "And do I have Mr. Lowell to thank for this . . . honor?"

"Lowell has nothing to do with this."

"I don't understand. You're taking me to a private screening of *High Plateau II*, and Doug Lowell has no say? He *owns* the movie."

"I can't explain everything, not just yet. But basically—well, a professional opinion is required."

"You *stole* it?"

I said nothing, and after a while he withdrew into his own private gloom. Soon, the Carquinez Bridge, which spans the headwaters of the Sacramento River, was upon us. I fished some coins out of my pocket and maneuvered into the exact-change lane. Tossed the coins in the basket, zoomed through.

"Is this the Richmond Bridge or the Carquinez?" he asked casually.

"The Brooklyn."

A heavy sigh issued from him.

I said, "Did you really think I was some disgruntled viewer coming after you? Isn't that a bit . . . grandiose?"

"Listen. What do you think I get in the mail? Epistles from parochial-school girls? Oh, no, I get hate mail by the pound. Surely you must know that seriously disturbed people live out there, and anyone who's got a name is a target. Not just politicians anymore, either. Take the lone nut who shot Andy Warhol, or the one who shot John Lennon. Those people, they're the tip of the iceberg, the age shrunk down and concentrated in a couple of psychotic individuals. *They're* the avant-garde, not Warhol and Lennon. And unlike those cultural icons, I can't afford bodyguards. People live such feeble shadow existences that they get more worked up about movies than they do about their own lives. The good old days when the middle class lived lives of quiet desperation are gone. Yes, people *used* to be quiet with desperation. Now they're just bursting with it. Now the desperate grab a gun and storm into the nearest post office or fast-food outlet and let other desperate people have it. They want to register their desperation. Record it for posterity." He nodded. "And intellectuals are as much to blame for this messed-up state of affairs as anyone. Poor quotidian reality has been under round-the-clock ground assault this century from heavy hitters everywhere, from Freud's *Psychopathology of Everyday Life* to Lefebvre's *Critique of Everyday Life*. Finally, there's nothing left to good old reality. Check my inside breast pocket. It came today. It's *typical.*"

I slipped an envelope out of his pocket, shook out a folded typed note. I glanced at Alfred—tied up, blindfolded, miserable. Then, balancing the note above the steering wheel, I read:

> Dear Mr. Superior Movie Reviewer,
>
> I guess it must feel pretty good to get paid so high for being wrong so often. The only reason they keep you around KMUT is because of all the controversy you stir with your snotty reviews. Of course you're a movie reviewer because you don't have the originality to be a moviemaker. It's widely known that most critics are frustrated artists.
> Anyway, I've been seeing your damn face on the tube for too long. We got to sit down and iron things out. So what I'll try to do is find out when you get done at KMUT.
>
> Yours truly,
> One Who Knows
> The Price Of Admission

I whistled softly.

"The relentless stupidity of people. Anyway, now do you understand that when someone sticks a gun in my back, throws me in a car, then handcuffs and blindfolds me, that I am disinclined to think they're about to do me a great big favor?"

"I see your point," I said, and meant it. "But basically you must enjoy your job, no? You spend half your day watching movies."

Alfred ventilated: "You mean do I like watching four hundred movies a year, then in December have trouble coming up with enough of them to fill a ten-best list? You mean do I like going to cocktail parties where the first thing strangers say to me after introductions is, 'What should I see this week?' Or, 'If you hate a movie, I rush out to see it.' " Alfred started flushing, incandescing, a mild-mannered man enraged by the passions of outraged moviegoers. "You mean did I steep myself at Ann Arbor in Aristotle and Kant, Heidegger and Habermas, did I study the phenomenology of perception, the transformation of the Darwinian animal eye into Marx's social eye, all in order to wind up explicating for TV viewers why *Friday the 13th Part 12* isn't quite as resonant as *Nightmare on Elm Street Part 10?* You mean do I like finding myself at each year's end, four hundred films older and four hundred films more desolate?" Alfred nodded fiercely. "Does that answer your damn question?"

Then, softly, he added, "Look, I don't want to become your 'pal.' 'Bonding' with the terrorist and optical illusions of that ilk don't appeal to me. That's all very well and interesting for the weak-willed and for the student of criminal psychology. But the age rushes toward decadence, confusion, chaos, and you're part of it. I don't like you, I *can't* like you. You're an adventurist."

I decided to push him no further. Alfred fell bleakly silent, as though running his credentials through his mind in an effort to understand how he had come to such a pass. To be sure, much aesthetic unhappiness resided in his looks, in the droop of his face and the drop of his eye bags, which hung well below the blindfold—a plethora of deadly movies sat on him like poison.

"Alfred, I need to gag you for the rest of the trip."

He shrugged fatalistically. I pulled onto the shoulder, gagged him, and then drove on in silence, occasionally glancing at him. A man whom Wilbur probably envied. Not an academic fathead who once in a while talked about films before a handful of cinephiles in a museum, but someone who lived in the real world and trafficked in movies and expounded on them weekly before tens of thousands. And he had paid the price. His success contrasted with Wilbur's failure, and his unhappiness was etched deeper; his submerged nihilism, when it surfaced, blasted angrier, blacker.

Which made me wonder anew about Lowell. A man whom Alfred probably envied. Not a media shrewdie but a high roller who lived in the real, real world and had outclassed, outsmarted, outgunned everyone else. The man made movies and believed in them and in himself so much that he had crazily staked his entire life luggage on them even as the economy took the low road to hell.

We passed through Sacramento. The highway started to rise and fall, then rise rise *rise*. The Porsche ate up the road, charging toward higher ground. On the ridges tall pines stood silhouetted against the dark sky.

Soon after Placerville, on a deserted stretch of Highway 50, up ahead through the pines I saw the flashing blue and red lights of highway-patrol cruisers. They were parked in the gravelly lot of the 7-Eleven where two days earlier Wilbur and the sales clerk, each in his own way, had misconstrued the situation. State troopers milled around with shotguns. Lights on their car roofs revolved silently. I pulled over onto the shoulder on the opposite side of the road and lowered my window. "What's going on?" I called out.

A big, blocky state trooper stood under a tree lazily chewing gum. He rotated his head toward me, no rush, and said, "The Convenience Store Killer. He was here just minutes ago. Second time he's knocked over this place."

"No kidding? You sure it wasn't a copycat?"

"Nah. The same kid was behind the cash register both times."

"Anyone hurt?"

"Fortunately, no. Scared the piss out of the kid, though. Last time the guy asked him if he had any stroke magazines. Sick stuff. Kiddie porn, dogs. But this store doesn't even stock *Playboy*. The clerk thought he was dead right there. The guy flew into a rage and ripped the place apart. Then he made the kid lie on the floor and put a sawed-off shotgun to his head. Three hours later a customer comes in for cigarettes, the kid's still on the floor saying Hail Marys."

I waved to the blocky cop. "Hope you catch him."

He waved back. "We will."

C h a p t e r   2 3

T he next morning Alfred, untied, was allowed to stretch and wash. What he saw: a stout, ponderous Tommy Mace who looked as though he'd stayed at the table too long; a shapely Tommy Mace, androgynous in the modern way; and a third, more reasonable—physically speaking, at least—facsimile.

"Trick or treat," said Alfred.

"No, we're just the greeting committee," Jolene replied.

The viewing table had been set up in the living room, the shades pulled, the curtains drawn. I watched Wilbur lift the lid off the first reel of the positive, then remove the reel from the can. After slipping the spool onto the flat mechanical bed, he expertly threaded the yellow leader through the rollers. Above the bed was the modular screen, about the same size and quality as a twelve-inch TV monitor, except wider. To the left of the screen, a single speaker was positioned.

All this brought back memories. The KEM was similar to the viewing table Arnie, Tony, and I used to sit around in the warehouse in the shadow of the Throgs Neck Bridge, trying to figure out what to do with Tony's psycho-killer slasher from Italy. Meanwhile, outside the warehouse, sea gulls had screeched and wheeled over dismal gray Long Island Sound, awash with garbage, used hypodermics, pre-owned condoms, sewer runoff, and worse. As children we used to swim there, off Orchard Beach, at the end of Pelham Parkway. And across the dreary Sound—for some reason I imagined sheets of rain slanting into it, riddling it, the driving rain veiling from view the North Shore of Long Island—across the Sound, unbeknownst to me, a pearl was form-ing in Oyster Bay, my future ex-wife, a blossoming mad beauty preening and prepping to haunt me. Now, watching the lumpish professor who looked so absurd, so seriocomical, in his Tommy Mace mask fiddle with the film, I started to feel a nostalgic attachment to those simpler days.

It was too painful. I turned on the TV while waiting for the professor to set up the film.

"At the top of our news this morning," announced Philip Longly, the Channel 3 anchorman, "is the extraordinary kidnapping of the popular, and controversial, San Francisco movie critic, our own Alfred Egert. We switch now to Cindy Anderson, our reporter on the scene."

Hmm I thought as a small rush of adrenaline, all on its own, slammed home. Life is about to become still more interesting. I glanced at Jolene. She stood, arms crossed, watching the screen, fascinated; even through the latex slits her brilliant stormy green eyes were beautifully registering disgust, though diluted by a reluctant thrill—the thrill known to connoisseurs of roller coasters, horror movies, and certain kinds of one-night stands, as well as to practioners of hijackings, stick-ups, mayhem, and murder. From Wilbur's slits, two eyes filled with dread peered out.

"Thank you, Philip." The TV now showed the front of the KMUT office building on Bay Street, the very building from which Longly was broadcasting. Cindy Anderson, cool, composed, a touch of irony quickening her eyes—for *on the scene* merely meant that she stood in front of the building she worked in—held a mike. I had spotted her once having a cocktail by herself in a Jack London Square bar and had asked if I could buy her a drink. Without the proscenium arch of the TV framing her, she had seemed somehow vulnerable, approachable. But I was mistaken. She had simply smiled and said no thanks.

"When Alfred failed to show up for a ten a.m. screening and calls to his home went unanswered, a few alarms were raised. Then a co-worker stepped forward. According to her eyewitness account, Alfred Egert was abducted last night at gunpoint as he left the KMUT building after work, at around ten p.m. He had just waved good night to a group of co-workers when a well-dressed man in a sports jacket was seen walking up behind him." The camera angle widened to include a young woman, flushed and jittery. "Peggy LaTell is a KMUT secretary. Peggy, you told police this morning that you saw the man put a gun of some sort to Alfred's head and hustle him around the corner?"

"That's right, Cindy," she said excitedly. "It was one of those little Jewish machine guns you can stick in your pocketbook, an Ozzy. And—"

"Peggy, why did it take you until this morning to report it?"

Jolene said: "The new American family of the nineties—Uzi and Harriet."

"Well, to be honest, Cindy, at first I thought it was just a gag. You know, like in the movies, him being a movie critic and all. But then, after I talked it over this morning with my boyfriend—"

"Peggy, I'm sorry. We've run out of time. Now back to Philip Longly."

I glanced at Alfred. He was holding down a full head of steam. "Unbelievable. *Well, to be honest, I thought it was just a gag,*" he mimicked nastily. "*You know, like in the movies.* Would you really like to know why she didn't report it right away?" he asked. "I'll tell you. It's because I *ignore* her. And for good reason. Her first week on the job, she collars me in the corridor. Tells me how impressed she is with my intellect, how turned off she is by Morgan's loudmouthed ways. And if I ever need someone to take to the movies. . . . But her mistake was in believing all those gossip columnists who write that Morgan and I never say a word to each other outside the studio. A week later I'm talking to Morgan, it turns out she told him how swept away she was by his flamboyance, and how cold the rigor of my intellect left her." Alfred shook his head. "People like that just blur the thought processes. I mean, what is the reality consensus on this sort of behavior?"

"Calm down, Alfred." I wanted to listen.

The anchorman was saying, "So far the police have no hard leads, but since we're looking at an apparent kidnapping situation, the FBI has been called in." An insert shot showed several men sifting through stacks of mail. "No, these are not postal workers sorting out early Christmas mail. These are FBI agents looking at Alfred's hate mail from the past year. A few cynics have suggested that all this is a publicity stunt to boost ratings even more for the popular KMUT show 'Popcorn.' But the FBI is taking it very seriously. And now, for a more intimate side to this sad story, we go to Morgan Meany, Alfred's partner. Morgan?"

"Thank you, Phil." Right away, Morgan, pumped up and manic, began gesticulating with both hands. "Look. Obviously Alfred and I have our disagreements. But what would the show be without disagreement? Does everyone have to agree all the time about every little thing with every little person? No, of course not, a bit of human tolerance is what is required here. That's why I find this just—just"—Morgan shook his head—"bewildering."

Interested, Alfred shifted his chair closer to the TV and leaned forward.

The anchorman said: "Morgan, let me ask you a question. Suppose—now this is just hypothetical—suppose Alfred doesn't turn up by Sunday. Then what happens? Does the 'pop' go out of the 'corn'?"

For an instant Morgan's deepest sense of self surfaced in his black bellicose eyes. No pity there. They flashed a look that said, *You mean does the "corn" go out of the "pop"?* Highly unprofessional of him. But immediately he adjusted, became emotional, and said, "Don't say that. Don't even say that. Knock on wood. I don't know." He pumped shakiness into his voice. "To be honest, I don't know if I could do it alone. We *need* each other. We are not able to do without each other. God, I just hope that whoever took him is interested in his money and not his celebrity."

"Thank you, Morgan. Coming right up after a few words from our sponsors: In other news this morning, police are investigating what they believe to be a drug-related double homicide in East Oakland, while in the Sierra Nevada the search goes on for the Convenience Store Killer—"

We switched to the national networks. The kidnapping of a San Francisco movie critic was not the top news of the day, but—so peculiar—they did cover it, as the fourth or fifth story. More interesting than a couple of dead eggplants in East Oakland. More imaginative than another footloose serial killer in the Wild West.

"Good work," Jolene said, watching me through her eyeslits.

"How the fuck did I know he'd be missed so soon? I swear, I didn't see that woman. She must've been hiding up a goddamn tree. Shit, you think I'm happy?"

"Our master of logistics. Our criminal mastermind. Bigtime. We've gone national."

"Hey, did you float a better idea in our 'story conference'?"

"This is pathetic."

"It was viable. Still is. What do you want, a guarantee? You want a guarantee, see a lawyer."

I looked at Alfred. Our squabble didn't interest him. Too materialistic, too profane. The bickering of grubby people. He was off on his own tangent.

Alfred said, "Gentlemen, I have an idea." He took out a spiral notebook, scribbled something down. Then tore out the page and handed it to me.

"Morgan's?" I asked, looking at an address.

"Another opinion can't hurt."

"Alfred," I explained, "if I bring Morgan here, it'll no longer be your exclusive."

He waved his hand dismissively. "On TV, two talking heads are better than one. You can cut away, zoom in for the expressive reaction shot, pan back and forth as one head interrupts the other. It's hard for one person to work himself up into a dither. The emotions are big, they need something to bounce off of."

I looked at my partners. Jolene, eyes cocked, said, "We need a word in private."

I nodded. "Alfred, I'm going to handcuff you to the chair for a minute."

"I understand. Go right ahead." Accommodatingly, he wrapped his arms around the back of the chair and clasped his hands behind him.

Out on the sun deck, Wilbur tore off his mask. "Jesus, now what?"

"Look. Maybe we should get Morgan," I said. "Two of them go on TV doing their shtick, praising the fuck out of the movie, Lowell'll be begging us to sell the damn thing back."

"You think maybe we can pay attention to the implications of what's going on here, Frank? The folks on TV are saying KIDNAPPING. Do you understand? Not h-e-i-s-t but, in big fucking caps, K-I-D-N-A-P-P-I-N-G. And now you're talking kidnapping times two? As in thirty years times two? You remember your multiplication tables, Frank?"

"Hey, you people brought me this. You said, 'Here, do something for us.' So I did. I've been breaking my balls trying to make it happen, and been getting a minimum of cooperation and a maximum of aggravation."

Wiping sweat off his forehead, Wilbur said, "I think this might work. It has a kind of lunatic logic."

Jolene shot him a look. "Hey, Wilbur, who is kidding who here? Where is all this unwarranted optimism coming from? The wishing well?"

"You don't love me," Wilbur cried suddenly.

"Wait a second. What are we talking about? We're—"

"See what I mean, Frank? She doesn't even want to *hear* about it."

"Whoa! Wilbur, you and her—take this up in private. Let's keep the professional and the personal in their separate principalities."

"The principality of the personal," Jolene muttered and shot me a brutal look.

"I love you, goddamn it," Wilbur shouted.

"Wilbur, please. Later, okay?"

"Goddamn it, don't you hear me?"

"*Wilbur,*" she said, and this time a plaintive note cracked her voice.

"How could you turn so cold so fucking fast?"

"I didn't, honey. Please. I mean I—I don't know what I mean. I mean—"

"Hey, you two. When I'm out of here you can thrash it out between yourselves, maybe get in a few co-counseling sessions. But don't make me referee this shit."

"Those are very kind words," Jolene said. "Very considerate. I mean, you wouldn't want to be a prick about it."

"I'm finding this fucking disquieting," I said.

"But it's an interesting distraction from that fantasy shit happening on TV, isn't it?"

"What the hell is going on here?" Wilbur cried. "*I'm* finding this disquieting."

I looked out at the lake, at the blue-gray mountains rimming the distant shore. I said, "I don't want to get in your way. Think I'll head back down the Bay Area, go ring Morgan's doorbell."

C h a p t e r 2 4

Once you've kidnapped one movie critic, the second one is a piece of—of—of—*shit*. Morgan lived in a one-story white cottage with a tile roof on a cul-de-sac high in the hills above Mill Valley. Set back off the road in a grove of eucalyptuses, the house was reached by a gravel driveway flanked by rhododendrons. Alfred had said that Morgan would probably be home and that he lived alone. I pulled into the driveway and eased behind a red Celica convertible with a California vanity plate: STARCRIT.

In the old days, modesty was a virtue, a low profile the preferred way of conducting business. You didn't want to attract attention. You didn't want a lightning bolt to seek you out. But today—when did we all become so full of ourselves, so puffed up with self-importance, each of us the star of our own nonstop movie?

I yanked the Gunborga mask down over my face, grabbed the sawed-off shotgun from under my seat, and stormed up the driveway. The gravel crunched beneath my shoes. I was about to bang violently on the door when inside I heard a girl shouting. I discreetly pressed the doorbell. The opening notes of *Star Wars* chimed. The shouting stopped.

A moment later Morgan yanked open the door. "Who the fuck—" He halted in midsentence. Behind him, a young blonde—by young I mean a voluptuous fifteen or sixteen—was running around the living room in black panties gathering up her clothes. On a glass coffee table was a small mound of white powder, leading export of the Upper Huallaga Valley.

"Jesus, you're always ranting about how coke has ruined the industry," I murmured, taken aback.

Morgan was too startled to say anything. The girl wasn't. "Yeah, he's always carrying on, the phony. The son of a bitch lies about everything. Told me he could get me a screen test with Francis Coppola. 'Francis has me up to Napa to taste his wines.' 'Francis invites me to his private screenings.' Turns out Francis wouldn't give him the fucking time of day."

"Morgan, put your shoes on," I said.

"Hey, you wanna take him down to the river, blow his fucking head out," she screamed, "be my guest. I'll even pull the trigger for you. And if you need an alibi, willing to weigh jailbait against homicide, I'll get the receipt for Motel 6." She looked at Morgan. "Shitty scumbag."

"I don't believe this," Morgan muttered. "I don't fucking believe this."

"C'mon, Morgan," I said, grabbing him by the collar. "We're taking a ride."

"Oh no. Oh no. I don't believe this is happening—"

Morgan magicked into a wiggling, writhing greased eel and slipped out of my grip. I grabbed him—he broke away. I aimed the shotgun as he dashed across the room. He noticed and froze. "NOW," I said.

The truth is, all this commuting between the Bay Area and Lake Tahoe was taking its toll. My nerves were jangled, raw around the edges; I was operating on a hair-trigger. I wanted Morgan to behave, to conform to the usual standards of hostage protocol. Because part of me suspected that killing a movie critic might prove therapeutic.

"What should I do about you?" I said to the girl.

Her eyes sought out mine through the latex slits, she fixed me with a fifteen-year-old's lewd-bold smile, worldly in a tentative sort of way, still testing the waters with an exploratory sexuality. She looked frightened. The girl might go far, she might wind up running with the Oakland chapter of the Hell's Angels, but either way, she'd know enough not to go to the police. "I'll be okay," she said.

"Take care."

I pocketed the coke in case I should have to ration it out later to Morgan, then I shoved-guided-pushed the wiggling jerky Morgan out to my car. His movements seemed made up of hundreds of little seizures occurring in rapid succession. I watched Morgan—his constant stop-motion: spasms: stillness: bobbing and fidgeting: forceful yet directionless—I watched Morgan's little cocaine dance and wondered if I had made a mistake. The speedy jumpy way he pivoted—I expected his Clarks to squeal like car tires. He seemed forever furious. Give substance to the light and shadows of the screen and he would probably hit it with a critical stick. In any other circumstances I would have found him interesting, even diverting, a kind of walk-on curio—but not today.

"Where're we going? Is Alfred alive?"

"Alfred's fine, Morgan. Relax. You'll be fine, too. We're going to—"

"And never mind her crap about Francis. I *do* know Francis. In fact, I've interviewed him."

"Lucky 'Francis.' "

"Francis is a great filmmaker. Fine. I am a great film critic. When I interview Francis, I do not feel intimidated or reverential. We meet as equals—two men at the top in our respective fields." He nodded to himself, pleased at this formulation.

"You know, a lot of people find you really fucking irritating."

"In this world," Morgan snapped, "if you do not say a thing in an irritating way, you may just as well not say it at all, because people will not trouble themselves about anything that does not trouble them. Where'd you say we were headed?"

"A sneak preview. *The High Plateau of Stars, Par*—"

"Right. And questionnaires will be distributed after the screening. 'Age? Opinion? Would you recommend this movie to a friend? How did you hear about this?' "

I pushed his head down and shoved him into the car, handcuffed and blindfolded him, then took a deep, deep breath. As we drove off I supplied the relevant narrative details, and when I was done he said: "Let me get this straight. Alfred passed up an exclusive to share this with me?"

"Nothing personal, but I got the impression he thought it would be good for business."

"That so?" Scrunched on the floor, he rested his head against the door and lapsed into silence, breathing raggedly.

The third time driving up to Tahoe I felt the scenery was losing its charm. I had worn it out. The bucolic had turned colic. My enthusiasm for the heist was leaking away, as though some teenage terrorist had let the air out of my tires. Too many conditionals. Too many rules I didn't grasp. And too many people whose behavior was below the line.

◆　◆　◆

I knocked on the door. A few seconds later Jolene, masked, opened it. She looked at me and smiled wonderfully—through her eye slits an intent, even innocent expression shone in her green irises. And in that instant I realized I had missed her, and that she, despite her anger over these "kidnappings"—or perhaps, in her own stubbornly perverse way, because of them—had missed me.

She glanced at Morgan, then turned back toward the room. It was very quiet, very still. Alfred sat in a chair reading about himself in the *Chronicle*. Wilbur, masked and distressed, sat on the couch staring at the blank TV screen—but not really. He was staring, I think, at the blackness at the end of things but not knowing it yet, trying not to pick up on the restless sexual weather that Jolene had begun to move in.

Alfred looked up and said, "Morgan!"

"So, Alfred, this is on the level?" Morgan was grinning, pleased to see his critical adversary. I unlocked his handcuffs, and he shook out his hands, then bent and unbent his fingers.

"Apparently so."

Morgan turned to me. "Okay. What's the problem? Lowell doesn't want his movie back? Probably because it's as awful as the rumors have it and he'd rather collect the insurance. Happens all the time in other areas of commerce. Look at the restaurant business, small retail stores in the garment industry. *Whoosh!*" He threw up his hands in imitation of an explosion. "You think these places just happen to be especially combustible? I'm surprised he didn't think it up himself."

"That's probably it," I said agreeably.

"So what do you need us for? What do you think is going to happen afterward?"

"We're going to sit at the table and talk about the movie, and then you're going to go on TV and tell the world it's a masterpiece."

"Sure. You want that I do this in prime time or on late-night cable?"

"I'll pay you twenty-five thousand each."

"Hey, you think we're prostitutes, our opinions for sale? Fuck you. *Fuck* you."

Jolene said coldly, "Two hundred and fifty thousand each. A quarter million."

Morgan studied Jolene. Then me. Then looked at quiet Alfred, who shrugged mildly, amiably. "Ordinarily . . ." Alfred said. "But this isn't ordinary. We both command sizable lecture and consultancy fees. Film departments and journalism schools want to hear what we have to say. So, why not? Besides, it might lead to national syndication."

I said, "You go on TV, explain you weren't kidnapped but taken to a private screening. Tell the world how great it is. Make it convincing. Then give us a week to work things out with an enlightened Doug Lowell. Afterward you can go back on TV, tell the world it's a piece of shit, you were forced to lie, gangsters threatened to hack up your children, whatever. No one will be the wiser. Your sterling reputations for critical integrity will remain intact."

Morgan, watchful like a hawk, said, "What guarantees you don't stiff us?"

"I'll give you the third reel of the negative and Alfred the fourth. We'll be negotiating piecemeal with Lowell, so we'll buy back your reels with our first two installments from Lowell."

Alfred said, "Sounds fair enough. I look on it as reparation for the fright you gave us."

Morgan nodded. "But I need blow. I'm gonna need blow."

"You're unbelievable," Jolene said. "You have the nerve to go on TV, bitch how coke has—"

"Hey, the age of innocence was long ago, B.C. We're all adults here. I don't mean to sound like the moralizing nihilist, but I think all of us understand that hypocrisy has its place so long as the passion underlying it is the genuine article."

"Let's get on with it," I said.

Morgan and Alfred, a couple of privileged characters, straightaway made themselves at home, positioning themselves directly in front of the KEM's screen. Wilbur once again threaded the tracks of the first reel onto the sprockets around the heads that led to the take-up cores. Then he pulled up a chair alongside Morgan. I pulled up a chair alongside Alfred. Jolene pulled up a chair alongside me. Even without the mask I would've known it was her. Her warmth, the essence of her carnal scent—woodsy, damp wild mushrooms—tinged the air, stirring me.

"You wouldn't want to sit next to me," Wilbur said darkly.

"Oh, stop getting paranoid about every litt—"

"Hey, let's just watch the fucking movie," I said, "see if Lowell put sixty-seven million on the screen or not."

The cabin was dark, the curtains drawn, the windows closed. All eyes focused on the small screen.

"Ready?"

"Just about," Wilbur said.

In the dark Jolene sighed theatrically. "Just think. The excitement. The anticipation. That heady surge of elation when the lights go down."

Wilbur leaned over and pushed a button on the KEM's console.

The machine whirred and hummed.

The bright yellow leader started snaking through the heads.

The High Plateau of Stars, Part II blazed to life.

The Movie Mogul

C h a p t e r 2 5

Big day. A big, big day ahead of me. The culmination of all my dreams, all my hopes, all my *money*—a small, ultra-low-budget home movie that would balance the books on my $67-million megamonstrosity, that would *close* the books on that monstrosity which had very nearly broken my heart. But this, my new movie, my "small gem of compression," would be different. Yes yes yes, I thought, as I bustled about the kitchen of the guest cottage, where the only guest is usually myself; I am the guest, I am the host, I extend to myself the utmost hospitality. *Small gem of compression* I kept saying over and over to myself, *Small gem of compression, small gem of compression*, until it assumed in my mind the mesmeric power of a mantra.

The kettle started to whistle. I listened to it for a minute; it was whistling—*impossible*—the theme from *The Black Pig*. But no, of course it wasn't, just a trick of the morning imagination, my imagination is always too active in the morning, for I wake abruptly, with a start, I rocket away from my dreams, which are left far, far below, invisible specks on the launching pad of my consciousness. And this abrupt waking, this eruption out of dreamland, has never sat well with my girlfriends, it does not sit well with my wife, they have all thought there is something suspect, something fishy, something *diabolical* about a man who regains full consciousness so easily, so instantly, who doesn't have to work his way into it, who simply wakes up, looks around, and *Bingo!* his mind is roaring at full throttle, wide open, making all the right connections, the synapses fully wired, everything racing right along. He's ready to read the morning news, assimilate and process new information, ready to sit right down at the computer with a cup of coffee and start banging away at a screenplay. They don't understand it, my wife doesn't understand it, she *hates* it. Dear Victoria wakes very slowly, in piecemeal fashion, brain cell by brain cell, in installments, floating up out of her hackneyed dreams, that surrealistic garbage dump of her unconscious, that jumbled assortment of bad Freudian stage props that she always insists on relating to me in painfully excruciating minutiae. Yes, she awakens slowly, she takes her sweet time, the alarm goes off, she hits the snooze button for another ten minutes of shuteye, I bring her her coffee, she sits up in bed propped on a cushion of goose down, she sips slowly, she warms her hands around her cup, she has her little patterns, her little routines, a cup of Viennese coffee, heated half-and-half, no sugar, she dips into whatever horrible novel she's been reading and lumbers through another four or five pages. Then she puts on her robe and draws a bath, a long hot soak with oils and salts, this followed by a light breakfast and a second cup of coffee, and an hour later she's finally achieved full consciousness—and that (she thinks) is the civilized way to start the day, none of this abrupt-transition nonsense.

Never mind. I was in a good mood. A good mood! I left the cottage and headed through the woods to my mansion. Inside the office, my secretary, Beth, blond Beth, delectable as a shiny purple plum in her tight-fitting plum-purple designer outfit, sat at her desk watching the office TV. At the sound of my entrance she turned, laughing, and said, "Doug, you wouldn't believe what happened."

I looked at the monitor ensconced in its walnut cabinet. My old friend Cindy Anderson stood in front of the KMUT building, telling a story about a man with a gun who had snatched a movie reviewer off the streets.

"Isn't this a kick?" Beth said.

"This country. In South America they kidnap U.S. business execs. In Germany and Italy they kidnap industrialists. Here, they kidnap movie critics. What's that tell you about our priorities?" I shook my head. "He liked the original *High Plateau*, didn't he?"

"Yeah."

"My loss. Any messages?"

"Slow day, Doug. It's the calm before the storm."

Unfortunate choice of words, I thought. I said, "All this free time on your hands, Beth, and what with my finances the way they are, maybe you can pick up a few extra bucks doing phone sex out of the office, help pay the rent around here."

Beth laughed and said, "I had a friend was doing that for a while, paid her way through S.F. State. Sometimes she'd come home from classes, be in a really foul mood, say to her boss, 'Route the masochists to me tonight.' "

I laughed. But then all at once—I don't know why—I said, "Beth, do you like me?"

"Do I like you?" She looked puzzled, perhaps even a touch distressed.

"You know, as a person. For myself and all that."

"Of course I like you."

"Or is it because I'm 'Doug Lowell,' famous moviemaker, that whole trip?"

"But Doug, that's who you are. How do I—how does anyone— separate out you as a person from you as, you know, who you are, as 'Doug Lowell.' I mean, you're the person you are. See?"

"I guess." A depression, mild but poignant, began to grip me.

"You okay, Doug?"

"I mean, if you were to meet me on the street . . ."

"What?"

". . . and didn't know who I was . . ."

"Oh, Doug."

". . . do you think you'd like me?"

"Oh, Doug. But I do know who you are."

"This is 'avoiding the issue.' "

"This isn't—isn't an *issue*." Pause. "I'd probably think you were a very charming and articulate man. With a nice sense of humor. Intelligent." She paused again. "Maybe just a touch cynical."

"Women like men with a good sense of humor, don't they? I read that somewhere, *USA Today* or something."

"They do."

"Do you?"

"Of course, Doug."

"So you would like me?"

"But I do like you."

"No, you like DOUG LOWELL. What about *me*?"

"Doug, we're going in circles."

"Working for me is addictive, though, isn't it? I mean, friends ask what do you do, you say 'I'm Doug Lowell's secretary.' "

"True."

"Which sounds a hell of a lot better than 'I'm Joe Schmo's secretary.' A lot *sexier*. After all, what else do we got in this society? Computers, law, business? Don't make me laugh. There's *nothing* like the movies."

"True."

"Nothing so exciting. So *addictive*."

"I know. And I'm very pleased to be working for you."

I paced around the office. I was feeling antsy, a bit nervous, wired, a big afternoon in the offing. I parted two slats in the blinds and peered out the window. "Phone sex."

"Huh?"

"If you did phone sex, Beth, what would you do?"

"Ummm . . ."

"I mean, what kind? Style? Content? These are all things you'd have to consider. How would you pitch your voice? Soft? Husky? Would you go for the vulnerable note? The dominant?"

"I—I—"

"What I'm saying is, it's a subset of the industry, no? You're acting, though maybe not exactly throwing yourself into the role. You're talking to some suburban goofball you're never going to see, miles and miles away, and you're moaning, 'Oh honey, how I wish you were here. My hands are wandering over my smooth round breasts, down my slinky waist to the flare of my hip. And now with my fingers I'm parting the moist lips of my tight young quim.' "

"Doug!" she squealed, and gave a little-girl giggle.

"Of course, you're saying all this crap while you're sitting there filing your nails, leafing through *TV Guide,* maybe throwing darts or something."

"I don't know what to say. . . ."

"Maybe the phone john asks, 'What're you wearing?' Your hair's in curlers, facial cream's smeared all over your face, you have on a shit-brown terry-cloth bathrobe. You look like hell, right?"

"Yeah . . . ?"

"So what do you tell him? That you look like a beanbag? *No.* You tell him you're wearing these sheer black seamed nylon stockings. This unbelievably tight-fitting, rich-smelling black leather miniskirt that you've hitched up to your crotch, the better to finger-fuck yourself. This silky see-thru black camisole that clings to your swollen nips. See what I mean? You become an actress, you get into it, you improvise, you create an illusion. You construct a whole other persona for yourself. You become *the other.* On the phone you can be anyone you ever dreamed of, do anything you ever fantasized about."

"Yeah?"

"But maybe while you're doing this, you cross some sort of line. Boundaries melt away. You find yourself getting turned on. Turned *out.* You've entered the Twilight Zone of Desires."

"I'm not sure . . . ?"

"Like your friend at S.F. State, thinks it's a lark, a joke. 'Send me the masochists, I'm in a bad mood.' Maybe normally she's in a bad mood she'd pop two aspirins, a Valium, go lie down."

"Okay. . . ."

"But suddenly it's 'Bring on the slave boys, Simba.' "

"Yeah?"

"Next thing she knows she hears herself saying to this guy, 'Are you *ready* to be schooled? Because I have my riding crop in hand and I'm just *ripping* to school you.' You follow, Beth?"

"Okay, yeah, I think so. . . ."

"And maybe she's saying this, her hair's in curlers . . ."

"Right. . . ."

". . . but maybe not. Maybe she's decked herself out like the fantasy call girl she's described. And maybe her bad mood starts to lift. She feels 'empowered.' She feels *turned on.*"

"I can see what you're saying. . . ."

"She's getting wet. She's doing a job on the guy but she's also doing a job on herself. She's talking herself into it. She starts to masturbate. So in fact what's happening is, she's not just 'working' to put herself through 'college.' I mean, fuck that, that's just bullshit. What's happening is, her excuse, her rationalization—college, work-study blah blah blah—is just an excuse, a rationalization for her to discover finally who she is. To delve into the deepest, murkiest depths of her personality. The secret core, the dark side. To feel herself out, to learn more about herself, her real nature. Self-delusion time is over. Kaput. Let us now stop lying to ourselves, you and I. You follow?"

"Kind of. I think so."

"We all have our dark sides, Beth. Even you."

"Maybe. . . ."

"It's just that most of us keep our dark side under pretty tight wraps, even from ourselves. Lockdown, numb-out, entrenched systems of defenses and all that."

"Yeah?"

"But not us, Beth. Not us. I mean, if I didn't have a dark side, would I have binged for sixty-seven million of my own fucking money on what should've been a sure thing?"

"Well. . . ."

"And if you didn't have a dark side, if you weren't in some ways a highly motivated piece of work, would you be here answering the phone for me? You follow? People don't just walk through the door, say 'I wanna work for Doug Lowell.' Isn't that right, Beth?"

"I guess so."

"You *guess* so? I mean, it's no accident you're NOT in computers, you're NOT in business, you're NOT in law. You're in the fucking MOVIES—"

"Right."

"—and you work for fucking DOUG LOWELL."

"That's true, too."

"So there's gotta be a reason. This isn't fucking lotto."

"I guess so, I mean *yes*, right."

"So what is it?"

"I—I—I—I don't know, Doug, I'm feeling all confused."

"How's your screenplay coming along, Beth? Ready to give me a peek?"

"It's—it's—coming."

I nodded. "Look at how you're dressed. This skirt. You can barely part your legs. This fitted silk jacket. The silk stockings." I started to laugh. "Jesus, what do I pay you, you can afford to look like this?"

She smiled goofily, nervously.

"I'm putting you on the spot."

"No, yes, I mean, it's okay, Doug. Really."

"You been working for me now—how long?"

"Three. Three years."

"I ever make a move on you, try to hit on you?"

"No. And I respect you for—"

"Fuck respect. Respect's got nothing to do with anything."

"All right."

"But you work for 'Doug Lowell'?"

"Yes."

"And you'd . . ."

" 'You'd?' 'I'd' what?"

"Stand up, Beth."

"Okay."

"Now turn around. Grip the edge of the desk with both hands. Right, like that, that's good. Now spread your legs a bit more. Get the skirt—I know it's tight—but . . . a little higher."

"Like this?"

"That's very nice. You're a beautiful woman, Beth."

"Thank you."

And then and there, several hours before showtime, several hours before Tommy Mace was due to drive through my gate in his Mercedes sportster with smoked windows to star in my home movie, then and there for the first time in the three years since I'd hired her I fucked my secretary—a shattering violation of business and pleasure, a dizzying breach of the personal and the public, an exhilarating infraction of work and play—then and there I fucked my secretary from behind, the two of us standing bent over her desk, her tight skirt hitched up above the tops of her silky stockings, my jeans tangled around my ankles, and it made me feel *good*.

Chapter 26

"Doug, why the front projection? Why the wind machine? I don't get it. What the hell is going on here?" Tommy was pacing back and forth around my small sound stage. He tripped over a cable and angrily kicked it. "This is supposed to be a screen test, a dry run, am I right?"

I stared icily at Tommy for several seconds—enough to put him on edge. But then I relaxed and smiled warmly. Margot, fortunately, hadn't shown up yet; she would require a whole other explanation. I said, "If you look carefully, you can select almost anything for background. But it is in the *choice* of background that true character is found. Between you and the background, we discover personality—"

"Doug, what're you talking ab—"

"An early Soviet filmmaker, Lev Kuleshov, conducted an experiment. First, he showed an audience a close-up of an actor whose expression was completely neutral. He followed this with a close-up of a bowl of soup. The audience thought the man looked hungry. Then Kuleshov showed the neutral shot of the actor again, but this time followed by a shot of an open coffin that contained the corpse of a young woman. Now the audience thought he looked sad. Next, the neutral shot again, but this time followed by a shot of a little girl jumping rope. What do you think the audience thought, Tommy?"

"That he looked happy?"

"Right. They praised the actor's extraordinary range. His versatility in portraying such different emotions."

"That's pretty funny."

"So, you see, it wasn't the actor per se who was important but the juxtaposition of him as an *object* alongside other objects. Emotional meaning grew out of the sequence of shots, not the actor's ability to emote."

"Okay."

"And that's what I'm doing here. I know you can act, that you're highly skilled. But I have to see if you're the *object* I need to place against the background. The vase against the wallpaper."

"If I'm the right object . . ."

"I mean no insult—"

"I think I understand."

"—but I need to coolly consider you apart from who you are, from the very talented human being I know you to be. I need to consider you as an *object* rather than as an actor."

"Okay, I'm following what you're saying."

"Hence the front projection."

Tommy nodded with dawning comprehension, with profound understanding, with deeply felt imbecility. If something sounds reasonably intelligent, it *is* reasonably intelligent. But he still looked a tad uneasy. "Doug, I would like to say 'I want to do your script.' But if you're not showing me—"

"Don't worry."

"At least give me an outline, a broad sketch. What's the story roughly? You said I play an actor. . . ."

"That's right."

Tommy walked over to the rumble pot filled with blocks of dry ice. He stuck his hands, palms down, into the rising stream of mist and rubbed them together, then blew on them. He turned and said, "Okay. So I play an actor . . . ?"

"A stolen movie negative."

"Excuse me?"

"A stolen movie negative."

"I don't und—"

"You play an actor. Royally fucked over by some producers, by a director. So you steal their negative."

"I steal the negative?"

"Correct. You, a disgruntled employee. Vengeance, crime, action. Social satire on the side. Which adds depth. And a girl. Romance. Devious, double-crossing. Of course sexy."

"Hmmm."

"Your ticket to stardom. Real stardom—not linked to the sci-fi horse-opera crap but to talent. Your talent."

"Well . . ."

"We're going to make art."

"Art."

"Critical acclaim married to commercial success—"

"Commercial success, okay—"

"—though, of course, not on the scale of *High Plateau*."

"Of course. Not."

"But then we don't want a blockbuster. Don't *need* a blockbuster."

"No, that's not—"

"The Academy never honors blockbusters anyway. Harrison, *Indiana*. Jack, *Batman*."

"Forty million in his pocket."

"Envy. Jealousy. Forget that."

"Envy, jealousy . . . Still . . ."

"Petty little people."

"That's true."

"Nonetheless, we want them to honor us. To respect us."

"For our art."

"Now you're talking."

"Forty million."

"Fuck that. Fuck Jack. Money's never meant anything to me anyway, Tommy."

"Of course not."

"It's the ones it means so much to who fuck up. Whose train never arrives at the gate."

"Right."

"You have to *force* the action yourself. You have to *know* what you want. The world doesn't make room for you, you make room for yourself."

"A room of yourself . . ."

"Exactly. You try to do good work, everyone lines up against you. This industry—full of treacherous, two-faced little pricks. People smile, stab you in the back."

"Can't be too careful."

"But me—I'm up-front about things. I don't like you, I'll stab you right between the fucking eyes. You see it coming. Know where it's coming from."

"The only way."

A door creaked open. Margot entered, stage left, nervously blinking her one-inch eyelashes, dressed, as usual, in sepulchral black: black lizard-skin boots, black jeans, black crewneck sweater, and a black sweatband to keep her frenzied black hair out of her mad bright unfocused eyes. She said, "Hi Doug." And, "Hi Tommy."

"The hell is she doing here?"

"Just a stand-in for today, Tommy. A kind of visual aid, a floor cue, if you will." I glanced at Margot and winked. She nodded just slightly, conspiratorially—a bit uncertainly.

"I don't like this."

"It'll be okay."

"It's not like I've agreed—"

"I do prefer you to Sean. . . ."

Tommy stared at me. I stared calmly back. He broke off and resumed pacing back and forth in front of the screen. "Couldn't you come up with someone better? Like the Guatemalan maid?"

Margot looked stung. "Doug, do I have to stand here list—"

"She'll do fine," I said. "Just like once upon a time, over the objections of the studio heads, an arrogant young filmmaker insisted on using an even more arrogant young asshole who until then had starred in a string of low-budget flops."

He stopped pacing and regarded me. Then regarded Margot. He sighed and said, "Okay."

I handed each of them a two-page script. On top of a rock that I'd had the Gonzálezes roll down from a mountain and place in front of the screen, I now set a briefcase filled with stacks of bills: hundreds on top, ones for padding.

"This, a dream role?" Tommy said, perusing the script. "Am I missing someth—"

"A dream role."

"You honestly think this is Oscar material?"

"In the context of the whole thing—Kuleshov, the neutral expression, the bowl of soup, the open coffin—yes."

For the next hour I ran Tommy and Margot through a dozen, *two* dozen exhausting rehearsals. Tommy, who had come a long way, was completely professional. Margot kept blowing her lines in fairly uninteresting ways—not even interesting as bad comedy. I allowed myself to drift, to direct them on automatic pilot, realizing that she would eventually gain command of her lines. But this part didn't interest me. So I drifted and waited patiently.

Patience. It is the secret virtue of the best artists—and, in the last issue, I consider myself an artist. It goes without saying that in the course of rehearsing my actors, of communicating to my cameraman the look, the feel, the atmosphere that I desire, of conveying to my editors the mood I want the rhythm of the selected shots to transmit, it goes without saying that I alternate the most ingenious flattery with the harshest criticism, that I know when to give them room and when to box them into a corner, that I frequently blow up and scream at them as though they were dogs, that I tell my actors they're delivering their lines like zombies, that I tell my cameraman that a bat operating by echolocation could compose better pictures, that I tell my editors that their rhythms are spastic and convulsive. It goes without saying. And such behavior naturally leads them to believe that I am mercurial, highly inflammable, the temperamental director prone to murderous outbursts.

But beneath that excitable exterior resides the person who understands that the outbursts are all for show, all part of the process, that if I appear to have a short fuse, in fact I possess a long-range patience that *never* loses sight of the final goal—a stronger, more beautiful work of art. Yes, patience. Patience while waiting for the actor to find just the right blend of precision and passion in his line readings. Patience while waiting for the sun to find just the right angle in the sky so that the light matches the shot from the previous day or week. Patience while waiting for my editors to coax out of all the assorted footage the true secret order of the shots. I have the patience to outwait the sun itself. I certainly have the patience to outwait, to out*wit*, an actor, to wear him down to the point where if I were to put a loaded revolver in his hand and say "Shoot her," he would.

"I think we're ready," I said.

"Shit. I'm ready to sleep."

"Yeah, can't we take a break?"

I turned on the wind machine, which was situated just behind the basin filled with dry ice. I walked to the projection machine and turned it on, simultaneously activating the interlocking motor of the video camera. White light bounced off the semireflecting mirror and seared the reflex screen. Next I attended to the video camera, which I had positioned a few branches in front of, for a camouflage effect. Tommy and Margot, who had assumed their positions flanking the open brief-case filled with cash, watched me curiously.

"All set?"

"I guess so."

The screen roared to life. The robust Mendocino coastline. Waves, in the grand style, crashing behind my actors. Scenic cypresses tossing in the wind. Sea gulls winging picturesquely over their heads. Reasonable facsimiles of mist drifting past. I looked at the video monitor, studying the composition of the shot. It wasn't perfect. The cypresses seemed to be blowing one way, the mist somewhat in another. But these were mere details, below the threshold of most people's consciousness.

I said, "Camera. Action."

C h a p t e r   2 7

An exhausted red sun—a sun on the blink, a sun fit for the dust
hole—lowers toward a motionless gray sea. This image then dissolves
seamlessly into another—the prow of a spaceship cutting restlessly
through space, the camera tracking with it past one dead orbiting planet
after another. Is that Earth? Is that Mars? Actually, not all the planets
are orbiting. The ones nearest the sun, itself just a bundle of embers,
appear to have fallen out of orbit and are simply drifting toward the
glowing ashen sphere. Some planets continue to turn disconsolately on
their axes, others wobble, and the planets farthest from the sun seem to
have pulled free of the solar system's gravitational field altogether. The
spaceship, moving faster and faster, speeds away from this lifeless solar
system—a solar system that hated God, and that God has fled. A
desolate spacescape where a human being could not begin to make his
or her presence felt. Not the toy-store outer space of Star Wars and Star
Trek or even the first High Plateau, but outer space as a howling
wilderness that sends you reeling back into your own private wasteland.

Not a solar system whose expansiveness suggests an infinity of space but rather an eternity of nightmares, of unending coldness, of bleak shining desolation.

Then that image dissolves as the spaceship alights in a forest—yet not, however, the kind of primordial forest that moviemakers so often use as a cheap stand-in for another planet. For on this planet things are the same, but not quite the same—something about the way the sun filters and shimmers through the trees, the peculiar pitch of the light; the colors seem subtly different, tainted, as though the very molecules vibrate to the music of a different god.

The door of the spaceship creaks open. Gunborga steps out. Behind him, other honorable explorers—and dishonorable ones, too. Gunborga's face registers the dread—but also the exhilaration, almost carnal in nature—of the unknown. But deeper than that dread and exhilaration is a new note, a new emotion—his recognition finally that he is spreading not light and knowledge but a seed, a virus, a madness into the farthest corners of time and space. To stamp the human race's dark destiny on all of creation.

There is no music. It is as though the director wants us to hear the quiet, the harrowing disquiet, to feel the sheer weight and terror of so much silence. . . .

Then it all starts up—

Two minutes into the movie and I felt unnerved. The screen of the KEM was small, the sound that issued from the speakers tinny. Yet none of that mattered. The opening images were so unexpectedly powerful, the visuals so confidently composed, the camera work so rhythmically, self-assuredly matched to the movement of objects within the frame, that I realized with no small shock, with *horror,* that I was watching a great movie.

Two hours later it was over. For a full minute no one said a word. Stunned, I sat oddly frozen, holding tight onto the arms of my chair. I shifted slightly. My body creaked under the weight of my thoughts. I felt fierce, flummoxed, rattled, murderous. The narrative of the last few days needed to be radically reconstructed. Yes, I wanted to lie down and grieve.

Alongside me Jolene started laughing quietly, then louder, she laughed and laughed, and said finally, "The son of a bitch pulled it off."

"What happened to that stupid trailer we saw on TV?" I asked uneasily. "It wasn't in the movie. Or the Five-Headed Vomit Monster?"

"Lowell probably cut the scene after the trailer had already been put together," said Wilbur, who had begun rewinding the film. He shook his head, amazed. "In fact, he just cut away *all* the parts that weren't *High Plateau II*, and there the film was."

"Maybe we should invite Lowell over, break out the champagne," Morgan said. Then asked, "Okay if I smoke?"

"Please, go ahead," I said.

"And can I get some coke?"

"Here."

He reached for an ashtray, tapped out a cigarette from his pack. Then laid out a few lines, snorted them right up. He seemed hyper, wired, terrifically on edge.

Alfred asked, "Could I trouble you for a Scotch—with ice?"

"Coming right up," Jolene said. "Hey, drinks for everyone. They're on the house."

"It's just fucking amazing," Morgan said, leaning back in his chair, cigarette in hand. "In these cautious, recessionary times the man took his own personal fortune and with absolute conviction seized the chance to make a world-class epic." He sprang up from his chair and started roaming the room restively, cigarette in mouth, hands in pants pockets. "This is the sort of movie you wait *years* to see. It's as though Orson Welles, David Lean, and Francis Coppola at the top of their game had been rolled into one." Shaking his head, he removed his hands from his pants pockets and clasped them behind his back.

"Stay away from the curtains," I warned.

Morgan halted, pivoted abruptly, and said, "Sorry." He stood abstracted for a moment, puffing on his cigarette. "Even the notorious $3.2-Million Heartbreak Sunset turned out incredible. Somehow the lens splintered the sun so it seemed as though ten suns were setting all at once across the bleak icy horizon. A melancholy multiple twilight."

"I'll tell you what amazed me most, though," Alfred said. "Tommy Mace. The guy started out in the first movie like some kind of comic-

strip hero defying the gods. But from the beginning of this one we can
see how his character has grown, how he's become so confident in his
greatness as an explorer that his generosity of spirit—just let me finish,
now, Morgan—seems pure courtliness. Yet as the movie progresses we
also see how the years have taken their toll, slowly driving him mad,
so that by the end, deified by his people, he has become a god
himself—a crazy lost outcast maniacal god bent on colonizing the
universe and then the universe next door—"

"King Lear crossed with Vito Corleone," Morgan said.

"Precisely!"

Morgan picked up the ashtray from the coffee table, was about to
tap ash off his cigarette into it, but then absently put it down and
resumed pacing.

"No way he could've made this movie under studio control," Jolene
said, laughing, and Morgan looked over at her. "It would've scared the
shit out of the executives."

Alfred nodded. "She's right, you know. All that money, all that
agony, all those lawsuits, delays, and disasters—"

"Worth every damn penny," Morgan said.

I went over to the table and poured myself another double Scotch.
The movie had been a terrific hit with everyone in the cabin. Fine.
But now I was depressed, confused, upset, no longer certain how to
proceed. It was as though Lowell had pulled yet another practical joke.
Contrary to expectations, he had brought off his movie—but he didn't
want it back, so he was in fact self-destructing but on a wholly unexpected level. Lowell was a complex man and his was a complex prank.

Grinning, Morgan turned to me and said, "So, you want to tell us
what this is about? You know and I know Lowell doesn't have a worry
in the world about this film making back its cost."

"I'll drop you off tonight," I said, turning away from Morgan.

"What about our half million?"

"That was for going on TV and lying through your teeth. You *like*
the fucking film. What am I going to pay you for?"

"You pay us because that was the deal. You don't pay us, we don't
go on TV," Morgan said.

"Your loss. It's money in the bank for you guys to weigh in with the world's first review—and one you won't later look stupid retracting."

"We had a deal."

"Based on the film being shit," I said.

"A *deal*."

Alfred chimed in, "This is not honorable."

"Alfred, cut the crap."

Frowning, Morgan said, "This smells fishy. This whole heist business—something's very suspect."

"The hell are you sugg—"

"Do you expect me to believe Lowell's made a masterpiece but now negotiations are stalled because he'd rather collect the insurance? C'mon! Do I look stupid?"

"Hey. He doesn't want it back. Why? I don't know why. Because he's fucking nuts is why. Because he isn't playing with a full deck is why."

"Doesn't wash," Morgan said. "Whatever your scam, I want my share. Put us through—"

"*Your* share? You got to be joking."

"—put us through the inconvenience of kidnapping, shove guns in our faces. Now you think we're going to deliver ten million in free advertising? Forget it."

"No way am I going to pay you to tell the world the movie's a masterpiece when in fact it is. Shit, *I'll* go on TV," I said.

"What? You alone? Or the three of you in your Gunborga masks?"

"Hey. Maybe I should just rip your fucking eyeballs out, you can read films by Braille."

That stopped Morgan cold. Oh yes, this is the fellow who barged into my house brandishing a sawed-off Winchester Ranger pump-action.

But it was no longer Morgan and Alfred who concerned me. I had been operating on the assumption that Lowell knew what he was doing, which meant that I could pull strings, push buttons, work relay switches. But Lowell didn't know what he was doing, didn't know what he had done, probably didn't know the month on the calendar.

"Handcuff and blindfold them," I said. "I'm taking them home tonight."

"Okay," Wilbur said. "But—"

I slammed the door behind me. Ripped off my mask, brushed back my hair. Started jogging toward the mall. The sun was too bright, it was overilluminating everything, it was the sort of light that bleaches out shadows; even the dark pine forests seemed to throw off light. Spots swam before my eyes.

In the booth I fumbled for change, spilling nickels, dimes, quarters to the floor while I jammed the phone between my ear and shoulder. Finally, I got coins in and dialed the Bonny Doon Road estate. He answered.

"I just watched your movie, Doug. It's quite beautiful and moving."

"Righto."

Light and sporty, that *righto* told me everything. I cast around for something to say. "The $3.2-Million Heartbreak Sunset turned out pretty good."

"Just terrific. Like some teenage nut case took a tire iron to the lens." A pause followed. Then Lowell, his tone strangely conciliatory, said, "Can I tell you a secret?"

"Go ahead."

"I *made* the film. And for better or worse I know just what I did. That sunset—it's second-rate, the colors not heightened but exaggerated and overblown, like some Grand Canyon picture postcard where the whole thing's been touched up. One thing I try not to do is lie to myself."

I felt at a loss for words. In his movies Lowell had reached for the stars and, amazingly, light-years ahead of the scientists and the poets, found them. But now he didn't know what planet he was standing on. So without even thinking about it I said, "Well, I'm not going to be tedious. But seeing as how you don't want your movie back, we went and burned the negative."

There was a silence. Then Lowell, with unexpected gentleness, softly, almost kindly, said, "Send me the ashes," and hung up.

The Movie Mogul

C h a p t e r   2 8

"It does not matter that you don't have a green card," I explained slowly to Pedro González, who stood carefully listening—or maybe not too carefully listening—leaning on a garden hoe, chin resting lazily on its wooden handle. "In fact, that is the beauty of this. You will step forward at the risk of being thrown out of this great magnificent country. You will testify that you trailed me at my behest—"

"Excuse me, man. Your . . . ?"

I studied him. His beady peasant eyes seemed to be mocking me —or perhaps they were beady death-squad eyes. I have never gotten his lusty tropical genealogy straight. "Because I asked you to. You trailed me in your car up the coast. Then after I met the extortionist, you trailed him to a spot farther up the coast, where you secretly videotaped him meeting with his confederates. To divvy up the money."

"Sí, Señor Lowell. But can you—how you say?—repeat that?"

I pondered Pedro carefully for a minute. "No, I've a better idea. How would you like to take a little trip?"

—————— **249**

"Trip? Sure, man. Where to?"

"You taped their meeting, just as I've explained. But then when you got back here and gave me the videotape and resumed weeding outside the front gate . . . an INS agent drove up out of nowhere—some nosy neighbor's anonymous tip—and checked for your green card—"

"You mean I gotta get busted, man?" Pedro González, still leaning lazily on the garden hoe, studied me back, his eyes not nearly so lazy. In fact, a touch of sporting glimmered in them.

"Yes, but let me finish explaining. There's money involved, of course—"

"Money?"

"Good money."

"Okay, no problem, man. I been meaning to take a trip back home, say hello to the family."

"So Immigration ships you out, and by nightfall you'll be getting laid in Tijuana."

"*Sí*, Señor Lowell. I think I understand. But I am Guatemalan, not Mexi—"

"Details. So they'll ship you to Managua."

Pedro raised his chin off the hoe handle, laughed good-naturedly, then abruptly rested his chin back on the hoe handle and said levelly, "Then what happens, man?"

"You get lost in Guatemala and *stay* lost for a month. Buy some new clothes, have a cold beer, whatever. You're not into that *santería*, *changó* shit, are you, sprinkling human blood around? Good. Within a month everything should be worked out. Then you can call me—"

"I call you collect, okay?"

"—collect if you wish, and I will arrange to get you back into this country but this time with a green card, blue card, whatever color they're issuing this year. Senator Waters owes me one."

"*Gracias*, Señor Lowell. This will make my family very, very happy."

Señor González bowed and, hoe in hand, departed for the front gate. For a moment I kept my gaze on Pedro, the humble *campesino*, the tiller of the soil—*death-squad* soil, *graveyard* soil—then I headed back to my cottage, phoned in my anonymous tip to the INS, and crossed the woods to my office. I should've felt all pumped up, delighted. I should've felt as though I were moving in an air of profound composure. But Pedro, shady Pedro, somehow put a damper on my spirits. I couldn't *read* the little bastard.

I opened the door. Beth was on the phone. "No, I'm telling you, Deborah's boyfriend was a pompous ass *before* his screenplay got nominated. Yeah, we're at this dinner party . . . right. Just incredible. I thought John was going to slug him. You know John." Glancing up, she noticed me. "Leslie, let me call you back."

"Beth—"

"Doug, you look terrible."

"Could you—fix me a drink please?"

"Of course." Beth got up and bustled to the liquor cabinet, where, with terrific secretarial efficiency, she mixed bourbon with ice cubes. Today Beth wore a green silk miniskirt which clung to her buttocks with harrowing elegance, with heartbreaking profundity—but I would have to sit on the carnal impulses. It wouldn't do to have animal urges in light of the terrible tragedy that had just befallen me.

"Doug, what's the matter?" she asked concernedly, handing me the drink. I felt the personal tragedy of my stolen negative melting.

"Beth, I—I—don't know how to begin. I—I—"

"Breathe slowly. In . . . out. In . . . out. A few more times. Good. Now, take a deep breath and start at the beginning. It's okay."

"You must swear not to tell anyone—"

"Of course, Doug."

So I took a deep breath, paused dramatically, then launched into my tale of woe, relating how my negative had been stolen, and how I'd been fervently negotiating for its return, but then negotiations had collapsed, then resumed, but then the extortionists had tricked me, and I'd just learned they'd destroyed the negative, and so on, and so forth. . . .

Beth looked puzzled. "That's terrible, of course. But it's not a total wipeout. You still have tons of outtakes."

"The fire," I reminded her—perhaps too quickly, for her eyes momentarily said, *Gee, that's a fishy coincidence.* But then she just nodded and said, "I forgot."

"That's okay." I tried to look lost. "Beth, I have a few calls—"

"Would you like me to—"

"No, no, I think it's best I handle these."

"Of course. If you need anything . . ."

I retreated into the inner sanctum of my office. I picked up the phone and dialed KMUT in San Francisco. I identified myself and asked for Cindy Anderson. I had to wait five interminable minutes while they tracked her down—five long irreplaceable life-minutes during which they piped young Midori over the line: violin music to soothe the nerves of the impatient. It had just the opposite effect. Child prodigies get horribly on my nerves, the jump they have on everyone else, I want to boil them alive, commit sex crimes upon their tender young bodies, *I* wasn't a child prodigy. When Cindy finally came on I said, "Do you still have access to a national network?"

"Of course, Doug. We're an affiliate. What's up?"

"How would you like an exclusive?"

The Gangster

C h a p t e r   2 9

I left Morgan and Alfred bound, gagged, and blindfolded on a suburban Sacramento lawn at three in the morning. Then drove back up
into the mountains, pondering the enigma of Doug Lowell.

A confession. Something odd happened to me after seeing the
movie: I decided I liked Lowell. I felt more respect for him. I don't
mean because he had made a great movie. I mean because he had
made a great movie and didn't realize it. This moved me more than
I can explain. It also made me, oddly, root for him—for him to come
to his senses and pay us. For him to stop acting so nutty.

Nutty indeed! Whereas our heist plan had been the very model of
rationality. Who was I kidding? I was a rank amateur, a dilettante when
it came to this ransom business. The Calabrian gangsters from the Plain
of Gioia Tauro who had kidnapped Paul Getty, Jr., had the right idea.
Hack off an ear. Air-freight it to the family. Then use the money, as
they did, for something beneficial to society, like buying the trucks
necessary for establishing a transport monopoly in the construction of

a new industrial port in Calabria. Fuck the film. We should've snatched Lowell's wife, then sent him a simple note: "$3 million or we chop off a finger. Then an arm. Then you get a hatbox."

I arrived back at Tahoe before dawn. Entered the cabin quietly and went into the bathroom. The fluorescent light was on. Jolene stood there naked in the pale light, one foot up on the side of the bathtub, the other on the tiled floor, reaching with several fingers inside of herself to slip out her gooped-up diaphragm. She looked up, startled, but on the instant regained her composure. Crisp and very ladylike.

"I thought you'd stopped screwing Wilbur."

"I started again."

"You don't like what went down with Morgan and Alfred, you show your disappointment with a grudge-fuck?"

"Don't be self-centered."

"Why then?"

"I do have feelings for him."

"And me?"

She paused, bending the rubbery diaphragm between thumb and forefinger, studying me. Then said, "You know I like you, Frank. Way more than Wilbur."

"I'm not in the mood for playing revolving doors with the prof," I yelled. "I swear I—"

"*Shh.* You'll wake him. Frank, please. I promise, you're not going to play revolving doors with him. Let me—I have to straighten out a few things. Just give me a little time."

I nodded inanely.

She changed the subject (I went along). "You really think letting them go, not paying them off, was a good idea?"

"No way was I going to give them half a mil—"

"Maybe a quarter million. We could've compromised. We could'v—"

"Look. The bottom line is, Morgan and Alfred don't matter. Just so long as they say something publicly—*anything*—the insurance company will be alerted and Lowell will have to deal. Yeah, this isn't what we originally had in mind, but . . ."

She nodded. "You're the boss."

The Negative

I was in bed by 5:15 a.m., fast asleep by 5:16. The next thing I knew, someone was shaking me. "Guess who's on TV," Jolene said, not smiling.

◆ ◆ ◆

We sat on the sofa watching "America This Morning." The host was saying, "Earlier this week we reported the kidnapping of San Francisco movie critic Alfred Egert. Two days later his TV partner, Morgan Meany, also disappeared. Since then, no one has heard from either of them. Well, this morning we have the second bizarre movie-biz story of the week. We go now to Cindy Anderson at our affiliate in San Francisco."

Cindy Anderson in the KMUT studio. "With us is Doug Lowell, director and producer of the hits *The Black Pig* and *The High Plateau of Stars*, here to tell us about another, different kind of abduction."

I sat on the couch staring at the set. Weary and glum, Doug Lowell, America's distinguished guest of honor this morning, garbed in faded blue jeans, a torn sweatshirt, and a navy-blue windbreaker, sat beside Cindy Anderson, his fingers combing his matted beard. "The negative to my new movie, *The High Plateau of Stars, Part II*, was stolen earlier this week. A negative, I should explain, is what the prints for the movie theaters are struck from. No negative, no movie. This all happened six days ago. I—"

"Doug, did you notify anyone at the time? The authorities?"

"I couldn't," he said, struggling to keep his voice from cracking. "The people who stole it said they'd destroy it if I did. They demanded six million dollars in unmarked nonsequential ones and fives, an impossible task, really. Even major-league drug traffickers couldn't come up with that kind of cash on such short notice."

"So what happened?"

"I talked them down to three, then arranged a meet. Up the coast, at a motel on Highway 1, just south of Mendocino. I left the money in a motel room as instr—"

"*Three million dollars?*"

He nodded. "I was supposed to go back to the room an hour later and find my film. It wasn't there. They took my money and kept my film."

Cindy Anderson was quiet for a moment. Then: "Do you have any idea who—"

"The money means far less to me than the movie," Lowell went on, pulling distractedly on his beard. "In the last issue, all that really matters to me is my work. One can become too enthralled by the glamour, which I think is just illusionary. If you took everything I owned away from me, I would still find a way to make movies."

Wilbur said, "What a fraud."

"I don't know," said Jolene. "Even if he's lying about everything else, he sounds like he means that."

Jolene was right—and wrong. Doug Lowell looked emotionally violent, his pellucid blue eyes, so piercing, close to tears. Aesthetic grief resonated in the set and plunge of his face. The man seemed far gone, in the grip of a supernumerary sorrow. If I hadn't known better, I'd have thought he was for real.

"Doug," Cindy Anderson said, "where do you think the negative is right now?"

"You asked if I knew who was behind this. I didn't at first. But I had my trusted servant, Pedro González, trail me at a discreet distance. Pedro has a gift for blending in, an invisible man who can fade into the background. It worked. He staked out the motel and was able to follow the thief to where he rendezvoused with a co-conspirator. Pedro surreptiously shot a videotape of them talking."

Startled, Cindy Anderson looked at Lowell, then at someone off-camera. Full of surprises, Lowell had apparently neglected to impart this to her before showtime. "You have . . . a tape?"

"Right here," said Lowell, retrieving the videocassette from his windbreaker's deep pocket.

Confusion in the studio. Technicians and anxious executives needed to consult. The camera cut back to the studio in New York, where the morning anchorpeople smiled at the camera, then the show returned to San Francisco. If KMUT refused to show this mystery tape before vetting it with their libel lawyers, Mr. Lowell might take his wares to another station. Ratings won out. The tape went on:

A filtered view through branches. Tommy Mace and a woman in her late thirties standing along a misty windswept coastline.

Mace, opening a suitcase stuffed with cash: "Three million dollars and he doesn't even suspect us."

The woman: "God, Jay was right."

Mace: "The egotistical bastard is too self-centered to notice anything that *really* goes on around him."

The woman: "And the negative?"

Mace: "I burned it."

The woman, startled: "What?"

Mace: "Hell, I'm doing him a favor. It was rotten. Anyway, my performance was not of a piece with the first film."

The woman: "Oh, dear. . . ."

Mace: "As for your husband . . ." Whereupon Mace embraces the woman, planting his lips on her lips, though with less-than-convincing passion, perhaps even a touch of irritation—regardless of which she tries to prolong the infelicitous contact. But then he freezes. "What's that?" he asks, looking almost directly into the camera.

The woman: "It was just the wind, honey."

Waves of visual static washed over the screen. When it cleared we were back in the KMUT studio, where Cindy Anderson, puzzled and wary, sat alongside Doug Lowell.

Jolene, sitting on the edge of the couch, said, "Jesus."

Puffing on his pipe, Wilbur said, "Something was off about that little home movie."

"Yeah, something was off," Jolene snapped. "*We* stole the negative. *We* have it. Remember?"

"No, no. I mean visually. It *looks* wrong. Kind of artificial. Stagy."

"It *is* stagy."

On TV Cindy Anderson, faintly puzzled, was saying: "Doug, what would be Tommy Mace's motive for stealing the film?"

"One, I think he wanted to get the money that he feels, however wrongly, I owe him on the last picture. As everyone knows, his lawyers and my lawyers have been negotiating for some time. And two, my guess is he planned to destroy the negative, as he says there, because he was unhappy with his performance. Which, to be honest, I thought quite interesting."

"How does the completion company which bonded your movie feel about these developments?"

The question, unexpected, threw him for an instant. Feeling his way, he said, "Well, my lawyers should be speaking with them sometime soon, I mean, if they're not already. I would imagine they're—or will be—upset, too. This will cost them tens of millions."

"In retrospect, don't you feel you should have contacted the authorities soo—"

"Look. I took the extortionist's threats very seriously. I believed I was acting in my—and in the insurance company's—best interests. Kidnappers might think twice about murdering a hostage. I had no reason to believe these people would think twice about torching my movie."

Jolene said, "This is insane. He's not going to get away with this. Mace is going to throw everything he's got at him." She shivered. "I wonder how Lowell got him to make that film, though. He must really be stupid. Or vain, which amounts to the same thing."

I said nothing. I was curious what Lowell thought he was up to. From my vantage it appeared he had flipped long ago. So why be surprised by more circus insanity? The man took risks, he was committed to recklessness. Okay, we would work around it.

We finished breakfast while monitoring other morning news shows, all of which were blitzing the story. Such a peculiar crime. Tommy Mace's female accomplice was soon identified as Margot Fugle; it was speculated that "Jay"—or "J."—was her husband, Jerry Fugle, Lowell's trusted, or once-trusted, lieutenant. A top Constellation executive was glimpsed leaving his Bel Air mansion shielding his face with a copy of *Variety* from the banks of cameras. A spokeswoman for Tommy Mace said he was not available for comment but that Lowell's charges were absolutely groundless and we could expect a major lawsuit. And a grim spokesman for the Crown Completion Bond Company refused comment.

◆ ◆ ◆

We stayed in that day. Playing poker. Monitoring the news. Sending out for pizza.

Then toward four—

"What're you doing?"

"What's it look like?" I said to Jolene.

"Oh man, you're slicing out another strip of the negative. Why the f—"

"We can't call him anymore. Crown operatives will probably have tapped his phone, he won't be talking on it. But we have to let him know the film *hasn't* been burned. So he'll deal."

"The way things are going, maybe you should just hire a plane and skywrite it."

I left the motel and walked over to Harrah's. To confirm my suspicions I first called the Bonny Doon estate. No one answered, no message machine clicked on. I slipped the strip of negative into a Federal Express envelope. Enclosed a simple note:

> *I lied. I didn't burn the negative. The price is now three million. Instructions will follow in two days. If you don't deal, Crown will. They must be pretty pissed.*

C h a p t e r   3 0

When I got back to the Ponderosa Lodge Motel, Wilbur and Jolene were sitting on the sofa watching the six-o'clock news: Morgan and Alfred, red-eyed and unshaven, flanked anchorwoman Cindy Anderson.

"Tonight," she said, "we have yet another nationwide exclusive. With us live in the KMUT studio is our own movie-reviewing team, Morgan Meany and Alfred Egert, back after forty-eight hours in the hands of their kidnappers. In fact, to everyone's surprise and relief, they walked into the studio unannounced minutes ago. And they have a story to tell. Morgan and Alfred say they were abducted—abducted in order to look at that other abducted object, Doug Lowell's new movie, *The High Plateau of Stars, Part II*. That's quite a story, gentlemen," she said, turning now to them.

"Yes, Cindy."

"Just what happened during your ordeal? And I'm sure everyone would like to know what you thought of the movie."

Both critics looked grim. Alfred said, "Unfortunately, it is not our prerogative to comment on a film before it opens."

Morgan agreed. "Yes, that would be unprofessional."

"Well, who kidnapped you? Why did they want you to look at the film? We had Doug Lowell on earlier, and he's quite upset."

Alfred said, "The people who kidnapped us claimed they had stolen the negative from Mr. Lowell and would return it for a large sum of money, just as Mr. Lowell said earlier. But there the stories diverge. Our kidnappers claimed that Mr. Lowell, contrary to what he is saying, does not want his movie back."

The anchorwoman: "I'm sorry. Did you say—?"

Morgan: "We believe we have been the victims of an elaborate publicity stunt, an act of self-promotion engineered by Mr. Lowell himself—and we are not amused."

Alfred joined in: "No, it is not amusing to have a sawed-off shotgun stuck in your face."

The anchorwoman: "You mean to tell me you believe Mr. Lowell arranged to have both his film *and* the two of you kidnapped?"

Alfred: "Some people believe Mr. Lowell is a genius. Some people believe Mr. Lowell is mad. Cultural history shows that the area of overlap between the two is considerable. But what Morgan and I know for a fact is that when Doug Lowell goes on TV and tells some cockamamie story about his lead actor stealing his film, he is lying through his beard."

The anchorwoman: "How do you—?"

Alfred: "In a moment."

Morgan shouted, "The son of a bitch scared the wits out of us, and all to generate publicity for his film."

Taken aback by such ferocity, Cindy Anderson said, "These are serious charges—potentially slanderous. Can you substantiate them? The movie's been getting enough publicity as it is. I don't see what would be in it for him." She was doing a nice job of maintaining her composure. It was the second time in a day she'd gone on live without realizing what she was getting herself into.

Alfred: "We don't pretend to know what goes on inside Mr. Lowell's head. Maybe he thinks he made a bad movie and by letting us see it early under such bizarre circumstances we would feel seduced into praising it."

The anchorwoman: "Are you saying it's bad then?"

Morgan: "No. We're not saying it's good or bad. We're simply suggesting the scenario that Mr. Lowell, in his own craziness and paranoia, might have sketched out in his mind."

Wilbur muttered, "Those idiots. How could they come up with such garbage? Are they mad? Or just stupid?"

I shrugged. "They were frightened. Add to that Morgan's cocaine jitters, which fuel his own paranoia. This will, you know, work to our advantage. Lowell has a lot of explaining to do. He *needs* to get the negative back. With charges like these, there's no way the insurance company is going to pay him off—not in this fiscal year or the next."

A skeptical Cindy Anderson shook her head. "Do you really believe he was behind your kidnapping?"

"Listen," Morgan said, tapping out a cigarette. He pulled a rolled-up copy of *Film Comment* from his inside jacket pocket. "Let me read you something Mr. Lowell said four years ago, after the box-office success of the first *High Plateau of Stars*. That film, I remind you, was studio financed. He was rich from *The Black Pig*, but, if you know what I mean, he wasn't *really* rich yet. I quote: 'Constellation wanted to take *High Plateau* away from me when I refused to trim it to a hundred and ten minutes. I insisted that my hundred-and-forty-minute cut be released. Contractually I did not have the right to final cut. But

morally, aesthetically, I did. They wouldn't even test-preview it. So
what I did was, I took the negative and told them that if they didn't at
least show my cut to a few preview audiences, something bad might
happen. Like the negative might disappear.'

" 'Question: You threatened Constellation with the theft of your
own negative if they didn't approve your cut?'

" 'Doug Lowell: No, no, no. Please don't misunderstand me. I
never threatened to steal it. All I said was, who knows, it might disappear. [Laughter] As it turned out, they sneak-previewed it in Pittsburgh,
Seattle, and Cincinnati, and audience reaction was overwhelming. The
studio went with my cut, and the rest is history. So in a sense I saved
the studio from itself.' "

Here Morgan laid the magazine down and looked at the anchorwoman. "What do *you* think?"

"To be honest, I don't know."

How interesting. All this talk of contracts and aesthetics and the
higher morality of the artist. I didn't remember reading that particular
interview, but then I had read and skimmed a surfeit of materials during
my several days in the University of California library. "Say, Wilbur.
How'd you get the idea to do this? It just 'came to you'?"

Wilbur turned to Jolene for help, but she was looking at the TV.
Slowly, Wilbur shook his head. "Frank, I swear I have no recollection
of that interview."

I stared at Wilbur, but then decided there would be no profit in
sitting on him. I turned back to the TV.

Cindy Anderson asked, "Who held you hostage?"

"Two men, one woman," Morgan said. "They all wore rubber
Tommy Mace *High Plateau* masks, the kind kids buy for Halloween.
One man was rather overweight, the second man had an average build,
and the woman was slender, mid-thirties."

"Mid-*twenties*," Jolene muttered.

Cindy Anderson saw a chance for comic relief and took it. "So it
could've been Tommy Mace after all hiding behind the Tommy Mace
mask?"

"Sure. It could've been Tommy Mace. It could've been Joseph
Goebbels."

She said briskly, "Doug Lowell claims the people who stole the negative contacted him about setting up an exchange up the coast in Mendocino. Do you have any idea where you were held?"

"Well, we were blindfolded and rode in a car for four or five hours," Morgan said. He crossed his legs. Took out a matchbook to light his cigarette. Taking his time. Drawing out the suspense. Enjoying himself immensely. Morgan arched his head back and blew a couple of smoke rings. "It probably wasn't Mendocino, though." The critic fished something out of his jacket pocket. "I took this from the room we were held in. A memento." Smirking, Morgan held up an ashtray. The camera zoomed in. Its logo read:

PONDEROSA LODGE MOTEL
SOUTH LAKE TAHOE

C h a p t e r 3 1

Wipe our prints—*thirty seconds*—throw together our belongings—*another thirty*—hell, the editing table—*fuck it*—out the door, into the Porsche and van—*twenty*—then clear the motel—*twenty more*—

"An ashtray!" I yelled, pounding the steering wheel.

"Just be glad those prima donnas played it for the ratings rather than go straight to the cops," Jolene said.

"Unbefuckinglievable. I want to drive straight to San Francisco—"

"Frank 'Grace-Under-Pressure' Furio."

"—rip out their wiring."

"Hey, Frank. You gonna be okay?"

"Me? Sure. Never been better."

Jolene and I drove up a deserted mountain road, Wilbur following in the van. Then I got behind the wheel of the van and bumped along on a fire trail a hundred yards into the forest, leaving the trail to nose the van deep into bushes. We camouflaged its rear with branches, then walked back out to the road.

In silence we drove to Harrah's. Farcical fugitive days. Jolene went to the hotel's front desk and got a one-bedroom suite on the tenth floor, Wilbur followed her up in a separate elevator, and I found a phone booth.

"Hullo?" A bit slurred.

"Wally, listen carefully. Report your van as stolen from a BART lot. You left it there three d—"

"Frankie, you're having fun after all. What happ—"

"Wally, I love you but I have no time for this. Now listen. You left it in the lot three days ago—you can make up a reason why—and only went back today. Repeat what I just said."

He sobered up and did so.

"You might get grilled. Stick to your story. Under no circumstances mention my name. You'll get five thousand for this."

"Just like the old days, hey Frankie," he said softly.

"Just like the old days," I said and hung up.

◆ ◆ ◆

That evening we gathered around the TV in our suite, sipping Scotch as we watched the news.

A spokesman for the FBI: "Morgan Meany and Alfred Egert should not have gone to the media first. It allowed the culprits to get away, could prejudice the prosecution, and will make it harder to catch this gang. But what do they care?"

A spokesman for Crown: "We plan, of course, to investigate this thoroughly before reaching any conclusions. And we reiterate our long-standing commitment to the movie industry. We have been insuring movies for decades, and if this turns out to be a legitimate claim, we will pay."

The president of KMUT: "This station apologizes to Doug Lowell for allowing its movie reviewers to go live on the air and suggest he might have organized their kidnapping when in fact there was no evidence. We were not aware before air time what they were going to say, and had we been we would never have allowed it. We at KMUT let our usual high professional standards lapse. We regret this."

Then the station cut from its San Francisco studio to Cindy Anderson standing in front of the Ponderosa Lodge Motel.

"Jesus," Jolene said, "they must've helicoptered her up."

Cindy Anderson, holding a microphone: "FBI agents have been interviewing motel guests and employees to get descriptions of the kidnappers. In the cabin that they rented, agents have found an editing table whose origins the FBI is now trying to trace. The kidnappers kept a generally low profile, but nonetheless there is a new, potentially very disturbing development. According to guests and employees, one of the men possibly involved bears a striking resemblance to the man widely known as the Convenience Store Killer."

Wilbur shook his head. "Great. The maid comes in to clean, she'll shoot me on sight."

"Just leave the Do Not Disturb sign on the doorknob," I said. "You'll be fine."

"Yes indeed," Jolene said. "Things are finally starting to break our way."

Lowell wasn't faring too well himself. Another station warned viewers that what they were about to see was violent and parental discretion was advised. They then showed old surveillance footage of the Convenience Store Killer making a clerk lie facedown on the floor in a 7-Eleven somewhere in North Dakota. Whereupon he put a .38 Special to the clerk's head and fired point-blank. Then the station played footage from Lowell's first movie, the R-rated *The Black Pig*, which showed a character firing point-blank into an innocent bystander's head. Such parallelism required no comment. It reminded people that Doug Lowell had another, darker side. It reminded people that before he had made the PG-13 classic *The High Plateau of Stars*, he had directed a far more unsettling movie that fewer people had seen.

Doug Lowell appeared finally on TV, drawn and haggard, combing fingers through his beard. "What Morgan Meany, Alfred Egert, and KMUT have engaged in is character assassination, pure and simple.

For that matter, when I want private critical feedback, I turn to my own people. I mean no disrespect, but I don't need those two. The idea that I'd steal my own negative is sheer nonsense."

A montage followed of suburban parents, interviewed in shopping malls across America, voicing outrage and vowing not to let their children see *High Plateau II* even if it were eventually released. Why, what sort of monster would recruit a serial killer to steal his own movie? The youth in the 7-Eleven reaffirmed that the Convenience Store Killer was working in tandem with others. The young woman who match-cut the negative was interviewed in her South of Market studio, saying yes, in retrospect one of the men did somewhat resemble the killer though he was apparently wearing a blond wig, while his accomplice actually had the gall to ask for her phone number.

"You tried hitting on her?" Jolene said.

"Oh, c'mon."

The language of litigation was in ascendancy. Plaintiffs and defendants everywhere. Lowell said he would sue Alfred, Morgan, and KMUT for defamation of character and interfering with his ability to earn a living. Morgan and Alfred responded that they would sue Lowell for kidnapping them and threatening their civil liberties. KMUT stood by its legal retraction and said it was considering suing its own film critics for criminal negligence and endangering the station's FCC license. Lowell threatened to sue Crown if it failed to live up to its contractual obligations, and Crown responded that it might yet sue Lowell for conspiring to defraud them. A chain of theater exhibitors threatened to sue both Lowell and Constellation for failing to meet their contractual obligations and deliver the movie on time, thereby leaving a gaping hole in their summer programming. Many multiplexes had booked the movie for two and even three screens. And Constellation announced it would sue Lowell for failing to deliver the movie on time. Of course, Lowell said he would sue Tommy Mace, his former employee Jerry Fugle, and Fugle's wife for stealing the negative, while separate lawyers for Mace and the Fugles said they'd be suing Lowell.

Sitting back on the sofa, watching the drama unfold dreamily on TV, I was starting to suspect that even if Lowell got the negative back he would find himself tangled up in lawsuits from now until the middle of the twenty-first century. And invited to fewer dinner parties. A New York anchorwoman asked a spokesman for the President if it was true that Doug Lowell was supposed to attend an arts reception at the White House in several weeks. The spokesman said Mr. Lowell was not on the guest list.

At the end of the eleven-o'clock news, Cindy Anderson weighed in live from Tahoe with an update: police were trying to track down Mr. Lowell's employee Pedro González, the man who had allegedly shot the incriminating videotape, but apparently the INS had packed him off to Guatemala the day before.

Finally, in San Francisco the U.S. Attorney announced he was convening a grand jury to consider charges against Lowell of grand felony theft, embezzlement, conspiracy to defraud, kidnapping, and more.

◆ ◆ ◆

We stared rapt at the TV, at the screen where life seemed to be unfolding independently of us, at the plastic box with its walnut-vinyl finish and its simulated chrome trim, radiating noise and light like some maniacal cosmic force. We still held the negative, but the story seemed to have passed from us. It was as though the screen were a window and we were on the outside looking in, nails scrabbling on glass. When I'd first gotten involved in the theft, the making of *High Plateau II* had been a back-page media event, not hard news—just your regulation saga of artistic madness and profligate spending recorded in the gossip columns, Sunday entertainment sections, and film magazines. Grand crank stuff. Public interest from certain sectors was deep but not broad, and that interest had developed gradually, not snowballed.

But now! And to be the unacknowledged catalyst for all this public brouhaha, all this noise and clamor—it made me feel oddly disembodied, unsubstantial, like a ghost. It made me feel sleepy.

◆ ◆ ◆

The sun beats down mercilessly. A high barbed-wire fence, broken at hundred-foot intervals by watchtowers, surrounds the exercise yard. Doug Lowell, Wilbur Blackfield, and I clank across the hot concrete. In addition to zebra-striped uniforms, we wear ankle and wrist manacles linked by chains. Lowell, oddly, also hefts a camera. The KMUT anchorwoman Cindy Anderson, smartly dressed in civvies, dogs our awkward steps with a mike, saying, "Mr. Lowell, is it true that your next movie will be one of those Andy Warhol–like experimental things shot in real time—Frankie, Wilbur, and Doug Do Twenty? Is it so?"

◆ ◆ ◆

I woke alone on the couch, soaked with sweat and trembling. The clock read five a.m. I dressed, left a note on the coffee table saying I couldn't sleep, then descended in the elevator to casino-hell.

I lost at blackjack. I lost at craps. I lost at roulette. I lost at slot machines. Cocktail waitresses in black décolletage and fishnet stockings kept bringing me more to drink. I continued to lose. I had thought that God, that gag writer, might let me win a million. But God's sense of humor wasn't running in that direction. At six I headed over to the Rendezvous Lounge, a darkened bar away from the floor action. Weary and frazzled, I sat on a stool and ordered a Bloody Mary. The TV above the bar was tuned to the ubiquitous news. The stolen negative, the serial killer. Someone slid onto the stool next to mine, obscuring my view of the screen. I tried to look around him. The guy shifted. I leaned far to the right. Oblivious, the guy shifted again.

"Do you min—" but then I checked myself. "Wilb—" but then I checked myself again. Something distinctly Not-Wilbur came off my neighbor. I took a better look at the fellow, who hadn't even glanced up. He possessed the same large hulking frame as Wilbur, the same half-cunning piggy eyes, the same sloping Cro-Magnon posture, and the same disheveled way of dressing.

I finished my drink. I signaled for my check. Farther down the bar I recognized a reporter from Channel 5. Some guy who'd won prizes for his investigative reporting. Right now he was busy watching TV and stirring an olive around in his martini. I casually got up, went to the lobby where the phone booths were, and put in some change.

First I dialed the Nevada State Police. Said, "The Convenience Store Killer. The Rendezvous Lounge in Harrah's, Tahoe." I hung up, moved to the next booth. Called the California State Police and repeated my message. Then moved to a third booth and called the FBI in Reno, reported the same.

I went back onto the casino floor and positioned myself at a twenty-five-cent slot machine that afforded a view of the Rendezvous Lounge. He was still there, drinking in the dark, hunched over his beer, perhaps brooding about his dark history. Keeping an eye on him, I steadily fed the machine quarters. After ten minutes he finished his drink and left the darkness of the bar to head out across the casino floor. I monitored his movements while continuing to work the lever on the slot machine.

No one looked up at him. No one gave him a second glance. No one noticed that a mass murderer walked among them. They were too busy throwing money away. Isn't this country something else? He was heading toward the doors that exit onto the parking lot on the Californian side of the border. I didn't want him to get away; if he was captured, the confusion with Wilbur would be cleared up and the feds would be back in the dark. I started to walk toward—BRRRRRRRRRRRRRRRRRRING! CLANG-A-LANG-A-LANG! CLANG-A-LANG-A-LANG! DING-DING-BRRRRRRRR-RRRRRRRRRING! Behind me the one-armed bandit lit up like a Christmas tree and started ringing like all the fires in the world. I looked at it dumbfounded. Four cherries lined up in a row! Two hundred dollars. Two hundred miserable fucking dollars. Quarters cascaded down, they clanged jangled crashed into the tin gutter. I was trapped. Gamblers at the neighboring machines, absorbed in their own play, glanced at me. I couldn't walk away while all that money clattered out. I grinned helplessly as the serial killer, *my* serial killer, the object of a regional manhunt, passed like a ghost out of the casino and into the California dawn.

◆ ◆ ◆

I grabbed two cardboard containers from an adjacent shelf and frantically shoveled my winnings into them. Then I hurried across the floor, threading my way between gamblers until, my heart thumping crazily, I reached the glass doors—

Out in the parking lot a crowd had gathered. Young, old, male, female, from all over the western states. The Convenience Store Killer stood in the center, shoulders hunched, hands cuffed behind his back. He looked nervous. What was the poor imbecile thinking about? The grandmother he had killed back on the Idaho farm when he was thirteen?

"I don't wanna *hear* it. I don't give a damn if he *was* in the casino. We grabbed him in the lot, and the lot's in California—"

"Hey, we were chasing the guy. Which is the only reason he ran into you."

A jurisdictional dispute. A California State Trooper and a Nevada State Trooper. It was interrupted by a middle-aged fellow in a gray pinstriped suit with a holster bulge under one arm who said, "Gentlemen, may I speak with you a moment?" Both troopers stopped to stare at him with undisguised hostility. The suit flipped open his wallet. "Agent Pete Hanlon, Federal Bureau of Inv—"

"Oh man. He's my catch and—"

"Yeah, butt out. It's enough I gotta deal with this asshole."

The FBI agent was civil. He tried to persuade them that because of the wide-ranging nature of this case, state lines and all that, the federal government would be better equipped to mount a strong prosecution, but that they would all share in the glory. The troopers listened dubiously; they had heard this before.

Then a fourth man joined the fray, wearing Gucci loafers and a pale-blue Armani suit—the kind that frankly would be frowned upon in the FBI. He took out a card, and the three law-enforcement agents leaned forward as one to inspect it.

"Private investigator John O'Connor. I'm working for Crown Completion Bond Company."

"So?"

"I have reason to believe," he said, "that this man is in possession of, or has knowledge of the location of, the movie negative for *The*

High Plateau of Stars, Part II." A gasp went up from the crowd. "You read the papers. You may have heard—"

"Hey, mister. Gimme a break. I'm more concerned that this guy's a killer than that he filched some movie negative or something."

"He did not 'filch some movie negative or something,' " the man in the expensive suit said, putting brass in his voice. "He stole a very special negative, a negative that is worth, to the people I work for, approximately sixty million dollars. Do you understand? Sixty million goddamn dollars. If you don't mind, I would like to talk to this—"

"Hey, mister, did you hear? I don't care he stole a hundred million. He's killed at least seven people. You take a number, get on the end of a long line you wanna talk to this guy—"

"All right, all right. He's killed seven people, whatever. I feel very bad for those seven people. Very sorry. But what's done is done. Those people—they're history. I don't mean to sound callous but you're not gonna bring 'em back. The negative on the other hand—"

"Hey," said the FBI man. "Didn't you use to work in the FBI's Denver office?"

O'Connor eyed Hanlon more closely. "Yeah. Do I know you?"

"I had a temporary assignment there once. Under Bill Ryan."

"No kidding? I knew Bill. Every first Friday of the month we'd get together, have a few drinks in the Brown Palace, shoot the shit."

"Yeah. Hey, you look like you've done well on your own."

"Well, I can't complain. It beats working for the feds. What a bunch of nickel-and-dime cheapskates. Listen, you ever want a recommendation for the private sector, I'm your man. Any friend of Bill Ryan is a friend of mine."

The FBI man made an exception and invited the private investigator to join him and the two state troopers in questioning the suspect, who had been standing idly by, gazing empty-eyed at the snowcapped mountains. They took the handcuffed killer back into Harrah's. The crowd followed but dispersed in the casino as the show went private in the security room. I had two hundred dollars' worth of quarters to blow, so I positioned myself at a slot machine near the security-room door. Soon I noticed TV crews crowded outside the glass doorways to the casino. Cameras weren't allowed inside—which was just as well. An hour later when the suspect emerged, cordoned off by FBI agents and state troopers, he had the beginnings of a black eye and had one arm in a sling. The Nevada state trooper said, "The suspect sustained injuries in the course of resisting arrest."

◆ ◆ ◆

A press conference convened at noon, just outside Harrah's, in the parking lot on the state line, to symbolize interdepartmental cooperation. The California and Nevada state troopers and the private investigator flanked the FBI man. A festive crowd of several hundred gamblers and vacationers had gathered, and reporters from all over California swelled the front ranks. The lot had filled with equipment vans, each bearing a television station's logo.

The FBI man said, "Okay, folks. We're going to keep this pretty informal. My name's Pete Hanlon, and I'm a special agent with the Federal Bureau of Investigation. At 6:33 this morning in Harrah's parking lot on the Californian side of the border the man tentatively identified as Henry Starkman, no known address or place of employment, was arrested for the murders of seven people in convenience stores across the nation. He has confessed to these crimes as well as to an additional two murders not previously linked to him. We'll do our best to answer your questions. Okay. Let's start with you."

A reporter asked, "Have you recovered the negative for *The High Plateau of Stars, Part II?*"

Excitement rippled through the crowd. The FBI spokesman held up both hands and shouted, "Ladies, gentlemen—please. We don't even know that this man is connected to the theft. We *are* sure he is the man sought in connection with the murders."

Insistent voices drowned him out. *"Is Doug Lowell involved in this?" "Has the negative really been destroyed?" "When did Mr. Lowell and Mr. Starkman first meet?"*

A serial killer? Old hat, yesterday's news. A $67-million movie negative? Now there's a crinkle.

The private investigator in the Armani suit and Gucci loafers spoke up: "So far, Mr. Starkman hasn't confessed to the theft of the negative. But I assure you he will."

KMUT anchorwoman Cindy Anderson said, "But he's already confessed to nine murders, including two not previously attributed to him. Why would he hold out on stealing the negative unless he wasn't involved?"

"Hey, lady, I'm no psychiatrist," O'Connor snapped. "I don't understand how the psychopathic mind works."

◆ ◆ ◆

We sat in front of the TV watching the evening news. With pizza and beer. Everyone leaning forward.

The anchorman asked, "Mr. Lowell, what is your reaction to the arrest of the notorious Convenience Store Killer?"

A weary Doug Lowell said, "It doesn't surprise me that he would confess to nine murders but not to stealing my movie. The reason is simple. He had nothing to do with it. The accusation that I would hire a murderer to hijack my own negative is not only groundless and base, but too preposterous for words."

I glanced at Wilbur. He looked worried. "Relax," I said. "It's over. People will no longer be gunning for a guy who kind of resembles you."

Staring at the TV, Wilbur nodded. But he didn't seem completely convinced.

For that matter, Lowell himself did not seem especially relieved by the arrest. A new glumness sat on his shoulders, he seemed to have drawn deeper into himself. Which might have had something to do with yet another development, reported earlier that evening.

On a six-o'clock newscast out of New York the reporter had said, "We have with us tonight live via satellite hookup from Zaire an exclusive interview with Mike Peterson, one of Hollywood's most highly regarded cameramen. It took some effort to track down Mike, who is on location shooting a film in Africa. Mike has twice been nominated for the Academy Award, and he has shot, among other films, all three of Doug Lowell's movies, *The Black Pig, The High Plateau of Stars,* and *The High Plateau of Stars, Part II."*

A cut-in to Africa followed as Mike Peterson appeared on a TV monitor in the studio. The anchorman, in the foreground, turned to look at the monitor. Unfamiliar trees and vegetation filled the screen behind Mike Peterson. A giraffe wandered into the frame and munched lazily on the top of a tree. The anchorman said, "Mike, what can you tell us about that videotape Doug Lowell claims shows the people who stole his negative conferring on the Mendocino coast?"

The studio-monitor image of Mike Peterson expanded to fill the whole TV screen. Doug Lowell's cameraman said easily, "It's a fake, Tom."

"How do you know this?"

"I'm a cameraman. I work in light and shadows. The sun is my principal lighting unit." The image of Mike Peterson was replaced by the now-infamous Mendocino videotape, which every station in the nation had been playing over and over all day long. In voice-over Mike said, "It's my job to be able to calculate the elevation of the sun from the length of the shadows on the ground, and I can tell you that in this movie people's shadows fall at four o'clock, tree shadows fall at seven. Also, the sun is coming in from the south, as in winter. At this time of the year, as we approach June and the longest days, the sun should be falling from the north. Moreover—and this is really elemental stuff—the fog is blowing in one direction, the tops of the cypresses in another."

"You're sure of all this?" the anchorman asked.

"Oh, absolutely. Positively. Also, if you look really closely you will notice that the background is not quite as sharp, not quite as crisp, as the figures of Tommy and Margot in the foreground. This is because the background is front-projection footage and hence a generation older than the live-action shot of Tommy and Margot."

The TV showed Mike Peterson again. Behind him an elephant galloped through the underbrush from left to right. In voice-over the anchorman said, "Let me get this straight, Mike. Are you saying this is a trick film?"

"Without question, yes."

"Do you—do you know this for an absolute certainty?"

"Yes. *I* shot the 35-millimeter footage—minus the people. It's an outtake from Doug's first movie, *The Black Pig.*"

The anchorman, pensive, brows furrowed, allowed a second for this to sink in. Then leaned forward and confidentially asked, "How could a man as talented, as savvy, as knowledgeable about film as Doug Lowell, a man who has pioneered so many special effects, a man who has always been praised for his visual craft—how could he have made such a blunder as to think this wouldn't be found out?"

Mike Peterson shook his head and smiled wistfully. "People have it," he said, "and people lose it."

C h a p t e r 3 2

People have it and people lose it. People have *it* and people lose *it*. People *have* it and people *lose* it. *People* have it and *people* lose it. People have it *and* people lose it. *People have it and people lose it.*

I left the TV on and wandered out of my cottage into the woods. Why was Mike Peterson turning against me like this, with such viciousness, such vindictiveness, such petty small-minded infuriation? Where did all this pent-up resentment and hostility come from? Hadn't I always treated him fairly? Of course, somebody with as expert an eye as Mike Peterson would have picked up on the minor flaws—extremely minor flaws, inconspicuous, if you will—flaws that would have been below the threshold of perception of most anybody else, lesser camera operators included. After all, Mike's vision is so keen, so sharp, so fast, he can follow light bowing through the air as it traces the curvature of the earth. So what if the mist blew one way, the treetops the other? So what if people's shadows fell at four o'clock, tree shadows at seven o'clock? This was nitpicking.

I felt angry. Mike could at least have exposed the fraud while praising me for the artful job I had done—if, indeed, fraud is what one wishes to call an artful hoax perpetrated for the higher good—that is, to secure the money necessary to remake my film. But no. He didn't think to do that. On the contrary. He had chosen *of his own free will* to mock me, to belittle me, to heap public scorn and ridicule on my head, to taunt and to twit me, to suggest that my little home movie was the work of a rank amateur rather than of a world-class artist, that it was the sleight of hand of a Reno cardsharp, an imposter, a mountebank, rather than of a consummate film director, a visual poet.

Yes, I was irritated that Mike Peterson had not even bothered to say, "Good work, old boy, but you can't pull the wool over *my* eyes." Hurt that he had instead chosen to jeer me *on national television*, pouring out his vituperative scorn. I am not a vindictive man, but Mike Peterson was finished, history, all washed up, kaput.

Yet maybe my little home movie was a touch off. Maybe it wasn't up to my usual standards. After all, I felt *High Plateau II* had missed the mark. And the truth is, I would never have contrived in the first place, when first setting out, to make movies if I had thought of myself as just merely talented, simply clever, as are most of my fellow filmmakers. Nor do I say this egotistically. Because in a very real sense I envy my fellow filmmakers. I *admire* them. For I find nothing more intolerable, more capable of filling me with self-loathing and disgust, than producing a work of art that is anything less than great. But they don't, it doesn't bother them a bit, not at all. They are able to go blithely about the business of producing "buddy pictures" and "romantic comedies" and "crime procedurals," moving from one job to the next as easily as a traveling salesman moves from doorbell to doorbell. I *envy* them.

I emerged from the woods and went into my office. Beth hadn't gone home yet; she sat glumly watching the news.

"Not good, Doug," she said. "Not good at all."

I watched. Apparently Mike had thrown open the floodgates, for my precious little Mendocino videotape had become the butt of jokes by film critics, *film barbarians*, from all over the country; they didn't have my new movie to practice their art, their *non-art*, of criticism upon, so they were practicing their *non-art* upon my Mendocino video, and relishing the task with gusto, too. Critics are such cretins, they wouldn't dare criticize Mike; after all, he is the professional, the technician-artist, the one whose *scientific* explanations of what was wrong with my videotape were irrefutable, beyond aesthetic dispute. So now I had to bear the indignity of a montage of film critics saying, "This home video is so miscalculated, it makes one cringe." Saying, "How could Doug Lowell of all people make such a technically shoddy film?" Saying, "A jejune little spectacle." Saying, "It's not even an entertaining fraud."

"Would you like a drink, Doug?"

I nodded. Kindly Beth wasn't even pretending to believe my videotape was genuine, that I was right and the world wrong, she was simply saying nothing, no longer taking sides. Fair enough. I recognized defeat. I *accepted* defeat. It was all collapsing. Moreover, the gang that had abducted my negative had burned it. I had nothing left, nothing to negotiate, nothing to straighten out. I was finished. Kaput. I felt as though I had become the villain of some internationally financed epic.

"Doug, look. They caught the Convenience Store Killer up in Tahoe. The guy they say might've been mixed up in the theft."

I hadn't even paid attention to *that* media sideshow. "Beth, hon. I have more serious matt—"

I stopped. The TV showed the so-called Convenience Store Killer, now identified as one Mr. Henry Starkman—a real sad sack—stepping into a police van against a sunny backdrop of the sparkling Sierra Nevada. It was the first time I had seen him.

And instantly I knew he had nothing to do with the theft of my negative.

Because as I stared at the killer's picture on TV I felt a queasy sense of recognition. For even as I stared, a second person began to peep out from behind the hunched, nervous, handcuffed wreck of the first—to peep out, see that the coast was clear, then start to reproduce himself from the killer, molecule by molecule, limb by limb, until finally, his project completed, he stepped forth and split off from the flesh and blood of the first, like a glimmery movie ghost stepping forth from the real, corporeal person; and this second person, this lustrous double, this ghost image, this astral projection, this specter, this phantom, this—this—this *wraith* was far more familiar to me than the first person.

Yes, I saw my old friend Wilbur Blackfield.

Part Four

The Movie Mogul

C h a p t e r   *3 3*

I sat slumped in the aluminum lawn chair at the pool's edge, macerating in the drizzle, sipping bourbon from a tumbler, watching the rain beat gently against the bottom of the pool. Several days earlier people from the Monterey Aquarium had come at my request to remove my pet dolphin who, though I loved, I felt was in for bad times if he stuck around with me. Then, at dusk, I had sat watching the pool drain.

But now, watching the rain, I was having second thoughts. Nothing seems bleaker than a pool standing empty in the rain, with its melancholy off-season patina, its sides cracked and peeling. Yet even decay has its beauty. Weathered, faded beige tiling runs in a band around the top of the pool. Beneath that, a grayish-aquamarine water line runs, fading to rusty mauve, shot with striations of rusty ecru. And these subtle shifts and gradations of coloration, these varied tonalities of blues and greens, already extraordinary in the sunlight, change and deepen even more in the rain, achieving a kind of somber poetry.

I could of course repaint it, refill it with water, and then—secret dream in which I take refuge—turn my estate into a campground and myself into its anonymous keeper, the man who gets up before dawn and, armed with a butterfly net, scoops leaves and twigs off the pool's surface in the first delicate light before the campers awaken. But, for now, even decay has its charm.

The frozen passions, the calcified dreams! How I got here, how they stayed there. Old friends—failed poets, broken novelists, unemployed actors—would in years past cry to me; cry unbearably that I do not understand paralysis of the spirit, prostration of the artistic will; that I have had it easy; that the motor of my talent was like a powerful locomotive, while they have had to struggle ferociously every inch of the way for the tiniest victories. And I used to reply that I *do* understand, but that—immodest as this may sound—it is just that my paralysis exists on a higher level, a more complicated but just as bleak plateau; and that if I appeared to them, to the world, to be a fantastically successful moviemaker, in truth I did not experience myself as half as successful as I appeared; that in the darkest, most secretive recesses of my heart I felt like a fraud. Yes, I know my subtle failings, I am aware of the precise locations in my movies where I turned coward and substituted technique for substance, where I was too frightened to push harder, to explore deeper, that I do not feel on the inside the way I project myself to the outside.

But such explanations do no good. They do *no good*. For the poets we love and respect and *pity*. We can afford to. For no matter how great, how inspired, how *mad*, they still count as nothing, as failures, marginal figures of no consequence, children lost in the vast mercantile jungle of American capitalism, a couple of kids trying to find their way in the dark dangerous forest with wolves and witches everywhere. But mad moviemakers! What a glory of a different fit. Artists who *score*. Artists who can hold their own with the best of American dealmakers. For a filmmaker, finally, is a poet who understands technology, who has married technology to poetry, who has a feel for the dramatic interplay of light and dark, of sound and silence—but who also understands human beings, with all their frailties, imbecilities, and fears. And so, one by one, by the *bushel*, the old friends dropped away—

envious of me, jealous of me, and deeply, profoundly *frightened* of me. They did not understand just how profoundly I frighten myself.

The impossible longing for just one true image—

The rain was starting to come down harder. I watched a leaf float on rivulets of rainwater, float this way, then that, in fits and starts, in slow motion, in zigzags . . . yet basically in one direction, following the slope from the shallow end of the pool down to the deeper end, whose ulcerated patina was looking more and more heartbreaking.

Wilbur Wilbur Wilbur. *Why?* Slumped in my rusting lawn chair, feeling increasingly wet and forlorn, I toyed with the foot-long strip of celluloid in my hands—a foot from the negative that had, after all, *not* been burned. It had arrived this drizzly morning by Federal Express. So—I was back in business. I was still alive, still in the running, though God help me I'm not sure whether that pleases me or not. But at least I had to credit Wilbur and his cohort. They had flushed me out. Moreover, they had cut the foot of film from the end of a shot, where a dozen or so frames would be just a blink in the moviegoer's eye. In fact I could probably even reattach the thing if I didn't let the rain ruin it.

When Wilbur and I had first met at USC, we had hit it off right away. We loved going to the movies together and almost always had the same take on a film. In those days we'd smoke some grass together or drop some acid, then catch a triple bill of horror flicks or spaghetti Westerns at the local grind house. Ah! We felt marvelously alive and in synch back then.

But today! Today his presence infuriates me. What a bilgebag he has become. What a sad sack. What a sad, sad sack of sad, sad bilge. Even back then Wilbur was mad, half-baked, and full of half-marvelous ideas. But he hadn't yet become sad. And we took a vow—a vow that the more successful one of us would always help the less successful one, would serve as his brother's keeper. Some vow. Even now, when I recall the two of us sitting in the luncheonette over ice-cream sodas, almost religiously intoning that vow, I seem to remember that in fact the vow was *his* idea; and that even as I was being tricked into swearing on our friendship, on our love of cinema, on our eyesight—*our eyesight!*—I remember that I was thinking, I am somehow, in the years to come, going to get the raw end of this deal. Yes, that is what I was thinking even as Wilbur, *fifteen years ago*, upon cementing our deal, upon *nailing the coffin shut*, leaned over and proceeded to suck up through his straw, in one preposterous slurp, the last of his strawberry ice-cream soda. *Belch.* His piggy eyes twinkled craftily as he pushed the soda glass away and wiped his sticky mouth with his shirtsleeve.

Wilbur was brilliant. He'd sit before the VCR for hours, *for days*, watching the same movie over and over again, and each time he would find something new in it to elaborate upon. "Did you see the way he used grays for contrast in that cut?" "Did you catch that long, seemingly impossible crane shot?" "Could you even figure out the light source in that shot? No wonder it makes the viewer feel so uneasy without his quite knowing why." Brilliant and stupid. And I had drained him— drained him of his knowledge of screwball comedies, Westerns, *films noirs*, epics. But the title *The Black Pig* was my disguised, perhaps pedantic homage to Wilbur Blackfield—the wild boar of *noir*. When I got my chance to make that first movie, against my better judgment I hired him as my editor. But for all his encyclopedic knowledge, for all his ability to meticulously analyze every cut and frame in every great film, he was terrible in the editing room. A complete washout. His knowledge to no avail. Useless. *Academic.* All the time that I was cutting *The Black Pig*, I had to order my poor assistant editor to stay late to undo Wilbur's work of that day—the poor assistant editor, who would then stay up till dawn reassembling the mangled footage. (I can at least thank God that Wilbur chose to become an editor rather than a cameraman.)

I tried at first to be politic. To explain to Wilbur why I requested editing changes. That it wasn't that his cuts were bad so much as just not right in the context of what *I* had in mind, and of course the failure was mine for not explaining properly just what it was I had in mind. Wilbur would listen politely, puffing on his pipe, and nod. What else could I have done? People *have* to lie to one another. If people did not lie, life would become intolerable. In such circumstances, lying is the *moral* thing to do.

Except he knew I was lying. And even then, before our break, before our final rupture, his resentment started to creep in. He resented the fact that *I* had gotten the chance to make a film before he had. That *I* was making a film while he was busy patching together a living out of part-time teaching jobs and low-rung editing assignments. He resented me even while we were collaborating, even while we were still *getting along*.

The Black Pig opens with a nightclub sequence, widely praised for its dizzying, lurid, hallucinatory fervor, where the main character walks into his favorite Hoboken tavern. The camera fluidly glides beside him as he greets his friends one by one along the bar while advancing toward the runway, propelled toward the topless dancer, who teasingly beckons him while the jukebox pumps out Bruce Springsteen's bleakly erotic "Hungry Heart." He is in a trance—and the strength of the camera work is such that it puts the viewer in a trance. Almost every critic would later single out that sequence as particularly astonishing.

At any rate, one day during the sound syncing I slipped into the darkened screening room unannounced and stood in back in the shadows while Wilbur, unaware of my presence, projected the scene for the assistant technicians but with "Hungry Heart" replaced by "The Nutcracker Suite." Ballet music. His idea of a joke. The hoodlum became Diaghilev; the stripper, Isadora Duncan. All the technicians sat in the front row cracking up; Wilbur grinned, his moment in the sun. I wheeled around and left before anyone noticed me.

The next day when I returned, "Hungry Heart" had been restored. I said to Wilbur, "An idea came to me in a dream last night. Why don't we drop the Springsteen and try something a little more risqué?" Wilbur looked at me, puzzled. What did I have in mind? The Clash? The Sex Pistols? I put on "The Nutcracker Suite." Wilbur didn't say a word. He just spun around and walked quickly out of the editing room. I didn't see him for a week afterward—a very productive week by the way. And when Wilbur finally did return, neither of us referred to the incident.

Nor did he work for me again. What was I to do? I couldn't watch over him forever, couldn't watch over him watching over my poor films. It is enough that every day I struggle to supplant one strong image with an even stronger one. I should have to contend with Wilbur Blackfield, too?

And my lieutenant! I don't know what to make of the fellow. I hired Jerry soon after Wilbur had been reduced to just a kind of hanger-on, an appendage rendered superfluous by evolutionary advances in my career. And Jerry actually seemed to feed on, *batten* on, my old classmate's disintegration (if someone fell overboard, Jerry would toss him the anchor). *Why* did I keep Jerry around for so long? Sometimes I think Jerry lives in contempt of me, bringing around all these foreign and experimental directors who spend days casing my mansion, pocketing the silverware, screwing the help, swigging down my fine wines. After all, how can I, with my commercial blockbusters, my blustery American know-how, my flair for the public jugular, possibly occupy the same high moral plateau as these financially strapped but dedicated-to-their-art fellows?

Which nonetheless doesn't stop these *avant-gardists* and these *video artists* from raiding *my* icebox and using *my* expensive editing equipment to finish their own rinky-dink films because they've run out of the foundation money that enables them to exist on the federally endowed "cutting edge." Foreign directors would call collect from Munich, Stockholm, Paris, Belgrade, to chat with my lieutenant, who is always abreast of the latest trends, who uses his festivals to *cook up* these trends. After a minute or two Jerry would say, "One second, Wilbur would like a word," and he'd put Wilbur on the line. But of course Wilbur *never* says a word, no, not if he can say ten thousand. So Jean-Marie, or Fritz, or Sergei would be stuck on the other end, stuck on *the other continent*, politely listening to Wilbur, who'd be assaulting Jean-Marie, or Fritz, or Sergei with some nonsense about *the politics of the camera angle*, or *the dialectics of lighting*, yes, they would be *forced to listen* to Wilbur's nonstop nonsense, since Jean-Marie, or Fritz, or Sergei would not want to risk offending Jerry, who has the power to place—or replace—Jean-Marie's, or Fritz's, or Sergei's next film in his, Jerry's, next film *festival*. And all the while Jerry, that well-adjusted personality, would be sitting off to the side, giggling like this was the greatest fun in the world, as Wilbur—who was then just weeks away from the nut house—would keep up his unceasing verbal assault on the ears of these poor, trapped foreign filmmakers. Jerry didn't see the coming crackup because he found Wilbur so diverting. I saw it but looked away.

Finally, during one particularly disastrous dinner party, Wilbur launched into a twenty-minute unstoppable ecological tirade about how the table we were eating off, my one-hundred-foot-long shellacked redwood table, my sculpture-slab, my slop trough, represented what I believed to be my ascendancy over nature. Indicated that I believed I had become *godlike*. He was smiling stupidly, smugly, ferociously the entire time he delivered this juvenile pap, this soft-diet discourse, while the rest of my guests listened uncomfortably, staring at their plates like they were especially fascinating works of art. It was the last straw. I banished Wilbur from my home.

But then I would drive into Santa Cruz for dinner, emerge from the restaurant afterward, and find that someone had spray-painted along the flank of my car, the flank of my eighty-thousand-dollar Maserati, "Art Whore." Finally I had no choice but to get a restraining order. He violated it several times, was arrested, acted crazy in the holding tank, and, following a court-ordered psychiatric evaluation, was committed.

He never understood my own frustrations, the depths of my despair, and how I could not afford to cater to his. He was so self-centered. Sometimes during the weeks of editing I would wake in the morning so nauseated and with my head so knotted that I would just roll over and, with a cry, go back to sleep. On such mornings I viewed walking into the editing room the way Roman slaves must have viewed walking into the gladiatorial pit where the lion, licking its chops, awaited them. That is correct. I would look at the reels of unedited film, and they would seem animated, alive, breathing. I would look at the reels of unedited film, and I would see *a pack of pacing lions*. It is the easiest thing in the world to let the film become your nemesis, your arch-enemy, and the editing table become the gladiatorial pit into which you must descend to wage life-or-death combat; and unless you arm yourself properly, you can get eaten alive in there, the film kills you or you kill the film.

Sometimes it simply became too much. *Too much.* One day, after too much editing and too much Wilbur, just like that I jumped in my car and drove up the coast and across the Bay to Berkeley. I had heard about an exhibit at the University Art Museum called "Anxious Visions: Surrealist Art." I thought that somebody else's anxiety might soothe my own. And at the museum I found myself gazing at a grim photograph of a devastated World War I battlefield. To make a rather obvious point, the curator had placed it next to Yves Tanguy's 1927 *Shadow Country (Terre d'ombre)*, as if to say, "See how one influenced the other." For, indeed, the surrealistic landscape resembled the war-torn landscape. And a young woman standing behind me said to her boyfriend, "What a crazy time to live, between the two world wars, and being sensitive enough to feel and express it. I almost feel like I've missed out on something." And I thought: Yet our own times are even crazier, even more frightful and anxiety-making, even more terrifying. The eye-opening evidence is everywhere, if you'd only look around you.

But that notwithstanding, a lot of the Surrealists, to be honest, give me a pain in the ass with all their hyperbole and apocalyptic jabber. They would go to a matinee of *The Perils of Pauline* and discover "nothing less than the poetry and passion of our age." They would go see some cheap German Expressionist horror flick and start blathering about how it excited in them "an impatient desire, a radical passion, for love and revolt, for poetry and sensuality." They would read a comic strip and decide that its "mission lay beyond fashion, beyond taste, that the comic strip taught one how to write the century's true history of disruption and upheaval, the century's grand passionate reality." A bunch of bilgebags with all their windy manifestoes. And it pained me no end that this attractive young woman, no doubt quite bright, should buy, lock, stock, and barrel, into all the Surrealists' self-promoting garbage and as a consequence feel *left out*. That she should not realize that her own time is just as charged and diabolical and frightfully insane. And I also thought, standing quietly beside her, that *I* am recording the new age, which is already quite old, decrepit, and crepuscular.

Splash. A big raindrop splattered in my tumbler. An involuntary shudder shot through me. It was raining harder and harder, I was feeling wetter and colder. I pushed myself up from the lawn chair, drew the strings that tightened the hood of my windbreaker around my head, my fragile overloaded head, and began walking through the woods. I felt lonely. Yesterday, in a kind of ironic tribute to Wilbur, I had had the table, the slop trough, the one-hundred-foot-long shel-lacked redwood *sculpture-slab*, cremated, its art-ashes swept into a sack. Then I ordered that the sack be emptied from a helicopter over the Northern California coastal forest from which the poor noble tree had been abducted. First the dolphin, then the redwood table. I felt like I was doing a kind of spiritual housecleaning. Besides, my poor solitary dolphin, multiplied in the media into a school, made me look like a kook.

I also heard from my wife yesterday. She called—collect, as usual—from her father's grand place in Shaker Heights.

"Doug. That fire Orson started . . ."

"Yeah?" My guard went up.

"I was watching TV. A spokesman for Crown said it might've been arson—"

"Arson, Orson! You mean you're going to believe an insurance spokesman over *me?*"

"Kidnapping your own film is bad enough—"

"Goddamn it. I am swimming in a sea of red ink and now I have to contend with my own wife—"

"—but setting our cat on fire for *insurance* purposes?" She gave a heart-rending little sob. "That's as low as you can go."

"*Not true*," I roared into the receiver. "People have been known to go lower. Husbands have been known to hack up their *wives* for insurance purposes. Children have been known to slaughter their *parents* for insurance purposes. Adulterous lovers have been known to—"

The line went dead. And, holding the receiver, I was left to ponder why I had married someone who didn't even know me. That was yesterday. Today—well, today it is raining. I emerged from the woods into the empty dirt parking lot, now muddied and puddled. In the middle sat my dull battered spaceship. It looked as though it had crash-landed on earth. And, yes, there were times when this lot had filled with the cars of the very rich and very powerful as they came to my fabulous parties and posed with me alongside the spaceship. Such parties!

But those times are past. Tonight—just stillness. Stillness and the sound of falling rain.

Black conifers grew out of the liquescent shadows around the lot's edges. Beyond them, the silhouetted hills loomed through the veil of rain. I stared at my dilapidated spaceship, at its hulking silhouette in the rainy darkness.

And then, balancing my tumbler in one hand, I climbed up the ladder and into the cockpit, and made myself comfortable in the pilot's seat. Feet propped up on the dashboard, I sat sipping my bourbon and listening to the oddly comforting patter of the rain on the metal roof.

Tomorrow I would make my peace with Wilbur.

I really didn't have a choice.

But tonight—tonight I could push all my troubles to the side.

I sipped some bourbon. I watched the rain. I smelled the wet pine-scented air infused with the salty sea breezes that gusted up the canyons, and I thought, *I feel sad.* Then I sipped some more bourbon. And then some more. And finally, to the sound of rain pattering on the roof of my battered spaceship—my spaceship, which had crash-landed in a pine forest in a mountain range beneath a foreign sky—finally, to the sound of falling rain, I fell asleep.

The Gangster

C h a p t e r   3 4

Wilbur's eyes, desperate with craftiness, scanned the personals page of the *Tahoe Daily Tribune*, his pen moving restlessly down the columns.

"What if he *doesn't* think to try and reach us through the local paper?" I said, sitting down. I needed to relax. "And even if he does, why are we so special we'll be able to decipher his message when the FBI and the private detectives can't?"

Hunched in an armchair, Wilbur didn't appear to be listening. His pen stopped midpage—actually, midflight. His pen *hovered*, as though it were an aircraft whose pilot wasn't sure whether he had clearance. Then Wilbur sighed, much more heavily than usual for him, and circled a notice. "I think I found it," he said softly, blinking.

I stared. "No kidding?" I thought I heard Jolene draw a deep breath—by deep I mean the sort of serious breath one might draw before diving underwater for two or three minutes, as an evasive maneuver to avoid gunfire, or a nuclear conflagration. But when I swung around to her she smiled brightly and shrugged, as though to say, "Who knows what to expect anymore?" I reached over and tried to take the paper from him. He wouldn't relinquish it. I tugged. He tugged back. I tugged harder—the paper started to rip—he let go.

My eyes settled on the personal ad he had circled in red: "WB. I'm sorry. Please meet, Tallac Trailhead, noon, Thurs."

I turned and stared at Wilbur—but he was gazing, with extravagant absentmindedness, out the window. I turned to Jolene. "What's wrong?" she said. I handed her the paper and monitored her reaction. Pokerfaced, she handed it back.

"You 'think' this is it, Wilbur?" I said quietly. "I 'think' you have a serious problem, and every moment you don't explain yourself your problem's getting worse."

"I edited *The Black Pig.*"

"You *what?*"

"We were buddies at USC. We made that first film together. Then things went sour. He fucked me over."

I stared at Wilbur, awestruck. "He 'fucked' you over? You mean this is a *vendetta?*"

"I got my Ph.D. at USC. Doug didn't even complete his master's. Got thrown out for stealing film equipment. Which is when he moved to New York and did his SoHo-loft thing for a few years."

"I don't believe I'm hearing this." A thought occurred to me. "That's why you didn't want to rent *The Black Pig.*" Even Wilbur's one apparently street-smart idea sprang from an unrelated source of anxiety. "You thought I'd spot your name in the credits."

He nodded painfully.

I turned to Jolene, her hair tied back in a ponytail, casually beautiful in blue jeans and an olive T-shirt, her legs slung over the arm of her chair, the stunning woman I had been—God help me—falling in love with, and I said, "You knew about this, didn't you?"

"It was never supposed to come down to this, Frank."

" 'It was never supposed to come down to this, Frank,' " I mimicked. Then shouted, "But it did. And you know why? Because things don't always come together as planned, especially when you're working with a couple of fucked-in-the-head assholes." I shook my head. "Doug. Does he know you, too?"

"No," she said quietly. "Just Wilbur. I met Wilbur later, when he was teaching at Hayward State." She stared intently at me, as though she wanted to say something further—she didn't.

I nodded and started pacing the floor. I was in too agitated a condition to sit still, to plot, to muse.

"Frank, please tell me what're you thinking." It was Jolene.

"About tomorrow."

"Like what if it's a trap?"

"Yeah. Could he have gone to the FBI and already fingered Wilbur?"

"Probably not," Jolene said. "I've thought about this. If Wilbur showed without the negative, it would be Doug's funeral as well as ours. We could implicate him for *not* wanting it back."

I nodded. "Which would make him, at the least, a co-conspirator."

"He'll want to get the lay of the land. But most importantly, he wants to get the negative back, even if he believes it's a bomb. Because that's the only way he can salvage his career at this point. Lawsuits he can survive. But if he doesn't come up with the negative, he's dead. No studio will ever hire him again. Because no bond company will ever insure him again."

I went over to the closet and picked up the duffel bag that contained the cans of the positive and the negative.

Jolene, her face expressionless—carefully expressionless—asked, "What're you doing, Frank?"

"From this point on, *I* hold the film. You have an objection?"

"Fine. But where are you going?"

"To cool out. To be alone."

◆ ◆ ◆

At four in the morning, with the duffel bag at my feet, I sat in the dim red glow of an airport bar in Reno, half an hour over Spooner Summit from Tahoe. For security reasons I had decided on the larger, more anonymous Reno airport rather than the tiny South Lake Tahoe airport. Arnie Goldblatt, L.A. porn distributor, dear friend from the old neighborhood, sat on a stool laughing:

"Oh man, this is great. After your call the other day I had a feeling I'd be hearing from you again."

"But can you do anything? Pitch it to the right folks? After all, buying this would be like buying a stolen Rembrandt. A special kind of status for that special CEO."

Arnie got serious. "I don't know, Frankie. You're right, this is heavy. But—hell, no trouble moving porn no matter how nasty it is. Christ, even a snuff loop, though I wouldn't touch that shit. Cost about ten thou and one poor screwed-up runaway chick who wouldn't be missed by no one. Line up twenty or so select parties on the Coast, New York, D.C., Miami. And don't forget Dallas. Weaned on those weird home movies ever since November 22, '63. Get, say, five to ten thou a head. Takes time, you gotta be careful, move through the proper channels. But you can clear half a mil in several months."

"Well, at least this wouldn't make you an accomplice to Murder One."

"The snuff film, they want it simple," Arnie went on, almost distractedly. "Technically, the simpler the better. A single-shot pic, no cuts. Like Hitchcock's *Rope*. Of course, there were cuts for reloading the camera. But you can't even see them. A snuff flick's gotta be like that. The buyer doesn't want to feel cheated—fancy editing, special effects, swirling camera movements. That film-school crap doesn't wash in snuff. You want documentary realism, not Industrial Light & Magic."

"We're going afield here, Arnie."

He drummed his fingers on the bar counter, watched a plane lift into the night. "I don't know, Frankie. There's no established market for this sort of thing. I mean, it *isn't* a stolen Rembrandt. Yeah, serious bespectacled Doug Lowell freaks might be interested. But who wants to deal with goofballs? Besides, they're kids, got no real money. They might scare up a hundred bucks to see the film. But not ten thou. Maybe a computer nerd or two would. But how you even gonna find them? Advertise in *Computer World?* Shit. If I took this thing off your hands for five thou I'd be doing you a favor." He shook his head. "Tell me something. Is it any good?"

"If that's the problem, I'll screen it for you."

Arnie chuckled, then his mind wandered off again. "Fisting to the elbow. Guys in black hooded robes with electric cattle prods. Barbed-wire bondage. Home movies with little kids. I mean, the sickest shit imaginable—no problem. But this? Who needs it? The aggravation. Sorry, Frankie."

I sighed and sipped my drink. "Do you ever miss the Bronx, Arnie?"

"Do I ever miss the Bronx? Lemme tell you something. People think you grew up in the Bronx, you must be a tough guy. But listen. It was Cub Scout camp compared to L.A. and environs. A year ago, guy comes to me. Wants to commission a home movie, his wife getting hacked to bits. 'Can it be arranged?' he asks. 'Sorry,' I say pleasantly. 'I'm in distribution, not production.' I mean, I may exploit women but I don't kill 'em. Jesus, Frankie. Where do these people come from?" Arnie shook his head. "And you know what? I know the answer. *The suburbs.* They come from the fucking suburbs."

I laughed, said, "You know, you should've gotten into mainstream production when you had the chance. Right after *Love You to Pieces.*"

"Ah . . . that was terrible. I wouldn't have cut it, Frankie. Really. I know my limits as a filmmaker." He finished his drink, looked at his gold Rolex. "I saw your father in New York a couple of weeks ago."

"Yeah?" I said unenthusiastically.

"He worries about you."

I didn't encourage further talk.

Arnie stood up. "Listen, no hard feelings, but my flight to L.A.'s in ten minutes. I got a breakfast meet. Say hello to your old man for me, will you?"

We shook hands and hugged. Then I remained by the window for perhaps twenty minutes after he had left. Pondering the intricacies of film distribution. Debating whether I should just hop on the next flight to anywhere. Change my name, my hair, the color of my life.

Instead I went into a phone booth and dialed a Westchester number. The phone rang once, twice—

"Yeah?" Harsh, clipped.

"Hi."

"Frank!" said my father. Genuine pleasure infused his voice. Then he caught himself. Adjusted his tone to something more businesslike. "What's up?" But then checked himself yet again—he'd always been like this—and corrected his tone to something midway between formality and familial warmth. My father, a mystery without clues—no chance at understanding. "How're things?"

"Oh they're . . ."

He heard my voice trail off. "What's a matter? Something a matter?"

"Maybe."

"Gimme your number. I'll call you right back."

While he ran outside to a pay phone—for some reason I pictured it raining—I waited in the airport booth, wondering what kind of life it is where you're always worrying about being tapped, monitored, electronically surveilled. I suppose for him it had evolved into a game of sorts, a contest, his notion of the sporting life. A kind of mental exercise to keep you on your toes, like reading Wittgenstein or listening to Schoenberg. The phone started to ring—flat atonal rings—and I picked it up.

"What's the problem?" he said.

I drew a deep breath and said, "I got something but—it's a bit hot. Your friend from Philly, maybe he can . . ."

A silence. Then: "How hot?"

I hesitated. "You keep up with current events?"

"Current events?" He pondered. Then, softly, he said, "Shit."

Nobody said anything for almost a minute. It had always been like this. The pretense might have been that we feared the phone was tapped; the reality was, words failed us, they *always* failed us, we could never express our fears or our doubts or our love. It was as though conversation were something to be fought off, like attacking troops.

I felt like I was in solitary.

I looked out the booth's glass door. A beautiful blonde in a sleek blue jumpsuit walked by, giggling and tottering on high heels, arm in arm with some guy who was about two hundred years old. The high desert country of northern Nevada. All that spooky wide-open empty space. A wonderful place for meditation, for cleansing the soul, for recovering the essential core. But build in the middle of it a gambling town, and you also get one of the highest per capita rates of divorce, alcoholism, prostitution, and suicide.

Sixty seconds of long-distance silence echoed and resonated and stretched out like sixty hours. How to keep the man talking. Interminable. Unbearable. I thought my head would split.

Finally he spoke. "Forget it."

"Forget it?"

"Yeah. I could go see our friend. A truckload of TVs, a Picasso, no matter. He's the man can move it . . ."

"I hear a 'but.' "

"Only I don't recommend it. Some of the cut will go to this guy, some to that . . . you'll wind up with a roll of nickels. Plus you gotta figure we're so riddled with informants and assholes these days . . ." He paused, then said: "Just burn it. The aggravation, you don't need it. Burn it and walk away. *Don't look back.*"

I gazed at myself in the glass door. I thought: a person who liked himself wouldn't be in this situation, wouldn't be staring at his reflection like this in a Reno airport phone-booth door at five in the morning. I pushed the door open slightly so the circuit broke and the overhead light blinked out. It was always easier in the dark.

Then I heard my father say, "I'm sorry I didn't do better by you."

I felt an instant hotness. Almost reflexively my hand tightened on the receiver. Then I heard myself say, "I love you."

There was a silence. A long silence. Impatient, irritated, I drummed my fingers on the phone-book counter. After a while he said, "Yeah." Flat and unemotional. After another while he said, "Take care." Click.

The sky was starting to lighten. In seven hours I was supposed to meet Doug Lowell. This time I felt certain he would show up. I watched an Alaskan Airlines DC-10 lumber down the runway, then lift into the first cold light like a great prehistoric bird. I turned, started back to my car. Heavily, as if mounting to the gallows.

C h a p t e r   3 5

Jolene dropped us off at the gravel access road that wound through the woods to the trailhead.

"You got the walkie-talkie?" I said.

"Yeah, yeah. It's cool."

"Now, you're going to—"

"—park twenty yards up the road. If I see anything funny, like a clown with a meat ax . . ."

I stared at her.

"Hey, Frank. I'm as tired of this as you are. Okay?"

"Please. Can we just go?" Wilbur said.

I glanced at him. His face, flushed pink, radiated a faint heat. He was breathing hard, as though trying to get a purchase on the thin mountain air. That wasn't it, though. What it was: he was all worked up at the prospect of confronting Doug Lowell. Too many bad years had passed, too many bad dreams and bad movies.

"I still say we should've brought the negative with us," Jolene said. "Get all of this over with and just go home."

"It makes me happier knowing it's in a hotel gym locker," I said.

I took the sawed-off shotgun out of the car. We started up the access road and soon arrived in a dusty clearing, a parking lot for wholesome types heigh-hoeing it into the wilderness. It wasn't backpacking season yet, though, and only one car sat in the lot—a battered blue twenty-year-old Volkswagen bug.

I took a rock and smashed open the trunk. No suitcases inside packed with money, no electronic surveillance equipment. I smashed a window and opened the door. No registration, no insurance certificate, nothing in the glove compartment.

The trail wound through an alpine meadow abundant with wildflowers, then climbed through sagebrush, dwarf junipers, and pine forests. We had gone about a hundred yards and just reached a point where the grade began to steepen when above us a voice rang out:

"That's far enough. Stay where you are. I have a gun."

I stood stock-still. A man says he has a gun, maybe he has a gun. Ten yards farther up the trail, the bearded face of Doug Lowell peered down at us from over the top of a boulder.

"Why the shotgun?" he called out.

"To protect *you*. From your old friend Professor Blackfield."

"You don't need a gun for Wilbur. You need rubber truncheons, a straitjacket." Doug Lowell's face betrayed a faint inner amusement, the eyes registered an almost roguish lilt. "Hello, Wilbur. It's been several years, hasn't it?"

"Yes, it's been several years," Wilbur shouted, shaking with fury. The rumpled professor metastasized into a wild boar filled with buckshot braying in the bramble. I feared he would fly apart. "We had a deal, Doug. An understanding founded on trust. On friendship. On mutual respect. We became blood brothers. Never to let the other down. A pact. And you shoveled dirt on it. You unzipped your pants and with your stupid dick pissed on it. And do you know why? Can you admit why? I'LL TELL YOU WHY," Wilbur roared. "Because you *envied* my talent, my intellect, my learning. I believed in Art but you believed in Mammon. In fattening the Golden Calf so you could grill it over mesquite."

"Art!" Lowell said, exasperated, then sighed. "Look. Art, beauty —those things are okay if you stumble upon them in the course of what you're doing. A sort of by-product of your work. But my desires were simpler. I didn't want to 'affect the consciousness of my generation.' I didn't want to set off fireworks in the next galaxy. I just wanted to make movies."

"Oh, bullshit, Doug. You were an *artist*. But you've degenerated into an *artistic racketeer*. You might think you're a success, but in my book you're not. In my book you're nothing but a cheap two-bit artistic *whore*. You've become an enemy of culture, a terrorist of the screen."

Here I was. A marvelous mountain panorama, a diaphanous pale-blue sky. The day seemed to say: Life is lovely. Enjoy.

"You're a child, Wilbur," Lowell said. "So caught up in your esoteric pursuits. You used to go out every night to see the most obscure boring useless movies in the world—long after the rest of us had had our fill of them. That's where life was for you. Yes, they had their uses. An interesting shot here, a nice composition there. But they weren't *life*."

"So just like that you wrote me off?" Wilbur cried. "As a fucking deadbeat? A loser? A guy with brains who could never figure out the angles?"

"I hired you as my editor because I loved you. But your editing was so crummy, so lousy, so *demented* that you were wrecking my film. It was as if you didn't understand the most fundamental things about cutting. I would tell you to match up, to make the weaker shots conform to the stronger. You would match down, so that the good conformed to the bad. I would ask you to cut in movement; you would cut so that the scene came out static and strained. On the theoretical level, you understand everything. On the practical level—nothing. Every night after you went home my assistant editor had to stay up till dawn unraveling and recutting your work—the assistant editor who got only an assistant editor's credit. Your credit read 'Edited by Wilbur Blackfield.' It should have read 'Nearly Killed by Wilbur Blackfield.' But I still cared for you. I still considered you my friend."

"That's not true," Wilbur said feebly. Then tapped into a fresh pool of resentment. "And you robbed me. You—"

Up by his boulder perch, Lowell suddenly put his finger to his lips and pointed down the trail behind us. I turned and saw two orange Day-Glo backpacks bobbing above the bushes, coming up toward us. A trap? I stuck my right hand in a bush, the shotgun concealed but at the ready.

Soon, two red bandannaed heads—a boy and a girl, about seventeen or eighteen—bobbed into view, the orange backpacks riding above them. They passed us, nodded warily, and continued up toward Lowell's position. I flashed a modest smile of apology. Had the girl looked askance at my blue linen Italian sports jacket, my Bally moccasins— not the ideal footwear for negotiating rocky trails? A copy of Han-shan's *Cold Mountain Poems* stuck out of a side pocket of the guy's backpack, stirring up undergrad memories. A girlfriend at Cornell, in a kind of carnal blackmail, had pressured me into reading them. And, to be frank, I felt I could've used some Zen meditative poetry just then, some bitter laments on poverty, avarice, and pride—along with demulcent descriptions of the natural world. The orange Day-Glo backpacks disappeared into the bush, reappeared—smaller—up the mountain, and moved on, bobbing above the shrub line before disappearing for good into the wilderness.

"You were saying, Wilbur."

"I was saying?" Wilbur shouted. "I was saying that you turned FALSE and VULGAR and—"

I tuned out. A clear light rinsed the mountains. The air was warm and fragrant with sagebrush and piney resins. The sky was blue like you seldom see except in the Sierra. A marvelous day—and it all had an air of unreality. I didn't even know what Wilbur was ranting about. He *liked* Lowell's films. He thought the newest one a masterpiece. Yet at the moment his voice rang with schizzy conviction. Such muscular mental maneuvers must have been required of his mind, a kind of proficiency in intellectual double-stopping.

And here I am, I thought, mediating between these two maniacs. Doing just what I had always dreaded most. Resolving a labor dispute. Wilbur, the former employee. Lowell, his onetime employer. And I, the Cornell School of Labor Relations dropout, refereeing. Wouldn't my father, the old labor enforcer, be proud?

"—and whatever happened to those gorgeous experimental movies we used to talk of making at USC? A couple of which you actually got around to making when you were living on Broome. We were going to shake up the film industry, make it shudder and splinter asunder. Deconstruct phony reality and reveal false consciousness for the racket that it is. Therapy for the artistically abused American soul. But instead of shaking up the film establishment, you *became* it, you remade it, you redid it in your own monstrous image."

"Righto. *You*," Lowell shouted out, addressing me in a voice that was suddenly commanding, directorial. "You look level-headed. I would like to get my goddamn movie back."

I said nothing. I was reeling, spinning, whirling from their repartee.

Wilbur had over the years gone crazy with jealousy, with spite, with outsized insanity at the size of his old classmate's achievement. And I did feel that Lowell had a point or two. Yet I felt for Wilbur. All the poor bastard had ever wanted was to work his heart out, even for Lowell, and he had been so frustrated, suffered such monstrous letdowns, seen his hopes dashed and smashed on the shoals of his own incompetence. Lowell had channeled his splendid madness, Wilbur had gone mad.

"And that crap you said in the *Playboy* interview to that bum, about how art grows out of the search for an accommodation between Eros and Thanatos, and how the artist is nothing more than the suffering servant of the sadomasochistic truth—*I* said that, that time we were discussing *The Black Pig*, trying to figure out what it was about. Yeah, just across the lake from here, in that cabin you rented that summer —the last time you'd rent a cabin instead of just buy it outright. We'd stay up till dawn discussing what the movie was about. Because *I* made you understand that even a cheap crime thriller, to be any good, has to be about something. You were very cavalier in that interview, dropping bits of learning you'd gleaned not from books but from me—me, who's read and absorbed it all. You quoted Céline and said that the passion of his nihilism made the Surrealists, despite their critique of the bourgeoisie, look like a bunch of dilettantes dabbling in dream imagery and the occult. *You* never read Céline—you tried to but found him too *depressing*. You talked about Ravel's *Jeux d'eau* and how his primary stylistic influence was Liszt, not Debussy. *You* never listen to Ravel. His compositions are too melodically complex for your three-chord ears that should've been weaned from the Beach Boys and the Rolling Stones years ago. You talked about Frank Stella on Caravaggio and how great paintings are great not because of what is present but because of what is absent. Absence! You're an absence. You got it all from me."

"I think you always did misread my faux cultural illiteracy, Wilbur."

But now Wilbur, off in his own world, shouted, screamed, *roared*: "You think I like getting shunted from cow college to cow college, from pasture to pasture, lecturing about the same damn movies over and over while you streak around the world in a Learjet, always meeting

NEW and INTERESTING people? I've come to HATE *films noirs,* to positively loathe them. You think I wouldn't like to be RICH and FAMOUS
and POWERFUL? To have BEAUTIFUL WOMEN throwing themselves at my
feet? Like that unidentified cutie standing next to you in the Radio
City Music Hall photo in *People.* Who was she by the way?"

"Who was who, Wilbur? I don't know what you're talking about.
Or when. Christ!" Lowell shook his head. "Tell me something, Wilbur.
Weren't you recently offered a two-semester gig at Columbia? Which
you turned down for reasons known only to yourself?"

Wilbur looked startled. "How did you know?"

"How do you think?"

"Shit. I should've known you were behind that, trying to get me
removed from the West Coast—"

"Get you removed? I was trying to help you. Jesus, some of the
insane—absolutely paranoid—things you accuse me of. I steal your
ideas, your mistress, your *soul,* for chrissake—"

"Anita at that party—"

"You didn't even know her. You met her that night. You were
drunk and coming on to her, and she politely tried to brush you off.
But you never could read a woman's signals very well. As the host I
felt obligated to shield her from you. She hardly qualified as your
mistr—"

"You ass. I *brought* her to that party. I'd been having an affair with
her for a year."

"You had?"

"Shit."

I was beginning to feel that this touching rapprochement, this
heartwarming alumni reunion, had just about run its course. Business
remained—the business of three million dollars.

Apparently Lowell felt the same way. "Look," he called out, ap-
pealing to me. "We need to talk about the negative."

"One second." I turned to Wilbur. "You have had your conversation with Doug. You have cleared the—"

"Oh bullshit. Nothing was resolved."

"You aired your grievances. You—"

"Oh shut the fuck up, you gangster asshole. You know nothing, you understand nothing. I'm as sick of your bullshit as his. And if you don't like it, break my legs."

"I understand," I said soothingly, and I did. Wilbur was entitled to a bit of huffiness—so long as it stayed within bounds. "But it's time to move on. I need to negotiate with Doug, and it will go easier one-on-one."

Wilbur, tired from the anger exertion, nodded reluctantly.

Lowell shouted, "What about your gun?"

"What about yours?"

"I don't have one."

"Should I give mine to Wilbur?"

He snickered. I broke the gun, unloaded it, flung the shells into the marvelous woods. For the squirrels to secrete away with their acorns.

Wilbur whispered, "What about Jolene?"

"She's in the car. She'll be okay." I turned again and stared up the mountain, whose highest slopes, far beyond Lowell, still shimmered with snow. I wondered if the world looked radiantly different to Lowell, if he saw possibilities everywhere, visual opportunities waiting to be exploited, if a mountain really looked like a mountain to him, a tree a tree, a lake a lake—or if they all suggested backdrops, trompe l'oeils, scenery to be dismantled at the close of a shot, stage sets to be struck at the end of the day. I wondered if *I* looked like scenery to him. "Doug, I'm coming up alone. All right?"

"Come on up," he shouted from his rock.

C h a p t e r   3 6

I hiked up to Doug Lowell's position, scrambling over rocks. He looked me over. I looked him over. He warily offered his hand. I warily shook it.

"I expected you to look more postmodern," he said. "Something about the *sui generis* nature of the crime. Like bad dada."

"Turn around. I have to pat you for a wire."

He turned and put his hands on a boulder, careful to avoid the mossy green patches of lichen. "And kidnapping a couple of movie critics—that was truly inspired. How do you know Wilbur?"

"Not important. What is important is that for me this is business, not some half-assed vendetta." I pointed to the trail beyond, which wound through the woods, ascending Mount Tallac. "Let's walk."

"What do I call you?"

"Frank will do."

"Frank. Do you actually *know* Wilbur? Is he a close friend? A colleague?"

"Not relevant."

"Look. If you haven't already figured it out, Wilbur is *nuts*. He is obsessed with 'Doug Lowell.' He goes bonkers on 'Doug Lowell.' " Lowell shook his head. "*I* betrayed him. *I* had him committed. *I* cheated him out of women. Out of *millions*. Incredible!"

"Can we stick to the subject?"

Lowell blinked rapidly, as though he had forgotten I was there. "Right." He nodded. "Well, does the negative still exist?"

"We didn't burn it. You're still in business."

"Who else is in on this?"

"No one."

He nodded. Birds were tweeting, pines emanating their resiny scent. He didn't seem in a particular hurry to discuss the negative.

"Three million? Do you have it?"

"Do I have three million?" he said, a trifle too sarcastically for my taste. "I have mortgaged everything I own to make this movie. I am twenty, maybe thirty, maybe even forty million in debt. And you want to know if I have three million."

I turned and started walking away.

"Look. I can show you graphs, charts, projections, estimates, accounting books filled with more red ink than you've ever seen. You've obviously done your homework, I'm sure you can read them. And this is without even factoring in the pending liens and frozen accounts."

I kept walking. Doug shouted, steadily louder, to keep up with me:

"You don't understand, damn it. My estate is under twenty-four-hour surveillance—the FBI, the insurance people. With all the suits filed against me and a rumored grand jury investigation, the courts have frozen my accounts. And they will *stay* frozen until the matter of the negative is resolved. Christ, if I went to my safe-deposit boxes now, they'd arrest me for breaking and entering. I'm practically under house arrest. I snuck out by hiding in the trunk of my old VW bug, with my mechanic at the wheel." Lowell paused. I stopped and turned to look at him. He said, "I had always hoped to move beyond this successful-industry-maverick shit and attain a sort of peaceful *éminence grise* status."

I walked back and said, "We have a problem. You can't get your assets back unless you come up with the negative. But you can't get the negative back unless you come up with some assets."

He didn't answer. Instead he said, "I'd been trying to get Paul—that's my lawyer—to work something out, a lie-detector test, say, with the insurance folks. But I can't even iron out the details with my goddamn lawyer. I say to Paul, 'Look. The insurance folks can ask me questions like, *Did you steal your own negative?* But they can't ask, *Were you happy it was stolen?*' But then Paul says that if he presents it that way, their lawyers will say that that implies intent on my part not to get it back, and then where am I?"

"Your lawyer sounds reasonable to me, Doug."

"That's not all. He also said, 'Besides, Crown's lawyers might suggest you're a sociopath, clinically speaking, *DSM-III* and all that. And everyone knows sociopaths are notoriously successful at outfoxing polygraph machines.' Son of a bitch had this funny little smile when he told me that. I could've smacked him."

"Seems like you're having a problem with the loyalty factor."

"The loyalty factor! Lawyers. Lieutenants. *Wilbur.*" Lowell got an abstracted look in his eyes and stared through the trees at the distant peaks. "As undergraduates we were infatuated with the bohemian mythology of marginality, parasitism, opposition, and withdrawal. Rimbaud disappearing into Abyssinia. Hans Jaeger in the Christiania-Bohème: 'One cannot treat one's parents badly enough'; 'Thou shalt never soak thy neighbor for less than five kroner.' Huelsenbeck in Zurich banging away on his drum in the Cabaret Voltaire. *But one grows up, one moves on.* But not Wilbur."

"About the three million."

Lowell sighed. "I could come up with two hundred thousand. Tops."

I started walking away again.

"Hey, wait."

I continued along the dirt footpath.

"Listen, I am in fucking trouble. If I scrape around maybe I could come up with a hundred thousand more. But there's no way I can put together what you're asking. *After* I get the movie back and it's been released, I could get you the other two million. But not a moment before."

"Doug, for two hundred thousand I will burn the negative. I piss on two hundred thousand. Understand? If this is the bazaar, I am willing to come down from three mil to two. But that's it. So if you can't come up with it, we both lose. And please, don't insult me with this 'after' crap."

Lowell studied me. His pores exuded sweat. He began pacing back and forth on the trail, scratching his head, kicking pine cones, combing fingers through his scraggly beard. Finally he stopped and said, "Let me run something past you. First, I cannot come up with two million. It's simply impossible. If I could, I would, believe me. If you destroy the negative I am ruined. Ring down the curtain."

"I'm still here."

"Here's what I propose. I give you two hundred thousand now. Then we'll make a deal. I'll contract with you and Wilbur to write a screenplay for me for which you'll be paid $1.8 million. The contract will be predated. It's a touch steep for unknowns, but not unheard of. A disadvantage to you will be taxes. An advantage will be you won't have to play hide-and-seek with the IRS."

I looked carefully at Lowell, wondering where the trap was in this.

"But it's imperative that I get the negative back. Without it, I cease to exist. With it, even if the movie bombs—"

"It won't."

"—I'll still be able to find work. I'll always be the guy who directed *The High Plateau of Stars*. They gave Spielberg work after *1941*. They gave Cimino work after *Heaven's Gate*. They gave Coppola work after *One from the Heart*—"

"They gave Polanski work after he screwed that child."

"Never an issue. What counts is they gave Polanski work after *Pirates*."

We walked on. "Doug, didn't you ever suspect it was Wilbur?"

"No. Not for a moment. I didn't think Wilbur had the cunning, the resourcefulness, the daring. Petty vandalism, slashing car tires, sure. But stealing the whole damn movie? No. Also, it would've required several people, and, no offense, but I couldn't see Wilbur recruiting, especially from among those who knew him. If it was his scheme, it was sure to be cracked." Lowell shook his head and laughed. "Maybe I underestimated him."

We climbed above the tree line and saw the rugged mountains to our east, pristine Lake Tahoe sparkling below to the north, the summit of Mount Tallac looming ahead. This hinterland environment had a strange, vibratory quality for me today.

"I think Wilbur probably got the idea from you," I said. "That time you threatened the studio. Said the negative to the original *High Plateau* just might disappear if you didn't get final cut."

"Maybe." Lowell shrugged. "In addition to all my other troubles, my wife's asking for a divorce now. I should let her have it. Community-property settlement, half of nothing is nothing." He laughed to himself. "The love of my life—I don't mean my wife—and she arrived out of left field. Our babysitter. An undergrad at UCLA when I was cutting the first *High Plateau* in Burbank. A bright, lovely girl with a keen sense of humor and an excellent eye. I used to tease her about becoming an actress. But she knew better. God, sharp as a whip. She actually suggested a lot of good cuts and ways to restructure the movie by shuffling scenes around."

"Doug, I am not the *National Enquirer*. Your love life doesn't interest me."

"And I could *talk* to her about what I was doing. The girl knew movies, from *Alphaville* to *Zulu*. You know what she once said to me?

We were in bed, she said, 'This isn't working. You only love me for my mind.' And we laughed. Because we had a great time in bed. And yet, in some awful way, it was true. I kept promising I'd leave my wife, marry her. It wasn't even that she was pressuring me. *I* wanted to marry her. Yet I was scared."

"Doug, save it for your analyst."

"My wife had done nothing. She wasn't at fault." Lowell slumped, looked depressed. "Do you know whose idea it *really* was to threaten the studio with the disappearance of the negative if they denied me final cut? Who pushed and goaded me into threatening them?"

I had been listening to Lowell's story—an old story, really—without paying close attention. But suddenly an odd tingle, cold and shivery, started at the base of my spine, tiptoed up it, then went "Knock-knock. Anyone home?" on the door to my skull. I remained quiet.

"I told her I'd leave my wife. I didn't. Christ, was she hurt. Really, really hurt. I was surprised at how hurt she was. She couldn't believe I was behaving like such a coward. But she also felt injured. She suspected it was in part a status thing, because she wasn't glamorous, a trendy L.A. type. And unlike my wife, who's from old Midwestern stock, she was lower-middle-class Southern Cal, two generations out of the Dust Bowl. 'From the Bowl to the mall,' she used to joke. And she might've been right."

"Did she know Wilbur?"

"No. She came after. He was persona non grata by then. She knew *of* him, of course. Wilbur's always been a great conversation piece— the demented way he cut *The Black Pig*, his crazy jealousies and paranoias. Oh yes, I talked about Wilbur. But she never met him."

"What was her name?"

"Excuse me?"

"*Her name.*"

Lowell looked at me and blinked. "Jocelyn. Why?"

I said nothing. A woman, a long-legged stranger, had installed herself in the black leather bucket seat of my Porsche—which had a $67-million movie, unbeknownst to her, stashed in its tire well—and that woman might as well have been from another planet. "Time to head back, Doug. How—"

"Oh, come on. It's only half an hour to the top. I'm enjoyi—"

"Maybe your next movie. How do we work out this contract business?"

He sighed. "Pick a restaurant. We'll go there, write it all up."

I nodded. "When we get back to Wilbur, I want no more scenes. Don't even talk to him. If either of you has a question, I'll relay it— even if you're only two feet apart. Understand?"

"Whatever."

"Also, leave your car in the trailhead lot and come with me—"

"I don't underst—"

"A security precaution. I'll bring you back afterward *with* the negative."

Lowell shrugged. "You're the boss."

Wilbur sat like a fat lizard on a rock, stewing beneath the overhead sun. He started to say something. I cut him off. "Wilbur, we've worked out a deal. Not exactly what—"

"What do you mean, not exactl—"

"Shut up and listen. Not exactly what we'd planned, but still pretty decent. I think you'll agree. But I want no more discussion until we're all comfortably seated in a restaurant."

" 'All'? What's this restaur—?"

"Enough." I turned to Lowell. "Excuse me one minute, please. I have to micturate." I moved off into the bushes. Took out the walkie-talkie. Pulled out the antenna and signaled Jolene.

"How'd it go?"

"Pretty well. Me and Wilbur will be coming out in a few minutes. Is the coast clear?"

"Far as I can tell. No traps in there?"

"No."

"And you slashed one of his tires?"

"Yes. See you soon." I pushed the antenna back in, stuck the walkie-talkie in my pocket. When I stepped out of the bushes I found Doug and Wilbur sitting on rocks ten yards apart, backs to each other, sunning, silent, sullen.

"Let's go," I said, and the three of us began hiking down the mountain trail.

Chapter 37

The Porsche, its sides faded with dust, sat on the shoulder of the highway, just off the junction of the gravel access road. Jolene—or was it Jocelyn?—in a yellow T-shirt and snug-fitting blue jeans, leaned against it, her slender arms folded across her chest. She hadn't discovered the film stashed in the tire well. She hadn't vanished with my car. I smiled. She smiled back. Right behind me, Wilbur emerged from the dark pines. She smiled at him. He smiled at her. Then Doug Lowell emerged from behind Wilbur—

The day dazzled and dazed me. Distant peaks blurred into the throbbing blue sky. Birds sang soprano. Heat shimmered up from the Porsche's black roof. And somewhere in the Tahoe basin, formed by eruptions and glacial actions millions of years ago, Doug Lowell was shouting at Jolene, Jolene was shouting at Lowell, and Wilbur—as soon as he realized with a shock that Doug and Jolene were old acquaintances—started shouting at them both.

My feet, cramped in my fine Swiss moccasins, were beginning to hurt. I refreshed myself by removing my jacket and sitting down on a log. It was my brain though that needed to be refreshed. These people were a workout.

Lowell, injured mightily, to Jocelyn: "How could you betray me like this?"

Wilbur to Jolene: "You mean you once took up with this double-crossing douche bag? How could you do this to me, knowing all he's done?"

Jolene to Wilbur: "How could *I* betray you with *him?* He came first, you moron."

She glanced—glared—at me, as though to ask, "And when did you figure all this out?"

The shouting, loud and angry, raged for five minutes, echoing off the mountainsides, coming back at me in vibrato, sending Steller's jays and sparrows to flight. I imagined deer, bears, squirrels, chipmunks, martens, weasels, all streaking and leaping away, as in the forest-fire scene in *Bambi*. Furious Doug. Cyclonic Jolene. Dumbfounded Wilbur. Yet the professor seemed oddly pleased, for Doug was enraged that she had betrayed him with Wilbur. Emotions warred pleasantly on the professor's face.

I zoned out. I felt calm—more calm, I suppose, than circumstances warranted. I had stolen a movie negative for money. Now I had no money, but I had a woman (which was uncertain), and the woman was a lying, thieving, manipulative wonder . . . more talented at lying and thieving than any of us.

Soon though, they would calm down and then we'd repair to a tasteful lakeside restaurant, where we would work out the remaining details of the contract, large and legit. After which we would pop open a bottle of Dom Pérignon and all four clink glasses. *So this is the industry?* I thought. You plot to steal two and a half million from a guy and wind up shaking hands on a business deal. What would my father, a man who didn't believe in the high lope of progress, make of these folks? A new breed. The evolution of the species. Would he approve? Or squint and say, "And you signed a deal with them?"

The Movie Mogul

Chapter 38

"Look. I have to get a screenplay credit," Jocelyn was saying sullenly. The four of us sat at a window table in Casa Donner, my favorite restaurant for a nibble, right on the lake just past Emerald Bay, farther out from the turnoff to Tallac Trailhead.

"Of course," I said expansively. "To protect your end." Jocelyn looked as excellent, as beautiful, as ambrosial as ever. I might even have still been in love with her.

"But I'm supposed to get *half* the money," insistent Frank piped up, "not a third."

I inspected Frank. This was the punk Prometheus who had stolen my fire. Even sitting still the fellow suggested busyness, a riotous flurry of motion. He hummed. Dressed in a vivid blue sports coat that looked like some newfangled blend of silk, Lycra, and electricity, with a subtly dark silk shirt beneath and—I peeked under the table—expensive moccasins of the wafer-thin leather variety, he was slimly muscular, intelligent-looking, and almost handsome. No matter. Clothes might make the man but they can't hide the man. He also looked like a hood. A refined racketeer fury radiated from the guy.

"If that was the arrangement the three of you worked out," I said smoothly, "no problem. We'll also give you an original-story credit to justify your higher fee." Also to get rid of him. I hadn't yet sounded the depths, or shallows, of whatever was going on between him and Jocelyn.

The waiter arrived. I ordered forty oysters for our party. My finger moved down the wine list, then stopped. "Give us a bottle of Dom Pérignon"—my finger, such a fine finger, resumed its cursor search —"and how about a bottle of the '83 Sonoma-Cutrer Chardonnay Les Pierres." The waiter nodded and moved off. "The thing is, though," I continued, "we need a story. It can be anything, it just has to be within the ballpark." I thought about it. "Though it wouldn't hurt if it was actually good. Maybe we could all make money on this. *Real money.*"

Wilbur said softly, "I have an idea."

I braced myself. "Yeah?"

"I've been wanting to make a documentary about people who think they've seen flying saucers." He paused.

"I'm still here, Wilbur."

"Only they haven't. They're the sort of people you read about in the *Weekly World News* and the *Midnight Globe*. Kind of sad and fucked up. They invent these things to fill a vacuum in their lives." Wilbur hesitated, as though wanting, waiting for, *desperately desiring* my approval—none was forthcoming—then he bravely plunged on. "Maybe there's a way to turn this into a feature."

Now I turned the full force of my beacon on Wilbur. He had put on some weight over the years. *We've all put on some weight over the years.* But he had turned into a Saint Bernard, a mastiff, a portable Dumpster, a mobile mountain unit. I stared hard at Wilbur, I drilled into Wilbur—and Wilbur seemed to wilt, to shrivel up, to atrophy before my eyes. "Tell me something, Wilbur. What did you plan to do with this documentary after you made it?"

"It'd be funny. Funny and sad. It would make money playing on the midnight cult circuit. Like *The Rocky Horror Picture Show*. Of course, it wouldn't be in the same ballpark as *High Plateau* but it would be commercial."

"Commercial!" I cried in despair. "You're joking, right, Wilbur? I mean, this is the industry, not the Pacific Film Archive. We, the people in this industry—great people, smart people, better-read and more cultivated than most other folks think—nonetheless realize that we were put on this planet to make a pile. That—"

"It'll make money."

I shook my head. "Where is the story in this, Wilbur? Where? You haven't changed one bit. A movie about people who *think* they've seen flying saucers but really *haven't*? Righto. The studios will be falling over each other to greenlight it first. Wilbur Wilbur Wilbur, you ever hear of 'the moviegoing public'? Of 'grosses' and 'box office' and 'legs'?"

"You just don't get it. It'll be seminal."

"It'll be *marginal*. I mean, are you *nuts*? Nobody wants this shit. I produce it I'll be the laughingfuckingstock of the industry. I'll be Z-list. A dog wouldn't lift his leg to piss on this picture, Wilbur."

The waiter arrived with our wines and eight glasses. He popped the cork on the Dom Pérignon, then poured it into four glasses and pushed the bottle down into the ice bucket. He showed me the label on the Chardonnay.

"Hey, what did I say?"

"You said Sonoma-Cutrer Chardonnay."

"Yes, but from Les Pierres vineyards, not Russian River Ranches. Pay attention now and you might learn something. This one has a very forward, *fruity* taste. It delivers a tart appley flavor—Granny Smith, Pippin. A really nice wine. But not for oysters. For oysters you want a more classic, austere, mineral-scented Chardonnay, from grapes grown higher up the mountain, in flintier soil. You got that?"

The waiter nodded stonily and removed the bottle from our table. I shook my head. "A simple fucking thing, waiting, and he can't do it right. Shit." I turned back to Wilbur. "Look, Wilbur. These documentaries you want to make—they're already made. I can see them in my mind's eye and I don't like them. You interview some poor pensioneered retiree who lives in a trailer park in Flagstone, Wyoming, or a retirement village outside Tucson, and they rattle on to you about their beliefs in flying saucers and how they saw one one night, and it'll take them a fortnight to say this—which monologue you'll capture in a single, head-on, uninterrupted shot—and it'll all be sort of sad but also sort of amusing, and the whole thing will be a touch condescending and patronizing, and maybe some *Village Voice* writer will do a few riffs on it about Americana this or that, and it'll make a couple of smartasses in Berkeley and Cambridge laugh—"

"I had hoped it would be a little more artful than that, Doug," Wilbur said sullenly. He looked crushed. Good. I wanted to crush him, I wanted to pulverize him, I wanted to smash this stupid idea right out of his fat head. The waiter arrived with the bottle of wine. I glanced at the label and nodded. He opened it, poured a little into my glass. I swirled it around, sniffed it, tasted it, and nodded again, and the waiter poured the Chardonnay into our glasses and departed. The others began sipping theirs immediately, but I let mine stand so it could aerate, so it could swell and enlarge with rich telluric layers of rare-earth scent, so it could open up and develop complexity, so it could develop *personality*, for if I have learned anything from my art it's that personality *is* complexity.

I sighed and looked at Frank. "What do you do for a living besides stick up moviemakers?"

He laughed. Wilbur said with pride, "This is the guy who was renting mansions, then selling them. Remember that Hillsborough scam?"

I felt somebody kick somebody else under the table. Too late. But it was no matter, no matter at all, I was feeling expansive, emotionally generous, I was feeling *relieved* that I was still in business. So I laughed with pleasure and said, "Oh yeah, I remember that. No kidding. That was pretty good." What I also recalled, if my memory served me, was that this guy was the son of a New York Cosa Nostra type. How in the world had Wilbur and Jocelyn hooked up with him? At any rate, this confirmed my earlier intuition that he radiated next-generation hood-iness. So now: Was this Frank fellow who sat across from me acting as a member of an organized-crime group when he stole my negative, or was he merely a freelance white-collar agent? I decided there was no point in asking. It may well be that the guy had nothing to do with his father, as I remembered him claiming in an interview; but, like it or not, in his business dealings with people he certainly must benefit from his old man's reputation and the mythology surrounding the Mafia.

I said to Frank, "This housing business would make a lousy movie, though. Who the fuck wants to watch people setting up escrows and arranging mortgages? It'd be 'Lifestyles of the Rich and Famous' with paperwork. You ever get into more visual stuff, like the Lufthansa heist at JFK?"

Frank laughed and said, "Sorry, Doug. No."

"Too bad." I scratched my jaw through my beard. "Look, Wilbur. Let's say we take your premise. People hallucinate aliens because in fact they're lonely and fucked up. Okay. They feel alienated from existence. In a metaphorical sense they're aliens themselves. That's what you're saying, right?"

Wilbur nodded—a touched depressedly I thought, probably because I had picked up so quickly on what he was trying to get at. I turned to Frank. "Now, let's turn things around a bit. Aliens arrive on earth and they're able to assume the form of humans. But they're not invaders, more like Margaret Mead and Claude Lévi-Strauss. Anthropologists from outer space. Martians with Minoltas. They want to move into a normal suburban community and observe human life firsthand, by participating. They buy a home.

"But then it turns out they bought the home from a real estate swindler. A scam artist. The aliens get all entangled in American laws and courts. It's completely beyond them. They're bewildered. People are treating them like *they're* the criminals, because that's how we treat victims. So everything seems alien to them. It's sort of a comedy with pathos. The familiar turned bizarre. The moviegoer winds up identifying with the aliens and finding the 'normal' suburbanites to be the true aliens."

Jocelyn was laughing, enjoying me. "You son of a bitch," she said. And I could tell by the way Frank was grinning that he too was impressed with the speed and agility with which I had combined the disparate elements of his real estate scam and Wilbur's documentary idea.

Getting right into the spirit of the thing, Jocelyn said, "Maybe the swindler turns out to be connected, a gangster. The aliens get run through the Federal Witness Protection Program. Relocated to another part of the country. Relocated dislocated aliens."

Everyone laughed. God, I had missed Jocelyn. I smiled warmly at all of them. "What a team we'll turn out to be yet." I reached for my notepad, took out a pen, and began writing rapidly. "Okay. Here's the deal. I contract to buy the rights to Frank's real estate story and the rights to Wilbur's alien story, which we'll say is Wilbur and Jocelyn's, with the understanding I'm going to combine them. My production company will purchase the rights to Frank's story for $666,000, and to Wilbur and Jocelyn's story for $333,000. An additional million will be paid for the screenplay, a third of a million to each of you. Straightforward and clear-cut. None of this 'structured' deal shit, where something is optioned, you get the money in drips and drabs, a little when it goes into preproduction, a little more at the start of principal photography, and so on and so forth." I rubbed my hands together. "And I'll tell you something. I *like* this. We're really going to do this. It's not just a way of paying you guys off." I nodded enthusiastically. "A full-length movie. First-run. Open wide on two thousand screens across the USA. The multiplexes. Syufy. United Artists. RKO. None of this art-ghetto, midnight-cult shit." I looked around at them. "Do we have a deal?"

Wilbur, Jocelyn, and Frank all looked at one another. Frank nodded. Jocelyn nodded. We all looked at Wilbur. He said nothing. I started drumming my fingers on the table.

"I don't know," he muttered.

"Wilbur," Jocelyn said sharply.

"What do you mean, you don't know?" Frank yelled. Oh yes, I could picture this Frank character working himself up, spurring himself on into a really beautiful state, lashing himself into a magnificent fury, propelling himself into an exceptional frame of mind. Awe-inspiring. Our boy, I felt sure, could be quite the terror when he applied himself to it.

"I just don't know," Wilbur said. "I had this idea for a documentary and now Doug wants to twist it and pervert it and—"

"Oh for chrissake," Jocelyn snapped. "You're hopeless. Doug's idea happens to be sound—"

"And you can always go off and make your documentary with your own money afterward, anyway," I said soothingly. "C'mon Wilbur. Be realistic."

"Be realistic?" Wilbur shouted, suddenly indignant. People turned and looked. He lowered his voice. "You're telling *me* to be realistic. You, who spent sixty-seven million dollars on a movie that should've cost thirty. You, who spent 3.2 million alone on sunset in Antarctica. 'The $3.2-Million Heartbreak Sunset.' Jesus, spare me."

I shrugged. What could I say? How the press loves to castigate me for throwing my millions away on a movie—but, I ask you, does the press ever castigate a poet for throwing away decades to eke out two or three flimsy books of poetry, two or three *pamphlets* of measured malarkey and high-sounding hoopdedoodle? Does the press ever go after a poet for the human wreckage of his or her life? I am not being facile. An old friend from the Lower East Side used to write poetry, and I always used to ask when his first book was coming out. He grew fond of tossing Rilke back in my face: " 'Ten years is nothing in the life of a poet.' " *Fine.* Ten million dollars is nothing in the wallet of a moviemaker. But, truth to tell, I had neither the energy nor the heart to say this to Wilbur.

So I just let it go and instead said, "I screwed up. I lost my sense of proportion. I admit it. My heart, though, was in the right place. I was trying to capture beauty. But now we're moving on." I leaned across the table, closer to my old classmate. "C'mon, Wilbur. I'm trying to do you—all of us—a big favor. Please."

Wilbur fretted and stewed a while. We all waited patiently, understanding it was necessary he get this off his chest. And, eventually, finally he did. "Okay," he said softly.

And then and there I drew up four identical contracts on four pieces of notepaper—wrote them out in the sort of plain, unadorned language that would hold up in any court of the land—then predated them several weeks before the theft. I stipulated that the monies were due two months from now, by which time the movie would be released and my funds no longer tied up. "Everything's legal. The unstated clause is, the only way you don't get your monies is because my company has gone bankrupt and me with it. Because I didn't get my negative back. So now you have your contracts, but they're worthless unless I get my negative. Everybody's protected." Frank, Jocelyn, and Wilbur nodded. Everyone signed everyone else's contract. Then we filled our glasses with the remaining champagne and clinked them.

It was now early dusk. Sitting in this tasteful lakeside restaurant, gazing out at the crystalline waters of Lake Tahoe and the surrounding snowcapped mountains, I felt serene, at ease, luxuriously limp. I *believed* in the idea for the movie we had just brainstormed. The waiter passed and I signaled for the check. He took my Visa card and removed the plates of oyster shells from our table. I turned and said, "That was just an appetizer. We'll eat tonight at the Forest. Magnificent lake view. Truffles. Red meat. Lobsters. Salmon. Ladles of butter and cream. None of this California nouvelle cuisine shit."

"No," said Wilbur. "That'll just make me fat."

"You *are* fat. Jesus. One rich dinner won't kill you. You've probably been sitting around eating takeout pizzas while we were negotiating."

The waiter reappeared with my Visa card and a pair of scissors. A malicious smile lit up his face. "Your card," he said, "has been canceled." Then, as I tried to contain my surprise, he took the scissors and cut the plastic rectangle in half.

"Frank, there's been some kind of misunderstanding. Would you—"

"No problem," he said, and took out his wallet. I noticed he had about a dozen Visa cards, though he paid the waiter two hundred and fifty in cash for his lunch with the movie mogul. All those credit cards went with the Disabled parking sticker on the dashboard of his Porsche.

"Don't let that disturb you," I said. "Once I get the negative, I'm back. Speaking of which—"

"We'll drive back to South Lake Tahoe right now and get your two hundred thousand dollars—the first installment, so to speak," Frank said, smiling, "and I'll retrieve the film from the hotel gym locker I stashed it in. Then we'll change and go out for dinner. A happy ending for all."

I nodded. "Which hotel?"

Frank said pleasantly, "None of your business."

It was already dusk. Out in the lot, Frank and I squeezed into the Porsche's tight back seat. He had said that as long as he had my ear, he wanted to ask me a few questions. Jocelyn, her long legs squeezed into blue jeans, climbed into the front passenger seat. Wilbur, who apparently had been aching to drive, wedged himself behind the wheel. Off we roared.

"Doug, did you really once issue an order that all memos be neatly handwritten on three-by-five-inch white lined index cards?"

I looked at Frank in the closeness of the back seat. I felt strangely, curiously intimate with him, as though there were some supramundane bond between us. "Yes," I said. "I suppose I did."

"Why? You're not that much of a flake."

I sighed. "It plays well in Peoria. In the Polo Lounge, too. People *like* driven artists. They look upon eccentricities as divine attributes not conferred upon ordinary mortals. Studio heads want to associate with you. You're an artist. It ups your fee." I shrugged. "It also gives me credibility with the highbrows. Not that I need them," I quickly added.

"And what does putting down your old man in an interview do? You remember, that stuff about your being 'a block off the old chip.' Jesus, that was disrespectful."

"That!" I cried. "Christ. My 'trusted' lieutenant set me up. He befriended this son of a bitch, some freelance writer, and was bringing the guy around to my place so often I got accustomed to his face and mistook him for a friendly. The guy's constantly flattering me, telling me I belong in the pantheon with Welles, Hawks, Hitchcock, Ford." I looked at Frank. "Can you believe I fell for that shit? So the guy comes around one day asking to interview me for *Film Comment*. Sure, I say. Why not?

"The day of the interview he shows up with a few Thai sticks, some uncut coke, and a magnum of Bordeaux, 1959 Lafite-Rothschild. Can you believe it? A freelance writer laying his hands on that? We start with the wine, he waits till I'm good and snookered before springing the other stuff on me. I don't usually do this—the drugs I mean, besides uppers and downers, at least not much since undergrad days anyway—but now I'm a touch drunk and thinking, What the hell! I'm feeling expansive, effusive. The guy's flattering me like a whore. He gets me going, and damned if I know what I'm saying. There I am, running down my poor father, who expected to do so much with his life and wound up doing so little. So it's true enough what I said, my father would be nothing without me, he'd never have graduated from carpenter to set designer. But these are things ordinarily best kept to oneself. Then the interview comes out. I'm on the cover. The worst stuff about my father finds its way into the pull-quotes. Naturally I never see the guy around my place again."

Frank shook his head. "I don't know. Even drunk and stoned . . ."

I shrugged. "Did Morgan and Alfred really like the film?"

"You should've heard them. And we did, too. Seriously, you got a winner."

I nodded. Maybe, maybe not. But, for the moment, no matter. I looked out the window. In the rosy high-altitude twilight the whole landscape seemed burnished, to hum and sing with heaven's light. Frank was all right. And it was good seeing Jocelyn again. God, now that my wife was decamping maybe I could win Jocelyn back. It was even good seeing demented overweight Wilbur. The road climbed several hundred feet and curved around Emerald Bay, affording a glorious view, then followed a ridge that fell steeply away on both sides to shorelines below. On our right, the dark polished brilliance of Emerald Bay. On our left, miniature Cascade Lake. Straight ahead, Lake Tahoe stretching for miles and miles, its rippling glassy finish throwing off sparks and fiery highlights from the setting sun. And everywhere, as far as the eye could see, magnificent peaks, their western exposures ablaze with the last light.

"Christ. I've always loved it here, especially at dusk," I said. "Wilbur, pull over."

He signaled and steered the Porsche onto the narrow shoulder. Wilbur parked, then maneuvered his noble carriage out of the bucket seat. "They shouldn't make cars people can't get in and out of easily," he fumed. Jocelyn emerged from the other side on her long limber legs, then Frank and I got out. Everyone stretched and walked around, awed by the splendor of the place.

"Wilbur," I said, "do you remember that summer I was finishing the screenplay for *The Black Pig* up here? At dusk we'd walk along the road—"

"—passing the wine back and forth." Wilbur smiled at the recollection. Professor Blackfield was okay. Maybe I would hire him as a gofer.

Then I noticed Frank's Porsche rolling slowly toward the edge of the cliff. An exhilarating three-hundred-foot drop. Good old scholarly Wilbur had apparently forgotten to set the hand brake. Hmmm. Should I say something? No one else had noticed.

I decided not to. Watching a car go off a cliff without a movie camera in sight would be, for me, a pleasure of a rare sort. After all the ardors and rigors of the past few years, after repeatedly working out the proper angle and lighting for a shot and then saying "Action" to my cameraman and to my actors, after repeatedly *worrying out* the proper angle and lighting for a shot and then *screaming* "Action!" to my cameraman and to my actors; after shouting "Action!" under all kinds of perilous conditions, in all kinds of insanely rotten weather, during all kinds of life-endangering stunts; and after then spending weeks, months, *years* locked up in the dark, cramped, airless editing bunker as I ransacked the miles and miles of footage in search of the best explosion, the best smashup, the best collision, the best *catastrophe*, why, after all that it would be a sheer pleasure to simply watch a real car go over a real cliff—an expendable sports car in the overbudget production of life.

The car went over.

Jolene/Jocelyn

C h a p t e r   3 9

Once a prick always a prick, is what I say, and on the road in front of me three pricks walked in the deepening Tahoe twilight: famous moviemaker Doug Lowell and obscure untenured professor of film Wilbur Blackfield, a couple of old chums reminiscing, and behind them, sunk in his own weird volatile thoughts, self-styled gangster Frank Furio, Jr. It gave me feeble pleasure to think that I had fucked all three of them, for my mind was more occupied with such fundamental questions as *Who are these people?* and *How did I get here?*

When I first met Doug I was just an undergraduate studying film at UCLA. I had been working part-time as a bartender in Westwood, but the job had been leaving me increasingly rattled: the way on nights that I wore especially short miniskirts I'd get more orders to scale the ladder for top-shelf drinks, and as I climbed I'd see their faces reflected in the back mirror—the boozy flirts, the fresh frat boys, the mild academics emboldened by two beers—the customers not realizing that if it excited them to watch my legs move provocatively up the rungs,

326

it gave me a small unexpected rush to see them beneath me gazing so hungrily up.

That rush made me decide it was time to move on. A friend passed me the number of a young filmmaker looking for a babysitter, and, shruggingly, I checked out his one movie, *The Black Pig*, whose quirky, slightly sick brilliance caught me off-guard and induced me to give him a call. I thought the babysitting work, however menial, might enable me to observe the genuine article, a living breathing working filmmaker—if not up close, then at least at a reasonable proximity. The next day I found myself driving out to a house on Pasadaro Drive in Tarzana, where one Doug Lowell was deep into postproduction on his next movie. The small success of the first film might have marked him as a talented comer in a minor genre, but *The High Plateau of Stars* would fix all that. Of course, no one knew it back then.

Right away I saw he was different. When I arrived at his rented mini-mansion that evening, he was pacing the living room in a frenzy: a large unkempt bearded man surrounded by unruly stacks of books, videotapes, laser discs, and CDs, who kept switching back and forth between tape decks playing Beethoven's "Moonlight Sonata," one version by Vladimir Horowitz, another by Alfred Brendel, a third by Steven Lubin. Skipping introductions altogether, he launched straightaway, as though we'd known each other for years, into an explanation of how he wanted to use the adagio for a scene in the movie he was completing. "What do you think?" he asked. "Horowitz of course is the best-known. And he's grasped the piece intellectually, mathematically, even artistically. He's thought it through—"

"But the Brendel is moodier, not so slick," I said, flattered by his attention. "Nicer actually. He's grasped it emotionally, right down to his nerve endings. There's a dynamic quietness there."

"But the Lubin—"

"Fragile. Yet curiously bracing." I paused, wondering if I'd gone too far—then decided to go further. "On the other hand, the choice of 'Moonlight,' no matter who plays it, is going to strike some as a touch complacent. What kind of effect are you after?"

He fell quiet for a moment and then said, "Thank you," and instantly left the room. A minute later his wife arrived and, formally gracious, coolly beautiful, spelled out the babysitting instructions. At first I thought I'd done something wrong, said something unaccountably stupid to Mr. Lowell. I didn't see him again that evening, and for days afterward I felt mildly anxious—a feeling which irritated me no end.

But a week later he called and asked if I could babysit that Wednesday night. I said I'd like to, but my car was in the shop. He said don't worry, he'd send someone to pick me up. He picked me up himself —which did something distressingly schoolgirlish to my insides—and asked would I mind if he first swung by his editing room in Burbank, he had to get something. "No problemo," I said. He invited me in. He told me, a tad defiantly I thought, that he had decided on the Horowitz (in the end he discarded Horowitz as well and instead did something bold, almost perverse: he used a scratchy 1923 acoustic recording of Gustav Holst conducting his own "Saturn" from *The Planets*—and it played beautifully, imparting a spooky, antiquated grandeur to a traveling shot of a beat-up rocket gliding out of the solar system). No one else was there, and he began running the film on the KEM. He seemed completely absorbed—I'd never seen such concentration. It made me feel locked out, yet also privileged. I felt I was witnessing a species of love I was unfamiliar with. But then, as with the sonata, he started asking for my opinion on different takes. And when he talked he looked straight at me, which I appreciated. Carefully, I offered my views. Several times he'd ask me why, and I'd explain. He'd nod, take notes, then fast-forward to the next shot. After an hour we left, and he dropped me off at his house, picked up his wife, and drove off.

This became the pre-babysitting routine, and I found him an interesting mix of boldness and bashfulness. Indeed, I found him attractive. He never came on to me—not the first time in the editing room, nor the second, nor the third. I wanted him to, but didn't want to risk a first move myself. I started feeling confused. Did he like me or not? Something was going on but I didn't know what. And not knowing made me edgy.

Then the fourth time he got stuck on a particular shot of Tommy Mace delivering a key line. He didn't know which of twenty-three takes to use—including three takes of Tommy sneezing midway through the line. Laughing, Doug told me that Tommy had been flubbing the line so badly, delivering it so clumsily, that finally Doug had requested black pepper, ordered Tommy to snort some as though he were doing coke, and then recite the line while trying not to sneeze. Annals of moviemaking—it worked. Tommy was concentrating so hard on not sneezing that he delivered the line effortlessly, as though it were a nuisance, with an offhanded naturalness, though punctuated by sneezes, except on the last two takes, which he got through with neither sneezes nor flubs. For Doug the question was whether to use one of the takes where Tommy sneezes or one of the poststernutation takes, which I favored. I thought Tommy had delivered the line well but that the sneezes themselves came out sounding scripted. To make my point, I kept sneezing midway through my own lines, until Doug, laughing, begged me to stop. But the serious business of which take to use plagued him. He kept playing the five takes over and over, one after another, getting increasingly wound up, less and less certain of what he wanted.

Finally he picked up the phone and called his wife. "Hon, the film's driving me nuts, but I think I have this one problem almost licked. Unfortunately I'm not going to be able to make it to the symphony." As I walked around the editing room, examining strips of film that hung from racks, fingering splicers and take-up cores, I casually eavesdropped on their conversation. And when I heard him say, "No, no, of course I haven't picked her up yet," my heart started pounding arrhythmically. I tried to conceal my excitement but felt suddenly aroused. After he hung up he told me he'd pay me anyway and if I wished he would drive me home now, though I was welcome to stay. What do you think I did? What would *you* do? He sent out for pizza and beer, we gradually loosened up, got more jokey, more flirtatious —at one point while we were playing the permutations of Tommy Mace's sternutations back to back, or hack to hack, I heard myself drunkenly saying, to my horror, to my *amazement*, that I could fake orgasms even better than sneezes—and by midnight Doug Lowell and I, intoxicated, tremendously primed, flushed with secret excitement, were clawing each other's clothes off and making fierce love on the editing room's beat-up corduroy couch. Our fucking felt barbaric, convulsive, as though we were detonating each other to bits—until finally, laughing, we fell back, blue in our faces and soaked with sweat.

Our affair continued throughout the rest of postproduction. A mercurial man, given at times to intense self-absorption, or at least absorption in his work, he nonetheless made me feel good, better than I'd ever felt. Sometimes a particular person likes you, and it allows you—frees you—to like yourself better. I had come to believe that Doug was a genius of sorts (and I suspected he himself knew that, though he was not in any way conventionally arrogant or affected); and I felt flattered that he should choose me, a UCLA undergrad, as his artistic confidante and lover, when surely he had access to so many more talented and beautiful women.

I also quickly realized that, aside from a fetish for sports cars, money meant little to him—his or other people's. He spent nothing on clothes, luxuries, vacations, and a lot on his movies, constantly pressing and extorting the studio for more money to reshoot a scene or loop in new sound—whatever. Once, when a Constellation executive told him he shouldn't be so free with other people's money, he whipped out his checkbook and shouted, "How much? How much will it cost me to get this shot? *I'll* pay *you* for it, you cheap no-account scumbag." The executive, red-faced, humiliated by the ferocity of Lowell's passion, caved in and authorized the additional expenditure. I thought it was brilliant bluffing—then got to know him better and realized it wasn't, he *would've* paid for it. (Doug later told me that all art is a bluff and that the best artists are those most deeply and passionately committed to the bluff—indeed, those who will stake their lives on it.)

Money also meant little to me. It meant freedom more than status, though as Doug once said, freedom *is* status. I had grown up in a lower-middle-class suburb of San Diego, my parents were one generation removed from the Dust Bowl, and they had inherited from their parents a desperate carefulness about money—a carefulness that had, with them, degenerated into a venal, churlish meanness of the spirit. And I had reacted against that with a positive loathing, determined to do what I wanted and not be constricted by monetary considerations.

So I had refused Doug's offers of gifts—an apartment in Westwood, jewelry from Frances Klein, a Toyota Supra. And I think that impressed him even more, that he couldn't buy me.

Yet he had bought me already with his confidence, his faith in my opinions. What I thought *mattered* to him. And *I* took confidence from that, felt emboldened by his respect and love for me.

So when Constellation said they wouldn't release the two-and-a-half-hour cut of *High Plateau* he had delivered, and demanded he recut it to under two hours as per his contract, it was I who suggested, who pressed him, who emboldened *him* to threaten the studio with the negative's disappearance if they didn't release his version. Which he did, and once again the executives, intimidated by the passion of his conviction, caved in and agreed to at least test-preview the long version. Audiences loved it, and the rest is history. (In retrospect I sometimes think that he had emboldened *me*, so that when a crisis came and he faltered, I would be there to embolden him—to spur him on.)

The phenomenal success of *The High Plateau of Stars* might have been unfortunate. Before the movie's release, Doug had started talking about divorcing his wife and marrying me. Nothing definite, just floating trial balloons. I didn't encourage him, I didn't discourage him. Of course I wanted him to marry me, I wanted to marry him, but felt it was too much to hope for. So I played it cool. I teased him: "You say that to all the girls." And: "It's just that we both get a thrill out of horror flicks, and your wife doesn't." And: "You only love me for my mind." My coolness, naturally, inflamed him all the more.

But the movie's success unhinged him. It let the megalomaniacal and paranoiac sides of his personality, which had always been held in check by his basic good sense, come out and play in the expanding sphere of his personality. He moved from Los Angeles, which he considered corrupt, a company town, to the Santa Cruz Mountains, where he had a beautiful home constructed—and I saw less and less of him. An occasional distracted dinner date in some out-of-the-way place in Venice. A spur-of-the-moment invite to a friend's private screening in Beverly Hills, where we would hold hands in the dark. Then nothing. He no longer needed me; now the whole country adored him. I felt angry. This guy is a moviemaker, a genius at creating illusions, I thought—illusions he can sell to people all over the world. And to me he sold the convincing illusion of love and marriage.

Doug had promised that, at the least, he would serve as my mentor, help me get an editing position, and, when I'd had enough experience, perhaps a directing job. He didn't deliver; he was too distracted, too busy, and I lacked the confidence to follow through on my own. Nor did my encounters with his crowd encourage me. While he was still living in Tarzana I occasionally attended his parties and would wander around talking to industry people. At one party I found myself chatting with a well-known young actress who asked what I did, and I told her I hoped one day to direct. She put her hand on my arm and told me, confidentially, that though she wished me all the luck in the world she herself would never *think* of working for a woman director because she felt they lacked the "toughness," the "sense of tyranny" necessary to dominate a set. She added with a giggle, "Female directors don't know how to stroke actresses the way male directors do." I nodded and smiled stupidly, and thought to myself that if I ever did make a movie it would be a buddy picture, heavy on the male bonding, so I could avoid dealing with idiots like her. At another party I found myself chatting with a woman who had actually just directed her first movie—the fourth installment in the popular *House on Cemetery Street* series. She told me she had landed the job only after spending six years directing TV shows. Then she had to assure, hammer home to, some half-dozen studio executives, nervous about the loss of authority on the set and consequent budget overruns, that she was neither "sensitive" nor "emo-tional" nor "girly." She landed the assignment and proceeded to prove herself, to (as she said, laughing) "make her bones" by directing a picture that was scarier, sexier, and bloodier than the previous three. (It also went on to do better.) I stared at her. She winked and wished me luck. I was left standing by the drinks table thinking, Is *that* what it's going to take? Is this what I really want?

Then one night after I had just about given up on Doug, he called from Bonny Doon.

"My wife is visiting her folks in Ohio this weekend. I'd really like it if you drove up."

"Oh you would, would you?"

"Yes, I really would. I can't tell you how much I miss you."

I decided to sit on my anger and save it for when I saw him. So I drove up—in a rage of ambivalence—for an hour or for the weekend I wasn't sure.

But when I arrived that night I found he had dismissed all the staff and made dinner for me himself. I decided to put my anger on hold and wait for an appropriate moment to bring it up. After dinner we wandered out into the woods, laughing and talking and drinking straight from the evening's second bottle of wine. We climbed up into the cockpit of the spaceship from *High Plateau* that sits in the middle of the dirt parking lot out in the woods. It was a warm clear spring night. Crickets chirped away. Thousands of stars shined down. I forgot how angry I had been. And we made love right there in the spaceship's open cockpit. It was the most wonderful time we'd ever had—other times had been wilder, more inventive. But none had been so special. There was something about huddling in the privacy of the space-ship's cockpit—the spaceship that a hundred million moviegoers had marveled at on the big screen. It was as though public and private had been turned inside out; and we sat there feeling the salty breeze that drifted up the canyon, smelling the pines, hearing the crickets, and seeing the black silhouettes of low mountains that loomed around us and the stars shining above. And when I came that night, sitting astride Doug in the pilot's seat, I threw my head back and looked up, up, *up* at the stars—and I swear they splintered and fell away on all sides, as though I were shooting out through them faster than light. And Doug whispered, "We are the only ones here. We have crash-landed on the third planet of a completely insignificant solar system, on an unpopulated place called Earth. Which of course makes us, brave explorers, the first Earthlings."

Then he said, "I love you. When my wife returns on Monday I'm asking her for a divorce."

I scrambled out of the cockpit, screaming, "I've heard this before, you bastard." I was shaking with rage.

"Jolene, I swear on my eyesight," he said, standing up in the cockpit and spreading his arms in a gesture of helplessness. "Please, I understand your anger. But the success of my movie completely unglued me. For months I didn't know what I was doing. But now I've gotten my bearings back and I know what I want, and that's you."

"You didn't even call, goddamn you."

"I'm sorry. I should've. But I was a mess."

"Didn't even drop me a *note.*"

"I fucked up. I admit it. Please forgive me."

I felt confused. He had disarmed me as adroitly as if he were from the L.A. bomb squad. So I just said, "She'll fleece you. You're no longer just rich. You're rich-rich."

"No matter," he laughed. "All we need is our spaceship in the woods. We'll set up housekeeping right here."

And I climbed back up into the cockpit and snuggled alongside him.

The next morning, as though under a spell, I drove back down to Los Angeles. I never heard from him again. I could no longer reach him at his studio, and once when I called him at home, his wife, that boreal bitch, answered and said coolly, "We no longer require your services." I wondered what he had ever said to her about me, if anything. For all I knew their marriage was far stronger than he'd ever let on. Several times I sat down and wrote him a letter, and each time I tore it up. Once I sat down and wrote her a letter, and tore that up, too. I felt humiliated running after him like I was some crazed little art groupie, some cultural social climber. *I* hadn't chosen him, *he* had chosen me. For a few months after that I would sometimes telephone him at home at two or three in the morning. I would hear him say, "Hello." And I would catch my breath, not wanting to say anything for fear he would hang up on me, hoping that just once he would acknowledge that I was on his mind as much as he was on mine by saying, "Jocelyn?" He never did. He'd just hang up. After a while I started getting his answering machine.

It made me crazy. The silence made me flat-out crazy. Was it my halitosis? My déclassé background? Did he detect in me some profound character defect of which I hadn't the slightest clue? I felt as though I had been thrust outside the gates. I felt insane.

And then hurting angry. Furious. I was aching so badly. No one had asked him to fall in love with me. I hadn't sought him out, I hadn't come on to him. Nor could I just simply walk away and forget him. No, for he was *Doug Lowell*, whose name popped up everywhere, in newspapers and magazines, on the radio and TV; and every time I heard *Doug Lowell*, it triggered in me such rage, such hurt, such loss that I would throw down the paper or zap off the TV.

And, damn it, I missed him. I missed his chatter, his murderously funny unmuzzled monologues, his scurrilously wicked talk, reserved only for me, in which he'd lampoon and vilify and rain down maledictory abuse on various deadbeat artists and overesteemed celebrities. I missed lying in bed with him, sharing a glass of bourbon, touching him, hearing him describe how Jerry had recommended some modern experimental composer, but "listening to the guy's music is like hopping hurdles in a sack on a contrapuntal obstacle course." Or about a film-maker widely praised for the chase scenes in his action thrillers: "Actually, Billy gave up directing movies long ago. Now he just stands in the intersection with a whistle and directs traffic."

Or another time. We'd driven to San Francisco to take in some South of Market galleries and wandered into a place that featured a video installation. Some performance artist was telling his life story in two hours using six separate tapes running simultaneously on six video monitors. On one tape he told the story of his spiritual development, starting with his memorization at age six of the Ten Commandments, which he then recited one by one. On another, his sexual history, STDs included, in numbing medical detail. On another, a chrono-logical record of his IRS returns, with every work-related deduction painstakingly itemized. And so on. Any one tape alone was capable of boring a person to tears—but all six taken together! After ten minutes of impatiently glancing from one monitor to the next, Doug whispered, "Let's go. Two hours in this avant-garde bedlam will give me whiplash."

"You just don't get the significance," I said, laughing. "There are six tapes because the artist has multiple personalities, and life has become so fragmented. I suppose your old-fashioned linear mind would have preferred digesting the tapes one at a time."

"On the contrary," Doug snarled. "I think the fellow made a mis-take. He should have doubled the number of monitors and thereby halved the time. Then everyone could have gone home early."

I *missed* that man.

Missed him and hated him. In my own mind I became a movie-maker directing all the sequels to a single horror movie: *Doug Lowell Dies.* Yes, through the viewfinder in my mind's eye I saw Doug Lowell dying in a bloody car crash on a winding coastal road during a storm. I saw Doug in a hospital wasting away painfully of twenty AIDS-related complications, which he had contracted after schtupping some trampy blond intern who had been my replacement. I saw him slitting his wrists in his bathtub after his film had bombed so totally that it wiped out all his assets as well as those ancillary feelings of artistic supremacy. My imagination knew no limits: I envisioned sequels stretching away into infinity.

But these movies existed only in my imagination. My pride, my sense of self, had been damaged, deranged, and I determined finally to hurt him back in reality. But how? I suppose becoming successful on my own in the industry might have worked, just to show him what he had thrown away. But I felt the odds were against me, especially without him in my corner. Besides, my pain and my anger and my humiliation blinded me. All I could think was, *How can I hurt him most?*

And the answer came echoing back: Shaft him the way I once suggested he shaft the studio. Steal the negative to his next movie.

That was at least a year in the offing, though, and would require assistance and the laying of groundwork. But in Wilbur Blackfield, whom I had heard much about, I knew I would find the perfect malleable accomplice. The rest was, in its way, easy. Revenge became my job, my full-time occupation, my—as the poet said—avocation and my vocation; and with the methodicalness of the mad, as though sleep-walking, as though deep in the grip of posthypnotic suggestion, I moved north, enrolled in a class Wilbur was teaching at Hayward State, and shone. He was drawn to me as his old buddy once had been. And, in his own way, he felt just as betrayed and enraged—only he didn't know that I too felt that way, or even that I knew Doug.

I experienced a touch of guilt about deceiving Wilbur, but I believed it was necessary that he think I was operating with a cool objective head. Which I was—and wasn't. But it's what gave me the upper hand.

I was discovering that the wonderful thing about lying to people is that you know something they don't know and therefore feel more powerful. And I did like Wilbur. His love of movies was passionate, his knowledge broad and deep, and his willingness to share that passion more than generous. In many ways he was a nicer man than his old school chum. But he wasn't in the same league as Doug—or, for that matter, Frank. He was a loser, someone who had things done to him, not someone who did things. And he brought out in me a protective, almost maternal instinct—which surprised me. Even though I didn't feel strongly attracted to Wilbur, I came—for a while, anyway—to like sleeping with him. He was like a cuddly, depressed bear.

Still, I eventually realized we would need a third accomplice, someone with a bit more of a larcenous bent, and who Doug wouldn't recognize during the negotiations. Of course Wilbur thought Doug wouldn't recognize me, but I persuaded him a man would serve us better. Then one day I read in the *Chronicle* that convicted real estate swindler Frank Furio, Jr., by way of the Bronx and Cornell, with a shady minor in film, was getting released from prison. His résumé seemed right, and I suggested Wilbur contact him.

I liked Frank right away, or, more accurately, felt an antagonistic attraction to him right away. He was a case, different from the others. Refined. Yet raw. A crazy vitality animated him—a vitality even Doug lacked. Someone who had done time in Allenwood as well as in the Ivy League. Someone who had hobnobbed with murderers. Whose own father probably had murdered. And he had this quiet intensity—intensity and an unnerving unpredictability. The day I became most aware of it was the day he took down the 7-Eleven. Totally nuts. Yet completely calm and quiet. He simply let it happen, without calculation, beautifully detached, as if he had this curiosity to see where this might take him, might take us. That was the day I realized he was for real. That was the day I realized he was dangerous. Not the careful, methodical planning of the heist. But the random play of the 7-Eleven. And, I hate to admit it, that was the day I started to fall for him.

But he was also somebody I resented falling for. He was a good lover—energetic, playful—but I had the feeling he could be good with anybody, that he wasn't just responding to something special in me the way Doug had. Consequently when he said he was falling in love with me I didn't believe him, didn't want to believe him, didn't *trust* him. Of course by then I had created so many layers of deceit—between myself and Wilbur; between myself, Wilbur, and Frank; probably between myself and some other self that had long since gone out the window—that I had become my own best argument for not trusting anyone else. But then again, after Doug I had convinced myself that I had good reason never to trust a man, and that the best protective covering for my vulnerability would be to make myself a chameleon, as changeable as possible. Which gave me the feeling I wielded control, the whip hand, even if the tradeoff was a loss of closeness. But at this point I felt my past had instructed me that control was more profitable than the dubious pleasures of the heart.

And, strange to say, this feeling of a deliberately created alienation gave me a peculiar new freedom, as though I had put myself outside the limits and as a result could see farther. So when Wilbur asked me to work "undercover" in the topless bar for the sake of his preposterous research, I said, "Sure, no problem." In fact, I *reveled* in it. I felt it was someone else up on the runway rotating her hips in a suggestive manner and thrusting her pelvis forward as she coolly scanned the male patrons. The rush that several years earlier in the Westwood bar had so rattled me—now it exhilarated me. I felt liberated, unshackled, curiously free. Of course it would occasionally occur to me that my career plans seemed to have been derailed a bit, but I would quickly push such thoughts aside.

But then the heist didn't quite go as planned. When I had earlier suggested that Doug hide the negative from Constellation, I had figured it was in the studio's interest to let Doug have his way rather than forfeit the summer box office. As a result of that success, I had presumed it would likewise be in Doug's interest to just buy the negative back as quickly and quietly as possible.

But the day I read in the *Chronicle* that a fire had gutted his editing facility, I knew all bets were off. I knew we were in trouble. I knew once again that I had fatally misjudged this reckless, unpredictable man. (Yet why should I have been surprised? He was an artist, and his ace in the hole, what gave him his edge, was that ability to surprise people again and again.) But then I had on my side someone who was, in his own disturbed way, just as savagely unpredictable. Which evened things out a bit. Gangsterism as artistry—opposite sides of the same crazy coin.

It seems so long ago.

Then, just an hour ago, sitting in the lakeside restaurant, when my eyes met Doug's and I saw, *felt*, the ragged remorse in them, the abject longing, I realized with a start, with a helpless feeling, that he didn't even hate me for this sick stunt. That he might even, in his own perverse way, respect me for it. And with that I felt all my rage, all my pent-up hostility, against my will, collapse, go *poof!* I felt a wrenching sensation bolt through me, and I wanted him again with all my heart, all my might, and there was nothing—*nothing*—I could do to kill that feeling.

So now I hung back in the cool Sierra Nevada dusk, inhaling the fragrant piney mountain air, walking behind the three of them, three pricks, three lovers, and knowing which one it would be, and that this time he would accept me.

Doug and Wilbur paused by the edge of a cliff and gazed out upon the dusky, shimmery expanse of Lake Tahoe. Deep rose hues accentuated the shallower sections of the lake. Doug stretched his arms and scanned the panorama. Frank, too, stopped a little ways ahead of them to gaze at the water.

Then I noticed Doug smiling. The sport's smile. I turned to see what so transfixed him . . . and saw Frank's Porsche rolling toward the cliff.

"*Frank!*" I yelled.

Too late. The car kept rolling toward the edge . . . *rolling* . . . *rolling* . . . hung there a second—dropped off. The Porsche seemed to take a long time going down, turning leisurely as it descended. It was a three-hundred-foot drop, and time stretched out and yawned. As the car tumbled through the soft, dusky light, an eerie silence transfused the air. It was as though existence itself had slowed way down.

Then—*kaboom!* Time snapped back. The Porsche smashed onto shoreline boulders and exploded.

I looked up. Dear, sweet, incompetent Wilbur stood at the edge of the cliff, wringing his hands; he must have forgotten to set the hand brake.

Frank balanced on the edge, staring in amazement at the flaming wreckage far below. He looked stricken, shocked, like he had taken ill.

Laughing, Doug stepped alongside him. Doug seemed fine, the child, the moviemaker delighted by the fiery spectacle. He put his arm around Frank's shoulders and said, "You should've put a roll bar in."

"A roll bar?"

"Never mind," Doug said jovially. "We must think of an epitaph."

Something was wrong. I couldn't put my finger on it, but something was wrong. Seeing one's car roll over the cliff like that has got to be a shock, but certainly it was insured.

"C'mon, Frank. Snap out of it," Doug continued, punching Frank in the arm. "We'll get you another Porsche. Hell, we'll get you a Ferrari. There's sure to be a Ferrari dealership in Sacramento. After all, Sacramento's the capital of the seventh wealthiest nation-state on earth."

Why was Frank so stunned? He was a sport, like Doug. The car was replaceable. He too should've been laughing. But he looked terribly out of sorts—faintish.

More. An emotion gripped his face that I had never seen there before, an emotion I would have thought foreign to him. Frank looked . . . frightened.

And then I thought, *Fuck.*

"Hey, you paying attention?" Doug said, shaking him. "Forget the car. Stop brooding. Look around you, for chrissake. It's beautiful out."

Doug was right. Deep glowing reds highlighted the peaks to the west. It was a breathtaking sunset, a magical sunset, a beautiful melancholy lyrical sunset. Can you put a price tag on such a sunset? All right then. Call it a $67-Million Heartbreak Sunset.

"Okay," Doug said, guiding Frank away from the cliff. "Here's my idea for the opening shot of our Martians-with-Minoltas movie. . . . *Hey!*" He shook Frank. "Pay attention. Stop brooding. Forget the car."

Doug still didn't get it. No matter. There'd be plenty of time in the slow years to come, I thought, for all of us to reflect on whether

Wilbur, however dimly, by whatever maladroit medium, had divined the secret cargo of the car and so forgotten to set the hand brake; or even on whether Frank, shrouded in his own stormy cloud system, inscrutable even to himself, had decided to delegate the driving to the professor, faintly auguring that Wilbur could only screw up; or, for that matter, to meditate upon my own Dionysian malice in this breathtaking anarchic mess.

Plenty of time.

And so we hiked on in the cool Sierra Nevada dusk beneath the first glimmering stars.

Epilogue

The rain falls gently on my spaceship in the forest. It is falling on my mansion, on the guest cottage, falling laterally into the pool, on the woods, upon the mountains, *everywhere*. It has been raining intermittently for three days and nights now, and I cannot see the stars. But I know they're shining brightly beyond the dark gauze of rain— whole other solar systems, universes, pearly galaxies beckoning to me. That is where I want to go. Here, the welcome mat has been rolled up with a snap.

A battery-powered transistor radio, installed in my spaceship's control panel, harvests from the air news of this strange grim planet that I like to think I have crash-landed on. But the news has not been too good lately, so I listen instead to a classical-music station. At the moment, the adagio from Beethoven's Sonata no. 14 in C-sharp minor, Op. 27, no. 2. Its unworldly passages, its ghostly bars, fill my soul with a cold brittle light. Conjure up images of moonbeams slanting through a midnight forest. The damp scent of sequoia. Melancholy disciplined by rigor. I like to think Beethoven was from another planet, an alien making a brief pit stop here on way station Earth before moving on to more hospitable climes.

Hospitable! Yes, lately the news has not been so . . . *hospitable.* Two days ago in New York it was announced that several publishing houses were bidding for the rights to Jerry Fugle's memoir, *My Days with Doug.* And on the West Coast a spokesman for Mr. Fugle said that he and a group of creditors were filing an involuntary Chapter 11 bankruptcy petition against Doug Lowell's estate and company. According to Mr. Fugle, he plans to head up a consortium of Australian and Japanese real estate developers who will purchase the estate out of Chapter 11 and establish on its grounds the First Pacific Rim Artistic Film Festival, as well as a year-round coastal resort with condos, spas, and golf courses (the festival, I have been assured, will not kick off with a Doug Lowell retrospective). Already the plan has my neighbors up and down Bonny Doon Road in an uproar. One neighbor, a gentle poet sort, even showed up at my front gate with a petition. I signed with a flourish.

Other news arrives almost hourly. My gardener, Pedro González, was picked up at a garbage dump on the outskirts of Guatemala City, apparently doing a little gardening of his own—something about burying a decomposed body believed to be that of a missing American volunteer health-care worker. U. S. Embassy officials have agreed not to press the government to investigate, provided Mr. González give a signed deposition attesting to the culpability of his former employer regarding the production of a certain fraudulent home movie. A little matter of state, the art of diplomacy. Then a van believed to have been used in the theft of my negative was found burned on a back road in the Tahoe basin. Its plates had been stripped and its serial numbers filed down, though the lab boys from Quantico were able to raise the number off the engine block and trace the van to one Wallace "Wally" Thompson, identified by the FBI as a suspected onetime drug-trafficking associate of Mr. Frank Furio, Jr., in Ithaca, New York. Reached at his home in Walnut Creek, California, Wally, grinning madly, a touch tipsily I thought, denied any involvement, declared

"Frankie is a swell guy," and parted his fingers in a V for the TV cameras. Oh boy.

With all this, I half expected to learn that my former secretary Beth had sold her story to the *National Enquirer*. But dear sweet consoling Beth has managed to duck the brutal public spotlight and, I hear, is planning to leave the business altogether and return to graduate school to roam in the gentler pastures of English literature. Just as well. She'd been forgetting to give me my messages lately and misfiling important documents. As for Morgan Meany and Alfred Egert, the kidnapping turned out to be a good career move; the major networks, I understand, are bidding for their show. Yes, the boys are about to take their act national. Critic-celebs as big as artist-celebs. So the century winds down. Meany and Egert have also since announced, with deep regret, with profound sorrow, with truly heartbreaking anguish, that my film—the one the world will never see—belonged up there in the pantheon with *Citizen Kane*, *Lawrence of Arabia*, and *The Godfather I and II*. That's what they don't understand, they say on TV, shaking their heads in amazement and grief. How could he have gotten involved in all this madness when he'd just come through with such a beautiful work? Are they right? Do they taunt me? I hardly possess the faculties anymore to consider the myriad implications.

Pitter-patter, pitter-patter. I love the sound of falling rain. What else? Oh yes. Constellation announced a $120-million three-picture deal with Tommy Mace, who will direct his pictures as well as star in them. If I had stock in Constellation I'd dump it double-quick. It was also announced last week that San Francisco KMUT anchorwoman Cindy Anderson, on the basis of her fine coverage of this whole fiasco, has landed an anchor position in New York. Congratulations, Cindy. Maybe I'll see if I can sell her the audition tape of Tommy's eloquent reading of *Hamlet*, a little something to inaugurate her show. If the IRS hasn't already put a lien on the tape.

Other things have been happening as well. Willy Keenan, former radical trial lawyer for the Dafton Ten in 1969, has won bail for alleged serial killer Henry Starkman. How he managed that I'm not sure, but something like, You cannot beat a confession out of a suspect unless his lawyer is present. Judge Bob Arnado of the Eldorado County Court, who grouchily ordered the release of Mr. Starkman, has asked the Eldorado County Sheriff's Office to keep an eye on the guy.

And several days ago my lawyer, Paul Meltzer, informed me, with great tact, with special discretion, with really tremendous delicacy, that I should expect to be arrested soon on federal racketeering charges. These would include conspiring with a member of organized crime to defraud an insurance company, manufacturing false evidence to cover up the crime (my little home movie starring Tommy and Ms. Fugle), polluting the environment with hazardous products (not my movies: something about a fire at a toxic-waste dump), kidnapping, extortion, and possibly murder. *Possibly murder?* Apparently the FBI is investigating two killings that might be connected to the theft of the negative. In Los Angeles, Arnold Goldblatt, a pornographic film and video distributor and alleged associate of the Capriccio family, was found shot dead in the usual execution style in his office on Melrose Avenue. I wonder what he had to do with this. Poor fellow should've stuck to the sleaze. And on the East Coast, Frank Furio, Sr., an alleged capo in the Capriccio family, was found shot dead in the trunk of his black Lincoln Town Car in front of De Lillo's Bakery off Arthur Avenue in the Bronx. It looks as though Mr. Capriccio was doing a little spring cleaning—severing the links to himself, to whatever extent they existed. Too bad. All things considered, I sort of like Frank Senior's son.

At any rate, according to Paul, the indictments, recently handed up by a federal grand jury in San Francisco, are expected to be unsealed tomorrow. In fact it was only this morning (I think) that Paul drove out in the rain, parked in the muddy lot, then, in his three-piece Hart, Shaffner & Marx suit, climbed the rain-slicked ladder to my spaceship's cockpit, tapped on the dripping windshield, and informed me that I was supposed to turn myself in this afternoon. Or was that yesterday? At any rate, he also informed me that he is no longer my attorney since I can no longer afford to pay him, since, more importantly, I no longer even seem to listen to him. But, true-blue gentleman and old friend that he is, he did wish me well before climbing back down the ladder, getting into his mud-splattered Mercedes-Benz, and driving off in the rain and out of my life, the windshield wipers swishing softly.

◆ ◆ ◆

I feel so tired.

◆ ◆ ◆

The rain is coming down harder, my bourbon is running low. Somewhere through these majestic woods the rain is slanting into my empty pool. I used to fantasize that even if my film bombed, even if it failed to recoup its costs, I could probably, after selling off all my other properties, still hold on to my estate, which I would then convert to a campground. Yes, in the misty early mornings before the campers awoke I would wander down to the pool with a butterfly net and—*no no no*. What in the world am I thinking of? Such inner peace, which I never put much of a premium on anyway, is most decidedly not to be mine. After all, Jocelyn once said I'd be happier with her and she was right and look what I did to her. But of course happiness, poor old happiness, was not what I was looking for: I sought a permanent state of slight unease, of accommodable alienation, of productive tension, so I could create.

Pitter-patter, pitter-patter. I spent last night listening to the heavy rain beating against my spaceship's hull, a steady, gentle sound, and I will spend tonight the same way . . . unless I get a last-minute dinner invite. Highly unlikely though. It's so cozy here, so comforting, if a touch lonely-making.

I once made love with Jocelyn right here, in the cockpit of this battered spaceship, in the middle of this forest, hemmed in by the mountains under a canopy of stars. And now . . . What happened? How in the world did I come to this pass? If I could just untangle the skein of my life since then and trace the thread back to that night.

But let's not get too nostalgic. To be honest, it was not the most erotic experience of my career, though afterward Jocelyn couldn't stop blathering about how beautiful it was, a great gush of mawkish erotic nonsense. And perhaps for her it was. Sitting astride me, she was able to arch her head back and gaze heavenward at the stars and feel herself, as she came with all her might, rocketing out into them. Me, I was stuck staring into her chest, feeling my penis wrenched forward at a particularly incommodious pitch, and listening to the racket of cicadas. I suppose I should have said something but she was really enjoying herself, lost in her own little galaxy of swirling sensations. For relief I thought not of another woman but of the shot breakdown for a scene in my next movie that had been particularly troubling me, and I had even worked out a new sequence of shots . . . when suddenly I heard her saying that she felt closer to me that night than ever before. I told her I did, too. It is a terrible thing, but the thoughts and feelings of two human beings, even two human beings who are especially close to one another, even two human beings sharing the most intimate of moments, don't necessarily dovetail, don't as a matter of course interlock (it is only in the haven of my art, when I join one strip of film to another, one image to another, one *emotion* to another, and realize with a jolt that they fit perfectly together, realize that I have created a completely new image, a completely new and unexpected *emotion*, it is only then that I experience anything like a shudder of aesthetic bliss at the unity of an otherwise fragmented, blasted existence). But these things mustn't be dwelt upon too closely or you can go insane.

Isn't that right, Jocelyn? *Isn't it?* Tell me, is it pouring where you are tonight? Can you hear the cicadas? Is the rain lashing the treetops back and forth? Are you thinking of me? Does it matter?

I long to bequeath just one true image—

It's raining harder and harder, I'm running out of bourbon. I heard on the news last night that George's new film opened. Dead time. Also heard that one columnist, reporting in from his little plot of turf in that weed patch he writes for, actually accused me, on the basis of all this nonsense, of gunning for a *"succès de scandale."* While another journalist, another *war correspondent*, complained of my "wretched excesses" and of the way I "manipulate" people's fear of death.

But why manipulate people's fear of death? More important issues exist than that of simply dying.

The fear of being $67 million in debt.

Lately, memories have been assaulting me. Memories of my father searching high and low for carpentry work in Hackensack, New Jersey, so he could pay our winter heating bills. (This was before he followed me west and became a Guild "set designer.") Memories of lying in bed in the New Jersey darkness, wondering when my father would get home, feeling my child's stomach knot up harder and harder as the hour grew later and I knew he would be drunker, nastier, louder.

They cannot understand, but I remain *at heart* an austere street kid from the tenements of the Northeast.

My worthless memories, my ashen glories. Playing out my dreams upon the psychic landscape of the country.

Now my country is primed to play out its dreams upon me.

And whatever happened to that small, audacious, autobiographical film I had once hoped to make? What *happened* to it? A chilling, scandalous artwork; a radical, nihilistic film.

Yet why waste my time making a scandalous avant-garde film that the vast public would simply ignore? *Why?* So it could be lapped up by a "cultural elite" inured to scandal? *Above* scandal? Cultural elite! That collection of cretins and imbeciles who, every last one of them, used to be pushed around and bullied in the schoolyard and now are just getting theirs back. Public punishment, private art. Reality, actually, is quite a horrendous thing, perfectly intolerable. Wilbur used to say, "No matter how bad the movies get, they're never as bad as real life." So why try to transmit one's experience of reality directly in one's art? What one needs to do is outwit it. *Outrace* it.

◆ ◆ ◆

The rain has really started to come down now.

◆ ◆ ◆

Wilbur was right when he said, while we were making *The Black Pig*, that even a crime story has to be about something. What he didn't realize: I already knew that. In my two *High Plateau* movies my protagonist's quest for new worlds, to keep pushing on to new frontiers, to new *little cosmos*, represented in my own mind a drive that lies the other side of nihilism. For the human race, when all is said and done, is clinically insane. We propel ourselves forward, individuals as well as the whole species, our instinct to survive trying to outrun our instinct to self-destruct, trying to reach the stars and get a fresh start before we completely botch, totally butcher, our planet. And in making *High Plateau II* I felt that my own personal headlong race between my most brilliant visions and my darkest nightmares was rapidly approaching some finish line. My protagonist's quest represented a protest, *my* protest, against limitations, against biological and astrophysical imperatives—a protest ultimately that stinks of death. For my hero, traveling out on a thunder road through the cosmos, reaching for one new planet after another, committing one *transgression* after another, was in the last issue only trying to outstrip that greatest transgressor of them all: death. I had tried to get much more of that into the second film—though one critic had had the wit to see through the general good nature of the first and say that the film, contrary to what other reviewers were saying, was actually "imbued with a presentiment of death," and that my "playfully elastic treatment" of time and space actually meant to implicate the modern world's negation of history. Or something like that.

I feel cold.

Still, it is a frontier and I like pushing back frontiers. I take an almost sensual pleasure in breaking the rules, in destroying the boundaries. In art, as in sex, we seek ever greater degrees of intensity, to shatter limits, to cross borders, to discover *new worlds*. We seek to explode some final, maybe impossible, barrier—beyond which lies perhaps only death, just death. As for my art, I have found that it guarantees me nothing, no relief, no freedom, nothing but a still more keenly felt solitude.

◆　◆　◆

Just one true image—

◆　◆　◆

The rain is falling gently on my ramshackle spaceship. I feel sad. And groggy. How did I get here? Must have crash-landed. Crash-landed in this strange and hostile terrain beneath foreign skies. What kind of planet is this anyway?

Through the sheets of falling rain I can see the black conifers growing out of the darkness; and I can hear the rain beating on pine boughs, soft as a whisper; and farther back, beyond the trees, I can see the dim silhouettes of low mountains. It is all so unfamiliar—unfamiliar yet oddly recognizable, as though I had passed through here once ages ago. And above me, even though the rain obscures them, the stars shine—the stars, which I should be getting back to.

Quiet.

What was that?

And now, in the wet darkness, I can see the lights of several strange vehicles approaching through the forest. Their headlights weave and seesaw as they bounce along the bumpy, winding road. The blue lights on their roofs flash and revolve. Earthlings coming to see what strange manner of creature has landed his spaceship in their forest. Earthlings coming to take me away, to interrogate me, put me on display, their prize captive. Mustn't let that happen. Check the instrument panel.

Fuel gauge: half-full.

Booster rockets: active.

Radarscope: working.

Well then, through the black rainy night—

Blast off.